Son of the Star

Also by Janice Dietert

Illusions in Time
Origins of the Alad Udug Lama
Between Two Worlds

Compendium of Scottish Silver (coauthored with Rodney R Dietert, PhD)

Son of the Star

Janice M Dietert

www.lulu.com

Cover Art by: Felix Eddy
http://www.felixeddy.com

Son of the Star/

ISBN 978-0-6151-4341-5

PROLOGUE

A pale, grey fog shrouded the dense forest from view as the thick mist shifted aimlessly across the tall meadow grass. Suddenly bright flashes of light exploded through the murk, and a body sailed through the air, landing with a muffled thump on the ground.

The dark-haired young man, surrounded by wet dripping weeds, lay still for a long moment – eyes open, lips curled back in a grimace of pain, and teeth clenched tight to stifle a moan. Finally he managed a wheezing gasp for air.

"Mike!" a girl screamed from nearby.

With effort, he sat up and shook his head, then rubbed his sore back. The crash of branches at the edge of the forest arrested his attention as pounding footsteps headed his way.

"Mike! M…." the girl screamed again only to be cut off abruptly.

Alert now, he jerked his head about squinting to peer through the fog. Suddenly he heard the roar of engines. Seconds later, a large dark blur whizzed past just overhead.

"Mike! He-elp!" trailed behind on the breeze.

He leapt to his feet and raced after the vehicle. As he jumped up to grab hold, it jetted straight upwards then skimmed the treetops.

Though it was lost to view, Mike listened hard and sprinted into the thick undergrowth after it. Following the whine of the engines, he dashed on heedless of the wet leaves that smacked his face and neck or of the briars that stretched out spindly, barbed fingers to snag his muddy jeans and rip at his shirt. He dodged wildly past the tall pines that sprang up around him, leaping the occasional fallen log with athletic ease.

Mike blundered through another thicket, tumbled into a mucky ditch, picked himself up, and crawled out onto a rutted logging road. Through the fog he could just make out the vague outline of the vehicle that hovered above the ground. Several figures were struggling on the platform that outlined its perimeter. With a shriek, one tumbled to the ground.

"Pat!" he yelled, once again setting off toward her.

Unexpectedly a bright flash of light blinded him, while a low throbbing hum assailed his ears. Mike dropped to his knees, at once trying to both shield his eyes and cover his ears. A shot rang out and he jumped.

Mike jolted, finding himself sitting bolt-upright in bed with the early morning sunlight streaming through the blinds on his window. A loud, persistent buzz blared in his ear. He shook his head as he turned toward the nightstand.

"The alarm," he groaned blindly groping for the clock and pressing the snooze bar.

"Need a few more minutes," he mumbled falling back into bed. He grabbed his pillow and pulled it over his head to shield his bleary eyes from the merciless sunlight.

"That nightmare! Why won't it go away?" he moaned. "It's been years!" At last he lay quietly on the sweat-soaked sheets.

"Michael!" The muffled voice of a somewhat older man penetrated his bedroom door.

Mike tore away the pillow, threw it to the floor, and buried his head in his arms.

"Michael!" the man called louder. "If you don't get up now, you'll miss that lecture that Dr. Raymond's giving on ion propulsion."

Mike moved only to cover his ears with his hands.

"Michael! Did you hear me?"

"I'm up! I'm up!" he retorted crossly.

With a good deal of effort, he struggled to his feet and dragged himself into the shower. The pulses of hot water hit his neck and back, massaging his taut muscles. Gradually the tension eased and his brow relaxed.

Half-an-hour later, he sprinted out the front door of the older brick Cape Cod to his 1960's Triumph. Its tires squealed on the pavement as he backed it out of the drive and roared away down the road. He tore into the parking lot of the nearby university, squeezed into a spot between a Ford Bronco and a Mustang, hopped out and dashed over the grounds toward an impressive building close by. He bucked the outgoing foot-traffic of the nearest door in order to get inside and just slid into a seat in the conference lecture hall as the engineering researcher stepped up to the podium,

With a quick rustle of his notes, the distinguished speaker began. At first Mike attempted to take notes, but soon abandoned his attempts as the man at the podium flipped through slide after slide of what should have been riveting research. Instead, Mike watched the lecturer through half-closed eyes. Then, in a sudden move, the presenter turned to write on the expansive blackboard behind him. He rubbed his watchband across it and produced that unmistakable high-pitched screech everyone hates. Mike winced hard, the sound hurting his especially sensitive ears. In a blink, the lecture hall seemed to disappear.

"Pat!" he was shouting.

Fighting the glare from the lights and headache from the hum, Mike forced himself to move again and ran with all his might. Yet, his feet hit the hardened mud with the thud of lead weights. Fumes from the vehicle overhead drifted past his nose. The instant he inhaled them, they burned his lungs and made him gasp. He stumbled as he coughed and wheezed, clutching his chest to relieve the pain.

Mike looked up, just able to make out the figure of a girl who was struggling to her feet. Behind her, the machine settled to ground level and revved its engines in preparation to run her down.

"I won't reach her in time," Mike groaned inwardly, digging in as if to tackle a quarterback. "Pat! Jump!" he yelled to the dazed and terrified blond.

Slowly she turned to face the behemoth as it accelerated toward her. She screamed just before it hit her with a dull thump, and her body flew off to the side like a limp rag doll. The machine then turned and faced Mike, preparing for its final attack.

Just then, the headlights of a car stretched up over the hill behind Mike and bounced toward him. Uncertain, his assailants hovered over the girl's body. Ignoring both the car and his opponents, Mike dashed to the crumpled heap on the ground and knelt over the entanglement of distorted limbs. They were bloodied and all but unrecognizable, her legs twisted at violent angles.

Overhead Mike's assailants took off with the whine of exotic engines just as the car screeched to a halt beside him, kicking up dust and loose stones. Doors opened and several people rushed over.

"Call for the emergency chopper," a voice barked, while two hands firmly grasped Mike's shoulders and pulled him to his feet.

He crawled into the backseat of the car and doubled over. He remained hunched as they sped down the twisting logging road.

Later, Mike sat in a small waiting room and stared at the clock, while an anxiety-ridden man in his early fifties paced the floor. At last a doctor in operating scrubs entered and led the man to a small room in the far corner. Mike watched as the man nodded slowly then bowed his head covering his face with his hands. The doctor hovered a moment over the man then left. Mike rose and hesitantly approached the room where the grief-stricken man sat.

"I-Is she…?" he began.

The man looked up then shook his head. "She's alive," he managed to whisper.

Mike sank onto a chair. For a long moment there was silence.

"Michael," the man began again after taking a long, struggling breath. "Your science teacher told me all you did to try to save Pat's life on that field trip. Thank you."

"B-but you said she wasn't dead," Mike protested.

The man shook his head. "Not dead…paralyzed and in a coma."

Shock registered on Mike's face then pain and grief. The man laid his hand on Mike's shoulder.

"I know how much you cared for my daughter, Michael. But no one could have saved her. Don't torture yourself over it. You did everything you could have."

With that, Pat's father quickly got up and left the room. Mike sat alone, his eyes squeezed tightly shut and his fists clenched to hold back the tears.

A loud buzz squealed and Mike jumped. He opened his eyes and self-consciously brushed away the hot tears that had trickled down his cheeks. The lecture hall was a hub-bub of conversation as its occupants rose to leave. Below him, technicians helped Dr. Raymond remove his lapel mike. Slowly Mike pushed his notes back into his briefcase and stood up. Exhaustion etched haggard lines across his handsome face even though the day had just begun.

Chapter 1

Mike headed across the campus to the science lab he shared with William Shepherdson. More affectionately known as Will, the African-American researcher and university professor had been Mike's lifelong guardian since his parents' death well before his first birthday. Together they were working on developing a new space propulsion system. To fulfill their university responsibilities, they team-taught an upper level nuclear physics course while Mike also taught an introductory physics class. All-in-all one busy schedule by anyone's standards.

Entering the building by a side door, Mike descended to the basement level, walked down the empty, eerily quiet corridor and opened a lab door bearing a symbol denoting radioactivity. He wound his way through humming machinery where several graduate students ran tests and pushed open an office door with his shoulder. Will looked up as Mike swung his briefcase onto a desk and clicked open the dual locks.

"So how was it?" Will asked swinging his chair to face him.

Mike shook his head. "Your guess is as good as mine."

He took out a legal pad full of scribbled notes and slapped it on top of an unsteady pile of also full pads. "Looks like I managed to go on autopilot again, though."

"Yeah, now if someone could just decipher this scribble so we would know what it said," Will complained tilting the last pad upwards and squinting at Mike's scrawl.

A soft knock at the office door went unnoticed by either man.

"Well, if the Research Foundation would come through with that grad intern we requested," Mike grumbled as he turned toward his desk and clicked on his computer.

"A-hem."

Both men looked towards the door where a petite blond woman in her mid-to-late twenties stood eyeing them uncertainly.

"I believe that I may be that grad intern."

"So what took you so long," Mike snapped and swung back to his computer screen.

The young woman looked taken aback, but Will gestured for her to ignore him and have a seat. He moved a stack of books and set them on the floor while she made her way into the office towards the offered chair.

"I understand that several other interns applied for this position then turned it down," the young woman said pointedly.

"It involves a lot of paperwork," Mike said swinging around to gesture toward the stack of notes.

His hand brushed them and they began to topple. He and the young woman both leapt up to grab them bumping heads in the process.

"Ow! Watch it!" Mike exclaimed then froze at the look of hurt in her blue eyes. He muttered to himself and quickly returned his attention to the computer.

Will helped her restack the notes. "William Shepherdson," he said, extending his hand, "and this is Michael Stellan."

"Janielle Childen. I'm...uh...not sure my qualifications fit this position. I'm an English major with a computer background," she explained. "I know very little about physics."

"Can you type?" Mike asked.

"Up to 60 words per minute."

"How are your organizational skills?" he continued.

"I've worked both as an office assistant and in the special services department of a bank during summer breaks."

"Can you work on your own without constant monitoring?" Mike drilled.

"Yes...always."

"Who says you need to know physics?" he spat. "We weren't asking for another research assistant, just someone to log and catalog research notes. If you can't handle that, the door is this way," he continued rising and walking out into the lab.

Jan sat back in her chair, the wind all but knocked out of her. "Is he always so 'pleasant'?"

"Only on his good days," Will quipped looking over her resume.

She picked up Mike's latest set of notes and began trying to read them. "He's in the wrong profession," she remarked flipping to the next page.

Will looked up, an eyebrow raised in question.

"He should have been a doctor. His handwriting is terrible."

"Only on his...."

"...good days. I think I'm getting the picture."

"Look, Janielle...."

"That's Jan."

"Jan," Will corrected. "The honest truth is that we need someone to compile these notes. I wish we could be choosy, but we can't. Are you able to read what Mike has written?"

Jan lifted another page and looked. "For the most part, but I have no reference for a lot of these abbreviations."

"Mike has his own system, so you'll have to ask him."

Jan looked less than enthused.

"I'll have a word with him, ok?" Will offered.

Jan took a deep breath and let it out slowly. "The honest truth is that I need the stipend this internship offers."

"Looks like we're in the same boat," Will said rising and shaking her hand. "You need to see Laura in the Physics department office to fill out some paperwork."

"Now what program do you want the notes typed on? Does it matter if I use WordPerfect or Microsoft Word, or do you have one of your own you would prefer?" Jan asked as Will handed her several notepads to get her started.

"I would prefer Microsoft Word," Mike said entering the office and plugging a flash drive into a USB port on his computer. "You'll need to use one of the computers on our sub-network so I can access the notes as you complete them."

"Which computers do you want me to use?"

"Any of the ones in the lab," was the curt response.

Jan left to complete her paperwork, and Will turned toward Mike. "If you continue to jump all over her, we'll lose this intern, too. At this point in our research, that's the last thing we can afford."

Mike nodded.

"You had one of those flashbacks again, didn't you?"

Mike froze.

"Forgive yourself, Mike. Let it go...before it kills you." Will quietly left the room.

A couple of days later, Jan sat at one of the computer stations in the lab and rubbed her eyes for the hundredth time. She picked up a yellow highlighter, ran it across another abbreviation and made a note of it on a separate sheet of paper.

"All right, enough of this," she groaned, got up from her chair and picked up a sheaf of paper. She looked at the office door, squared her shoulders and marched in.

"Yes," Mike asked not glancing up.

"I need some help."

"Thought you 'always' worked on your own," he snapped.

"I have been for the past four days," she retorted, "but you have your own code or something, and without some kind of key, I'll never get these notes typed up."

He stopped moving the mouse, leaned back in his chair and turned to look at her. "I'm not changing how I write just to suit your sensibilities."

Jan's mouth dropped open in shock then she glared at him in indignation. "Excuse me, I think I heard myself say I want some sort of key. I'm not asking to be babied, just informed. However, I can understand why every other intern you hired walked. You have an attitude problem in the worst way."

She stalked back out into the lab; Mike followed. Jan reached out to shut down the computer without saving her work.

"What are you doing?"

"I'm leaving, too!" Jan declared. "I'm a human being and I deserve to be treated like one. Whatever your problem is, you don't need to make it everyone else's too."

Her finger touched the power button.

"Stop! Stop!"

Mike heaved a sigh as she backed away.

He grabbed the notes from her hand, took her arm and roughly maneuvered her through the lab.

"Let go of me!" she demanded.

He immediately dropped her arm and gasped for air.

"What is wrong with you?"

Mike looked at his shoes then placed his hand gently in the middle of her back and guided her down the hall. They walked up the stairs and out into the bright sunlight. He led her to his car in the parking lot.

"Where do you think you're taking me?" she demanded.

"For pizza. I thought we'd go over these 'codes' of mine over pizza."

Jan's eyebrows arched in shock. "Do you ever let anybody else in on the plan?"

Mike unlocked his door and slid in. "Are you getting in?"

Jan cautiously opened the door. "Is it safe?"

"My bark is a lot worse than my bite. Been defanged, don't you know. Can't bite." He gave her a crazy grin that showed all his teeth.

Jan just had enough time to buckle her seatbelt before he squealed out of the parking lot and down the street.

They entered Tony's pizza a few blocks away and took a booth all the way in the back.

"Make it a pepperoni, Gina," he ordered.

"Um, can half be plain cheese?" Jan requested.

Mike raised his eyebrows.

"I can't eat sausage-type stuff," she volunteered.

"Half pepperoni, half plain cheese," he corrected.

"And a coke," Jan called after the waitress.

Mike took the notes she had made on all of his abbreviations and slowly began going through them. He said nothing all through lunch, just scribbled definitions for each one. By the time he was ready to pay the bill, he had barely completed the first side of the first page. He sat back and scratched his head.

"Gee, I didn't know I used this many," he said, genuinely surprised.

Jan stifled the urge to scream, "He's human!"

"I can't get this all done today."

Jan took a look at what he had done. "That's ok. It'll take me a bit to find all the places you've used these and replace them."

"Word has a neat trick that'll make your job easier," Mike said, laying the tip on the table. "I'll show you when we get back."

"So when will we work on the rest of these?" she asked following him to the counter.

"I'm busy until Friday. We'll come back then and work on them here."

"Over lunch?

"Yeah."

"Settled just like that?"

Mike did not answer but headed out the door towards his car with Jan following.

"Do you ever consider anybody else's schedules or needs?" she demanded.

"Why? Got a conflict?" he asked smugly.

"As a matter of fact I do. I have a three hour graduate seminar starting at noon on Fridays. How about we meet here again next week?"

Mike looked at her as if a whole new world had just opened up to him. "You do have something else."

She nodded.

He considered this for a moment and nodded, "Next week."

They made their way to Tony's each week for several weeks. Jan watched him as he studiously deciphered his codes for her. On this particular day, he had not yet touched his pizza and rarely glanced in her direction.

"Oh well," she sighed inwardly. "At least he's quit being so cross in the lab."

At that moment Mike went to take a bite of his pizza. He

glanced up over Jan's head, and his face drained of color.

"It was better hot," Jan quipped, but he gestured for her to be quiet.

Mike grabbed a twenty from his pocket, slid out from the table and grabbed Jan's hand. "Whatever I say, just do it," he growled. "No questions."

Jan's eyes widened in wonder. "Yeah, sure," she said swiping the notes off the table and stuffing them into her backpack.

They moved slowly toward the counter, Mike's eyes riveted on the figures of two tall blond men who had just seated themselves in the booths on either side of the door. He looked around, spotting the kitchen door near the restrooms.

"When I say 'Run,'" Mike whispered, "duck into the kitchen."

"What?"

"No questions, Jan. Not now."

"Ok, ok."

They sauntered past a waitress who was working her way toward the swinging cafe-style doors to the kitchen. At that moment, the men by the door spotted Mike and stood up blocking the exit. With a tug, he yanked Jan toward the kitchen. A shot rang out hitting the wall just above Mike's head.

"What the...?"

"Run, Jan! Run!" Mike yelled.

Dodging cooks, busboys and waitresses, they dashed through the kitchen and out the back door. Realizing their quarry was escaping, their two assailants were pushing people out of their way in an attempt to follow.

Mike yanked open the back door, and he and Jan leapt outside. Hand-in-hand they raced down the alley toward a side street. Suddenly Jan tripped and fell sending Mike flying. He stumbled into a pile of boxes and fought to disentangle himself. At last, he crawled to his feet and turned to help Jan.

Two tall blond men stood over her. While one reached down and jerked her to her feet, the other stepped toward Mike, a weapon in his hand.

"Leave her alone!" Mike ordered sharply.

The men began backing up dragging Jan with them.

"I said, 'Leave-her-alone!'" Mike yelled. He started forward.

"One more step and she dies," her captor stated flatly.

Mike stopped in his tracks.

"Never mind her any more," the other man said waving his weapon at Mike. "Forget you even knew her."

"Mike! Help!" Jan cried hoarsely. "Mike!"

Without warning, a busboy threw open the back door and dumped a tub of water onto the stairs. Seizing the opportunity, Mike leapt at Jan's kidnappers. He slipped on the wet pavement falling on his face. When he looked back up, the men and Jan were half-way down the alley. Scrambling to his feet, he dashed after them watching as they stuffed Jan into a black sedan with smoked windows. He skidded to a stop as they peeled out having barely enough time to catch part of the license number and see the direction they were taking.

Without hesitation, Mike dashed back through the alley to where his car was parked on the other side. He jumped in and started the car before he had even slammed the door shut. He burned rubber as he gunned the car out of the lot and onto the street then expertly wove his way through traffic. Anxiously he looked for the black sedan. At the next light he spotted it. He hung back a car or two just maintaining visual contact. Yet, as if sensing his presence, Jan's abductors screeched around corners and through alleys at every opportunity. His car might have been small and fast, but Mike was having a difficult time keeping up.

Finally they approached a light that had turned yellow.

"They're slowing down!" Mike exclaimed under his breath. "Now I've got them!"

He pulled alongside them and stopped. Without warning, the sedan shot forward just in time to miss the red light, but Mike was stuck. He slammed his fist onto the dash yet carefully watched the direction the sedan took.

As soon as the light turned green, his little car charged forward and he screeched around the corner after the sedan. He nearly came to an abrupt stop. The street was bare except for an ice cream truck and some kids on skateboards and inline skates.

Quickly Mike rolled down his window. "Hey," he yelled to the ice cream vendor, "did you just see a big black sedan turn down this street?

The man poked his head out his window. "Sorry, I've been in the back getting the ice cream for these here kids. You're the first car I've seen in the last five minutes."

"Thanks. How about you kids?" Mike asked, turning his attention to the skaters. "Did you see a big black car go by?"

"Yeah, what's it to ya?" a skinny, freckle-faced boy of ten asked.

"He was goin' pretty fast," his friend said, whirling around on his skateboard.

"The dude took the corner down there on two wheels," a boy, who appeared to be an older brother to the first boy added.

"Thanks, guys," Mike said, hopeful once more. He waved as he took off and turned the same corner the sedan had taken.

But that street was even more deserted than the previous one. The only thing that moved was a fat tabby cat, and that was only to curl up into a ball of fur on a sunny patch of lawn.

With his anxiety quickly growing to full-fledged fear, Mike began to work a grid work of all the streets and alleys in the area. He drove slowly up one, down the other, and through an alley he came to. He doubled back and worked the streets in the other direction. Finally he pulled to the curb and stopped. Jan had been kidnapped and he had no idea where to look for her.

Her kidnapper's words rang in his ears. "Forget you even knew her."

A knot gripped his stomach and a band tightened around his forehead. He just had to find her. Fast.

Chapter 2

"I can't give up," Mike declared through clenched teeth. "God knows what they'll do to her."

Images of Pat's mangled body flashed through his mind. He squinted his eyes closed in an attempt to block out the painful memories.

"Better try one more time," he breathed starting the car back up and heading down the streets he had just combed so very thoroughly. "Maybe this time I'll see something I missed before."

At half the 30 mile per hour speed limit, he rolled down the streets and crept through the alleys. He stopped at the end of the third alley and looked both ways. An erratic movement to the right caught his eye and he turned toward it. Near the middle of the block, a disheveled young woman staggered down the sidewalk then collapsed against a tree. He squinted until he was close enough to make out the details then let out a sigh of relief.

"Jan!" he yelled out the window.

Stepping on the gas a little, he did a perfect one-eighty and parked the car under the tree. He shot out the door and ran up to her side.

"Jan, are you all right? Did they hurt you?"

Dazed, she barely recognized him and was panting too hard to speak. Putting his arm around her shoulders, he gently led her to the car and helped her in. She sank back into the seat and closed her eyes. Worried, Mike checked her pulse. Though beating fast, it was still strong. He checked her eyes for responsiveness until she waved him away.

"Jan, are you all right?" he asked again.

This time she nodded. "They didn't hurt me, just scared me. I just never thought I'd get away," she replied. "In fact, I still don't know how I managed to outrun them."

"Do you want to go to a hospital? Maybe a doctor should check you over?" Mike persisted.

Jan shook her head. "No, I'm all right. Really. I just want a shower and a good night's sleep."

"Do you remember where they took you?"

"It all happened so fast," she moaned.

"Try," Mike urged, "think."

"After they grabbed me in the alley, they drove around in circles for a while."

"I know. I was right behind them most of the time," he muttered.

"Then I heard something open, like a big garage door," she continued. "The car drove inside and the door clanged down behind us. When they dragged me out, it looked like an old gas-station garage, except it was empty."

"An abandoned garage," Mike mused. "Seems to me I remember having seen one while I was driving around looking for you."

Mike stood up and looked back toward the tree. "Where's your backpack?"

Jan waved aimlessly out the window. "It was with me, that's all I know."

"We've got to try to find it," Mike said hurrying around to the driver's side of the car.

"We're going back there?" Jan cried in alarm as Mike started the engine.

"Yes, but don't worry. I have a feeling those two are long gone by now."

"I hope so. I didn't exactly enjoy my little adventure with them."

"Just what did they want?" Mike asked heading the car back down the street.

"They kept asking weird questions over and over again."

"Weird like what?" he pressed.

"Weird like, who you were; where you were from; where you lived. Stuff like that," Jan told him. "After a while it made my head hurt."

"Then what?"

"When I couldn't answer their questions, they got mad. Then they just got disgusted with me. They put this cloth that smelled sickly sweet over my face. The next thing I knew I was lying under a tree in somebody's yard. I saw their car coming along the road like they were looking for me, so I tried to run. You must have scared them off, because they turned around as you headed up the road.

Mike gave her an appraising glance. Color had returned to her cheeks and her eyes were brighter now. She was sitting upright in the seat, following their progress down the road.

"There's a place around here that used to be a muffler shop before it went out of business," Mike said matter-of-factly. "I think we'll try there."

Fifteen minutes later he approached a one-story cinderblock building with three big bays and a boarded up office.

"Does this look like the place?" he asked.

"Sort of. I don't know," Jan replied uncertainly.

Mike drove around the back and parked in the alley. They got out cautiously and approached the back door. Mike tried it but found it locked.

"Well, they certainly didn't come out this way," he commented.

He cupped his hand over the lock, a blue glow showing through his fingers. Seconds later, the door popped open. He pushed the door open further, and they cautiously crept inside. The interior, though dusky, had enough light shining in through the bay windows for them to see around. Three long pits that were five or six feet deep were sunk into the concrete floor opposite each bay door. Old hydraulic lifts remained in place beside them. The air smelled musty with a tinge of grease and gasoline. Oil splotches remained on the floor, dried and ugly.

"This look at all familiar?" Mike asked as they edged inside.

Jan shivered. "Too familiar."

"Let's look around."

"Do we really have to?"

"We've got to find your backpack," Mike insisted. "We'll make it quick," he added as an afterthought.

Reluctantly Jan followed him about the empty building. He spotted something on the floor by a stack of old tires and hurried forward. He picked up a crumpled canvas pack.

"This yours?"

"My backpack!" Jan exclaimed.

Mike opened it and stuck his hand in. The notes were still there. They had been crumpled into a ball, but they were still there. He handed the backpack to Jan then picked up a damp cloth, took a whiff then held it away from his nose. "Ether," he surmised. "Just enough to knock you out for a short while. Probably just long enough for them to get you out of here and dump you.

"So I didn't escape?" Jan remarked quietly.

"Doesn't appear so."

"Does that mean they wanted us to find this place?" she wondered.

"Maybe," Mike said bending over a spot near one of the overhead doors. As he scooped a shiny object off the floor and pocketed it, the garage doors began to open.

"They're back!" Jan whispered hoarsely.

Mike leapt into action. Hurrying to her side, he grabbed Jan's hand and nearly dragged her across the floor. "We've got to get out of here!" he said shoving her out the back door.

They dove into his car and he pulled out. But as he bumped out of the alley and onto the street, the sedan rounded the corner and the chase was on. Mike wove through the neighborhood then headed out of town. He climbed into the hills where his little sports car had the advantage on the narrow roads with their tight turns. Still, every now and then, they could see the lights of the sedan behind them. Jan gripped the seat, her knuckles white.

Mike turned onto a dirt road and roared off. Moments later, the sedan followed, its back end fishtailing on the loose gravel and dirt. Up ahead, a sign said "Bridge Out." Mike gunned it.

"What are you doing?" Jan demanded.

"Just hang on," he told her. "The ride's going to get a little bumpy."

Behind them the sedan's driver either had not seen the sign or had chosen to ignore it. The sedan increased its speed closing in on the little red Triumph. With a last burst of power, the car shot through the barricade and out into open space. Jan screamed with all her might. The car touched down on the other side with a horrendous jolt, and Mike spun it around.

On the opposite bank, the sedan had slid to a stop, its front wheels dangling in thin air. Neither driver nor passenger got out, but it was obvious that they were going nowhere soon. Satisfied, Mike backed up his Triumph, spun it around and headed home.

Both of them heaved a sigh of relief as they took off down the road. For a long while they rode in silence as Mike guided his car over the many bumps and ruts. But once they had returned to smooth pavement, their tension eased.

"What I can't figure out," Jan remarked, "was what they wanted with me since all they asked about was you."

"Industrial spies," Mike replied.

"Spies?" Jan asked incredulously.

"There may be a show of cooperation between the nations in the space race, but the competition is fierce. The country who can get its hands on the winning propulsion formula will be the first to travel to the stars."

"You and Will didn't exactly mention industrial spies or espionage when I signed the paperwork to get my stipend."

"It doesn't happen very often," was Mike's dry reply.

"It's happened before. How often do your assistants get kidnapped," Jan demanded.

Mike looked straight ahead remembering all too well all the times 'they' had been back. "It hasn't happened before. I suspect they think we've made a recent discovery and are trying to get some info."

"Do you think they're satisfied now?"

"Did you tell them anything?"

"I didn't know anything to tell them!" Jan exclaimed.

"There you go."

"You're a real help," Jan said crossing her arms in front of her. "I'm not exactly interested in meeting up with them again."

"And what makes you think that you will?" Mike asked smugly.

"Well, they kidnapped me to get information about you. Now that they know what I look like and that I work for you, they'll probably be back," Jan said seriously.

Mike broke out into a cold sweat. "I-I never thought about that!"

Jan gave him a hard look. "You know, ever since I was hired on, I've noticed one thing about you. You're so wrapped up in your own little world that you don't notice anything that happens to anyone but yourself."

"It's all this research," Mike retorted defensively.

"No," Jan said quietly. "It's not. Will's not like this and neither are your lab assistants. Say what you might, Michael, but something's eating the life out of you to the point that you can't see what's right under your own nose. Problem is, if you don't wake up and come out of your shell soon, it could cost you your life or someone else's."

Mike did not say a word for a long time. Jan's words had hit him like a jack hammer. Here he had been trying to keep people out of his life to protect them, and instead, he was endangering them further.

"You going back to the lab?" he finally choked out.

Jan shook her head. "I'm done for the day. Would you mind taking me home?"

She gave him directions, and he soon pulled up in front of her apartment building and parked the car.

"I'd better walk you to the door and check things out before you go in."

"And how would they know where I live?" she asked.

"They went through your backpack."

"Oh, right. Please help yourself," she said gesturing toward her apartment.

They got out together and walked up to her door. Jan already had the key out, but her hands shook so hard she could not get it in the lock. Mike gently put his hand over hers. For a moment he smiled down at her then he turned the key and opened the door.

Pushing Jan behind him, he crept into the apartment. She waited by the door while he snuck about her little efficiency. He checked behind the couch, under the table, in the shower and in the closet. Finally satisfied that no one was there, he flipped on the lights and closed the shades.

"Feel safer?" he asked.

"A little," she said, "but I think I'll be glancing over my shoulder for a long time to come."

"I know that feeling really well."

"My car is in the university lot. Can I get a lift in tomorrow?"

Mike nodded then left.

He backed his car out of its parking spot and hesitated at the entrance to the street. Finally he turned away from the university and headed out toward a nursing facility in a nearby town. He walked up the tree-lined sidewalk and checked in as a visitor at the front desk. He made his way through the familiar maze of halls until he found the skilled nursing floor. He hesitated outside a room, took a deep breath and entered.

The room was dark and life support machines whooshed quietly. He made his way to the bedside of a comatose young blond woman and sat down. He stared deep into her face, memories and guilt etched on his own.

"She wouldn't want you to be living like this," an older woman spoke from nearby.

Mike startled and looked up to see a woman turn from the window to face him.

"I know the guilt you're carrying. Don't you think I tortured myself for not being there for her when it happened. For being so busy on an overseas business trip that I wasn't by her side when they took my own daughter to the hospital?" the woman demanded.

She moved away from the window and to Mike's side. "I lived that guilt for too many years, Michael. I finally had to let it go. It was eating me up inside. Pat would never have wanted it that way for me…or for you," she said as she left the room.

Mike stared at Pat for a long while then hung his head.

That evening he entered the home he shared with Will who was sitting in the living room surrounded by piles of lab reports. His guardian looked up as Mike walked in and instantly noticed the worried frown on his friend's face. Will took off his reading glasses and set them on the coffee table as Mike came around the couch and sat in the chair nearby.

"I missed you during the lab session today. Did something happen?

Mike nodded then pulled a small, flat, shiny black case from his pocket and handed it to Will.

"What's this?" Will wondered turning it over in his hand.

"I was hoping you'd know. I picked it up in an abandoned muffler shop," Mike explained going into a brief recounting of the afternoon's events.

Will frowned as he listened and eyed the small box more closely.

"So, I thought you might know what it is," Mike finally concluded.

Will sprung a hidden door and a small probe popped out. "Hmmm. I do now."

Mike leaned forward to get a closer look.

"It's a device used for extracting the truth from a person under intensive interrogation."

It was Mike's turn to frown. "'They' kidnapped Jan this afternoon then let her go. Do you think they used it on her?"

"Most likely. What do you think Jan might have told them?"

"Not much. She said they kept repeating the questions but she couldn't tell them what they wanted to know which made them angry. Now, who are we dealing with? The usual?"

Will nodded. "The Saracens have used this device. You're certain Jan couldn't have told them much?"

"The notes on the codes in her backpack told them more. She knows nothing about us and understands nothing about our research."

Will nodded. "That's probably just as well. It's likely that after this encounter, they'll leave her alone."

"What about us?"

"Oh, they'll keep looking for us," Will replied wearily setting the small device on an end table. "What we need to know now is what else they may have wanted from Jan."

Mike frowned. "Like what?"

"Like…was she really kidnapped or was she an operative used to decoy you out of hiding?"

"What if she's not an operative?" Mike pressed.

"They may still be using her as a decoy without her knowledge. You might consider keeping a closer eye on her from now on," Will suggested.

Mike frowned again.

"I didn't say date her, just be more attentive to her life. What happens to her could have a big impact on us," Will pointed out as he headed upstairs to bed.

Chapter 3

From that evening on, Mike started looking for Jan on campus whenever he was not in the lab. She would often be heading toward the library only to spot him sitting on a bench outside and reading a journal. He would glance up, nod at her, then go back to reading.

On one particular occasion, Jan felt a tingle in her neck. She glanced over her shoulder but saw no one in particular except Mike. For once he was glancing away. Setting her jaw in a determined fashion, she marched over to him and grabbed his arm. Startled, he swung his head around to meet her blazing blue eyes.

"Mr. Stellan. I have had just about enough of this!" she declared angrily. "I don't seem to be able to go anywhere on this campus without you following me, and I'm either going to know the reason for it right now, or I'm going straight to the Office of Affirmative Action and file harassment charges."

Mike put his fingers to her lips and tried to hush her as passersby began to stare. "Do you have a study carrel?"

She nodded.

"I'll explain there."

They entered the library, rode the elevator to the second floor, and made their way through the book stacks. Finally Jan pulled out a key and opened a door. Mike grabbed a nearby chair and propped it just inside the door.

"Ok. What's this all about?" Jan demanded in a loud whisper.

"They've been on campus."

"Here?" Jan asked alarmed.

"I've been keeping an eye on you from a safe distance. So far, that's all they seem to be doing as well," Mike explained.

"You could have said something," Jan replied. "You could have warned me…anything. Why do you insist on being so closed?" She fought back angry tears.

Mike looked at his hands uncomfortable with her justified outrage. "It's a long story."

"Unfortunately I don't have time to listen right now. I have two twenty page papers due next week and I'm behind in my research for them because of all the notes I have to type for you."

She got up to leave, but Mike caught her arm.

"I'm sorry. Really."

Jan sank back onto her carrel chair. "Why can't we just be friends. I work for you," she reminded him. "I work hard."

"Very hard," he corrected.

"And I do a good job," she persisted.

"A very good job," he added.

"Then why do you treat me like I'm poison?"

Mike sighed heavily. "It's a long story."

Jan placed a hand on his arm. "You know, I get the feeling that it's not just a long story, but it's ancient history as well. When you've decided to join the rest of us in the 21st century and are ready to be friends, let me know."

With that she climbed over his feet, which blocked the doorway and stalked off into the stacks. Mike watched her go and swallowed hard.

The next day Jan ran into him while she backed into the lab. She grabbed his arm pulling him in with her. She dragged him into the office and closed the door.

"What's going on?" he demanded.

"I saw them, and they kept following me," Jan replied lowering herself into a chair and breathing deeply to calm herself.

"Did they follow you here?" Mike asked pointing down at the lab floor.

She shook her head. "I took some of the tunnel walk ways and lost them, but they gave me a good scare."

Mike breathed a sigh of relief. "Call security to walk you to your car when you leave," he instructed.

He opened the office door to leave, paused then turned back. "Will you be ok here in the lab alone? No one is due in for another hour."

She nodded.

He remained in the doorway a moment longer then went back to his computer, turned it back on and typed in his password. "Use my computer and keep the office door closed. Only Will and I have the keys."

"Thanks."

He tried to leave one more time but stopped and turned toward her, his hand outstretched. "Friends?" he said hopefully.

A big grin spread across her face as she shook his hand. "Friends."

That Friday afternoon Jan was in the lab as Mike and Will held a meeting with their research assistants. Though concentrating hard on the notes she was typing, she could not help but overhear the group discuss a planned trip to an small aircraft launch field where they planned to test some new designs. After the meeting adjourned, Mike came over and rested his hand near her work station.

"The research assistants, Will and I are going to a dirt strip in the hills tomorrow to test out some designs. I know you're an English major, but you might find it interesting anyway. Some of our engineering students have developed some pretty cool stuff."

Jan mouthed "pretty cool stuff" before turning to look at him.

"Will it be all day?"

"All day," he confirmed.

She thought for a moment then nodded. "Sounds like it could be fun."

Mike turned to head into the office.

"Mike."

He stopped.

"Thanks for asking."

He smiled to himself then closed the office door behind him.

At breakfast the next morning, Will folded the paper so that only one article was showing and laid it in front of Mike.

"What's this?" Mike asked curiously.

"Read it."

Mike picked up the paper and read aloud.

LATEST UFO SIGHTINGS

"Last night residents between Crest Ridge and Clear View Heights were once again treated to a UFO display. As with every other evening this week, spherically-shaped objects were reported hovering over rooftops and scaring residents with their flashing multi-colored lights. Many claimed that, following the ominous special effects, the crafts took off at high speeds then suddenly vanished.

Forest Ranger Joe Cantelli said, "Hikers have been coming in all week with reports of finding charred depressions in the meadows up in the mountains."

When we asked what he thought was causing them, he replied, "Everyone has a theory, but no one really knows. The ones I've checked out, though, were definitely not the remains of campers' fires."

Ranchers in the valley have reported that their livestock have been spooked each night this week and several nights last week. Said Sheriff Toni Runo, "The first couple of calls we chalked up to local kids pulling pranks. But now we're not so sure. The incidents have gone on for far too long to be just kids."

We also talked to Meteorologist Bob Collins and asked him what weather conditions might possibly cause the phenomena that we have been seeing.

"Nothing would act like this with the possible exception of low-lying patches of fog, which we have not had in the valleys lately, and not at the time of day that people have reported the sightings. Evening and morning weather conditions have been clear all week."

Local law enforcement officers, as well as astronomers from the Mount Wilson Observatory, are presently investigating the alleged UFO sightings."

Mike groaned. "Them again?"

Will nodded. "That's my guess. I can't be totally certain, but their description and MO certainly fit."

"And we're going into the heart of the sightings with Jan in tow? Maybe I should call her and cancel," Mike said rising from his chair and heading for the phone.

"No," Will said stopping him. "Let's take her with us and see what happens."

"A test?"

Will nodded. "This is the perfect opportunity to see if she's being used as a decoy."

Mike resumed his seat and finished his coffee, a dark cloud settling about him.

Half-an-hour later they pulled up at Jan's apartment. She hurried out locking the door behind her. She slung a gadget bag over her shoulder while a camera dangled around her neck.

"Hi!" she said climbing into the front seat beside Mike. "I thought I'd take pictures, if it's ok with you guys."

"Terry's already been assigned to take specific shots," Will replied, "but some backup shots would come in handy."

They drove through town then headed into the hills. Mike flipped through the stations before landing on a retro station. Jan rolled down the window on her side and let the breeze blow through her hair. For a while, they relaxed and enjoyed the scenery.

The news came on and Jan's ears perked up when the announcer mentioned the recent UFO sightings in the Crest Ridge area. Will smartly snapped the radio off, while Mike looked uneasy.

"I thought I'd heard something about UFO's being seen in the area," Jan remarked. "I've always wondered if they were real."

"These UFO's?" Will scoffed. "Not likely."

"You don't think so?"

Will shook his head. "These 'sightings' are the result of pranks and mass-hysteria. One jokester scares a bunch of kids in a neighborhood, someone else burns some circles on the ground. One person sees them and tells another. Before you know it, the media has fleets of UFO's mutilating livestock and zooming over middle-class homes. Suddenly everyone is looking at airplanes and having a UFO experience."

"And that's all there is to it?" Jan asked skeptically.

"It's close."

She settled back to watch the scenery. "Well, I'm a romantic, so I'm hoping you're wrong."

Mike and Will rolled their eyes and said nothing.

Soon they were bumping along an old logging road which was narrow and rutted. Will had difficulty negotiating the acute turns even in his Suburu Outback. After a while, the trees parted and a large clearing showed up ahead. They pulled onto it, parked and got out.

Jan watched as other vehicles pulled in and parked along side them. Soon a bustle of activity hummed about the field. She picked up her camera and bag and began meandering around the field. She asked questions and took pictures on occasion.

Will joined Mike as they watched some tests in progress.

"Think they'll bother us today?" Mike asked.

"They may get curious to see what we're testing," Will replied. "Just be on your guard."

By late afternoon the tests were complete and everyone called it a day. Will waited till the others had headed off the field before putting his car into gear and heading back down the road.

"No UFO's," Jan said disappointedly, as she tucked her gadget bag at her feet.

"What?" Mike exclaimed.

She turned red. "I thought that since the reports came from this area, we might see one."

The two men stared at her in disbelief.

"Well, I told you I'm a romantic at heart. Sheesh, I'm an English major. I'm entitled!"

"Look, Jan," Will said gently. "No one is going to see something that doesn't exist. It's a 'product of mass-hysteria,'" he reiterated.

"Yeah, I know," she said glumly, "but I couldn't help hoping anyway."

She sank back against the seat between the two men and closed her eyes for a while as they meandered down the twisting mountain road. As the light began to fade, clouds rolled in overhead and the shadows grew to ominous proportions.

Soon tension settled oppressively about them. Now and then Will glanced nervously into the rear and side view mirrors. Mike anxiously scanned the dark woods on his side of the road. Jan's eyes had popped open of their own accord, and she stared straight ahead, arms crossed protectively before her.

They came to a fork in the road where the other cars turned off to head back to Clear View Heights. Alone, the Outback continued to bump down the empty logging road. The sun had set completely and the dark of night closed in around them. When the last car's tail lights had disappeared, a throbbing hum suddenly joined the refrain of the car's engine.

The hair at the nape of Mike's neck stood on end as he cocked his head to one side. "Will, is something wrong with the car?"

All three of them strained their ears listening as the hum deepened and grew louder.

"It doesn't sound like an engine knock," Mike said pensively.

Will scanned the gauges on the dashboard. "It doesn't sound like the car at all." He worriedly knit his brow.

"It's not! Look!" Jan exclaimed pointing out the window. "Here comes your 'product of mass-hysteria.'"

"What?" Will cried twisting in an attempt to see behind them.

"She's right," Mike said hoarsely, a cold sweat breaking out all over his body.

They glanced up through the windshield just in time to catch a glimpse of the spherical object that hovered just overhead pacing them.

Chapter 4

Will's mouth dropped wide open and Jan gazed in fearful awe. Suddenly a blinding white light bathed the car.

"Your eyes!" Will yelled. "Cover your eyes!"

Mike's hands flew to his face to shield his sensitive eyes from the strong light.

"Jan, look in the glove compartment. There are some special prescription sunglasses in a vinyl case. Get them…hurry!" Will commanded. "This bright light could blind Michael permanently," he added straining to see through his own Ray Bans past the glare while trying to keep the car on the narrow road.

"Will, the light's too bright. It goes right through my fingers," Mike cried. "It hurts!"

"Hurry, Jan," Will urged. "Please, hurry!"

She shielded her own eyes with one hand while pawing

frantically through the glove compartment with the other. "Found 'em!" she cried pulling them from the case and placing them in Mike's groping hand.

He hastily put them on and breathed a sigh of relief. "Thanks. That's much better!"

Jan grabbed her camera and dove into her gadget bag for a telephoto lens and her darkest filter. She snapped them onto the camera body and quickly aimed at the beam of light.

"What are you trying to do?" Will asked.

"I'm trying to get a picture of this great 'practical joke' that's causing the three of us to experience 'mass-hysteria'." The shutter clicked.

You didn't believe me, did you?"

"Let's just say I was hoping you were wrong."

"It's too bright! The picture will never come out," Will corrected.

"And we won't stay on the road unless you watch it," Mike snapped.

Will swerved to avoid the cliff edge, and Jan pressed the shutter release again. In response, the UFO dove at the car aiming its light through the front window. Will grit his teeth and squinted his eyes to mere slits.

"That thing's out to get us!" Jan gasped as it made another low pass overhead. "This is no 'practical joke.' That thing's serious!"

One wheel edged off the road pulling the rest of the car toward the cliff. Mike grabbed the steering wheel while Will shielded his eyes. They swerved and lurched sickeningly as Mike fought to bring the car back onto the road. They bumped, jolted, then drove steadily once more.

Abruptly, they found themselves in total darkness. The sudden black of night was as blinding as the glare of the light had been.

"Whoa!" Mike exclaimed ripping off the sunglasses and giving the control of the car back to Will. "Now I really can't see. My eyes don't adjust this fast."

In an instant, the steering wheel jerked from Will's hands and rolled back and forth on its own.

"What's happening?" Jan cried in alarm.

"That thing has control!" Will gasped.

The car bounced and zigzagged drunkenly along the road. Will's hands were violently yanked back and forth as he fought to regain control. Mike quickly placed his hands on the dashboard and closed his eyes. A blue shimmer encircled his hands before disappearing into the car. Little-by-little, Will was able to steer the car once again.

Gradually though, he and Mike became painfully aware of a low, thrumming sound that seemed to pulsate through their veins. Mike covered his ears and writhed, while Will vigorously rubbed his throbbing forehead.

"What's wrong?" Jan asked glancing anxiously at both of them.

"Don't you hear it?" Mike gasped, wincing.

"Hear what?"

"A low-frequency, throbbing sound," Will replied thickly as the car once again swerved drunkenly.

Jan turned her head straining to hear the sound that was bothering her colleagues, but all she heard was the whine of the UFO and the laboring of the car's engine. Yet, as she placed her hand on her chest, she could feel a throbbing pulse in her sternum like the beat of a great bass drum. Finally she, too, heard the thrumming – like the heartbeat of some enormous creature. Mike suddenly grabbed his head and slumped to the dashboard, groaning.

"Mike, are you all right?" Jan asked, shaking him slightly.

His head rolled to one side.

"Can't drive anymore," Will slurred, his head falling back against the seat.

The car lurched toward the cliff and picked up speed. Jan grabbed the wheel and tried to steer. She caught a fleeting glimpse of the speedometer as the fluorescent arm edged past eighty. Panicking, she glanced down. Will's foot was jammed down on the accelerator. She frantically kicked at his ankle and pulled on his leg but to no avail. He was frozen in place.

Jan looked back up and screamed. The car roared up a steep embankment with its last burst of speed and crashed through the brush alongside the road. Branches scraped and thumped against the hood and sides of the car. By now, her neck all the way into her head was throbbing in response to the thrumming that had increased in pitch.

Her reactions slowed as her brain quickly became muddled.

"Can't-pass-out," she declared through clenched teeth.

But the world had gradually become a slow-motion nightmare. What little she could still see was thick and shaky, like looking through a bowlful of Jello. Out of the corner of her eye, she glimpsed a slow movement. Mike had raised his head up, but she could not see his eyes.

The car broke through the bushes with a bound and hurtled into a clearing. Jan's face drained of color and her mouth opened wide in a silent scream of horror. Ahead of them loomed a huge boulder. She tried to move her foot toward the brake as tears streamed down her face but she, too, was frozen in place.

"I'm steering us to our deaths," she breathed silently.

Slowly, painfully slowly, Mike opened his eyes and raised up his right hand. He gritted his teeth and sweat streamed down his face as he fought to extend his index finger and concentrate. The car was nearly on top of the boulder now. He pointed his finger straight toward it. Jan shrieked as they hit – a giant marshmallow.

There was a sickening jolt as the car bounced backwards. Mike's head snapped back slamming into the window. His body limply slouched forward. Will, still frozen in place, barely moved at all. Jan braced herself against the dash with both hands as she was whipped back and forth. The car miraculously came to a halt. Exhausted, she glanced up at the great blinking sphere that hovered menacingly over them. It flashed its lights threateningly before the world around her went black.

The huge craft lingered bobbing overhead for nearly an hour while it blinked its lights on and off like a Christmas display. Now and then it bathed the car in the white light and, once or twice, turned on the thrumming sound again.

Eventually when no movement could be detected or roused, its lights dimmed. It lifted upward with a soft whoosh then jetted away at an abrupt ninety-degree angle. It skimmed along just above the treetops till it neared the airstrip at the top of the hill. It hovered over the open patch of ground a while before its lights blinked out. When the full moon finally came out from behind a solitary cloud, the craft was gone.

Next thing any of them knew the light-grey fingers of dawn were creeping over the mountain top and into the clearing. Mists shifted eerily in the increasing light and surrounded the still car. Jan awoke sobbing and shaking uncontrollably. Will shook his head, momentarily disoriented, before turning to the distraught young woman beside him.

"Take it easy, Jan. Take it easy," he soothed. "That thing's gone now. Everything's all right."

"Don't…want to…C-can't…s-stop," she chattered, wrapping her arms around her knees and slowly rocking back and forth.

Mike groaned and haltingly pushed himself away from the dashboard. "Oh, my head," he moaned. He doubled over clutching his stomach, his face paling. "Gotta get out," he whispered.

He hastily pushed open the door, rolled out of the car, and crawled a short distance away before his stomach heaved violently. Shivers ran up and down his spine as he broke out into a cold, clammy sweat. Finally his stomach eased enough for him to drag himself back to the car. He leaned weakly against the wheel, his limbs shaking and his teeth chattering, until the uneasiness in his stomach had subsided.

Eventually he managed to climb back inside. As he slid in beside her, Jan glanced over worriedly noticing his ashen-white face and trembling hands.

"Are you all right?" she asked putting her hand on his arm.

Mike nodded slowly. "I think so. Just have a whopper of a headache." He leaned back against the headrest and closed his eyes.

Will rubbed his hands over the stubble on his face and massaged his forehead. He climbed out gingerly and shuffled around the car. He kicked the tires and knelt beside the fender checking the underside for damage. He staggered to his feet and scanned the fenders and grill before climbing back inside, a puzzled look on his face.

"Does anyone remember what happened after I passed out last night?"

Jan nodded drying her eyes on her sleeve. Even though the sobbing and teeth chattering had ceased, her hands and legs still shook.

"You passed out with your foot on the accelerator," she answered. "I couldn't move your leg, so we just kept going faster and faster. Before I could do anything else, we ran up the bank. Then I froze and steered us straight for that…." she said pointing toward the front of the car, "that boulder. Only I could have sworn we hit a giant marshmallow." She looked to Will for reassurance she had not gone crazy.

"It was probably just the effects from the UFO," he replied patting her shoulder reassuringly.

"Then how come the car isn't totaled and we aren't dead?"

Will looked at Mike who ducked his head sheepishly.

"A 'giant marshmallow'?" Will's voice echoed inside Mike's head even though his lips had not moved. "Why not a foam-rubber rock? At least that would have been easier to explain."

"Sorry, Will. Guess it was all I could come up with at the time. Right now, I honestly don't remember any of it," Mike replied, his lips as still as Will's had been.

"Still want to see UFO's?" Will asked Jan aloud.

Jan shuddered at the thought. "I'm a romantic not a masochist. Last night cured me."

"We'll have to push the car off that boulder and back it up a ways in order to get out of here. Plus, the wheels have dug into some pretty soft ground. There must be a spring around here," Will surmised then studied Mike's drained face. The young man looked quite ill. "Michael, do you feel well enough to help me push?"

"I think so. Now that my stomach has quit rolling, I feel a bit better."

"Wonder why you're the only one who got nauseous?" Will mused.

Mike shrugged.

"Well, for now, let's get out of here." Will opened his door and slid out. "We'll have to check you out when we get home."

Mike climbed out after him, and the two men headed toward the front of the car.

"Put your back to the car and brace your feet against the rock," Will instructed.

He turned and yelled to Jan. "Put the car in neutral and crank the wheel all the way to the right. Hold it there till the car's off this rock."

Jan quickly shifted the car into neutral and frantically tugged at the wheel. Without the power steering, the wheels were difficult to turn.

Finally Will yelled. "Hold it! That's good!"

He turned back to Mike and studied him carefully. "Do you think you can add a little something to our push, or do you feel too sick?"

"I'll try, Will," Mike replied gamely, "but I don't know. I feel pretty fuzzy right now."

"Just do the best you can. We'll make it," Will assured him then yelled over his shoulder to Jan. "Ok, let's go."

The two men put their backs against the car and pushed. Meanwhile, Jan fought to keep the wheel turned as the tires slid in the ruts they had made. Little happened at the start other than the car's rocking back and forth. After a while, though, Mike's eyes began to glow and a blue aura grew around his hands. As the car moved off the rock, sparks kicked up around the hood near him. After two strong heaves, it finally broke loose from the stone with a loud scrape and rolled away from the boulder. Mike staggered to the car and crawled alongside it till he could slide into the seat next to Jan. He sat with his eyes closed, sweating and panting from the exertion.

"Hadn't you better check under the hood?" she asked as Will opened his door.

"Why?"

"I saw sparks flying when you two were pushing."

"That was just part of the bumper scraping against the boulder. Trust me, the car is just fine."

"If you say so."

"Trust me."

Jan held her breath as Will turned the key in the ignition. The car sputtered to life and rumbled terribly. Will shut it off immediately and got out. He lay down and scooted under the car. A moment later, he was rummaging in his toolbox in the back. He returned, screwdriver in hand, and disappeared under the car once more. Finally he got back in behind the wheel.

"What was the problem?" Mike asked.

"Bent rotor guard. The fan blades were scraping against it. Should be fine now."

Still, Jan held her breath again as Will turned the engine over. This time nothing happened other than the motor roaring to life. She breathed a sigh of relief and relaxed. The poor car wheezed, squeaked, rattled and knocked as Will eased them out of the clearing and back down the logging road. A little while later they were limping into the parking area at Jan's apartment building. She crawled over Mike and stumbled inside.

Once home themselves, Will staggered inside with Mike whose arm lay limply across his guardian's shoulders. Will dragged him upstairs and gently laid him on his bed. Carefully he checked him over then sighed.

"You don't seem to have any internal injuries," he concluded shaking his head.

"I'm just exhausted, that's all," Mike replied wearily. "Fighting their mind control to keep us from crashing, then adding that extra boost to my push this morning really drained me. I'll be fine, Will. Just let me sleep."

"I suppose you're right," Will replied, yawning as he fumbled for the knob and closed the door behind him. He stumbled the few feet to his bedroom, climbed into his own bed and drifted into a deep sleep.

Chapter 5

Monday afternoon Jan walked through the lab, set her backpack by her station then pulled out a large manila envelope. She walked to the office door and saw that both men were present. Stepping inside, she closed the door behind her.

"Hey, what gives?" Mike demanded.

She ignored his rudeness and handed Will the envelope.

"What's this?" he asked putting on his reading glasses.

"Take a look. I think you'll find them interesting."

Mike stood up and peered over Will's shoulder while his colleague opened the envelope and pulled out several black and white eight-by-ten photos.

Will's eyebrows raised sharply.

"Wow!" Mike exclaimed. "How did you get these through all that glare?"

Will passed the top photos of a spherical craft to Mike while he looked at some of the bottom photos.

"I stopped my telephoto lens all the way down to f/32 and used the filter I bought for photographing solar eclipses," Jan explained.

"You just happened to have it with you?" Will asked sarcastically.

"I'm always prepared," she replied coolly. "Anyway, what do you think it is? It's too round for a helicopter, and it can't be an airplane. A blimp looks like a cigar, so…"

"Weather balloon?" Mike proposed. "They're round and fly low."

"Oh, sure…and a weather balloon just happened to have a blinding spotlight on board and could maneuver to run us off the road."

"No, this isn't the norm," Will broke in. "This is something I can't explain…yet."

"Hmm, Daryl could digitally enhance the negs," Mike mused.

"Think we could identify it then?" Jan asked.

Mike did not reply but kept staring at the photograph in his hands.

"Could we borrow the negatives?" Will asked.

Jan pointed to the envelope. "They're inside. I was hoping you guys could do something with them."

Mike took the envelope, dumped out the negatives, and held one up to the light. "I'll drop by the audio-visual department later and see what Daryl makes of these."

He slipped the negatives and photos into the envelope which he placed into his briefcase. Snapping it shut, he saluted Will and Jan, opened the door and headed out through the lab.

Later that afternoon Mike returned to find most of the research assistants gone to a class or lab of their own. Jan occupied her corner near the office. As he neared the door, he realized that she was holding her head instead of typing. He set his briefcase down inside the door then stepped over to her workstation.

"You all right?" he asked quietly.

Startled, she jumped and her pen went flying under a nearby lab table. Breathing hard she looked up. "You scared me out of my wits," she accused.

Mike pulled up a lab stool and studied her hard. "Are you all right?" he persisted.

Jan looked down and shook her head.

"What's wrong?"

"My neck has been killing me, and I've been getting the worst headaches…blinding. Sometimes I can't even see what I'm doing."

Mike rolled the stool over behind her and began massaging her tense shoulders.

"Would you believe I went to a chiropractor this afternoon?"

He stopped rubbing and looked at her in shock.

She nodded confirmation, as he began kneading between her shoulder blades and working his way up to her neck.

"I swear the pain is worse now since I went than it was before," Jan complained then drew a sharp intake of breath as Mike hit a spot directly behind her left ear. "Ow! That's the worst. That and my left temple."

Mike rubbed her left temple, discovered a small puncture mark and depression then went back to the spot on her neck, his brows furrowed with deep concern.

"I know my grandmother started having migraines when she was 25," Jan went on wincing as his fingers touched a small disc just under her skin. "I guess they caught up with me at 27 instead."

Mike stopped rubbing her neck. "You're just doing your grad work at 27?"

Jan pulled away like she had been slapped.

Mike put out a hand to stop her from fleeing. "Look. I-I didn't mean that the way it sounded. I had just automatically figured you were around 22 or 23 like the other grad students."

"Sorry. I'm edgy with this headache," Jan apologized.

Mike picked up her pen from under the lab table then guided her into the office and had her sit down.

"I spent a year in England after I got my bachelors," Jan explained. "It was a graduation present from my dad. I'd had to wait a year to start college while I helped take care of my mom."

"What was wrong with her?" Mike wondered.

"She had cancer and it was terminal. She and dad decided it would be better if she died at home instead of in some sterile hospital room, and I stayed home to spend what time she had left with her," Jan explained matter-of-factly. "When I got my bachelors, dad decided I should enjoy life a little."

"Hence the trip to England," Mike surmised.

She nodded.

"Dad never told me he was sick, though. I found out he had heart failure when I got back. So I got a job for a couple of years...."

"And took care of him, too."

Jan nodded again. "I'm not sorry I took the time to do that. If I had gone away to school, I would have missed making some great memories with him. In the end, dad died in his sleep."

"And you came here."

She smiled but tears welled in her eyes. "I'd lie if I said I didn't miss them, but I've still got a life to live."

Mike nodded, quieted by this new revelation of Jan's.

"Look, why don't you knock off. I'll talk to Will about those migraines of yours. He's tried just about every remedy in the book. If he doesn't know what works, no one does." Mike smiled.

Jan closed her eyes and sighed. "Thanks. I think I'll take your offer. Maybe a good night's sleep will help."

Mike walked her to the door. She turned and looked back at him.

"You know, you're not half bad when you're being a friend."

"Thanks."

She waved and walked away down the hall.

That evening Mike sat in the living room and stared, without seeing, at a picture on the wall. Will entered from the kitchen, spotted that well-known gaze of focused concentration and took off his glasses.

"Michael," he called. "What's up?"

Mike blinked then turned to look at him. "Jan's having migraines."

Will sank onto the couch. "Welcome to the club."

"No. Not regular migraines," Mike countered.

Will's eyebrow raised. "And you would know how?"

"I gave her a shoulder rub."

Both of Will's eyebrows shot straight up.

"I found something I don't like."

Will's brow furrowed. "Like what?"

"I found the insertion point from that probe near her left temple," he began, "and a homing disk behind her left ear."

Will nodded gravely.

"They're-using-her," Mike said vehemently.

Will studied him a long moment. "You seem to care quite a bit that's she's being used."

Mike's face softened for a brief moment before the armor dropped over his visage once more.

"Want some help with that disc?" Will offered.

Mike nodded. "I told her you had some great migraine remedies."

"Why don't you bring her by tomorrow evening and let's see what we can do?"

The next day Mike brought Jan home with him. Will was already there, sitting in the living room. He pulled his glasses off and looked up as they walked through the door.

"Mike told me about your migraines," he commented, as Mike brought in a dining room chair and motioned for her to sit in it.

"Yeah, nothing touches them. Nothing."

"I deeply empathize. I've suffered from migraines for years, but I have learned a trick or two in dealing with them."

Jan closed her eyes and rolled her neck to relieve the stiffness. "Well, I'll certainly try about anything you have to offer. My grandmother described hers, but I don't think they were ever this bad."

Mike brought in another chair and placed it facing her. Will sat in the chair and Mike sat behind her.

"So what do I do?" she asked.

"Just get as comfortable as you can and relax," Will said in a soothing monotone. "Just relax and stare at a point on the wall. Got a spot?"

She nodded.

"Good, now let your eyes relax till things are just blurry. Allow your eyes to relax. Now, look straight up just moving your eyes," he instructed. "Now, bring your eyes back down to focus on your point. Good," Will said watching her. "Relax your eyes once more then raise them straight up again. Hold your eyes up and close your lids. Hold it. Hold it. Now, bring your eyes down and let yourself relax completely."

Will continued droning instructions until Jan was completely unaware of her surroundings. Mike quietly left for the kitchen and returned a moment later with a scalpel and a first-aid kit. Carefully he felt along her neck until he found the tell-tale bump. He nodded to Will.

"Right now we're going to take care of those migraines. You will feel no pain or pressure," Will droned. "You will remain completely still throughout the entire procedure. When you awaken, your neck and shoulders will feel soothed and relaxed, and your migraines will be gone. If you heard me and understood, raise your right index finger."

In response, Jan raised her finger and put it back down.

"Ok, Mike," Will telepathed. "Go ahead."

Mike took the scalpel and delicately cut around the bump till he could brush back a flap of skin. Inside lay a round disc the size of a dime. Both he and Will held their breath as Mike lifted out the disc. He passed the scalpel to Will, treated the open wound with antiseptic and a Band-Aid fluid then took the scalpel from Will and hurried outside to dispose of the disc.

Meanwhile, Will slowly brought Jan around, bringing her from a level of deep relaxation until he was counting her up to wakefulness. "When I finish counting, you will be awake and aware and feeling fine. Ten…nine…eight…becoming more ware…seven…six…five…four… feeling fine…three…two…eyes open…one."

With that Jan's eyes flickered open. At first she looked a little bewildered, then a big smile spread across her face. "It's gone!" she exclaimed. "My migraine's gone!"

Mike returned her smile. "I told you Will knew all the right remedies."

Jan stretched her neck from side-to-side. "You're not kidding. I was wondering if I'd ever feel this good again. Thanks, both of you."

"C'mon. I'll take you home," Mike offered.

She headed toward the door. Mike quickly stowed the first-aid kit in the kitchen cupboard. Will watched him follow Jan out the door.

Mike dropped Jan off at her apartment then made a late visit to the nursing facility.

"Visiting hours are over in skilled nursing," the woman at the desk told him.

Mike looked at her and a quiet gasp escaped her lips. Slowly her eyelids fluttered then closed. Mike left the desk and threaded his way through the maze of halls. Once on the skilled nursing floor, he traveled more cautiously, opened Pat's door, then closed and locked it behind him.

Making certain no one else was in the room, he stood beside her bed. He concentrated on her still figure until a blue glow surrounded her body. Her double rose above her and stood beside him.

"I won't leave you, Mike," Pat's glowing form said.

"Pat, I need to be free. I need to live again," Mike implored her.

"But you need me," she reminded him. "Our bond. You need our bond," she said approaching him and reaching out to touch his arm. He stepped back avoiding her caress.

"I can't be bound to a corpse," he said, gesturing to her still body kept alive only by machines. "I need a living, breathing, walking, talking woman, Pat. I need to live again."

"But, you can always come to see me!" she protested. "Just like you have for years."

Mike shook his head. "What if I leave the area? What if I leave," he emphasized, "period. Then what? Where does that leave me?"

Pat again tried to advance on him.

"No, Pat. I need you to set me free."

"But I'll die!" she protested.

"Pat, look at what you're calling life now. Look!" he demanded pointing to her body. "You're only being kept alive by machines. You were hurt too badly. You will never come back to me whole. Please…give me my life back! Let-me-go!"

Pat shook her head. "No!" she protested. "You said we would always be together."

"But I never meant like this, Pat. If you don't let me go, I'll die, too."

"Then we'll always be together," she said a smile spreading across her face and she reached out to him again.. "Always together. No more separation like now."

Realization struck Mike as to what she was implying. "No, Pat. I want to live, fully."

She backed him against the wall, touched his hair and let her hand glide down his cheek to his neck. She brought her body closer until she started to melt into him. The sharp crackle of electricity filled the air as Mike's knees began to buckle.

"We've always had each other like this," she crooned. "Now we can have each other fully."

"No. Got-to-live," he gasped.

Slowly he forced himself to stand once more and his eyes

glowed bright blue. Pat backed away from him, the blue aura that enveloped him disappearing into her shimmering figure as if she were sucking it in. He gritted his teeth in concentration and a light shot from his eyes at her glowing figure. For a moment she was caught in its intensely bright field.

"What are you doing? I only want to be with you." Her protest faded as the glow vanished back into her comatose form on the bed.

Mike heaved a sigh of relief and breathed deeply to regain his composure. He took a moment to compose himself and regain a sense of inner balance before opening the door and entering the hallway. Quietly, without attracting attention, he made his way out of the building.

When he arrived home, the house was quiet and the lights were off. He let himself in without his keys and tip-toed upstairs. He sat upstairs on the edge of his bed thinking about his latest exchange with Pat. With resolve he swung his legs up onto the bed and lay staring at the dark.

Chapter 6

The next day Mike entered the lab with a determined step. Rather than pushing right through, he stopped to chat with assistants who were running tests. He tapped Jan on the shoulder and waved hello as he entered the office.

"Good-morning, Will," he said cheerfully flicking on his computer.

Will's hand froze in mid-air, just short of bringing his coffee cup to his mouth.

"Looks like Terry's getting some good data," Mike continued.

Will turned slowly in his chair and stared at him. "You checked?"

Mike glanced up at him and nodded.

Jan knocked at the door and Mike turned to face her. "What's up?" he asked pleasantly.

She paused and looked at Will who shrugged. She tentatively held out a print out of the latest set of notes.

"To be honest, this stuff is so beyond me, I'm not sure if the notes I'm typing make any sense," she related hesitantly.

Mike skimmed the first couple of pages and frowned. "Mm-hm. I need to help you with some of this."

Jan mouthed “help” to Will.

“Give me half-an-hour to get this program running. Once it begins the number crunching, there won’t be anything else for me to do and I can help you make sense of this.”

He handed the notes back to a shocked Jan who left. Will continued to stare so hard at him, Mike finally had to stop entering commands and look at his colleague.

“What?”

“I’m surprised, that’s all!”

“I could growl and snap.”

“No, no. I prefer this,” Will replied. “Just tell me…why the sudden change? How?”

A dark shadow crossed Mike’s face.

“Mike, something came between us years ago,” Will began. “Things have never been the same. But I haven’t seen you act this much like your old self in….”

“Ten years. It’s been ten years, almost eleven,” Mike murmured. “I’m sorry, Will. Something happened…has been happening that I couldn’t talk about…still can’t.”

“Not even to me,” Will asked in amazement.

Mike swallowed hard and looked away shaking his head.

“Let’s just say that I finally heard you, and I’m taking my life back.”

Will studied his friend wondering at the depths of meaning beneath his words.

Mike quickly set up the computer to begin analyzing his research assistant’s data. He went out into the lab and pulled up a stool next to Jan. He looked over what she had been typing.

“You’ve got all the right words there,” he commented, “but it’s obvious you don’t know how all of these terms relate.”

Jan held her forehead in her hand. “I almost feel like you would be better off finding someone with at least a background for this stuff. I’m beginning to feel like I’m doing more harm than good with these notes.”

Mike laid a hand on her arm as if to prevent her from leaving. “Let’s see if we can’t familiarize you with some basic concepts first. You’re the first person who has at least been able to decipher my handwriting and put up with me.”

"I don't know."

"C'mon, let's give it a shot," he implored.

She sighed heavily. "Ok. I'll try."

"Great! I have to go teach now, but how about we grab dinner and I'll try to explain some of the basics?"

"Some place other than Tony's."

"No, I've got another place in mind," Mike assured her.

He grabbed his briefcase from the office and headed out to teach. "Don't worry," he called back over his shoulder. "We'll get you up to speed."

Jan watched him leave in wonderment. Will stood in the office doorway watching, too.

"Is this just a passing phase?" she wondered aloud.

"I don't know," Will replied. "I almost don't think so."

Around seven that evening Jan sat with Mike in a Mexican restaurant ordering enchiladas. Once the waitress left, he took out the notes and started relating the concepts to her almost as if he were telling a story. By the end of the evening, as they shared fried ice cream, Jan was feeling far more confident about the material.

"You know, I can see why so many of your intro physics students think you're really good," she commented digging in for another spoonful.

"They do?"

"Yeah. I've heard several students say you're the only prof who makes physics understandable. Given the way you just explained this to me," she said lifting the notes as evidence, "I believe them."

Mike thought about this for a moment. "Wow! I figured they thought I was a grouch and a jerk and were just happy to get out of my class."

"Well, that, too, but…." She stopped and looked at him squarely. ""Why the sudden change, Mike? It's as if someone has breathed new life into you."

He looked down at his napkin. After a long silence, he finally looked up. "I guess you could say, I decided I wanted to live life again. I had felt so choked off, drained. I decided…no more."

She looked at him quizzically but asked no more.

On the way back to the campus Mike glanced at her noticing her tired, pale face.

"Any plans for the mid-semester break?" he asked.

"I'm working on a forty page paper for my 19th Century Literature class. It's the only grade for that class so it has to be good."

"What about some R and R?"

"Oh, I plan to catch up on my sleep. Recreation will have to wait until the break between semesters," she replied.

"That won't do," he said in a mock serious tone.

"Yeah, but such is life."

He shook his head. "You need to take one day and actually do something fun."

"With all the work I have to do?" she protested. "You have no idea!"

"It's only been two years since I defended my dissertation," Mike informed her. "I'm not that much older than you, and I keenly remember the work load. But you have to do something fun. You'll be able to think straighter afterwards."

She looked at him quizzically. "So do you have any suggestions?"

"As a matter of fact, I do. I have an ultralight, a two seat training model. Come fly with me Saturday."

"For real? What about your research?"

"It'll be waiting for me when I get back," he replied. "It always is."

She thought for a moment. "All day?"

"Most of it."

"Just flying around in the ultralight?"

"Yeah, it's a lot of fun."

Jan bit her lower lip. "The temptation is terrible." She squinted her eyes closed then said, "Oh, all right. I'll go."

"Great! I'll pick you up around nine Saturday morning."

"I'm actually looking forward to this," she said getting out of his car as he stopped behind hers in the parking lot.

Saturday morning dawned bright and clear. Mike knocked on Jan's apartment door. He waited till she came out locking the door behind her. They headed for a small plane airstrip half-an-hour away and pulled into the lot beside Will's Outback.

"My Triumph only holds two so Will's our carrier. We'll take off from here and land at another strip. Will will pick us up there,"

Mike explained.

The ultralight was in separate pieces and it took them another half-an-hour to get it all together.

"You two all set?" Will asked, as Mike pulled on a protective helmet.

"Should be. I checked it over last night. The engine's running fine and it's got a full tank," Mike replied. "Plus, once we catch a thermal, I can always cut the engine and let it glide for a while."

"Good enough. Give me a call when you want a pick up," Will said, getting into his vehicle and driving away.

Mike handed Jan a helmet which she pulled on.

"Ever been up in one before?" he asked.

She shook her head.

"They're a lot of fun. I used to fly regular planes, but there's nothing like the feel of an ultralight. Climb in."

Jan climbed into the seat without the controls and gripped the slender frame tightly. Mike eased in, checked the air strip's windsocks and started the motor. He eased the throttle open, revving the engine, then taxied down the dirt strip until the wheels were off the ground.

Jan gazed about them as they soared over the treetops. "Not bad. You get a great view from up here," she remarked. "Just one thing wrong."

"What's that?"

"I'm scared to death of heights."

"Why did you agree to come?" he asked.

"You said it would be fun."

They buzzed off over the treetops and headed out along a ridge. After a while, Jan got used to the hum and the bumps and wobbles and eased back into the seat.

"Feeling better?" he asked.

She nodded continuing to look at the scenery below them and off toward the horizon.

Eventually they crossed the narrow neck of the valley and swept along another ridge.

"Hey, isn't that Crest Ridge Heights down there?" Jan asked, pointing.

Mike glanced down then nodded.

"Think that thing's gone?" she asked.

"I haven't heard about any more sightings," he replied. "There are moments when I could almost believe it was nothing but a nightmare."

The Outback still has some scrapes on the fenders," she reminded him.

"Let's just take a look," he suggested heading the ultralight towards the nearby hills till he found the logging road and the test site on top. As he circled the large open field, Jan tugged at his sleeve and pointed. Off to the north was a small clearing surrounded by tall pines. Something about the clearing caught his eye and he swung back toward the field and landed the little plane.

"Didn't that almost look like something had crashed there?" Jan asked, unbuckling her helmet.

He shook his head. "Those branches were bent straight up and the tops of the trees were pretty charred."

"That's bizarre. Are we going to have a look?"

He nodded and led the way toward the scrub at the edge of the field. Soon the underbrush gave way to stout tree trunks, bracken and moss. Water oozed from the ground around their feet squishing as they skirted a swampy area. Suddenly they burst through into a clearing that was strewn with broken and charred branches. They stopped in their tracks and stared.

"Wow!" Jan exclaimed. "Something big crashed here."

"Or landed," Mike said under his breath.

"You don't think it was that thing, do you?" she asked, becoming alarmed.

"Maybe. Let's have a look around."

They began to cross the clearing shuffling through the tall grass and periodically picking up charred pieces of wood. In the woods behind them, branches rustled then quieted and a pair of amber eyes glowed eerily.

Jan wandered off to the left and spotted a circular scorch mark in the grass. She knelt down and picked up some of the white powdery substance inside it. She smelled the powder, its acrid odor tickling her nose. She took another whiff, scrunched up her nose and sneezed. Pulling a tissue out of her pocket, she began to scoop some powder into it. Behind her a hand reached out toward her through the bushes.

Just then Mike yelled for her. She looked up and the hand shot back into the bushes. She hurried over to him to see what he had found.

"No wreckage except for this," he remarked showing her a small piece of curved metal.

"I found one of those weird burned circles," she told him, "and I got some of the powdery stuff from it to take back."

A shiver ran down her spine, and she glanced over her shoulder. "You know, it could be me, but I've gotten the feeling that we're being watched."

Mike looked around at the forest's edge but saw nothing abnormal. "I know what you mean because I've felt it, too."

"Maybe we're just edgy because of that thing," Jan suggested.

"And it appears to be long gone," Mike added.

Still, uncomfortable tingles made them both wary and a breeze started blowing.

"We'd better head back before the wind makes flying difficult," Mike said heading across the clearing.

They began at a swift walk, but by the time they dove into the woods, Mike and Jan were running. Now and then Jan glanced over her shoulder as they crashed through the bracken and broke out of the underbrush. As they hurried onto the field, the breeze picked up and tossed their hair.

They wasted no time in donning their helmets and clambering back into the ultralight. Mike revved the engine and headed them into the wind. The ride was bumpy, but once they were airborne, Jan heaved a sigh of relief.

"Mike, someone was out there with us," Jan said. "I could swear someone was following us back."

He circled the field once but it was empty. Satisfied, he headed back toward the other landing field.

From the forest eaves, two glowing amber eyes watched them leave then blinked out.

They took the metal and the powder back to the university. Mike headed straight for a friend's chemistry lab.

"Ken, got a minute?" he asked.

"What's up?" his friend asked watching him enter.

"Got a couple of anomalies I'd like identified if you can."

Mike handed him the scrap of metal and the powder.

"Where'd you get this?" Ken asked.

"From one of those UFO sites the news was talking about a couple of weeks ago."

Ken raised his eyebrows.

"Just run some tests and see if you can identify it, ok?"

"Yeah, sure. Should be a piece of cake."

A week later, Ken entered Mike and Will's lab with a very puzzled look on his face. When Mike saw him, he drew him into the office.

"So? What've you got?" he asked.

"I don't know," the chemist replied.

"Wood ashes, right?"

Ken shook his head. "I ran some standard tests, ph, stuff like that. It's highly acidic, but not wood, plastic or any vegetable matter. There were traces of silica, but otherwise…." he shrugged his shoulders.

"And the metal?" Mike asked.

"Nothing man made or known to Earth. Whatever this is, Earth has never seen its likes before. Depending on temperature and the angle of the light hitting it, it randomly changes shape. It's unbendable, can't be cut by either a diamond blade or a laser, and I have no clue what it's made of," Ken replied.

Mike let out a low whistle. "And you're the best."

"And when the best can't crack it…."

"Right. Thanks anyway, Ken."

"Hey, anytime. Next time make it something I can figure out. I'd like to get one right now and then," he said and headed out the door.

That evening, Mike showed the find to Will. "What do you think?"

Will examined the powder and the piece of metal for a while. "Earth has never seen this alloy."

"How about Saracen?" Mike pressed.

Will shook his head. "Not the last I knew, but a lot can happen in nearly thirty years. Maybe they're mining in new territory."

"Could they be partnering with another alliance?" Mike wondered.

"If they are, we may be in more danger than we have ever been in," Will said gravely.

At that moment, the phone rang with an almost insistent edge to it. Mike got up and put the receiver to his ear.

"Hello?"

"Mike, help!" It was Jan; she sounded terrified and nearly hysterical.

"Jan, what's wrong?" Mike asked tensing.

"They're here. They're trying to break down my front door."

"Who? Who's 'they'?"

"Those spies. Help, Mike! What do I do?"

Mike's eyes widened in fear as he listened to the pounding in the background.

"Mike, that door's not going to last much longer. I'm scared."

"Stay put, Jan! We'll be right there," Mike assured her and hung up.

"What's wrong?" Will asked.

"They found her. Even without the homing disc they found her."

Will stared at him in shock.

Chapter 7

Mike slammed down the receiver and grabbed a jacket. "C'mon, Will. Let's take care of those two."

They hustled out to Will's Outback and hopped in. Will paused a moment before starting the engine. He watched as a blue glowing image of Mike detached from his body and hovered like a mannequin above his lap. In a flash it collapsed into a shimmering blue ball of energy, dissolved through the car window zipping through the night like a streak of blue lightning.

In seconds the ball of pure energy reached Jan's apartment, stopped and lengthened into Mike's form. He looked at the door that was ajar and rushed forward. In the narrow entry hall the two tall blond-haired men heaved their shoulders against Jan's bathroom door in an attempt to force it open, also. From inside, Mike heard her muffled sobs.

Without warning, a bolt of blue light shot from his eyes and hit the closest attacker squarely in the chest. He was knocked off his feet and flung against the far wall like a limp rag doll. His companion turned and received a lesser dose of the same treatment.

Mike pursued them into the main room of the apartment and stopped as the second spy scrambled back to his feet and prepared to attack.

"You have come," he growled. his eyes glowing amber. "We could not find you, so we drew you to us."

Mike braced his feet well apart, prepared for any move the man might make. Outside, he heard the screech of tires as Will swung the Outback into the lot. The door opened and his footsteps pounded toward the door.

Just as Will leapt inside, the spy dove for Mike who simply disappeared and reappeared behind him. The spy sprung to his feet and grappled with Mike.

As the two locked in hand-to-hand struggle, each trying to out power and thus subdue his opponent, Jan crept out of the bathroom and met Will in the hall. Cautiously they edged into the main room, and Jan darted past the wrestling opponents to the other side.

By now a blue glow had begun to surround both men, and Mike had managed to force the spy to one knee. They wavered like that for a moment, and Will glanced about for something to use as a weapon. He spotted a movement and watched as Jan picked up a heavy antique iron lamp, raised it over her head and brought it crashing down against the back of the spy's head. He looked up at Mike in open-mouthed shock, twitched, and crumpled into a heap on the floor.

Will hastily flicked on the lights as Jan sank onto her bed. For a moment Mike studied the two bodies on the floor then looked over at Jan.

"Are you all right?"

She nodded, her eyes never leaving the bodies on the floor.

"Who were these two?" Will telepathed.

"They're the same ones who abducted Jan a while back," Mike replied mentally.

"They're definitely Saracen," Will surmised still holding his mental conversation with Mike.

"Oh, I knew that from the first moment I saw them," Mike replied. Suddenly he spotted Jan reaching for the phone. "Who are you calling?" he demanded aloud.

"The police, who else?"

Mike appeared to glide from where he was until he stood beside Jan, all in a matter of seconds. She stared at him uncertainly. He took the receiver from her hand and set it back on its cradle.

"This is more of a job for the FBI," he explained, "only the police and the FBI usually have some difficulty working together very smoothly."

"Any investigation they performed on this could drag on for months," Will added.

"And since it probably involves some of our research findings, they could quarantine the lab and confiscate all our data," Mike continued. "We'd have to start all over again."

"If they even let us," Will said.

Jan sank back in defeat. "I never figured it would be this complicated, but you're right."

She looked back at the bodies. "What will we do with them?"

Mike looked at Will.

"I think we can take care of them and no one will know a thing," Will assured her.

That was when Jan looked up and noticed the scrapes and gouges in the walls of her apartment. "Then there's this place. How am I ever going to explain this to the super?" she fretted.

"Michael and I can help you repair this," Will offered.

"Yeah, by tomorrow evening it will look as good as new," Mike added.

Jan sighed and nodded. "As long as my super doesn't find out, that's all I care."

"Michael, do you want to come out and help me re-arrange things in the Outback so we can fit these two in?" Will asked giving Mike an almost imperceptible nod toward the door.

"Right now," Mike replied. "We'll be right back," he promised Jan.

They hurried out and she soon heard the car door open. She gingerly stepped around the two corpses and slipped into her bathroom to grab the cell phone she had kept with her out of the shower. She saw a shimmer of light through the window and glanced outside.

A limp Mike sat propped in the passenger seat, while a second shimmering Mike stood beside the car. The second figure collapsed into a blue ball of light that eased into the car and hovered in front of the still body. Slowly it penetrated his chest, there was a flash of light and only one Michael remained. He blinked his eyes and looked around.

Jan drew back from the window, her eyes wide. She shook her head disbelieving what her eyes had just seen. She snuck a quick peek back outside, and saw the two men heading back up the walk. The car itself was empty.

She muttered to herself as she walked back into the main room to place the cell phone in its charging stand. "More than espionage is at work here," she told herself, then shook her head. "No, I had to have been seeing things. A lot has happened tonight, and I'm hysterical. Once I calm down, everything will make sense…I hope."

A moment later Will and Mike let themselves in. They hefted the two bodies onto their shoulders in a fireman's hold, then staggered out the door to the car. While Will arranged them in the back of the vehicle, Mike returned for one last check on Jan. She was busily studying the door which sat open at an odd angle.

"The super is going to have to replace the whole thing," she groaned. "But until then, what do I do for a door?"

Mike sized up the bent hinges then tried to shift the door. "Do you have a hammer and a screwdriver?" he requested. "I think I can at least get it to close."

While Jan went to rummage in the drawers of her kitchenette, Mike placed one hand on the door and the other on the top hinge. A blue glow surrounded his hands, entered the door and the frame until they glowed, too.

Jan returned with the tools gasping as Mike swung the door open and closed, the hinges completely repaired.

"How in the world did you do that?" she wondered.

Mike shrugged. "You need to have the super put in a dead bolt."

"Yeah, I will. Still, how…?"

Mike ignored her question and went over to her cell phone. He punched in a number and a code.

"I just put our number in. If anything else happens, hit star one and it'll reach us."

"Thanks. I must admit you have an excellent response time." Jan laid down the tools and sank into a chair.

Mike studied her a moment then knelt beside her chair. "Are you going to be ok?"

She nodded. "I'm just really shook up, that's all."

He laid his hand over hers. "I'd feel terrible if anything happened to you," he murmured.

"Why? Because you would lose the only grad assistant who can decipher your notes?"

He slowly shook his head. "Because I care," he said quietly then left.

Jan listened to their vehicle leave, her head spinning with all of the events of the evening. Exhausted, she crawled back into bed and fell into a troubled sleep.

Meanwhile, Will and Mike had the dubious privilege of taking care of the "remains." They drove straight home, where Will backed the Outback into the garage. As soon as the door had clanged shut, they dragged the two limp corpses into the farthest corner of their backyard. Will felt around their shoulder blades, popping open a secret compartment in both.

"Androids!" Mike breathed.

"I had suspected as much," Will replied. "Head for the house. I'll join you as soon as I set the self-destruct mechanisms."

Mike sprinted for the back door. Seconds behind him, Will dashed in and crouched near the door. A moment later they heard two short explosions. Will cracked the door open, peeked out then sighed with relief.

"All done," he said getting to his feet and heading back outside.

Mike followed and they carefully examined the powdery residue that remained.

"I should probably have Ken analyze this, too," Mike said.

"Not worth it," Will replied heading back inside. "We would be better off getting a good night's sleep."

"Yeah, but how will we both fix Jan's apartment and run the data tomorrow?

"I'll go run the data," Will offered. "You're better with spackle. You've had more practice."

The next morning Mike showed up on Jan's doorstep at ten sharp. "Work crew," he announced cheerfully as she opened the door.

She pressed a finger to her lips. "Not too loud. The super already called to find out what all the noise was about last night."

"What did you tell him?" Mike asked stepping inside.

"That I'd fallen asleep with the TV on and probably had the volume up too loud."

Mike nodded and set down the bucket of tools he had brought with him. "The walls should be pretty easy to patch with spackle," he surmised. "The bathroom door will take a bit of careful artwork, though."

"You sound like you've had practice," Jan remarked.

"Now and then."

He pulled out a can of spackle, popped the lid with a screwdriver and set to work with a spackle knife. Jan watched as he smoothed the sticky white paste over the dents and holes, then feathered the edges to blend with the rest of the wall. At last he set the can down and stepped back to inspect his work.

"It's fast drying, so give it an hour and we should be able to paint it. Good thing your apartment's painted flat white. It makes getting paint to match real easy."

"What about the bathroom door?" Jan asked.

"That will take a bit. Would you mind going out and getting a can of white paint while I work on it?"

"Sure," Jan said grabbing her keys and her purse.

Forty-five minutes later when she returned, the bathroom door looked as good and new. She examined it carefully.

"I can't even tell that anything happened to it," she remarked. "You're a real pro."

"Not much to it," Mike replied taking the paint can, opening it, and dabbing paint on the areas he had patched earlier.

Once done, he packed up his tools, then sat down on her sofa bed a moment. Jan slid onto a chair eyeing her room distrustfully.

"You ok?" he asked.

She nodded. "I guess. So much has happened since last night it's hard to know."

She got up, ran her hands over the walls, then sat next to Mike on the couch. Mike stretched his arm along the top of the couch behind her.

"You know, I'm really glad you weren't hurt last night," he said holding her hand. "I can't imagine what they wanted with you."

"I'm just very glad I didn't have to find out," she replied shuddering at the thought and unconsciously snuggling closer to him.

He glanced down at his lap for a moment, took a deep breath, looked up and held her gaze. "I know we started off on the wrong foot because I was such a jerk," he said.

"You've mellowed out a bit since then," she affirmed.

"And you've had a big hand in that."

"Me?"

He nodded. "You wouldn't let me get away with treating you like a jerk. You also wouldn't let me stay in my own little world. I've started seeing and hearing and feeling things that I had closed myself off to until you came around."

She searched his eyes and found nothing but sincerity.

"I'd like to ask you out for a real date. No Tony's or the like, but an evening out without research notes between us."

Jan's eyes widened. "I'd…I'd like that…a lot."

That night as Mike lay in bed deciding where he would take Jan, a faint glow appeared in his room. It moved toward him and a voice called his name. He frowned and turned toward the glow.

"Mike. I have no form left. You haven't visited in so long," Pat protested. "I'll die if you don't come back."

"I made a mistake years ago, Pat. I thought that if I could share my energy with you, I could bring you back."

"And you did," Pat insisted.

Mike shook his head. "No. I kept some part of you alive, but I couldn't revive the girl I had known. I should have known that even in your state, you either had to find the strength within yourself to live or you would die, regardless of what I did."

"And I'm dying now. Help me, Mike, like you always have," Pat pleaded, a transparent arm stretched out toward him.

He closed his eyes tight. "I can't, Pat. What I've done all these years was wrong and I have to face that fact…as do you."

Pat's form began to flicker. "I need you, Mike. My life energy is fading. Share yours."

He shook his head not opening his eyes to watch. "I-can't."

The glow disappeared as her cry of "Mike" faded as if on a distant breeze.

Chapter 8

Mike sat at his computer in his office. Two assistants planned to stay well past midnight, but he was nearly ready to leave. He heard Jan's computer power down, and he got up to catch her before she left. He motioned for her to join him in the office.

"Yeah?" she asked, stepping inside the doorway.

"How about dinner at Martinelli's on Friday evening?" he suggested.

"Martinelli's? Oh, you mean that new restaurant on Costello Blvd?"

He nodded.

"Mm. I've been thinking about that place for weeks. One of my girlfriends went there, and she's been raving about it ever since," Jan said.

"So, it's a date?"

She looked at him and smiled. "Yeah. It's a date."

Mike left for home with a spring in his step. He hummed as he entered the house. Will heard him and looked up.

"You seem happy…finally."

Mike stopped and glanced his way. "I guess you could say, I finally found a reason to live again…fully."

Will nodded. "I'm happy for you. I've been worried about you for years, and I just didn't know how to help."

"You couldn't have, Will. I had to come to a point where I could see what I was doing to myself. When I did, I didn't like what I saw, but I couldn't have realized it any sooner."

Will nodded accepting this explanation. "Speaking of 'seeing things,' I get the distinct feeling there is something we aren't seeing."

Mike frowned as he went through his mail. "Like what?"

"You removed that homing disc from Jan's neck...."

Mike looked up understanding dawning on his face. "But they still found her."

"How?"

"Do they put homing devices on their operatives?" Mike wondered.

"Most of their operatives are androids."

"So, no need for the discs."

"Right."

"Could she be cooperating with them?" Mike postulated.

"Then why would they attack her? Why not follow her and get to you? No, Michael. There is something else that we're overlooking."

Mike sat down, a dark frown on his face. "If she isn't cooperating with them then they're using her...."

"Without her knowledge it would appear," Will added. "But how?"

A thought made Mike's blood run cold. "An implant," he whispered.

"What? I didn't hear you."

"An implant? Could they have fitted her with some sort of psychic implant?" Mike wondered.

Will looked at him then groaned. "Of course. Why didn't I think of that?"

"Because they let us think we had already taken care of the problem."

"Meanwhile, they're using Jan letting her mental circuitry work for them," Will said.

"And once they have what they want from us...."

"It self-destructs and no one is the wiser," Will finished.

"Except that Jan can no longer function, she's locked away in some institution and eventually dies of 'natural' causes."

They both took a deep breath as they thought of the ugly possibilities.

"We and Jan are in just as much danger as we were before," Will said.

"Yes, but I'll take care of that," Mike replied, fists clenched.

"A subliminal?"

"I hate them, but to save her life...."

"And ours, don't forget," Will reminded him.

"I'll do it," Mike declared resolutely.

Wednesday morning the phone was ringing as Mike entered the office. Will picked it up then handed it over.

"Who?" Mike mouthed, but Will just shrugged.

"Hello, Michael Stellan, here. Oh, Mr. Gregory, it's been a while since I saw you last."

He listened for a moment then slowly eased into his chair.

"When?" Will heard him ask.

"In the night?"

Will's interest was piqued.

Mike let out a long breath. "Well, she only had two options – wake up to whatever life she could live, or finally pass on...I agree, it's much better this way."

A long silence followed as Mike listened. "So the viewing is tomorrow and the funeral is Friday evening? Yes, of course I'll be a pall bearer. Yes, I'll see you then."

Mike handed the phone back to Will and just sat staring for a moment.

"Pat?" Will asked.

"She passed away last night...unexpectedly."

"I imagine it's a relief to her parents," Will began, but stopped as Mike squinted his eyes tightly closed and pinched the bridge of his nose to keep from crying.

Will got up and closed the door. "I know you really cared about Pat back in high school."

Mike shook his head. "All along. Some part of me hoped she would revive...that I could revive her. I had finally gotten ready to let go, but I didn't think it would hurt this bad when the end came. I thought it had all happened so long ago."

Will looked at Michael in quiet contemplation. "You will go on," he said. "You've already started the process."

"Too recently. Why didn't I see this sooner?"

"Want some time to be alone?"

Mike nodded and Will picked up his work and left.

An hour later the office door opened and Mike peered out looking for Jan. He spotted her at the computer and motioned for her to come inside.

"What's wrong?" Jan asked spotting his distraught face.

He motioned for her to sit down and closed the door. "I got some bad news this morning."

She frowned.

"An old friend of mine, who has been in a coma since an accident in high school ten years ago, died this morning. The funeral is on Friday."

"I'm so sorry. That must be awful," Jan said.

"It's good and bad. Even if she had awakened, she would have been vegetable. It's probably better this way," Mike consoled himself.

"Well, take your time to get over this," Jan said. "I'll take a rain check on that date for whenever."

Mike smiled weakly.

"Is there anything I can do to help?" she asked.

Mike looked at the backs of his hands. "I know this is a lot to ask, but would you mind going with me to the funeral? Will has to be in the lab Friday night. He can't leave to go with me," he explained.

Jan thought about his request. "Well, I'm really familiar with funeral protocol and I won't need to get a dress."

Her words struck him. "Oh man, what a jerk I am! I'm sorry. I was forgetting everything you've been through yourself. A funeral's the last thing you want to go to."

"It's ok," Jan replied lightly patting his arm. "I understand the request probably better than anyone else. I'll be there."

At five o'clock Friday evening, Mike and Jan solemnly entered the chapel of a large Methodist church. They made their way to the front of the room where an open coffin was settled before the altar. Mike gave Mr. and Mrs. Gregory a hug. Their eyes were damp but they shed no tears.

Next Mike edged over toward the coffin. He hesitated until he felt Jan's soothing, reassuring hand on his arm. He patted her hand, suddenly very grateful for her presence. He took a deep breath then led her over to the open end of the casket. Jan stood back as he approached Pat's body alone.

He looked down into the coffin. He was used to seeing Pat's body lying so still. The funeral home had done an excellent job of making her look lifelike. Without all the tubes and the ventilator, he could almost believe Pat would simply open her eyes and sit up. Yet, when he touched her hand, it was stiff and cold. A shock went through his body. No pulse, no breath, no aura to connect to. She was truly gone.

Mike bowed his head and whispered, "I'm sorry, Pat. I should have let you go years ago. Be at peace. You're whole at last."

A movement behind the casket caught his eye, and he glanced up. Pat stood bathed in a golden glow, her face radiant with health and her limbs whole and sound.

"Good-bye, Mike. I'm sorry I held on so long. I thought that somehow I could come back to you, but I was wrong. It's time for both of us to move on. Take good care of her," she added nodding toward Jan. "I give you back your heart and life."

She cupped her hands under her chin and blew towards Mike. He felt a warmth hit his chest and spread throughout the rest of his body. A weight lifted from his shoulders and he straightened up.

"Good-bye, Mike," Pat called and faded from view.

Jan, who had watched him throughout the unseen exchange, saw his features relax and peace melt into his eyes. As they walked to a seat in one of the pews, she squeezed his arm. He took her hand as they sat down and remained calm throughout the entire service.

After they had transferred the body to the cemetery and the casket had been lowered into the ground, Mike stayed behind. The cemetery was actually quite park-like, and he and Jan ambled along the walkways.

"Was she your girlfriend?" Jan asked.

Mike stopped beside a quiet pond and watched the ducks diving beneath its glassy surface. Finally he nodded.

"My first," he said at last. "Actually my only girlfriend. After Pat got injured in that accident, I closed off to everyone and everything. I didn't realize how much of myself was slowly dying day-by-day, year-by-year."

"But a sense of peace seemed to come over you back in the church. It's as if you got your heart back," she remarked.

He gazed at her for a long while then smiled. "I did. I have my heart back, my life back and I'm ready to truly live again."

She smiled up at him.

As he looked into her bright blue eyes, a flash from deep within caught his attention. Unnoticeable to any except the trained, Mike spotted the device that threatened to kill them all.

Keeping his fears to himself, he took her hand and led her into a garden area. Tall hedges marked out specific areas - some planted with roses, others with cactus, and others with more exotic plants. Off to one side was a deep alcove shaded by a leafy arch. Inside was a quietly bubbling fountain and a wrought iron bench. Mike led Jan inside and they sat down, screened from the world.

"I know a funeral may seem like a poor way to start on a new life, but I'd like to start it over with you in the picture," he said gently touching her hair.

"I can understand a funeral being a beginning, but let's take things a little slower," Jan cautioned.

"Given the rough time I gave you at the beginning, could we have had a slower start?" Mike asked.

Jan chuckled. "Probably not, but still let's take our time. If this is the beginning, we should have plenty of time to take."

Mike rested his hand against the side of her head and looked deeply into her eyes. "I agree."

But Jan heard his words as if from far away and down a long tunnel. One moment she had been aware of his warm protective presence, the next she was alone and scared. Echoes rang out all around her as if from giant footsteps on granite. She did not even know where she was anymore, only that she was alone.

Candlelight flickered from a short distance away and a tall menacing shadow stretched up and over her. Frightened she backed up into a locked door. She had no where to go and no where to hide. As she cowered before the door, a monster appeared, its face lit from below. It stalked her until it was nearly upon her, and she gasped.

"Mike! It's just you!"

He smiled, but his smile appeared hideous and menacing in the eerie light. "You have the key," he said motioning toward the door. "May I have it?"

She looked at him wide-eyed. "What key?"

"The key that only you can keep. I must open that door."

"No," she said shaking her head and crouching against the door. "No, I can't open that door."

"No, you can't," Mike said, his voice echoing, "but I can. Please, don't make this difficult, Jan. Give me the key."

She slipped her hand into her pocket and felt something metal with jagged teeth. "What will you do if I give you the key?"

"I'll open that door and let you escape," Mike replied.

She looked toward the door then toward Mike. "It will get me if that door opens."

"I promise, I will get it first," Mike assured her and held out his hand palm up. "The key, Jan."

Slowly she pulled the key from her pocket and laid it in his hand. He pulled her to her feet and set her behind him. Mike slid the key into the lock and turned it. The door swung open and a metal disc hovered inside. A beam of red light shot out from a knob near its center. Mike met this beam with a steady blue beam of his own. Gradually, with effort, he forced the red beam back to its housing where it exploded and the disc fell away into space. Jan looked past him into the void watching as the disc broke up into pieces that dissolved into dust and floated away.

Chapter 9

Jan awoke to a spray of cool water in her face as Mike flicked water from the fountain at her.

"Hey, has the day been that long?" he teased.

She looked around, trying to get her bearings, then noticed her black dress and the rows of headstones stretching out beyond the garden. Suddenly the funeral and Mike's hand against the side of her head flashed back to her, and she took a deep breath.

"Wow, did I fall asleep?" she asked still bewildered.

"Out like a light," Mike confirmed.

"I'm so sorry. I guess I was up too late last night working on a paper," she apologized. "Here I came with you for moral support, and I end up falling asleep."

"It's ok," he assured her. "It's just that I have to get back to the lab."

Jan glanced at her watch. "Oh-my-gosh! You're late!"

"It's ok. Will will survive, but I do need to get a move on."

They ducked out of the alcove, hurried along the walkways and were soon headed back toward the university. Mike dropped her off quickly then headed straight for the lab. He jogged inside and rushed through the lab, peeling off his formal jacket and tugging at his tie. Will was already packed up and waiting.

"What took you so long?"

"I did it," Mike said hanging up his jacket and throwing down his tie.

"Did what…oh the subliminal. How did it go?" Will wondered.

"It went very well…much better than I had expected," Mike told him fishing deep in his right pocket. "And this is the result."

He held out a shiny flat disc the size of a nickel. In the center on top was a tiny hollow dome.

"Well, I'll be," Will exclaimed softly under his breath. "I haven't seen one of these babies in decades."

"Seems to work across temporal zones and through the psychic field as well as presenting a physical appearance," Mike related. "But just what are they made of? Why didn't Jan's system reject it? And what was its purpose?"

"To begin with inserting an implant like this is like putting a titanium pin in someone's knee," Will explained. "By itself it's perfectly harmless."

"Then what does it do?" Mike wanted to know.

"It's something of a transceiver. They send directives to her brain to control her, and they pick up her brain wave patterns and translate them."

"In other words, whatever she hears and sees, they hear and see, also?" Mike asked.

"That's the basics. Now, has she seen anything or heard anything that would put us in danger?"

"How to get to our house," Mike said.

"Anything about our origins?"

"Not a thing. Seeing Pat's body at the funeral today is all she knows of my past," Mike assured him.

"Then we can handle what shows up on our doorstep. It makes me wonder, though," Will mused.

"What's that?"

"I wonder if the reason they attacked Jan at her apartment was because they found they couldn't control her or use her against you," Will speculated.

Mike considered the possibility. "That would make sense. We had removed the homing disc, possibly before they could get a fix on our location. And, while they could hear and see via her mind, they couldn't influence her actions."

"Therefore, she was a dud as far as they were concerned. Possibly they only have a couple of these," Will said flipping the disc in his hand, "so they came to get it back."

"They would have killed her in the process," Mike added.

"She was worthless to them at that point."

"What about now?" Mike wanted to know.

"They'll be furious that they lost the link and the disc," Will said, his eyes narrowing.

"Will they go after her…or us?"

"That, Michael, is an excellent question. I'm sure we won't have to wait long for the answer."

The next afternoon as Mike entered the lab, he squinted his eyes as the room momentarily spun. He braced himself against a lab table, shook his head to clear it, then continued on. Another dizzy spell overtook him as he nearly fell into his office chair. Beads of perspiration dotted his brow and his muscles began to ache. He turned on his computer but found he could not bear the glare from the screen. He sat in his chair with his chin sagging onto his chest.

Jan tapped on the door. "I have another batch of notes and I'm getting close to finishing," she announced.

Mike did not look up or even acknowledge her presence. She set down the notes and turned his chair so he faced her. His face was flushed.

"Mike, are you all right?" she asked full of concern.

"Think I'm sick," he mumbled.

"You look it. You'd better go home."

"Can't."

"Why not?"

"Can't drive."

"I'll drive you."

"Still can't," he insisted.

"Why not?"

"Lab work."

"I'll find Terry and see if he knows what needs to be done.

Don't go anywhere," she cautioned as she dashed away.

Thankfully she had learned where most of the lab assistants hung out. Terry, a graduate student working on a research thesis in their lab, always seemed to know what was happening. She found him and dragged him back to the lab.

"What's up?" he asked as they hustled down the hall.

"Dr. Stellan's really sick. He's got to go home," she replied.

Terry was about to groan and complain under his breath, but they had entered the lab and had gone straight back to the office. He took one look at Mike and turned back to Jan.

"There's a loading dock just outside. Bring your car around, and I'll help him out." He eyed Mike closely. "Maybe you should take him to the hospital."

"No!" Mike suddenly shouted then winced and held his head. "No hospitals. Go home."

Jan and Terry looked at each other questioningly.

"One way or another, we've got to get him out of here," she said heading toward the lab door. "I'm getting my car."

Terry got Mike's arm over his shoulder and managed to hoist him to his feet. Meanwhile, Jan dashed to the parking lot, dove into her Chevy Cavalier, and was soon racing across campus. She found the loading dock, swung the car around and opened the passenger door. Terry eased Mike onto the seat and swung his legs inside. He closed the door, Jan buckled the seatbelt and they were off.

As she got to the stoplight at the entrance to the university, Jan suddenly realized she had no recollection of where Mike lived. She shook him gently.

"Mike, how do I get to your house?" She shook him again. "Mike, you've got to help me out here."

He opened his eyes, pointed to the right, and closed them again.

"How far do I go?" she asked. "Where do I turn?" She shook him again to rouse him.

By fits, and with many wrong turns, she finally recognized the brick front of their house and pulled into the drive. She killed the engine, hopped out of the car and ran around to his side. When she opened the door, he would have fallen out if the seatbelt were not still fastened.

Jan held him in the car with her knee while she unbuckled the seatbelt then swung his legs out. How she managed to pull, push and lift him from the car, she could not remember later. The next thing she knew, they were standing in front of his door and he was sagging to his knees.

"Mike, where are your keys?" she prompted for the third time.

"At the office."

Jan groaned. "How will I get in?"

"Spare key in garage. Opens side door," he mumbled.

"Will you be all right if I leave you right here?" she asked easing him down onto the step.

He nodded.

Jan jogged around to the side of the house, entered the garage and spent the next twenty minutes searching for the key. She was about ready to give up when she spotted it dangling far above her head. She had to find a step ladder, climb up and get it down before she was able to unlock the side door and enter their house.

She stepped into the kitchen and suddenly heard a loud thump from the living room as well as the sounds of shots being fired. She clamped her hand over her mouth to prevent herself from screaming, and crept toward the café-style door.

A lamp broke and several thuds reached her ears. The struggle sounded fierce and she found herself trembling and not knowing what to do. Glancing around, she spotted a broom and picked it up. "Armed" she eased her way out of the kitchen and towards the living room where she just stopped and stared. Lamps lay broken on the floor, books were strewn about, the phone hung off its cradle and large scorched holes dotted the walls. Worst of all, Mike was no where to be seen even though the front door stood wide open.

At that moment tires screeched in the drive. Seconds later, Will bolted up the front walk and dashed through the open door. He skidded to a halt, his mouth open in shock at the disaster that met his eyes. He glanced up at Jan looking right into her terror-filled eyes.

"What in the world happened?" Will exclaimed. "And where's Michael?"

Jan just shook her head. "I-I don't know. I went into the garage after the spare key and the next thing I heard was fighting. This was what I saw when I came in."

Will looked in anguish at the scorch marks on the wall. Suddenly they both heard a muffled groan.

"Mike!"

"Michael!"

Jan dropped the broom as they hurried around the sofa and found Mike half-buried under the coffee table. While Jan pulled the table away, Will lifted him onto the couch.

"He's burning up!" Will exclaimed.

"That's why I got Terry to cover the lab," Jan explained. "He looks awful."

But Will only half heard her. "We've got to get him upstairs," he insisted.

Suddenly Mike's eyes fluttered. "Will," he whispered. "Tried to open the front door…all turned against me…exploded…powers… went wild."

"Shhh, Michael. Don't try to talk," Will warned.

"So hot," Mike mumbled. "Can't see."

"What is he talking about, Will?" Jan asked anxiously. "What does he mean that something exploded and powers went wild?"

"He's delirious, Jan. We've got to get him to his room."

"But shouldn't we take him to the hospital? He looks dehydrated. He needs an IV and some antibiotics," Jan said.

"I don't think any of our hospitals have seen what he has," Will replied. "We can't take him anywhere right now until I find out if he's contagious."

"And you can do that here?" Jan persisted.

"I hold several degrees – one in biochemistry and another in infectious diseases. I'm a man of many talents," he replied with a wry smile.

"Ok. Then let's get him into bed," Jan agreed.

"How about you take his feet," Will instructed. "I'll take his shoulders."

Nodding, Jan positioned himself near Mike's feet.

"Ready. One…two…three…lift."

Struggling with Mike's dead weight, they half-carried, half-dragged him upstairs. They rested at the top before completing the distance to his room and laid him on his bed.

"If you'll get his shirt off, I'll go get a syringe so I can take a blood sample," Will instructed.

Jan quickly began unbuttoning Mike's shirt while Will ran into his room and opened his closet. Reaching way to the back, he grabbed a portable lab on a wheeled cart and hurried with it back to Mike's room.

"There's a basin under the bathroom sink," Will said. "Plus, there are towels and wash cloths in the linen closet in the hall. Would you bring all of that back here for me?"

Jan sprang to her feet and hurried out.

Meanwhile, Will removed a kit from his portable lab and wrapped a tourniquet around Mike's arm above the elbow. He felt around for a good vein, took the cap off a syringe and gingerly slid the needle into the vein. Blood began filling the hollow tube, and he released the tourniquet. He took two vials before removing the needle and applying pressure to the puncture.

With the other hand, Will pulled out a small scanning device. He flicked it on and proceeded to run the scanner the length of Mike's body. Then he hit a button on the front and waited for a digital read out.

"Heart rate's high at seventy beats a minute...should be thirty-five," he said to himself. "Got to find out what this is."

Jan returned with everything he had asked for. "Do you want me to get water and ice?"

"Yes, please. His temperature is 103 degrees. We've got to get it down quickly," Will responded.

She headed out the door and downstairs.

Will put a Band-Aid over the puncture on Mike's arm then pulled two small bottles from a compartment in the mini lab. Using clean syringes, he added a drop of one to the first vial and a drop of the other to the second vial. Then he stuck them in a small centrifuge and turned it on.

"How long till you know what's wrong with him?" Jan wanted to know as she returned with a jug of water and a tray of ice.

"This will take a few minutes, then I need to put the blood on slides and run them through the computerized microscope. Meanwhile, let's get some cold compresses on him."

Will lifted Mike's head and shoulders while Jan spread towels over the pillow and bed. They began dipping towels and washcloths into the basin she had filled with ice and water. Carefully they applied the packs to his forehead, neck and shoulders. A "bing" sounded and Will returned his attention to the portable lab, while Jan continued with the cold packs.

Will transferred the blood in the tubes to two different slides, placed them in a tray, then watched the screens as two microscopes scanned the blood samples. He hit a button to stop the scans and to bring the focus closer. What he saw made his blood run cold.

"Biological espionage," he muttered. "Not contagious, but very deadly."

He typed some commands into the computer unit and waited while the program searched the data base for the proper anti-viral antidote. In seconds he had the information he needed. He read each "ingredient" carefully then groaned.

"I've got everything I need but that. Now what?"

Chapter 10

Will knit his brow in desperate concentration.

"What do you need?" Jan asked. "Is it possible that our chemistry department has it?"

Will shook his head and rubbed his eyes.

"What about the campus infirmary? Don't they keep some prescription medications on hand?"

"Yes, but I can't be sure they have this one?"

"Hospital, pharmacy, a-a clinic somewhere," Jan continued trying to be helpful.

Will considered all the options then looked at his watch. "Seven o'clock," he said quietly.

He took a long deep breath then looked at Jan. "Can you stay with Michael until I get back? It may be quite a while."

"Yeah, I guess. Where are you going?"

"To get what I need, but this will take time," Will replied, packing up the lab and heading toward the door. "I may be gone all night."

"Do I have time to go get some things?" Jan asked.

"I can give you half an hour," Will replied.

Jan dashed back to her apartment, threw some things into an overnight bag and was back at their house within the prescribed time. Will sat in his Outback waiting for her.

"If anyone comes around, we have a security system. The alarm will go off."

Jan nodded.

"There's a pistol in my top dresser drawer if you need it," he added.

"I've never shot one before."

"Just aim and pull the trigger. Chances are you won't have time to think more than that anyway," Will said picking up a large satchel.

"Will, are you going to be all right?" Jan asked, concern tightening her voice.

"I'll be back by morning," he promised and left.

Worried and anxious, Jan filled another ice cube tray with water and took the last batch of cubes upstairs with her. She sighed heavily as she changed Mike's cold packs. He was still burning with fever, and his skin had become hot and dry.

Meanwhile, Will got on the highway and headed toward the desert. About fifty miles from Crest Ridge Heights he pulled into a truck stop and got out his cell phone.

"Put me through to Lt. Lansky," he said with resignation. "Tell him, William Shepherdson is calling."

A few seconds later a triumphant male voice sounded on the other end. "So, Shepherdson. You finally made that call."

"Lansky, if the matter weren't life and death, I wouldn't be talking to you and you know it."

"Who's life – yours or his?"

"His," Will replied.

"You have a lot at stake," the lieutenant reminded him.

"You have as much to gain," Will countered.

There was a long silence on the other end then finally. "It's a deal. How much do you want?"

"I don't want money, Lansky. I want a chemical formula." Will quickly read off its molecular configuration.

"How much?"

"Four ounces."

There was a sharp whistle on the other end. "What am I getting in return?"

"The main component to an interstellar propulsion system and full diagrams," Will replied.

"Shepherdson, are you mad? That's your ticket home."

"I can't go home without our king," Will replied flatly.

"Point taken. Ok when?"

"Midnight."

"The site?"

"Yes, but you come alone," Will warned. "No weapons, no backup, no planes, no helicopters. Just you and me."

"You don't have your muscle with you."

"I survived long before Michael's powers developed. I'll deal with you if you double cross me, and it won't be pretty," Will growled.

"Yes, I guess you would have," the lieutenant said. "Ok, midnight…your terms."

Will returned to the Outback and headed out into the desert. Traffic died out to nothing until he was alone on the road. He came to a spot where a dirt track turned off the highway and pulled over.

"Lansky's lying through his teeth," Will muttered angrily. "I just hope he brings the formula. Otherwise, I'm sunk."

He opened a laptop computer, plugged it into an adapter, then into the cigarette lighter.

"Arm security system," he said.

"Password," replied a dry synthesized female voice.

"Q…U…E…N…T…A…S," Will typed.

"Confirmed. Security system arming."

Will watched the screen as the arming procedure took place. He picked up a pair of glasses and held them lens side toward the screen. Shortly a series of lines flashed across the screen, beeping at intervals, then the lines ended and one long piercing beep followed.

"Security system armed," the computer said. "Defensive armament ready. All scanners at full."

Will all but closed the top of the laptop and carefully slid it under the passenger seat while still plugged into the cigarette lighter.

"Ok, Lansky," he muttered turning down the dirt track. "Now, I'm ready for you."

Back at their house, Jan checked on Mike again and glanced at the clock. It was nearing midnight and Mike's fever had not budged in spite of all the cold packs. For the umpteenth time she went to the phone, picked up the receiver and began to dial 911, but hung up the phone with a heavy sigh.

She had plenty of time on her hands to think and was far too anxious and worried to watch television, read or work on papers. Instead, she kept replaying all the events that had occurred since Will and Mike had hired her. A piece of the puzzle was still missing, a very big piece. But intuition told her now was not the time for questions and independent action. Sooner or later the answers would come and all of the craziness would make sense.

A sudden noise from outside caught her attention. She sat straight up and listened hard. She could hear Mike's dry, raspy breathing, the clock ticking in the living room and the faucet dripping in the kitchen. Convinced she had just been hearing things, Jan was almost ready to slouch back into a comfortable position when she heard the noise again – the sound of a ladder against the house.

A chill went up her spine, and she silently tiptoed into Will's bedroom, opened his top dresser drawer and pulled out the pistol. It felt cold and foreign in her hand, but she was suddenly glad to have it.

Hurrying back into Mike's room, she grabbed a flashlight she had seen on his dresser then quietly eased herself down the stairs. Cautiously she tiptoed through the house, her heart racing until the blood pounded in her ears, and her hands sweated profusely. As she entered the dining room, she saw the ladder through the window. A dark silhouette was slowly climbing up to Will's bedroom window.

Will stopped the Outback in the middle of the dirt track. A wilderness landscape stretched out around him for miles, while millions of stars glittered brightly overhead. A shooting star crossed the horizon.

He grabbed a large satchel, opened the door and stepped out of the car. As he moved to walk around the door, headlights flashed on and blinded him. He shaded his eyes with one hand while he held the satchel in the other.

"Move away from the car, Shepherdson, and keep you hands

where I can see them," Lansky demanded.

Will squinted as he raised his hands high and walked away from his vehicle. He heard the sudden click of army rifles.

"You have a funny way of keeping your word, Lansky," Will said.

"That's because I decided to nab the motherload of prizes. What good is an engine part and blueprints, I asked myself? It'll take years to figure out what they mean and how it operates," Lansky said self-importantly. "However, I have the opportunity to actually obtain that working knowledge and be able to put it to use in a year at most. You see, Shepherdson," he said as three soldiers moved toward him, "I've got you."

"I'll never tell you what you want to know," Will declared.

"Oh, you will," Lansky said holding up the vial of serum. "You see, I know where you live and I can have this in his system in a matter of minutes via helicopter. It's your choice."

"You have no idea where we live," Will replied.

"Oh, I've known your location for quite a while. I've been watching you and waiting for the right moment."

'You're bluffing."

"Can you afford to take that chance?" Lansky asked.

Will remained silent.

"Think of what I'm offering you. The chance to build that return ship with a brand new interstellar engine."

"I'd build it but I'd never be on it when it took off," Will said.

"On the contrary. You and your partner would be very important 'passengers' aboard that ship. Without you, how could we convince your people to accept us? Trade with us? Give in to us?" Lansky asked sketching an ugly portrait of future plans for Will's benefit. "Oh no. You and your 'king' are far too important to us. We need you, just like you need me. Now put down that bag and move away from it."

Will slowly set down the satchel and complied. One soldier took it, another trained his rifle on Will, while the third soldier frisked him.

"He's clean."

"See, I know you're a man of honor, Shepherdson. I can trust you. That's why it was all so easy," Lansky gloated.

He set the satchel down and began to open its clasps. Will eyed him like a hawk, tensing like a tiger ready to spring. Lansky opened the satchel, Will flung himself to the ground and rolled under his car, and a beam of light shot out at Lansky catching him in mid-chest. He looked up surprised before he slumped to the ground.

A soldier fired under the car hitting Will in the leg. He gritted his teeth against the pain. He watched as each soldier dropped to the ground; each with a gaping hole in his chest. Finally Will crawled out from under the car, limped over to Lansky and grabbed the satchel and serum from his limp hands. As he hobbled back to his car, he heard the beat of approaching helicopters.

Will flung the satchel inside, slammed the door shut, put the car into reverse and swung it around. He floored it crying out with each bump and jolt the Outback flew over. Helicopter searchlights flashed over the ground behind him preparing to sight their quarry.

"Reflector shield up," Will said through clenched teeth.

He raced on barely keeping ahead of his pursuers.

At the house Jan rushed back upstairs, slunk down the hall and stood just outside Will's room, her back against the wall. Taking a deep breath to steady her nerves, she glanced inside the room and saw a flashlight playing over the wall. With trembling hands, she forced herself to enter the room and made her way to a spot beside the window. Just as a hand poked through a hole that had been cut in the window to allow access to the lock, Jan spun to face the intruder, the gun straight out in front of her. Simultaneously, the low deep growl of a large ferocious dog sounded from nearby.

The intruder had not seen her yet, but as he unlocked the window and began to slide it up, the growl turned into a vicious bark and the holographic image of a Doberman pinscher appeared at the window. The intruder took one look at the dog, glanced up and saw the barrel of a gun pointed at him and began flailing around. The ladder wobbled then toppled over backward. Jan watched as the intruder first lay on the ground dazed then slowly crawled to his feet and took off out of the yard.

She let out a huge sigh of relief, slid down to the floor next to Will's bed and laid the gun down on the floor. Still trembling, she finally got up and made her way into Mike's room where she collapsed into a chair.

In the desert the searchlights flashed over and around the Outback. Overhead, the helicopter pilots armed their air to ground missiles. A searchlight caught the car square on the roof and a pilot pushed down the trigger. A missile launched from either side of the craft and whooshed down toward the car. A second later a brilliant flash of light blinded him as the missiles exploded simultaneously above the car. He wobbled the joystick and the helicopter veered toward its companion. Its blades grazed against the side of his partner's craft and ripped a gash in the hull. Locked together, they tumbled from the midnight sky in a burst of sparks and exploded upon contact with the ground. A lone vehicle sped off into the darkness and away from the blazing inferno behind it that lit up the dark desert night.

Chapter 11

Somewhere close to 5:30 a.m., the screech of brakes in the driveway woke Jan up. She shifted in the chair and glanced at a clock. She heard a loud thud against the front door and a key turn in the lock. Seconds later the door opened and Jan heard a body fall to the floor.

Instantly awake, she jumped out of the chair and dashed downstairs. She found Will on the floor just inside the front door. He held his left ankle, and blood oozed through his fingertips.

"Will! Are you all right?" she exclaimed dropping to the floor beside him. "What happened?"

"Got-shot," he gasped between clenched teeth.

"Is the bullet still in the wound?" Jan asked helping him roll over.

Will shook his head. "Sliced right along my leg and hit a rock."

"We've got to get this bleeding stopped and clean that wound," Jan said sizing up the situation. "Got any alcohol or hydrogen peroxide?"

Will nodded. "In the bathroom upstairs."

"Let's get you to a chair and elevate that leg, then I'll go get something to clean it with."

At that Jan helped Will to his feet and half dragged him to a chair in the kitchen. She pushed over a step-stool, took his shoe off, pulled his sock off and placed his foot on the stool with several kitchen towels underneath. Grabbing a tray of ice from the freezer, she dumped it into another towel which she packed around his ankle.

Hurrying upstairs, Jan dashed into the bathroom and flung open the cupboard doors searching until she found the alcohol. She grabbed it and a couple more towels and carried them back downstairs.

"Is it feeling numb yet?" she asked setting the items on the kitchen table.

"A little."

"We'll leave the ice on a little bit longer." Jan glanced toward the entry hall. "Man, there's blood everywhere! How will we ever get it off?"

"There's a cleaning spray under the kitchen sink," Will instructed. "Made it myself. You'll be surprised at how well it works."

Jan checked under the sink, held up a bottle and Will nodded. To pass the time while Will's ankle numbed, she took the bottle out into the entry hall and started spraying the spots of blood. To her amazement, they reacted as if they were being eaten right off the rug. In minutes the blood was completely gone and the rug looked as if nothing had ever happened.

"I hope you have a patent on this stuff," Jan commented. "I've never seen anything like it!"

"I do have a patent."

"So why haven't you marketed it?"

"It has a side effect. It coats the fibers and prevents stains from ever occurring again in those spots," he explained.

"So someone could spray this all over their carpets...."

"And upholstery...any fabric for that matter."

"And they would never stain again. So what's not to like?"

"The lack of profit," Will replied. "After a while, with every fabric protected, no one needs cleaning supplies or laundry bleach...."

"And they wait till the rug wears out before getting a new one," Jan finished. "Too good. What a problem to have."

"Yeah. By the way, I can't feel the ankle or my foot anymore," Will informed her.

"Then let's clean that wound."

Jan peeled off the ice pack and looked at the deep gash along Will's ankle. It looked mean and painful. She unscrewed the cap from the bottle, doubled up a towel to hold under his ankle, then poured the alcohol into the wound.

At first Will did not react. Then suddenly, "A-a-a-a-h! Ok! Ok! Enough! Enough!"

Jan stopped pouring the alcohol and patted the gash dry. Will took in big gulps of air as the pain gradually subsided.

"Whew! That smarts bad!"

"Do you have a first aid kit so I can put some sort of dressing on this?" Jan asked.

"Under the stove."

Jan opened the cupboard and pulled out a large white box with a red cross on its side. She found several sizes of gauze, Band-Aids and medical tape. She pulled out a long, smooth, flat piece of gauze and opened up several butterfly Band-Aids.

"Can you hand these to me when I need them?" she asked passing the Band-Aids to Will who nodded.

Carefully she pushed both edges of the wound together, lay the gauze strip down and reached for a Band-Aid. She followed the wound along Will's ankle until she had closed all the edges. Then she took regular first aid tape and wrapped it over the Band-Aids and around his leg.

Finished with her task, Jan looked up. "Guess I can't convince you to go to the hospital, either?" she asked hopefully.

Will shook his head, and she sighed.

"What you can do is help me get upstairs. Now that I'm patched up, I've got to get the serum into Michael."

"Then you got it!"

"I wouldn't have returned without it," he replied solemnly.

Putting as little weight as possible on his left leg, Will hobbled into the entry hall and opened the satchel. He pulled out the vial of blue liquid and handed it to Jan. Then he shoved the satchel into the coat closet and closed the door.

"Ok, help me upstairs."

Will leaned on Jan and the wall for support and managed the climb upstairs. She got him to the chair beside Mike's bed and let him sink onto it.

"All right," Will said breathing heavily from the exertion. "I need my portable lab. Can you get that from my bedroom?"

Jan nodded, hurried into his room and returned pushing the cart ahead of her. Will opened it immediately, tugged open a small compartment and slid out a rack of vials. He chose one with red liquid and another with green. Jan watched as he measured out drops of each into the serum then set it in the centrifuge to spin.

"What do those do?" Jan wondered.

"They're enzymes that Michael's body will need in order to process the serum," Will explained returning them to their holding rack.

The centrifuge slowed to a stop, and Will withdrew one ounce into a syringe. Again applying a tourniquet to Mike's arm, he administered the serum intravenously. As he released the tourniquet, he felt Mike's forehead while Jan changed the cold packs.

"That fever didn't budge all night?"

Jan shook her head.

Will eyed Mike gravely. "Even once the antiviral serum has destroyed the virus, and that could take another twenty-four hours, he's still not out of the woods," he remarked.

"What do you mean?" Jan asked.

"As the virus dies off it will leave behind toxins that his body will have to destroy."

"Then his fever is actually a good thing," Jan said thoughtfully.

"How's that?"

"It will burn the toxins out of his system."

Will merely grunted then looked toward his bedroom. "Jan, I've got to get a few hours sleep, but no more than three," he said strictly. "Can you do a couple of things for me?"

"What's that?"

"Clean the blood out of my car, and move it into the garage. There's a cover you can drape over the car once it's inside. When you're done, bring the extra house key inside with you and lock the garage." He caught the weary look in her eyes and gave her shoulder a pat. "I know you've had a long night here, too, and I wouldn't ask, but this is really important."

Jan nodded.

While Will hobbled into his room and collapsed onto his bed without spotting the hole in his window or the gun on the floor, Jan went downstairs and took Will's special cleaner out to the car. She found it worked best to dump a large quantity on the blood stains and walk away for fifteen minutes. When she came back, the carpet and upholstery looked like new. In minutes she had completed her tasks, locked the garage and was lying on the sofa.

At 9:30 a travel alarm beside her went off, and Jan groggily opened her eyes. Disoriented at first, she slowly recalled the night and Will's request. She shuffled upstairs and into his room gently shaking his shoulder.

"Time to get up, Will," she said before moving into the next room to check on Mike.

Meanwhile, Will got changed, searched through a file cabinet until he found the car's title, and moved into Mike's room. He filled a slender syringe with Novocain and shot it into his leg near the wound. He checked on Mike while he waited for the Novocain to take effect. Finally able to put weight on his leg without pain, he walked downstairs.

"I'll be gone for a couple of hours," he told Jan. "Try to get some rest."

She heard the garage door open, the Outback start up, then the door clang shut. She stuffed another tray of water into the freezer, then stretched back out on the sofa and fell into an exhausted sleep.

Will's footsteps in the entry hall woke her four hours later and she sat up. He collapsed into a nearby chair, his face haggard and grey.

"You look awful," she remarked.

"Thanks for that warm greeting."

"Just stating a fact." She glanced out the window and saw a silver RAV4 in the driveway. "Where's the Outback?"

"I sold it to a 'friend' of mine who regularly takes cars across the border into Mexico and sells them on the black-market."

Jan stared at him in shock.

"I think the Outback was either bugged or wired with a transmitter of some kind," Will explained. "I wanted to get it as far away from here as possible."

"So where did the RAV come from?"

“The Toyota place on the main drag. Man drives a really hard bargain, too,” Will said shaking his head.

“He let you have it today? Did all the paperwork go through?” Jan asked in astonishment.

“Let’s just say, I didn’t give him any options,” Will replied then quickly changed the subject. “Right now I’ve got to check on Michael, and then I’ve got to get some sleep.”

Jan followed him upstairs where he drew another blood sample from Mike and once more checked it for the virus.

“How’s he doing?” she asked. “Is the serum working?”

“White count’s up…T lymphocytes are up…virus count is down, but not gone,” Will replied drawing another vial of serum and injecting it.

Finished with this all important task, Will stumbled off to bed. Jan changed Mike’s cold packs once more then headed home to finish sleeping. Later that evening, she grabbed a bite to eat, took a shower and put on a fresh change of clothes. She returned to their house and used the extra key to let herself in. As she entered the front door, she could hear Will speaking to someone. Hopeful, she dashed upstairs taking them two at a time.

Will spoke quietly to a groggy Michael who could barely keep his eyes open.

“You’re not out of the woods, yet, Michael. You aren’t to even attempt to get out of that bed,” Will said in that no-nonsense tone of voice that always lets the listener know he has lost the argument.

“The lab….” Mike protested.

“Will take care of itself.”

“It’s ruined…we were…trying something new.”

“Then it’s ruined and we’ll try again.”

“It’s not ruined,” Jan said from the doorway.

Both men turned towards her.

“I called Terry. He put a halt on the new assays and ran the data on last week’s, instead. You’re behind schedule and that’s all. He said that he’d like one of you to call him at the lab as soon as you're able. Seems this last run of data turned up something very interesting,” Jan related.

Will beamed and Mike relaxed back against his pillows.

Will got to his feet and hobbled out the door with the aid of a cane. Jan soon heard his voice on the phone in the kitchen as he discussed the latest news with Terry. Meanwhile, she sat on the edge of Mike's bed and began rearranging his towels and cold packs. He stopped her and took her hands in his.

"Will says I'm going to be ok thanks to you," he whispered.

"Thanks to me?"

"If you hadn't kept my fever where it was last night and it had climbed any higher, I might have been gone before he got back with the serum."

Jan stared at him, his words sinking in slowly. "I-I had no idea how bad…I mean I…I was so worried," she confessed. "I must have changed your compresses a hundred times."

Mike weakly squeezed her hands.

"I know that all night in the midst of these torturous flames, I'd feel this cool breeze. It felt like an angel had passed by.

Jan blushed and glanced away. "I-I'm no angel."

"You were my angel last night. You kept me alive in the middle of that inferno," he said earnestly.

Suddenly pulling her hands back, Jan leapt from the bedside and hurried to the door. "You need fluids and not just water. I brought some sports drinks with me. I'll go get you some."

With that she ducked out the door, and Mike lay wondering what he had said or done wrong. Then he heard a faint noise. As he listened intently, he realized it was the muffled sound of crying. He threw his covers off and tried to sit up. He fell back on the first attempt and had to struggle to sit on the edge of the bed with his feet on the floor. That small exertion winded him, but he was determined to reach the door. Stretching out his arm, he caught hold of the back of the chair. Ever so slowly he began to crawl his way across the room.

Jan stood outside his door trying to stifle her tears. Her eyes were brimming and her face was already red. Occasionally a soft sob would escape her throat, and she bit her lower lip to hold them back. Not wanting to go into the kitchen and have Will see her crying, she was desperately trying to overcome the tidal wave of emotions that welled up inside her. Just as she made the decision to lock herself in their bathroom, run the water and have a good cry, she felt a trembling hand on her shoulder. She spun to face Mike who was barely standing propped against the door casing.

"Mike!" she exclaimed in a whisper. "What are you doing out of bed?"

"What's wrong?"

"Mike, get back into bed," she urged trying to push him into his room.

"You're crying. What did I say? What did I do?" he insisted.

She got her arm around his waist and led him back to his bed where she gently eased him down. She sank onto the bed beside him and covered her face with her hands.

"Jan, I'm sorry. What did I do?"

"You just didn't know," she replied sniffling and wiping her eyes dry. "All the important people in my life called me their 'angel' – my granny, my mother, my dad – and all of them died."

Understanding dawned on his face.

"I couldn't stand it if I lost someone else because I was their 'angel.' I feel more like the Angel of Death," she said crying anew.

He took her hand in his. "Does 'angel who gave me the will to live' sound any better?" he asked hopefully.

"Only <u>if</u> you live. Will says you're still not out of the woods and here you are up walking around."

"How about 'you're the woman I love'?" Mike asked.

Jan stopped crying at his words, a warmth flooding her being.

"Is that better?"

She looked at him searching his eyes for confirmation that his words were not part of a cruel hoax.

"I love you," he said again slowly. "I will live, trust me. This virus hasn't beaten me. I will get better."

Jan wiped her eyes then leaned forward and kissed his cheek. "I care, Mike, but I'm not ready to love, yet," she whispered.

"That's ok," he replied. "As long as I rank up on your 'important people' list, that's all that matters."

She nodded then slipped out of his room and headed downstairs.

Chapter 12

Mike hung in there during the next few days, but his recovery did not go smoothly. His temperature spiked periodically without warning. At other times, all of his muscles ached from the build up of toxins. Meanwhile, Will and Jan took turns either staying by his side or making an appearance on campus. Finally, five days after acquiring the virus, he woke up feeling cool and hungry. Weak from his ordeal, he all but tumbled down the stairs to the kitchen. Will saw him stumble, caught hold of his arm and eased him into a chair. He felt his forehead and a relieved smile flooded his face.

"Welcome back, Michael."

"I'm starved. What can I eat?"

Will laughed for joy. "Those words are music to my ears."

"Means I'm better?"

"Means the battle is over and you've won!" Will exclaimed jubilantly.

"Good. Feed the warrior."

"You've got to take it a little easy on the food," Will cautioned. "You haven't eaten for almost a week."

"Whatever, just give me something," Mike insisted.

Will soon set some toast, soup and tea before him. Mike dug in like a starving man.

"Whoa! Slow down or your meal won't stay down."

From that moment on, Mike began to regain his strength. Still not strong enough to teach his class or go into the lab, he graded papers at home and went over lab data. One afternoon Jan walked in through the front door and found him sitting on the couch reviewing lab reports.

"Do you realize this semester is almost over?" she asked.

He looked up and smiled. "I know we just had Thanksgiving and Will's saving me some turkey and pumpkin pie."

"There's only three weeks left," she informed him as she walked around the far end of the couch.

Mike held out his hand to her which she took. He pulled her down beside him, upsetting a stack of reports in the process.

"Do you think you'll be back into the lab soon?" she asked.

"I'm going to try next Monday. I might get a little tired, but otherwise I should be fine."

Jan looked at him for a moment, opened her mouth as if to say something, then closed it and looked away.

"What?" he asked then touched her arm. "What?"

"Well, I've been wondering how you caught that virus and why none of the rest of us did," she finally confessed. "It's almost as if someone aimed it right at you."

"In a way, that's basically what happened."

"How?"

"Biological warfare is the best way I can describe it. Will and I have been a target because of what our research has meant, not just to the scientific community, but to the international community at large. Someone either knows or suspects that we're close to a break-through and is trying to stop us," Mike explained.

"That's what Will meant when he said the Outback had been bugged."

Mike nodded. "This goes well beyond what the local police can handle, so we've developed ways of dealing and surviving over the years."

"Yes, I've noticed that your first aid kit is well stocked, and that portable med lab is pretty amazing," Jan observed dryly.

Mike shrugged. "We do what we have to do."

"I know," Jan said, "but it's scary. Will the terror ever stop?"

Mike looked at her suddenly seeing recent events from another perspective. "I guess I've always just taken this stuff in stride," he said thoughtfully. "It just came with the territory."

"Well, it's new territory to me."

Mike's countenance darkened. "I can see how intimidating this must be for you."

"But does it ever stop?" she persisted.

He thought for a long time. "I don't know," he finally said quietly. "Researching interstellar propulsion systems was just something I had to do. I never gave the rest much thought."

Jan nodded.

"I can tell you've been giving it a lot of thought, though," he remarked gently brushing the hair back from her face.

She swallowed hard and nodded. "More so recently. My heart says I'm in love, my head says I'm crazy, and my feet are flying in the opposite direction," she admitted. "I-I want to follow my heart, Mike, but I'm scared."

He looked at her and his gaze was soothing. "Maybe this will help," he said pulling her closer and kissing her.

When their lips parted, she took a deep breath. "Maybe my heart will win out in time."

"I sure hope so. I'd like you to be around for a long time to come," Mike said earnestly.

"Well, for now I have two forty page papers to finish," she said standing up, "and Will has me proofing and editing a grant proposal.

"I bet he's glad you're doing it," Mike said smiling. "He usually gets a migraine trying to."

"He did look very relieved when he set it in my hands."

"Yeah, I can only imagine."

Jan gave him a quick kiss on the cheek. "I'll be back tomorrow to see how my favorite patient is doing," she said hustling out the door.

When Mike finally returned to the lab that following Monday, he looked pale and walked a little more slowly than usual, but he took an immediate interest in the most recent assays the lab assistants had conducted. Jan sat in on the lab meeting that week.

"The most recent results have been right on target with our original hypothesis," Will told the group.

"What's even better is that you've been able to duplicate the results several times with some good-sized samples. The last assays were the best yet," Mike added.

"Dr. Stellan and I have developed a new formulation. We want you to run the next assay using it. If everything goes the way we hope it will," Will said, "we'll be ready to add the component the engineering assistants have been working on."

"And if that works, we'll be field-testing over the break."

A few of the assistants groaned.

"We won't need all of you," Will assured them. "Just the graduate assistants. But that's all speculation based on these next assays."

The assistants nodded and the meeting broke up.

For all the notes she had typed up and the grant proposals she had proofed, Jan still had little true knowledge of what Will and Mike were actually doing. It appeared that they were combining some new chemical formula with some aspect of quantum physics, and the engineering assistants were creating a new "skin" and a craft to actually apply the technology to. While she did not understand how all of the pieces of the puzzle fit together, she was certain that the latest experiments were headed in the right direction, and Will and Mike were the happiest she had seen them all semester.

She sighed, swung her backpack over her shoulder and walked out to her car. "What is holding me back?" she muttered. "I know there's a part of me that really loves him. Why can't it break through?" Frustrated, she headed home to finish her work.

Two weeks later she walked into the lab with a spring in her step and headed toward the office. Mike caught sight of her, handed Terry back a chart and followed her.

"Well, you look like someone took the weight of the world off your shoulders," he remarked as he entered the office after her.

"I just handed in my last forty page paper, and I smell freedom for a month."

"So are you sticking around over break or going home?" Will asked.

"Actually home is pretty much where I make it," she replied.

"So are you sticking around?" Mike pursued.

She looked at the two men. "I had thought about taking a road trip, but now you two have got me curious. What's up?"

"We will definitely be field testing over break," Will replied. "We'll have two engineering assistants, Terry, myself, Mike and a foundation representative going with us."

"We wondered if you would like to come along…as a witness?" Mike asked.

"Where and when?"

"We'll be testing at a remote location," Will explained. "We'll have to backpack in and raft out."

"Are you up to a hike? You know we couldn't have got this far so quickly without all those notes you typed up," Mike added.

Jan looked from one man to the other. "You mean, you really want me to come along?"

They nodded in unison.

"I've been wanting to do some hiking," she mused. "Yeah, this sounds like a great idea!"

"Ok, we'll give out full details at the lab meeting we're holding on Thursday," Will said.

"We can't go during finals week. Will it be a problem if we go over Christmas?" Mike asked.

A dark shadow crossed her face and tears came to her eyes. "No," Jan replied in a husky voice. "In fact, I would appreciate the company and being away from the lights and glitz this year. Thanks."

She wiped her eyes as she left the office.

Will watched her leave with concern. "Is something wrong?"

Mike took a deep breath. "I'll tell you the full story later, but I think that taking her with us is probably the best thing we could do."

That evening, before returning home, Mike stopped by the local mall and fought the Christmas crowds to get inside. He gazed into shop windows with a frustrated frown. Suddenly a sparkle from a jewelry store window clear across the open center caught his eye. Like someone hypnotized, Mike walked across the center straight toward the store.

When he got closer, he saw what had caught his eye – a small Bavarian crystal heart pendant. As he stared at it, his focus softened, and he saw Jan's wistful face gazing longingly at the pendant. Mike shook his head, took a careful look at the pendant then entered the store. Several minutes later he left the store with a small box in a velvet bag tucked into his pocket.

Mike picked up the phone to make a call when he got home. "Jan, we are going to exchange presents before we leave for the field trial. I'd like it if you would join us."

There was a long silence on the other end of the phone. "I don't know, Mike. I'm not sure I'm up to it yet."

"C'mon, Jan. Life goes on. You've done so well. It'll just be Will and me," Mike urged.

Jan sighed. "Ok. You're right. I need to make some positive memories of Christmas. When do you want me to come over?"

"We have to turn grades in by Friday and we'll set up our tree that afternoon. Since we're heading out Sunday morning, how about Friday night?"

"Ok. But what do you guys want for Christmas? I don't know what colors you like, what your sizes are or anything," she complained.

"Ok, let's see. Will could use a new belt, size 36, or a wallet. I'm a fan of Mannheim Steamroller and the Broncos."

"All right. That's at least something to go on. I'll see you Friday night."

When that evening came, Jan pulled into their drive, turned off the engine and sat for a long while before she finally opened the door and pulled her packages out with her. She slowly walked to the front door and rang the doorbell. Mike answered and ushered her into the living room. Jan knelt to put her presents under their tree with the others and stopped for a moment to gaze at the ornaments.

"These are so unusual," she said pointing to prism-shaped ornaments. "It's almost as if there's an image deep inside them."

"They're unique," Will responded.

"One of your inventions?" she asked.

"Can't take credit for these," he replied.

She took one off the tree to get a better look at it, and Mike and Will held their breath. As the light from a candle touched the prism, a separate light seemed to burst from inside it and a woman's face appeared.

"A hologram! Wow!"

But Mike was no longer watching her. His eyes were closed and his face was strained with heavy concentration.

"Who is this?" Jan asked.

Will hurried over. "That's a portrait of his mother," he explained, carefully taking the ornament from her hand and placing it back on the tree. He took a second ornament off the tree and held it for her. "This one is of his father."

Jan studied the man's features as the hologram became clearer. "Mike looks just like him," she breathed, astonished. "If he grew a moustache, they could be twins."

In spite of their tension over the moment, both men smiled proudly.

"Michael's father was killed when he was a baby," Will explained. "For a long while we thought his mother was also dead. We later found out that she has been 'hospitalized' in an 'institution'."

"So, you've been Mike's guardian," Jan surmised.

"It was in his father's 'will'," Will replied setting the ornament back on the tree.

"I'm really sorry," Jan said. "I know how it feels to lose your parents."

She felt the tears brimming in her eyes and a catch in her throat. "I'll be right back," she promised dashing upstairs and hiding behind the bathroom door.

Will watched her leave then turned to Mike. "You did a good job of keeping the entire holoview from playing. Earth technology isn't up to their standards yet."

"I know," Mike replied. "I didn't think about that when we put them on the tree this morning. I just wanted to see them again."

"I know," Will said patting his shoulder. "We could never explain life-size interactive holographic movies playing out in the middle of the living room."

"I just hope I didn't jam the mechanisms," Mike worried.

"Try one now."

Mike picked up his mother's ornament, activated it and breathed a sigh of relief when the entire scene of his mother, surrounded by several attendants, played out in the midst of the living room. When it ended, he tried his father's ornament and let it begin to play. Mike's father sat on a marble seat. He was attired in royal blue with a gold circlet on his head.

Unbeknownst to the men, Jan had started back down the stairs. She caught a glimpse of this man in regal attire and stopped in her tracks, mouth agape. She stood on the stairs watching as the scene ended and Mike replaced the ornament. She leaned against the wall, breathing hard.

"That was his father," she thought. "But a crown and a throne? What's going on?"

She took a deep breath to quiet her pounding heart and continued down the steps and into the living room.

"Now, we can open presents," Will said rubbing his hands together.

Mike began passing the gifts around until the floor beneath the tree was empty.

"Jan, open yours first," Will said.

Jan carefully slid her thumbnail under the tape on her gift and pulled back the wrapping paper. "Will, how did you know my favorite 'flavor' from Bath and Body?" she asked holding up a gift basket of bath oil, talc and hand cream.

"Oh, I have my ways," he said smiling. "Michael, open yours. I've been saving this for years, but I think now is the time for you to have it."

Mike carefully opened a faded blue velvet box with a gold clasp. Inside sat a large blue sapphire set in a fiery gold band. Jan gasped as Mike lifted the ring from its resting place.

'It was your father's," Will's explained, "and he wanted you to have it."

Mike nodded unable to take his eyes off the gift. "Thanks, Will," he said quietly finally placing the ring back in its box.

He turned to Jan. "Open your other gift."

She untied the strings of the grey velvet pouch, pulled out the flat jewelry box and pried back the lid. Her mouth formed a large "O" as she gazed at the crystal pendant. A tear trickled down her cheek.

Mike watched her anxiously as she gingerly lifted the pendant and cradled it in her hand. "Is it all right?" he asked. "I-I was sure you'd like it."

Jan brushed away the tear and nodded. "I love it," she whispered. "I've been looking at it in Vales Jewelers in the mall for months. It's almost identical to the one my father gave my mother when they were dating. She wanted me to have it, but after she died my Aunt Joyce took it, and I was never able to get it away from her."

"I'm sorry. Wish I had known," Mike said.

She shook her head. "It's ok. I'm really touched…and happy." With that, she reached over and wrapped her arms about his neck, holding him for a moment.

As she let him go, Mike gently took the pendant from her and opened the clasp. While she lifted her hair, he slid it around her neck and fastened it in place. She held it up to look at it once more, a happy smile radiating from her face. She gave him another hug.

"Thank-you, Mike," she whispered. "That's the best present anyone could have given me this year."

Chapter 13

That Sunday, as the long golden fingers of the rising sun crept over the horizon, Mike and Will shuffled to the RAV and loaded in their camping gear. After one last check of the house, Will locked the front door, they climbed inside and headed over to Jan's apartment. Fifteen minutes later, they pulled into the lot, and Mike hopped out. He knocked on her door which opened just crack.

"Ready to go?" he asked.

Jan shoved her gear back with her foot and yawned as she opened the door wider. "My things are ready, but you'll have trouble convincing my body to come alive."

Still half-asleep himself, Mike picked up her gear, staggered outside, and began packing it in while Jan locked up her apartment. She climbed into the back behind Will, leaned her head back and promptly dozed off.

Will headed back onto the street, made a series of turns, then pulled into a local hotel. "Got to pick up that foundation rep," he reminded Mike.

They left Jan in the vehicle while they went inside. Minutes later they returned carrying the man's gear. Jan eyes popped open as soon as he opened the door opposite hers.

"Jan, this is Joe Kramer, a rep from the Hagger Foundation," Will said by way of introduction.

He slid into the seat next to hers and nodded in her direction. Jan promptly sat up, crossed her arms in front of her and shrank into the far corner. She glanced in his direction a couple of times then stared out her window. As soon as they pulled into the campus and stopped behind the Physical Sciences building, she opened her door and jumped out. She paced while their packs were unloaded, then grabbed hers before Mike could haul it over to the waiting van.

"Hey, what's wrong?" he asked, watching her dig into a side pocket and pull out a bottle of Motrin.

She popped open the lid, shook out two capsules, closed the bottle and stuck it back into her pack.

"You ok?" Mike asked, eyeing her with concern.

"That guy," she said nodding toward Joe who was now standing near the van, "gives me the creeps. It's as if he's radiating some sort of energy. As soon as he came near the RAV, I started to get a buzz in my ears and now I've got a headache."

Mike looked at her quizzically.

"Look, I'm not going crazy," she protested. "I was fine till he opened the door. It's really weird."

"No, I believe you," he replied.

"I'm just going to dash inside for a drink of water. I'll be back in a second," she said heading into the science building.

When she returned, the others were already climbing into the van. Joe sat up front to keep Will company while he drove. Mike had reserved a spot closer to the back. He let Jan in first so she would have a window seat then hopped in and closed the van door.

Will turned to look at all of them. "Everyone, this is Joe Kramer from the Hagger Foundation."

Five heads nodded hello.

"Joe, these two directly behind us are the engineering graduate assistants. This is Kimberlin," Will said pointing toward young woman with auburn, shoulder-length hair, "and her partner is, Ken," he said, gesturing toward the young Korean student who sat next to her. "You've met Jan and Mike, and our assistant who is already dozing in the back is Terry."

Joe nodded to all of them. He never smiled nor moved a muscle in his face, though he seemed animate enough when he spoke with Will.

"We have between five and seven hours of driving ahead of us, so anyone needing a pit stop, speak up now," Will called.

The van remained silent, so he pulled out and hit the road heading east. They were going into the desert near mesa country. Late that afternoon they would hike to the top of one and would perform the flight tests on its flat summit the next day.

For now, quiet filled the air as the passengers slept and the tires of the van hummed on the road. Jan's head nodded forward as she drifted off to sleep. Mike put his arm around her shoulders and leaned her head against his shoulder. He rested his cheek against the top of her head and dozed off, too.

Around them, the majority of the team gradually woke up and began talking quietly or staring out the window. Close to noon Will swung the van off the main highway and pulled into a small dry dusty town.

"We're picking up a guide here," he informed them. "I suggest you get out, stretch, and eat the lunches we packed in. Do what you have to, then we'll get back on the road by one."

The van slowly unloaded as the graduate students crawled out, stretched their cramped limbs and crowded around Mike who was hauling out a Styrofoam box filled with brown bag lunches.

"There's roast beef and turkey sandwiches," he informed them. "Take your pick."

Jan quickly grabbed a bag with turkey sandwiches then found a seat on a rail fence beside Kimberlin. They ate quietly and looked over the old buildings that made up the town.

By one, the van was loaded again, the guide was on board, and they were bumping down a narrow dirt road that wound up through a mountain pass, then down onto a plain. Several mesas loomed over the landscape, but Will headed towards the closer, shorter one. He pulled into a spot by a fallen log since a river stood between them and the mesa itself.

"End of the line, folks," he said. "We walk from here."

The crew jumped out, sorted through the gear and strapped on their packs. Once they were all ready, their guide, a Native American from a nearby reservation, took them through the river at the nearby ford and around to the north side of the mesa. Soon he found an ancient track that wound its way upwards. Here and there steps were chiseled into the stone, which made the going easier, however, occasionally they had to climb up the face of steep cliffs.

The ground leveled out in a spot near the halfway point. Their guide called a halt and they dropped to the ground drinking thirstily from their water bottles.

Jan watched their guide as he stood and looked out over the valley. She got up and approached him. “Hi. I’m Jan.”

He glanced at her and cracked a smile.

“I’m from back east and I’ve never seen country like this before. It’s beautiful.”

“All the earth is beautiful,” the guide replied.

“Yes, but not everywhere is as uncrowded and unspoiled,” she countered.

“This land? Unspoiled?” he grunted.

“It’s not?”

He pointed out across the valley floor to where the sun glinted off glass. “Men with off road vehicles ride through here all the time and tear up the ground with their tires. When the rains come, the good soil washes away. What is left can’t support the plants.”

Jan could see the dust clouds the vehicles were kicking up. “I’ve seen the destruction they’ve done to the hillsides back east. Guess it was a little naïve of me to think they wouldn’t be out here, too.”

The Indian nodded.

“What’s your name?” Jan asked. “I’d like to be able to call you something other than ‘Hey you’.”

The Indian smiled and held out his hand. “I’m Lawrence Little Fox, Larry.”

Jan smiled back.

He turned to their group and declared the break over. As they headed further up, they worked their way around to the other side of the mesa from which they could view the river as a thin blue ribbon that stretched off into the distance.

“We’ll be rafting back on the river,” Mike told Jan.

“That should be fun…and a lot easier than this climb.”

By late afternoon they reached the summit and made camp. Larry had them gather stones to form a circle for the fire. Then Kimberlin and Jan set up their sleeping bags on one side while the men set up on the other. Will helped Larry prepare the evening meal which everyone ate hungrily.

Jan and Kimberlin walked a ways away from the others and sat on a rock watching as the sun set behind the mountains. Reds, purples and oranges lit the sky along the horizon. When the last ray finally faded, they both sighed.

"I don't think I've ever seen a sunset like that," Kimberlin remarked.

"I know I haven't," Jan replied.

They sat for a while longer watching the stars explode onto the canopy of the night sky.

"You and Dr Stellan seem to be pretty close," Kimberlin said.

Jan nodded. "He'd like us to be closer."

"So what's stopping you?" Kimberlin wanted to know. "It's not like he'll ever be grading a Chaucer paper."

"No, that's for sure," Jan said chuckling at the unlikely thought then she grew more serious. "To be honest, I just don't know what's holding me back. There is a part of me that really cares about him and really wants to fall in love."

"Yeah, then there's this wall."

"That obvious?" Jan asked.

"I've noticed," Kimberlin replied. "Look, it's none of my business, but sometimes you look so miserable."

"I just lost my father last spring."

"Oh. I'm sorry. So now it's just you and your mom?"

Jan shook her head. "No, she died before I started college for my bachelors."

"Wow. Both of them. That's really tough," Kimberlin said sympathetically. "But I think I see what your problem is."

"Which is?"

"Everyone you've loved has died. If you fall in love, he'll die, too. Then you'll be alone again," Kimberlin explained.

"In other words, you're saying that I'm not letting myself fall in love for fear I'll lose Mike, too?"

Kimberlin nodded.

"Actually it does make sense."

"I know the explanation probably doesn't make you feel any braver, but you ought to let yourself go…."

"And fall in love?"

"Yes. You figure that unless we have a nuclear war tomorrow, everyone in the whole world can't suddenly up and die on you."

Jan chuckled again. "You're right."

The girls got up to move back near the fire.

"I'll give it some serious thought."

"Just DO it, or you'll think yourself out of it," Kimberlin warned.

Unbeknownst to the two girls, a set of glowing amber eyes glared at them in the darkness from behind a nearby boulder. As the girls turned toward camp, the glowing eyes blinked out.

Kimberlin and Jan said good-night to the men and crawled into their sleeping bags. For a while, Jan lay gazing dreamily at the stars twinkling in the dark night sky. Suddenly they were obscured from view. She blinked her eyes; the sky was once again clear with the stars twinkling in the heavens as before.

"Must have dozed off," she mumbled turning over and facing the fire.

The men had also crawled in and low snoring was carried on the breeze from the other side of the fire. Without warning, a dark silhouette sat up. Two phosphorus eyes blinked open. The glowing points stared fixedly ahead while the other campers slept soundly. Their owner got up and stealthily crept to the fireside. Not long afterwards, a low, spindly form jerkily detached itself from the flickering shadows cast by the campfire. It edged toward the sleeping campers.

Meanwhile, Jan began to toss from side-to-side. Her restlessness quickly escalated. She threw her hands up to her face as if trying to hide. Suddenly she and another figure across the camp both sat bolt upright; Jan screamed with all her might.

Mike leapt out of his sleeping bag and dashed through the camp with Will and Larry right behind him. Mike had nearly reached Jan's petrified form when he slid to a stop. Will plowed into him from behind.

"What's wrong?" he asked peering over Mike's shoulder into

the darkness.

"There, near Jan's feet!" Mike said in a loud whisper while pointing toward the ground.

Will looked toward Jan's feet squinting until he saw the huge black scorpion crouched there. It was larger than any he had ever seen. A brilliant blood-red streak ran down its back and up the whip to the very tip of its stinger. Its hand-sized pinchers were snapping open and closed as it scuttled back and forth in agitation.

"I've never seen anything like it before in my life!" Will hissed in exclamation.

"Where in the world did it come from?" Mike wondered.

"Let's worry about that later," Will said.

The others had also awakened and were gathering around. Threatened, the scorpion edged closer to where Jan lay propped on her elbows. The color had completely drained from her face as she watched the oversized arachnid's movements.

Joe edge towards it with a stick. Just as he got positioned to flip it away, the scorpion sprang backwards and landed on Jan's sleeping bag. Its whip vibrated menacingly while it crept toward her covered legs.

"Get it away," Jan whispered hoarsely. "Please, someone, get it away." She sobbed quietly as it inched toward her calf.

"Michael, use telepathy," Will whispered. "Try to draw it away from her."

Mike nodded then focused his eyes and will on the creature. Clearing his mind of all else, he projected thoughts of security and food to the arachnid. The scorpion spun around to face him, but backed up onto Jan's calf and began a slow march toward her body. Sweat broke out on Mike's forehead.

"What's wrong?" Will asked.

"There's a block. I can't get through to it."

"I'm going to get something from my pack," Will said. "Just try to keep it where it is."

He backed away then hurried across the camp.

In the meantime, the scorpion had reached her thigh and was making its way toward her hip and torso. It swung around looking at Joe then wavered between him and Mike. Suddenly its level of agitation reached its peak, and it tensed its tail, the tip swelling in size.

“Oh my God!” Mike whispered. “It’s going to strike!”

Chapter 14

Suddenly a flaming torch flared on the scene. Larry held it out at the scorpion blinding and confusing the creature. It beat at the air with its pinchers and began scuttling back and forth over Jan's stomach. With his left hand holding out the torch, Larry carefully maneuvered a slender branch toward the arachnid. He glanced up and spotted Will waiting on the other side of Jan. With a swift catlike motion, Larry knocked the scorpion off her. It fell onto the ground and Will slammed a glass jar down over top of it.

"Its pinchers won't fit in," Will cried.

Larry dropped the stick, grabbed the hatchet off the woodpile, and lopped off the pinchers in one clean move. Will slid the jar's lid underneath and, once the scorpion was encased inside, carried it to the fire. Terry and Ken had stoked up the fire, which now burned brightly. With a quick toss, Will dumped the frantic creature into the midst of the flames then watched as it scurried toward the edges. He, Terry and Ken grabbed sticks and continually poked it back into the heart of the flames. Soon it became a ball of fire.

Larry watched it carefully then called out, "Stand back! Hurry!"

In the next instance, just as Terry, Ken and Will had gotten out of range, the poison-filled tip exploded and flames leapt skyward. While Kimberlin watched from her sleeping bag, and the men worked to break up the flaming sections of the scorpion, Jan sat in place crying quietly.

Mike knelt beside her wrapping his arms around her shoulders. "Shh! It's all over now. It's gone. It's dead," he soothed.

"I know, but it was so big…and it felt…so awful," she sobbed into his shoulder.

Mike gently rubbed her back and shoulders, and Jan started to calm down. Together, they watched the others move around the campfire cleaning up and breaking up the scorpion.

"You know, Mike. Right before I screamed, I was having this terrible nightmare. I saw this cloud that turned into a hideous ugly face…."

"And it became that scorpion."

Jan stared at him in shock and nodded.

"I had that same nightmare. I was awake even before you screamed."

She shuddered.

"Are you ok now?"

She nodded.

"I'm going to go talk to Will," he said squeezing her shoulder reassuringly.

Mike headed over to where Will and Larry were talking.

"Are there many of those scorpions out here?" Will asked.

"That is not from here," Larry said. "Those have never been seen around here before. Someone brought it with them."

"Hopefully they only brought the one," Will muttered.

"They took an enormous risk to bring that one," Larry said. "One drop of its venom would have killed us all."

"Is it possible that someone left it out here or that it escaped from a collection?" Mike asked.

"If we were down there," Larry said pointing to the valley floor, "then yes. Up here…."

"No," Mike finished.

Larry headed toward his pack, took out a smudge stick and prayer feather and began humming and burning sage around the perimeter of their camp as well as down the entire length of Jan's body.

Mike led his friend out of the earshot of the others. "Will, Jan and I had the same nightmare right before that scorpion showed up."

"What about?"

"At first just images that kept melting into each other – like a cloud that turned into a hideous face then became that scorpion. Why did we both have that dream?"

Will frowned. "There is the possibility that Jan is clairvoyant," he speculated.

"But we both woke up and sat up at the exact same instant," Mike pressed.

Will rubbed his chin thoughtfully. "You weren't projecting your thoughts?"

"Not consciously. I had been sound asleep."

"It is possible that you developed a link with her when you performed that subliminal," Will began, "or…."

"Or what?"

"That you've begun to develop a bond with her."

Mike looked troubled. "I've heard you talk about the bond my mother and father had. How does that work?"

Will grew quiet. "When our people fall in love, Michael, they develop a lifelong bond with one person, their lifemate," he explained. "The other person can be worlds away, but the two of them never feel apart, never feel alone. Their life-forces intermingle to such an extent that even at death, the living partner rarely remarries. The sense of his or her partner lingers behind too strongly."

Mike whistled softly. "So that's what started happening between Pat and me?"

Will looked at him quizzically.

Mike frowned. "If I've started bonding with Jan, could that be why the scorpion attacked Jan? Is it possible that it was meant for me but got confused and went after her instead?"

A cold chill trickled through Will at the thought. "I hadn't even considered that, Michael, but you may be right."

"Then…whatever danger I'm in, she may be in, too?"

"Possibly, but not necessarily."

"What if they're homing in on her as well as me…?"

"Then it may happen again…yes," Will confirmed. "This particular instance was most likely a fluke, though; one they already regret."

"That isn't much consolation."

"I'm sorry, Michael," Will sympathized. "Coming to bed now?"

Mike shook his head. "I've got some thinking to do."

Will clapped him on the shoulder and headed toward his sleeping bag. Mike wandered over near the campfire, sat down on a long flat rock and put his head in his hands. He sat still for a long while hunched over until a crunch on the ground behind him made him sit up and spin around.

"Hi," Jan called making her way toward him. "Didn't mean to startle you."

Mike let his breath out slowly. "That's ok."

"Can I keep you company for a while?" she asked sitting next to him.

"Be my guest," he replied smiling and slipping his arm around her waist. "What's keeping you up?"

"That stupid scorpion." She shuddered. "I can't shut my eyes without seeing it."

"Mm, same here," Mike said slipping his sweatshirt around her shoulders. "I think I was as scared as you were," he added softly.

Mike gently brushed the hair back from her face and drew her closer.

"I've been doing some thinking, too," she confessed.

"About?"

"How I feel about you," she replied.

His arms tensed for a moment.

"That scorpion was poisonous, wasn't it?" she asked.

"Deadly," he confirmed.

"If it had stung me and I had died," Jan said, "I would have regretted only one thing."

Mike searched her eyes intently. "What?"

"Not having told you that I love you," she replied holding his gaze.

Mike cupped his hand alongside her face and leaned closer to kiss her. Jan's lips trembled and parted slightly. As his firm, sensuous lips caressed her mouth, he let his hand glide down her face and chin to her neck and shoulders. Her eyelids slowly closed and a soft glow crept across her face. Mike kissed her with increasing fervor as adrenaline shot through his veins. She opened her lips, and he slipped his tongue between them, exploring the sweetness of her mouth. Deeper and deeper he probed – hoping to reach into her very soul.

Reluctantly they parted lips each softly gasping for air. Mike held her close burying his face in her long golden hair. A warmth penetrated his heart as she snuggled closer.

For a long while they silently embraced each other. Mike enjoyed the feel of Jan in his arms and the weight of her head on his chest and shoulders. She thrilled to the touch of the strong arms that held her and breathed in rhythm with the rise and fall of his chest.

As the embers of the fire sputtered out, Jan's eyes closed in sleep. Mike listened to her calm even breathing then scooped her up in his arms and carried her back to her sleeping bag. He tenderly tucked her in then carefully picked his way around the others to his own resting spot. As he crawled in and stretched out, he caught a glimpse of gold that sparkled in the moonlight. He picked one of Jan's long hairs off his shoulder and held it up. Feelings were resurrecting inside him that he had not experienced since high school, and a host of new emotions were surging forward. Exhausted, he fell into a contented sleep.

The next morning, as soon as everyone had finished breakfast, they broke camp and hiked out across the mesa. They approached a section that was particularly broad and flat and commanded an excellent view of the valley floor and river.

Once there, Ken and Kimberlin dropped their packs and detached the extra sections they had strapped to the sides. Jan removed her pack and sat down to watch. Ken pulled out long thin pieces of frame, which he quickly began arranging on the ground. When done, they had formed a small circular dome. Meanwhile, Kimberlin pulled out a silver fabric that fluttered in the breeze. She unrolled it and worked with Ken to stretch it over the frame.

Mike and Terry helped the two engineering assistants tip the saucer over onto its dome. To Jan's surprise it rocked on its top as if the "skin" had become quite solid. Mike and Terry affixed a long tubular section to the underside, flipped it back over and hooked a short whip-antenna to the top.

Her curiosity getting the better of her, Jan edged forward for a closer look. She reached out to touch the saucer and was surprised at its cold metallic feel.

"Wow! How did this stuff roll up?" she wondered aloud.

"It has special properties based on quantum physics," Kimberlin explained.

"But I saw it flap in the breeze. It looked so thin and cloth-like. Now it feels like hard metal."

"Cool, isn't it?" Kimberlin said grinning.

"The real test is to see if it flies," Terry remarked.

"And how well," Mike said deep in concentration. "I just hope…."

Satisfied that it was completely assembled, Mike went over to where Will had set up a transceiving set. "I think we're all ready."

Will stood up and motioned for the group to stand back. Terry took control of the remote control unit, while Will turned on the transceiver.

"Trial one – lift off," Mike announced.

Dust began to kick up under the craft, and it hovered just inches above the ground.

"Take it up an inch at a time," he instructed.

Slowly the craft ascended until Terry halted it at eye level.

"Try the directional controls," Mike said.

"Forward," Terry called, and the craft moved several feet toward the edge of the mesa. "Back," and it returned to its lift-off point. "Left," and it maneuvered over towards Will. "Right," and it maneuvered over towards Jan.

"Ok, trial one complete and a total success," Mike announced. "Set her back down, Terry."

The craft returned to its lift-off point, Terry turned off the remote control and hurried to join Mike and Ken who were taking readings off the skin and engine.

Mike whistled. "Right in line with our hypothesis. Amazing!"

Readings taken and logged, the trio took up testing positions and readied themselves for the next trial.

"Trial two – begin," Mike called.

Terry again brought the craft to eye level and began a series of maneuvers in acute angle motion at increasingly more rapid speeds. Jan watched in breathless awe as the craft shot straight up, then moved forward only to reverse direction or swoop into a ninety degree turn in the blink of an eye. She could hardly believe what she was seeing. Within half-an-hour, trial two was complete.

The group took a break while Ken and Kimberlin made some adjustments to the frame and skin. Jan meandered over to Mike.

"I always wanted to see a UFO," she said. "If you flew this over Clear View Heights, they'd be seeing one for real."

He nodded concentrating on running some data on a lap top computer. He looked up and smiled. "This is as good as it gets…a perfect run so far."

Jan beamed back.

Soon trial three began. Before their eyes, the craft changed shapes. It got larger, smaller, oval, triangular, cigar-shaped and its color changed, too. Gradually Ken and Kimberlin sped up the structural change phases until it looked like a motion picture of changes in mid-air.

With trial four, Terry worked in concert with the engineering assistants to combine motion and direction changes with the phase changes. The effect left the entire group speechless. Finally they brought the craft back to settle on the ground.

"This is absolutely incredible!" Joe exclaimed, the first time anyone in the group had heard him speak besides Will.

"We have one more trial left," Will informed him watching Mike, Terry, Ken and Kimberlin ready the craft. "Then we'll call it a successful day."

Forty-five minutes later, they began trial five the most spectacular of all. Terry maneuvered the craft out over the valley and away from the mesa. Ken and Kimberlin enlarged the craft to make it more visible, then they re-ran the test patterns from trial four. The craft zipped and dipped over the valley at spectacular speeds. Suddenly one edge appeared to be blown downwards violently. Terry fought to regain control of the craft while the others looked on as it plummeted toward the river.

An anomaly in the atmosphere caught Jan's eyes, and she glanced upwards. A section of the sky appeared to melt and a tingle ran down her spine. The effect seemed so familiar yet totally out of place. Suddenly a scene from Star Trek flashed through her mind.

"Something's up there using a cloaking device!" she exclaimed inwardly.

She scrambled over the ground and tried to get Mike's attention. Too late; the craft plunged into the riverbank and could not be maneuvered out.

Chapter 15

Immediately the research team scrambled to pack up the equipment. Larry gazed intently towards the spot where the craft had gone down.

"How far do you think it is?" Will asked.

"From the base of the mesa, an hour or so," Larry replied. "But I don't want to rush down. One wrong step and someone could be injured."

Will nodded acknowledging their guide's concern.

"Once we get down, I could go on ahead and secure it," Larry offered.

"That may work out best," Will replied. "We'll discuss it again when we reach the base."

Larry nodded and hefted his pack onto his back. Jan struggled to get hers on and hurried over to Mike.

"That thing didn't crash," she asserted.

"Wind sheer," Mike countered. "We thought we'd taken it into account." He wrapped the cords around the transceiver and began stowing it in Will's pack.

"No, there was something up there," Jan said pointing to the place in the sky where she had seen the atmospheric anomaly.

"Jan, weather," Mike said with finality.

"But, I saw…."

Mike closed up Will's pack then moved on to get his. Jan stared after him in frustration.

"Then you saw the waves in the air, too," Larry said coming up behind her.

Jan turned toward him. "It made me think of a cloaked Clingon Bird-of-Prey from Star Trek," she confirmed. "That shimmery look in the sky."

Larry nodded. "Saw it yesterday."

"When we took a break?"

"Yes, I thought my eyes were playing tricks on me, and that it was just those ATV'ers."

'No," she said thinking seriously. "I saw it last night."

"Saw what?" Will asked with Mike behind him.

Jan went into a full explanation of the cloaking sensation she had experienced right before the craft crashed and the night before when she was drifting off to sleep. Will anxiously knit his brow.

"Could something have been up there and using a cloaking device?" Jan asked. "I know the army's been working on a cloaking device for ground patrols. Could they have something like that on a helicopter or a plane?"

"Something was definitely up there," Larry confirmed.

"We've got to get to that craft as soon as we can," Will said urgency in his voice. "Look, Michael and I will take responsibility for ourselves. Can you tell us the quickest way to get to that bend in the river?"

"You want me to stay behind with the others?" Larry asked.

"Yes. Get them down the safest way possible. Michael and I will rappel down the face of the mesa and head toward the river. Once we've secured the craft, we'll make camp and wait for you."

Larry nodded. "Ok. Over here." He took Will to a lookout spot and quickly showed him the landmarks to look for that would guide them to the river and the craft.

Meanwhile, Mike dug rope and rock climbing equipment out of his pack.

"Will you two be ok?" Jan asked watching him.

He glanced up. “Will and I’ve done a lot of rock climbing. We’ll be fine.”

“Once you’re down there?”

Mike glanced toward the river. “We can hold our own. It’s you guys we’re more concerned about.”

Jan nodded.

He stood up and gazed at her apologetically. “I’m really sorry I didn’t listen to you. I was just concentrating so hard on what I was doing.”

“It’s ok. Just be careful down there. My gut says there’s trouble,” she replied reaching over to kiss him.

“You’re pretty observant,” Mike noticed. “You go on instinct a lot?”

“I’ve never thought much about it.”

“Ready, Michael?” Will called.

“Coming.”

Larry helped them secure their lines.

They donned helmets and gloves and strapped on harnesses. After they had run the lines through and had made certain everything was secure, they backed up towards the edge of the cliff. Will took a look down then pushed off. Mike glanced up at Jan, gave her a thumbs up and a smile, then followed Will.

Larry stood for a moment and watched them descend then looked up into the sky at a hawk that circled overhead. He whistled and called to it in tones very similar to its own voice. The hawk let out a shrill cry and veered off heading for the mountains.

“Ok, folks. We’re going down,” Larry announced. “No rushing. We’ll join them this evening. For now, our biggest concern is that we get to the valley floor safe and sound.”

Silently the research team followed their guide down the steep trail. Tension hung over them like a thick fog and more than once Larry had to slow them down. Time seemed to be very precious and a sense of urgency filled them all.

“What do you think’s going on?” Kimberlin asked during a break.

“I’m not sure,” Jan said taking a swig of water. “I think we’re in for some trouble.”

“You mean you don’t think our craft just went down either?”

Jan shook her head.

"I hope they get to it in time," Kimberlin said gazing out over the valley.

"Me, too," Jan said standing up as Larry called an end to their break.

In the valley below Mike and Will were just approaching solid ground. They hopped out from the cliff-face and let the line peel through their gloved hands until their feet hit the earth. They ripped off their helmets, tore off the harnesses and quickly surveyed the landscape around them.

"Over there," Will said pointing toward a particularly shaped stone outcropping. "Let's go!"

The two men set off at a good pace stopping only for an occasional drink of water.

"How far did he say we were from it?" Mike asked.

"About an hour if we keep this pace up."

"I hope the others will be ok," Mike said.

"They're with Larry. He's the best. Plus, he sent for help," Will replied.

"The hawk?"

Will nodded.

"How long till his brothers get here?"

"Several hours, I'm afraid. We're on our own for the time being."

"So, the army? Or something else?" Mike asked.

"You mean, that thing Larry and Jan saw?" Will queried.

Mike nodded as they trekked along under the mid-day sun.

Will gave the possibilities serious consideration. "Given that scorpion last night, I'd rule out the government or armed services."

"Saracen?"

Will nodded. "They were working on a cloaking device years ago, but then so was Quentas. I'm sure they both have one by now."

"Seems like someone doesn't want us to leave planet Earth," Mike commented. "Jan said her gut said we're in for trouble."

"I think her gut may be right. Let's just hope we get to the craft before they do."

By late afternoon the research team finally reached the base of the mesa. They leaned against boulders panting from the heat and their exertion. Larry scanned the sky overhead, found the spec he was looking for and marked its direction.

"They've nearly reached the craft," he told Jan. "Plus, my brothers will meet us there, too. They can't get there much faster than we can, though, so hopefully they don't run into trouble before then."

A knot had been growing in the pit of her stomach, but Jan said nothing. If trouble found the two men, it would find them all.

Near the bend in the river, Mike and Will spotted the craft. One side of it was buried in the soft mud.

"It doesn't look too worse for wear," Will said starting to move forward.

Mike's hand sot out and he grabbed Will's arm. "No! I've got this feeling."

Will stopped instantly. Simultaneously they dropped their packs, then found a boulder and scrub brush to take cover behind. They watched the craft and soon saw several figures move toward it.

"They found it!" Will hissed through clenched teeth.

"Yes, and we've got to get it back!" Mike said.

"Any ideas?"

"We need to find out how many there are and even the score."

They lowered themselves to the ground and cautiously crept forward.

"I only count two," Will telepathed.

"You'd think there would be more."

"The team," the both thought in unison.

"Let's take these two out first," Mike suggested. "We'll get the others later."

Silently they moved apart and around the craft to places of cover. One of the tall blonde Saracens came within inches of Mike. He let him pass by, concentrating on a rock at his foot instead. In an instant the rock became a coiled rattlesnake and the Saracen stopped in his tracks. He stared at the snake dispassionately then brought his foot smashing down on it. Instead of crushing the snake, he slid on the rock and came crashing down. Mike was up in an instant and on him, but Saracens are bred for strength. The two opponents wrestled on the ground for a moment, before Mike broke away to try another tactic.

Now he was faced with the Saracen's laser weapon. He eyed it carefully as the two maneuvered around each other. Mike pointed at the weapon and it became a hot branding iron. The Saracen dropped it instinctively and Mike pounced on the weapon, rolled away and fired up at his enemy. The first beam stunned him. Mike heard a yell from Will, threw away the weapon and fired a bolt of pure blue energy from his eyes. It hit the Saracen squarely in the chest and he slumped to the ground.

Will found the other Saracen on the side of the craft closest to the river. He tackled him and found himself flying through the air. He lay for a moment with the wind knocked out of him before crawling to his feet. The Saracen brought the laser up to fire and Will kicked it away. The Saracen merely laughed and advanced on his opponent, forcing Will toward the river. Realizing that he was no match for his enemy alone, he yelled for Mike.

Just as Will's foot slipped on the muddy riverbank, a stunned look crossed the Saracen's face. An instant later, he collapsed face down in the mud. Mike stretched out his hand to Will and pulled him up onto solid ground.

"That takes care of these two," Mike said.

"Good. Let's go find the others."

Once on the ground at the base of the mesa, Larry set a good pace for the group. Hot and tired as they were, they pushed to keep up and no one spoke much. Once Jan thought she caught a flash of blue light and wondered at it.

From the mountains Larry spotted small puffs of dust. He stopped and studied their movement.

"Your brothers?" Jan asked.

He nodded frowning.

"Something wrong?"

He pointed to a slope opposite his relatives. They both saw the shimmering atmospheric anomaly.

"Do you think they see it?" Jan asked.

"We can only hope."

They turned toward the top and Jan suddenly realized that

someone was missing. “Where’s Joe?”

Larry glanced around quickly. “Anybody see where he went?”

They were all startled by the man’s disappearance.

“An ambush,” Larry muttered under his breath.

“What do you mean?” Jan asked.

“I haven’t felt right about that man since I laid eyes on him. Something’s not right about him.”

Jan thought about her first reaction to Joe, too. “I know what you mean. He’s weird. Do you think he’s in cahoots with them?” she asked nodding toward the cloaked device across the river.

“That’s my thought.”

“Then what’ll we do?”

“We must take another path. They may be just up ahead,” Larry replied.

“But what if Mike and Will head back for us?” she protested.

“They’ll walk right into a trap,” Larry breathed.

“What-do-we-do?”

Larry looked troubled. “Michael and Will are my brothers, and I should help them. Little Star, our people call him. But they can take care of themselves against these enemies; your people can’t.”

“What do you mean ‘they can take care of themselves and we can’t’?” Jan asked. “You talk like Mike and Will aren’t human.”

“You don’t know?” Larry asked.

“Know what?”

He frowned. “You’re in too much danger. We have to move out now!”

Larry hustled the team together and they took a sidetrack. Jan waited till they had all headed out. She took one more look towards the river then turned to follow the team.

Suddenly a hand clamped over her mouth, and she was dragged behind a large boulder. She squirmed, kicked and pounded on the arms that held her. When they did not budge, she opened her mouth as wide as she could, pressed her teeth against the flesh of the hand and bit down hard. The hand instantly jerked away from her mouth and she screamed at the top of her lungs.

On the trail headed toward the mesa, Mike heard Jan’s scream. “They’ve got her!”

“Run!” Will shouted as the two men put on a burst of speed.

Chapter 16

Jan managed to squirm around to face her attacker. She screamed again at the sight of the hideous man from her nightmare up close and personal. He pushed his misshapen face with its protruding eyebrow ridge that shadowed deep, sunken, sulphurous eyes at her. Thick red and blue veins undulated out from his temples while his cheeks ballooned into huge, hanging jowls. He looked as if someone had both melted and simultaneously stretched his features. As he bore down on her, she redoubled her efforts to escape. Behind him a tall blond woman closed in on both of them.

"The girl has alerted them," the woman hissed.

With that, the woman sprinted forward and brought the butt of her weapon down on Jan's head and the world faded to black. They quickly dragged her away and out of sight.

Moments later Mike and Will reached that spot and glanced around them.

"They didn't come past us," Mike said.

"Larry must have headed toward the river. Something forced him off his path."

"And they got Jan."

"We don't know that for certain," Will said beginning to look around.

Mike spotted a couple of drops of blood on the ground. "There's been a struggle. Something or someone was dragged away."

Will joined him and they began to follow the tracks in the dry soil. Mike spotted something discarded in the brush. He went over and pulled it out.

"Jan's pack. Will, we've got to find her."

Concern etched on their faces, they quickened their pace as they followed the tracks. Suddenly Will ducked behind some shrubs and Mike followed.

"What?"

"There. Something is cloaked and sitting there," Will said staring at an open spot in the scrub.

Mike followed his gaze and saw a shimmer like heat off a highway. "Think they're taking her on board?"

"I don't know, but where their ship is, they're bound to be close by," Will said. "Let's split up and look."

By now Jan had come to. Groggy and with her head pounding, she only gave a weak protest when her captors dumped her on the ground. The man shoved a laser in her face and she backed up against a nearby boulder and froze.

The woman came over, clamped cuffs over Jan's wrists and applied small metal discs to her temples. She pulled out a handheld device and turned it on. Immediately Jan felt a strong tingle near her temples that quickly escalated to the level of discomfort.

"Your pain will draw him," the woman said in a deep voice. "Then we will have their king and they will be helpless against us."

Not paying any attention to the woman, Jan fought to remain calm in spite of the increasing pain in her head. She closed her eyes and tried to breathe deeply from her diaphragm as she had once learned in the pain management classes she had attended with her mother, but the intensity of the pain kept rising. All at once a gasp escaped her lips and she moaned unable to manage the pain any longer.

"The woman's lips curled back into a cruel grin. "So weak. She might have given us some fun."

She motioned for her partner to hide and they waited.

As Mike searched the area, a wave of pain nearly knocked him over. He shook his head suddenly seeing Jan lying on the ground in his mind's eye as clearly as if she were in front of him.

"Will," he telepathed. "They're using her. They're hurting her."

"Where is she, Michael? Concentrate!" Will returned in kind.

Mike furrowed his brow tensely as the scenes of Pat's accident and mangled body clashed in his mind with the pain that throbbed in his head.

Will, who had been searching for him, hurried over. "Concentrate, Michael! Concentrate! We must find her."

Nodding, Mike inhaled sharply and focused on Jan's pain. Following it like a tracking beam, he suddenly "saw" her location in his mind. "Over there," he said pointing and opening his eyes.

"Carefully now," Will cautioned as Mike made to take off. "They'll be waiting for us. We want to surprise them instead."

In spite of their best intentions, they found Jan bound and gagged before they found her captors. In seconds, they raised their hands overhead as laser rifles were shoved against their backs. Mike glanced over his shoulder to see both Joe and the ugly man from his dream.

Their captors grunted motioning for them to move into the open near Jan. The woman rose from hiding and stood over her pointing a control device at her.

"Your life for hers," she said nodding at Michael. "Come peaceably and we will release her unharmed. Resist us, and we will kill her."

"They mean to kill her anyway," Will telepathed.

"I figured that."

Jan's eyes fluttered open and she recognized Mike. She glanced up at the woman, winced and looked back down.

"She can't hold out much longer," Mike worried. "They have that thing turned up too high."

"She's tougher than you think," Will replied. "She'll hang in there. Just think of a way out of this."

Mike focused on Jan and she raised her head to meet his gaze.

"Jan," his words echoed in her head. "Can you hold out a little longer?"

She nodded slightly.

"You say the word, and I'll give in."

Defiance sparked in her eyes and she shook her head slowly.

"Good girl. Hang in there. We'll get out of this real soon."

On the breeze came the call of a coyote. Mike and Will both listened carefully. Suddenly a shower of stones fell into their midst. Some bounced off their captors and themselves and they all ducked. As they stood back up, Mike and Will each jammed their elbows into their captors' stomachs. Joe doubled over and Will grabbed his weapon. With a second hail of stones, he brought the weapon down on the back of Joe's neck and the man crumpled to the ground.

Mike struggled with the ugly man. Though not as strong as a Saracen, he still presented Mike with a challenge. When the elbow to the stomach had not phased him, Mike had been forced to try a karate kick to the head. That stunned the man long enough for Will to swing the butt of the weapon around hit him in the temple. He finally fell forward onto the ground.

From all around them, Larry's brothers stood up and their rifles clicked in preparation to fire at the woman. Meanwhile, Mike went to take a step toward Jan, but the woman held up the control unit.

"Tell your friends to back off. If you come any closer, she dies."

Mike stopped dead in his tracks, and Will waved their friends back. They stood staring at the woman, no one moving on either side.

With her last ounce of strength, Jan lay back on the ground and kicked up at the woman's hands with both feet. The control unit went flying. The woman dove for it, but as her fingers closed around the unit, a boot slammed down hard on her wrist. She looked up into the angry eyes of a very tall black man and a half dozen rifles that were pointed at her head. Her grip relaxed and the unit fell back to the ground.

Mike scooped it up and reduced the signal to nothing. Jan lay back shivering and her teeth chattering. Mike rushed over and yanked the discs from her temples before ungagging her.

"Are you all right?" he asked helping her sit up.

"I hurt. Oh God, my head," she moaned tears squeezing out of her eyes.

Mike reached behind her and tried to undo the cuffs. His best efforts failed.

Suddenly Will yelled. "Michael! Look!"

Mike glanced up in time to see their attackers shimmer and dissolve. Simultaneously the control unit, weapons and metal bonds disappeared.

Jan gasped in astonishment. "Where did they go?"

Mike shook his head, but Larry pointed overhead. A shimmer in the air told the group that the ship was just above them. A second later, it was gone.

Will knelt beside Jan and examined the burn marks near her temples. He shook his head. "Those are nasty, but I've got something for them in my pack."

"Thanks," Jan said gratefully.

"Think you can walk, yet?" Mike asked.

"I can try."

He helped her to her feet, but she sagged and swayed. Finally he scooped her up in his arms. "Come on. Let's find the rest of the team."

Larry led them back toward the river and their craft. By the time they got there, the stars were beginning to come out and the others had a campfire ready. Mike lay Jan down while Will went for his pack which Larry had found earlier.

"Will," Mike asked telepathically. "Is it ok to give Jan our medications?"

Will pulled out a small round tin and popped open its lid. "We have no choice," he replied in kind. "Earth has no treatment for something like the Augmenter. A simple analgesic would never touch her pain. It disrupts the nerves' ability to conduct signals and upsets the neurochemical balance in the brain."

Mike nodded. Putting a strong arm around her shoulders, he propped Jan up. Will gently smeared the salve over her temples and back into her hairline. She murmured appreciatively as the soothing cream eased the pain.

"Feel better?" Will asked aloud.

"Mm, much. I'm just dizzy."

"Give it a few minutes, and you'll feel better," Will assured her.

Mike stayed with her, rubbing her shoulders and neck, while Will went to get them both a plate of food. He brought them back to the couple then went over to speak with Larry while he ate his own supper.

Jan took a few mouthfuls then leaned back against Mike's chest. "Larry talks about you and Will as if you guys aren't totally human. He said they call you 'Little Star.' Mike, what was he talking about?" She turned and looked up at him.

Mike gazed off into the distance for a moment. "He's right. Will and I aren't entirely human. We come from somewhere else."

"Where?"

"A planet named Quentas."

Jan thought quietly for a while. "Then your father really was a king?"

"Who told you that?" he asked in alarm.

"No one," she replied sitting up and taking another stab at her food. "I saw the hologram as I came back downstairs last Friday. I didn't say anything because I thought I was seeing things. Plus, nothing made any sense back then." She ate a mouthful then looked back up at him. "Did your other girlfriend know?"

"Pat?" He shook his head. "I've spent my life trying to protect the ones I love. I figured she'd be safer if she didn't know."

"Me, too?"

He nodded.

"Thanks for trying."

He smiled grimly. "Wish my best efforts would pay off now and then."

Feeling stronger, she sat up completely on her own. "How do you feel about my knowing?"

He half laughed. "How do you feel about knowing?"

She gazed at him for a long while before reaching up and kissing him. "I still love you."

He cupped the back of her head in his hand and held her lips to his. Soon he pulled her closer in a warm embrace. "I was always afraid that if you knew, you wouldn't love me."

Jan snuggled closer. “Things were already strange and a little scary before I knew. Tell me it can get any worse.”

She turned in early and Mike joined Will and Larry.

“Well, brothers. You have built your craft,” Larry said.

“Yeah, but we have a long ways to go before it can travel out of Earth’s atmosphere,” Mike complained.

“You need to find another way,” Larry countered.

Will nodded. “Those cloaked Saracen ships gave me an idea. If we could only find and capture one.”

“Could you fly it home?” Larry asked.

“I think they’re only designed to join a mother ship,” Mike said.

“Yes, but it would be easier to modify one of them and retrofit it with the technology we’ve developed,” Will mused.

“Then you need to find one of their ships,” Larry surmised.

“Yes and something tells me they’re hiding out here,” Will replied.

“And out here there are many eyes that watch,” Larry told him.

“Then you and your brothers will keep an eye out for one?”

Larry smiled. “If there’s a ship in this area, we’ll find it and you’ll have it.”

Weary from the long day, they all turned in. Overhead, watching and hovering in place, a shimmer temporarily obscured the stars.

Chapter 17

The next morning the research team packed up. Larry pulled out an inflatable raft he had had hidden along the shore. They handed their packs to him, and he strapped them down securely on the bottom. He waved his brothers on as the team climbed into the raft then pushed off and steered them into the main stream.

For a long while they drifted along with the current. With nothing to do, the team had time to take in the scenery along the banks. Now and then a fish surfaced nearby. They would watch as some bug on the water's surface was suddenly engulfed by a huge mouth and dragged down under the water.

As the raft approached the mountain pass, though, the banks drew closer together and the current picked up speed. Waves formed as they entered a section of rapids. The raft began to rise and fall rapidly and its occupants were jostled and tossed.

"Grab the paddles," Larry yelled.

All hands pulled on Velcro straps that held the paddles to the insides of the raft. Now huge boulders rose here and there in midstream, and the team dug their paddles in hard working frantically to keep the rafts clear of the rocks. Beyond the rocks were standing waves below breaking holes. Muscles strained to propel the raft forward to clear them.

"Hold on tight!" Larry called. "We're going though the jaws!"

Suddenly the cliff walls narrowed blocking out the bright sun. The raft was hurtled through a narrow squeeze, under low overhangs and down the steep drop through the gorge. Over and over again the raft was thrown into the air only to hit the water with a sickening thud. Water splashed over the sides soaking the team. Like a shot out of a cannon, the raft launched out of the gorge into the trough below.

"Paddle, paddle!" Larry yelled. "Keep it facin' forward!"

The team dug in hard sweat mixing with the river water. They plowed into the wave, crested it and slid down its backside, only to meet another head-on.

"Don't stop!" Will yelled. "Keep paddling!"

Finally they hit the boil and broke free of the rough water. The team held their paddles overhead and cheered then rested as the raft entered a broad stream of water. Jan glanced back and gasped at the sight of the sheer, narrow gap they had just descended through.

"Larry, are we close to the van?" Will called back.

"About another mile or two. Smooth water from here," he replied.

Breathing a sigh of relief, the team eased back and enjoyed the rest of the ride. All too soon, Larry asked them to help paddle the raft towards shore, and they were passing wet packs up onto the bank.

They had another couple of miles to hike over land, which they took at a leisurely pace. By mid-afternoon they reached the van. They flung open all the doors and slid up the windows then sat down to eat a quick bite before loading up the van. During the trip back to town there was excited talk about writing up the results of the trip's experiment. Mike, however, just quietly listened.

"Well, your lab assistants seem enthused," Jan remarked. "What about you?"

"Hm? Oh, I'm happy. The tests went really well," Mike said distantly. "There's just so much yet to be done."

She looked at him curiously, ideas forming in her mind. "This craft and propulsion system mean more to you than just a bid at the NASA space program, don't they," she asked quietly.

He looked at her for a moment then turned away.

"Mike, what else aren't you telling me?"

"Not now, Jan. When there's no one else around."

She glanced at the assistants and realized how far their voices carried in the close quarters of the van. "Ok, but I'll hold you to that."

He nodded without turning back toward her.

The van dropped Larry off in town. He stood by Will's window for a few last words.

"I'll call you, Dark Brother, very soon. A ship, even cloaked, can't escape detection too long."

"Just locate it," Will cautioned. "I don't want any of your people hurt trying to capture one."

"Don't worry, brother. Many coyotes live among us. We use our wits," he said smiling and pointing to his head.

Will shook his hand. "We'll be waiting for that call."

The trip back seemed longer than when they had come out, only because they were too excited to sleep. They pulled onto campus and around behind the science building near midnight. Tired, they shuffled out of the van, grabbed their packs and took off in waiting vehicles.

Jan sat in back again much more relaxed now that their extra "guest" was gone.

"So was Joe one of them?" she asked as they drove toward her apartment.

"One of 'them'?" Will asked feigning innocence.

"Will, she knows," Mike said quietly.

"About us?"

Mike nodded.

Will glanced in the rearview mirror. Jan waved.

"Um, Mike? Have you told him," she said pointing to Will, "about us?"

Mike ran his hand through his hair. "Well, there are a few details that I've left out…here and there…now and then."

Will raised his eyebrows in surprise. "Anything I should know about…I mean really know about?"

Mike looked sheepish and glanced back at Jan for moral support. He reached back and she leaned forward to take his hand.

"Uh, Will, Jan and I are in love…and I think it's pretty

serious," Mike finally managed.

Will glanced at their glowing faces as they exchanged loving looks. He nodded having suspected their secret for some time.

"How serious?"

"We haven't talked 'tomorrow' yet," Mike said using a phrase peculiar to their people.

Will nodded again. Out of the corner of his eye, he could see a faint blue glow that engulfed the two and he knew 'Tomorrow' did not even need to be spoken of. It had already overtaken them.

The next Monday the research team met in the lab to discuss the next direction they needed to take.

"To be honest," Will said, "we need to do two things simultaneously – publish our findings and take the research to the next level."

"We can't do both at the same time," Ken complained.

"That's why we need to put our heads together," Mike said. "There has to be a way we can do both."

The team sat around looking at the floor. Finally Kimberlin ventured a suggestion.

"We could take a collaborative approach," she offered. "Rather than Ken and I publishing our article separately, we could combine our data with yours."

Ken made a face that showed he clearly disliked the suggestion.

"If one of us begins the next leg of the research while the other one writes up our results, we could give them to you."

"Then what?" Will wanted to know.

"Well, supposing that your group was doing the same thing, you could pick one person to edit both sections together as a whole."

All eyes turned to Jan who began sputtering.

"Now, wait a second. Typing up notes and proofing grant proposals is one thing. Editing a scientific article is a whole other ball game," she protested.

"But you're a good writer," Kimberlin said. "Your Nineteenth Century Literature professor wanted you to publish that one paper."

"Actually when I dragged my feet on it, he submitted it for me," Jan replied.

"See, no one needs to teach you how to write."

"Yeah, but Kimberlin, literary analysis is one thing. There's a whole different structure to scientific writing and a completely separate way of citing the literature. I-I don't know," Jan said wavering.

"What if we provided you with sample articles we've written in the past?" Will asked.

"And someone were willing to field your questions on style?" Mike added.

Jan looked from one to the other. "But the English department wanted me to teach a course this semester," she said in a quiet voice. "I-I'd really been looking forward to that."

Mike looked down and Will glanced away.

"I'm sorry, guys. I wish this were an easy decision to make," she said. "Can I think about it for a couple of days?"

Mike glanced up and nodded, but she could read the disappointment in his eyes. She sighed heavily and put her head on her arm.

After the meeting, she went over to Mike. "Are you mad at me?" she asked.

He looked up, surprised. "No. I'd have a tough time making this decision, too. It's just that we need you to do this so badly…." His voice trailed off.

She looked down at the charts on the counter. "That's why I'm even willing to give it some thought," she replied. "I mean, being asked to teach a course as a first year grad student is a real honor. Plus, it's in the area I think I'd like to focus in. If I turn it down, I may never get offered the opportunity again."

"Will can explain how badly we need your help," Mike offered.

"I'm not sure the English department works that way, but I'm sure it would make a difference if he spoke to Professor Andrews for me."

She sighed heavily. "Partly I have to convince myself that I want to give up this opportunity to teach. I'd get a stipend plus benefits. I'd get a chance to show what I know."

Mike gently laid his hand on her shoulder and squeezed. "I really do understand, Jan. I would have had a hard time giving up my first shot at having my own class, too."

He leaned forward and kissed her forehead. "Just think about it, ok?"

She nodded and left for the day.

Mike did not see her that evening or the next, but she walked into the lab two days later and stood beside him waiting for him to finish talking to Terry.

"Hey, I was wondering when you'd be back," he said giving her a hug.

"I'm still thinking," she told him, "but I'm a whole lot closer to a decision."

"Anything I can do to help?" he asked.

"As a matter of fact, there is," she replied.

"Ok, shoot."

"Remember back when you told me who you and Will really are?"

He nodded.

"Remember when I asked if there was more to it, and you put me off till later?"

He looked down and pursed his lips.

"Later has come, Mike. I want to know and I want to know now. I don't feel I can make this sacrifice till I know what's really at stake."

He looked up at her and nodded. "That's fair enough. Let me get my jacket."

He told Terry he would be leaving for a while, got his jacket and walked outside with Jan. They hopped into his Triumph, headed to a park several blocks away, parked and got out.

"What do you want to know?" Mike asked as they walked along the sidewalk.

"I want to know what this project really means to you, Mike. There's an urgency in it for you that's more than scientific interest," she said.

"You're right. In some ways you could say the issue is almost life and death."

"How?"

"Jan, my father was the High King of Quentas, a planet your astronomers have yet to discover," he began. "When the Saracens invaded, they killed my father. I was just a baby and my mother was still too weak from an infection she developed after giving birth. She was still under a nurse's care and couldn't flee with me. She entrusted me to Will's care as my father had wished, and we fled our home."

She listened intently, her eyes never leaving his face.

"I've got to go back, Jan. My father made my people a promise with his dying breath that I would return to free them, and I have to find a way to do that."

Her eyes widened as she listened to his explanation.

"I've probably been entirely crazy for involving you and completely foolish for falling in love with you. I'm going to have to leave someday, maybe soon, and I don't even know if you'd want to come with me. I'd be asking you to give up a whole lot more than your teaching offer. I'd be asking you to give up your life for mine, and you would always be in danger."

Jan let out a long slow breath still reeling from the impact of what he had told her. "At this point, giving up the class for the semester seems easy. I can do that. But giving up my life, and the world I belong to. My God, Mike, why didn't you tell me before I lost my heart to you?"

Her lower lip quivered as she fought back tears.

He ran his hands through his hair then turned and embraced her. "I'm sorry, Jan. I never know when I'm trying to protect someone else, and when I'm just trying to protect myself from getting hurt. I'm sure I've done a bit of both."

Jan held him tight for a moment then pulled back. "Look, you've got your editor for that article. I'll do my best on it so you can keep researching."

Mike gently ran his thumb under her eye to wipe away the tears that were brimming over her lashes. "Jan, I'll release you. I won't ask you to sacrifice your life for mine," he said with a catch in his voice. "It won't be easy. I-I've already developed a bond with you."

He squeezed his eyes tightly closed.

"Not yet," she said shaking her head. "Don't release me yet. You've only just told me all of this. It's got to sink in a bit."

"Take your time," Mike said kissing her on the forehead. "Take as much time as you need. You've got to know your heart and mind for sure."

Jan nodded tears streaming down her cheeks as she struggled under the mountainous weight of the most important decision of her life.

Chapter 18

Jan immersed herself in the editing job for the research team. In return Will spoke to Professor Andrews of the English department on her behalf. Throughout the project, Jan worked closely with Kimberlin and Terry as she learned the scientific style of writing needed to merge the two separate pieces of research into one whole. She frequently went to Mike with questions, and he patiently answered them all. One day several weeks into the spring semester, however, he met her request for answers with a no.

"Take a break, Jan," he admonished. "Seriously, you've been driven on this project. The article is nearly finished. Take a break."

She put the papers down and heaved a sigh. "It's been such a struggle," she admitted. "I guess I haven't known when to come up for air."

"You've worked really hard on it, Jan. You don't know how much I appreciate that." He looked at her wistfully and half turned away.

She wondered why he was not more demonstrative like he used to be. "In fact," she thought, "he hasn't kissed me or hugged me since we talked in the park a few weeks ago." She frowned inwardly.

"Do you think you could take a break with me?" she asked him hopefully.

He ran his hand through is hair and glanced about the lab. "I don't know. I've been setting up a new series of assays, and the research is hitting a critical juncture," he replied. "I just…."

"Please, Mike," she said laying her hand on his arm. "Just for half-an-hour or so."

He took a shivery breath but nodded in the affirmative.

"Could we drive out to the preserve? I haven't seen it yet, and I'd kind of like to."

He nodded again but did not trust himself to speak. They took his Triumph, headed toward the coast and turned off the highway onto the shoreline drive. They pulled into a parking spot along the oceanfront and got out.

As they headed out along the boardwalk into the wetlands preserve, Jan reached out and took his hand. "Mike, you've been so distant these past few weeks. Why?"

An ocean breeze caught her hair and sent it streaming out behind her.

"I-I didn't want to influence your decision," he said swallowing back the tears that threatened to surface.

"Is that the only reason?" she asked quietly.

He faced her looking straight into her eyes. "Jan, just offering to release you felt like I had a knife turning in my heart. I was hoping that if I could just distance myself enough, it wouldn't hurt quite so much when you told me you couldn't go with me."

"And you're positive that that's what my decision will be?" she asked.

"Jan, what else can I think? I've been a complete fool, and I know it," Mike declared turning toward the ocean and letting the wind whip the tears from his face.

She put her hand on his back then slid her arms around him and held him close. "But I've decided to go with you," she declared.

For a moment his body stiffened and he caught his breath. He swung around and held her at arms' length searching her eyes for confirmation.

"Are you sure, Jan? Have you thought about what this will mean for you? Permanent separation from everything and everyone you have ever known. You'll be giving up your career, your interests, everything. Are you sure this is what you want?" he asked again.

"Mike, other than that article, this is all I've been thinking about," she assured him. "All night, all day, it's all I've thought about for weeks. My mother and father are gone. I was a bonus baby, my brothers were already out of the house when I was born, so I never really got to know them. My friends from high school and college are scattered all over, and my best friend is right here," she said patting his arm. "Lately, the more distant you've been toward me, the more certain I've been that I wanted no distance between us at all. I'll go with you, Mike. I love you."

Swallowing a lump in his throat, Mike took a deep breath. "I don't know whether to laugh or cry."

"Do both," Jan said tears of relief streaming down her face.

Mike laughed for sheer joy and smothered her in his embrace. "Lady, I never knew…not for certain. I could only hope. But you've made me so happy. If you only knew."

He slid his arm around her waist as they walked further into the marshes. Now and then they spotted birds like egrets, cranes and geese all cataloged on the endangered species list. They came to a point where a bench had been built into the railing, and he gently sat her down. Mike pulled a faded blue velvet box from his pocket and knelt on the weathered wood walkway before her.

"Jan, if your true intention is to go with me, will you take me as your lifemate? Will you marry me?"

She gazed at him gasping in astonishment when he pulled out the blue sapphire ring that Will had passed on to him at Christmas. "Mike, I-I…."

"Will-you-marry-me, Jan?" he persisted.

"Yes, Mike," she whispered, her heart swelling with warmth and love. She held her breath as he slipped the ring onto the ring finger of her right hand.

"Watch," Mike instructed.

As they did, the band molded perfectly to the shape of her finger – neither too loose nor too tight. Before she could be too amazed, though, the gem began to move. It turned ninety degrees sinking further into its setting. As it did, a spark in its center changed to a glow, which grew brighter and brighter until it shot forth an intense blue light. Mike and Jan shielded their eyes until the glow finally dimmed. However, deep in the center of the sapphire, a bright flame remained.

"Wow!" Jan exclaimed.

"It's taken on its own life!" Mike exclaimed to himself. "It really did it! I almost can't believe it!"

"You didn't think it would?" Jan wondered.

"I-I wasn't certain," Mike replied. "I thought it might reject you because you weren't Quentasian, but Will said the ring bases its decision on your heart."

"You talk about it as if it's alive?" Jan remarked incredulously.

"Something like that. I know it's not like any Earth gem. But now that it has accepted you, this ring will remain on your finger till the day one of us dies," Mike explained. "It will never hold your finger too tightly, and some of the archives have suggested it can even protect its wearer."

"That sounds a little like magic to me," Jan said.

"And what it just did wasn't magical?"

"Ok, you've got me there."

"Let's not go back to the lab today," Mike suggested on a whim.

"Where will we go?"

"Home," he replied decisively. "I want to take you home. I want to show Will. I want him to know."

For a moment his face took on a boyish expression. Jan caressed his cheek and kissed him.

"Ok, let's go home."

They hurried back to the Triumph and Mike sped toward his house.

"Good, the RAV is still in the driveway," he said parking his car beside it. He hurried around to open Jan's door and led her into the house.

"Will!" he called.

They heard his voice on the phone upstairs. "In a minute, Michael," he called down.

Mike wrapped his arms around Jan from behind and pulled her back to lean against his chest. They were still in that embrace when Will finally came downstairs.

"Michael, I just got a call from…."

"Will, look! It did it! Just like you said," Mike exclaimed, beaming.

He held out Jan's hand so Will could examine the ring. Will gently took her hand and gazed at the flame brightly burning in the center of the stone.

"So, you found a way to make this decision," he said gravely. "Do you understand the sacrifice you are making?"

She nodded sincerely.

Will looked up at both of them then engulfed them in a big bear hug. "Jan, welcome to the family."

To Jan's astonishment, he then got down on one knee before her and bowed his head. "I pledge from this day forth to honor and defend your life with my life. To serve you as I would serve myself."

Jan stared at him, wide-eyed in confusion and looked to Mike for understanding.

"We are his king and queen-to-be," he explained. "Tell him you accept his pledge and tell him to rise."

In a voice that wavered with uncertainty, Jan said, "I accept your pledge…and-and…."

"Tell him to rise," Mike prompted.

"You may rise," she said in a hurry to get the words out.

Will rose to his feet and looked down at her. "With that ring on, Jan, you are now both protected and that much more conspicuous to our enemies."

"So what should I do?"

"For now it would be better if we were all under one roof," he replied.

"Move in?"

"We have a spare bedroom, and it shouldn't be for too long."

Mike eyes narrowed. "What do you mean?"

"That was Larry on the phone as you came in. They think they've located the canyon where the craft is hiding. We should hear more by the end of the week."

"Then we could be leaving soon," Mike said.

"Very soon," Will confirmed.

"Let's get Jan moved in now."

With that a whirlwind of activity erupted around her as the men sprang into action. They picked up her car from the university, drove over to her apartment and were soon packing up her belongings, bringing them back to their house and unloading them. By midnight they had her things all arranged in the spare bedroom.

The first moment she had to herself, Jan gazed about her in forlorn confusion.

"You ok?" Mike asked popping his head in the door.

She just shook her head and stared about her. "I feel like one of those globes you shake and all of the snow swirls around the scene inside. My head is in a whirl."

Mike came in, sat on the edge of her bed and pulled her onto his lap. He kissed her fervently, loathe to let her go. "Any better?"

"Mm. Now my head is spinning for a totally different reason," she replied. "I like this reason better, though."

She leaned forward and kissed him again. After a while they came up for air. Mike's face was flushed, and she felt his forehead to check his temperature.

"What? I'm fine! Honestly!" he assured her. "Just a little drunk on love at the moment. That's all."

"Well, then, I guess I can allow that," Jan replied kissing him on the cheek.

She lingered at his cheek then kissed the corner of his mouth, moving on to his chin, the other corner and his other cheek. She kissed both of his eyes before running her fingers through the hair at the nape of his neck. His breathing quickened and he pulled her closer. With one hand on the back of her head, he maneuvered his lips over hers. The other hand let glide down her back and under her legs. He squeezed her outer thigh for a moment then ran his hand back up along her side. His thumb caught just under her breast and he rubbed the underside for a moment as she inhaled sharply.

Mike stopped for a moment, took several quick deep breaths, then pulled away and held her hands in his. She searched his face questioningly, but he closed his eyes and set her on her feet and got up.

"Is something wrong?" she asked anxiously.

He shook his head. "No, a little too much is right at the moment."

"I don't understand," she said putting her hand on his arm.

"Are you all right?"

Mike was breathing hard as if from great exertion. "I can't explain right now, Jan." He swallowed hard. "I'll explain later. I promise."

"Ok."

"Look, why don't you get some sleep. I'm willing to bet you're a lot more tired than you realize."

At that Jan yawned. "Now that you mention it, it was a big day."

He kissed her forehead letting his lips linger. "See you in the morning, lady."

Jan closed the door after him then crawled under her covers and promptly fell asleep.

Mike, however, laid awake for a long while. Ever nerve fiber in his body longed for her touch. He could feel her lips against his, feel the weight of her body on his legs, and he longed for her touch on his neck and back. In the back of his mind, one of Will's old lectures surfaced.

"The laws of Quentas are a lot different fro m those of Earth," he had told him. "As the future High King, a lot more is expected from you than from anyone else."

Mike remembered the stern, rigid look on Will's face.

"The boys on Earth can have sex with several different girls before they get married and vice versa. While the desire for sex is natural, you have a different calling from that of your friends, Michael. Your calling is to maintain your own sexual purity and to find a lifemate who has done the same."

Mike remembered feeling the injustice of the requirement. "And just how will I know she's a virgin?" he had asked angrily.

"The ring will reject her if she isn't."

"So what about my needs? What does staying a virgin do for me?"

"It proves two things," Will had replied. "One is your strength of character. It takes a lot of willpower and self-control to refuse what your body desires. The closer you are to a woman, and the stronger your bond, the harder it will be to maintain your self-control. If you don't practice that in casual relationships, you will never have the strength once you are betrothed to your lifemate and have begun to bond with her."

"So, what's the other?" Mike had wanted to know.

"To our people, maintaining your purity and the purity of the royal line is of paramount importance."

His moans of "It's not fair," faded from the moment.

"Maintain my purity," he said aloud to himself. He shook his head wondering if his ancestors had ever lived under the same conditions he was thrust into now. "She's only next door," he thought running his tongue over his dry lips. "Just next door."

Chapter 19

The next morning Jan woke to hear voices downstairs. For a moment she looked about her, baffled. The glint of sunlight that streamed through the window off the ring made her blink. She smelled salt air, felt a cool breeze and heard the cry of a seagull, and the memories of yesterday came crashing down around her like a wave.

She got up, slipped into a satin bathrobe, and walked out into the hall. Mike's door was closed so she brushed her teeth and hair in the bathroom and headed downstairs to the kitchen. She found Kimberlin and Terry sitting at the island and Will filling them in on the details of Larry's call from yesterday.

Will looked up and smiled broadly. "Jan, Kimberlin and Terry are two of Michael's cousins. They were exiled to Earth a decade after we were. We only located them just a couple of years ago."

Jan smiled and slid onto a stool beside them. Kimberlin spotted a flash from the ring and stared at in awe.

"He did it!" she exclaimed.

"It's alive," Terry added.

They both looked at Jan with new respect then to Will for instruction as to how to act. He nodded and they both slid off their seats and knelt before her, reciting the same pledge that he had given her the day before.

Feeling suddenly alienated, Jan accepted their pledges and told them to rise, but an awkward silence reigned in the seconds that followed.

"You guys don't have to get all formal now," Mike told them as he entered the kitchen. "Save that for after the coronation."

"And that won't be until after we've returned to Quentas," Will reminded them. "Since Larry's people are so close to finding one of those Saracen ships, I felt it would be best if we were prepared to act quickly. I called Kim and Terry over so we could develop a plan."

Will rolled out a map of the mesa area and reservation. Mike handed Jan a glass of juice and peered over her shoulder.

"Once they locate a ship, it will be up to us to capture it," Will began.

"Are we planning to retrofit it?" Kimberlin asked.

Will nodded.

From that point on a shimmer seemed to engulf them as they focused on the map. Jan looked from one of them to another, but could not make eye contact. Completely left out of a process she did not understand, she left her glass in the sink and went upstairs to shower and change. They were still entranced when she came back down, so she wrote a note, placed it in front of Mike and headed out the door to the university.

Around noon the huddle in the kitchen broke up. They all seemed surprised to find Jan missing from their ranks. Mike went upstairs to check her room, but Terry called him back down from where he stood by the front door.

"She took her car," he announced.

Mike frowned. "Why did she run off like that? Especially now. She knows better."

"Where do you think she might have gone?" Will asked.

"The store?" Terry wondered.

Kimberlin shook her head. "No, I'll bet she's at the lab."

She picked up the phone and dialed, but there was no answer. Worry creased their brows as they wondered where else to look for her. Suddenly the phone rang and Mike jumped on it.

"Jan!"

All heads turned toward him.

"Where are you? You've had us frantic!"

"I'm right where I told you I would be," she replied on the other end.

"You never told me anything about going anywhere," Mike countered.

"I couldn't," Jan complained. "I tried to get your attention, but you all acted like you were frozen in time. So I left you a note."

"I didn't see a note," Mike said. He looked around the island. "Anyone see a note?"

Kimberlin bent down, picked a piece of paper off the floor and handed it to Mike.

"*Will be in the physics department office printing out final copy of the article and the cover letter. Should be here most of the day. See you tonight. Love, Jan*," he read.

The others breathed a sigh of relief, and Mike leaned against the wall near the phone.

"I'm sorry, Jan. It must have fallen off the counter."

There was a moment of silence before Jan countered. "You know, Mike, it would be nice if you had a little faith in me. I'm not stupid enough to go running off without letting you know where I'm going. I was going to ask for the name and address of a contact but never mind. I'll find it on my own."

Mike heard a loud click and the line went dead. He winced, "Ouch!"

"Mad at you, huh?" Terry asked.

Mike nodded. "Guess I'd better go down and apologize. While I'm there I can make some copies of those schematics and our research notes."

Will nodded.

As he headed toward the front door, Kimberlin caught Mike's arm. "Get her a rose, Michael. It's the age-old way to apologize to a woman."

He glanced back at her. "Thanks. I think I'll be needing it."

Jan sat in the physics department office monitoring the progress of the laser printer and collating the copies as they came out. She spotted an error on the latest page, and turned to the computer to make the change. A velvety red rose suddenly appeared in front of her.

She looked at it, then up at Mike who gazed down at her hopefully.

Jan took the rose and smelled it. She let its sweet scent ease the tension out of her brow then stood up and gave him a hug. "You're forgiven."

"Thanks. So how's it going?"

"I must have written this final version on a late night," she replied sitting back down. "I keep finding typos, but I'm almost done."

"I'm going to be here for a while. We need copies of the schematics and research notes," he informed her. "And you're looking for the contact to the Journal of Space and Aeronautics."

She spun in her seat. "How did you know?"

"It's the only one not checked off on your list," he replied handing her a business card he had pulled from his wallet. "This should be the guy you want."

With that, he headed toward the lab and Jan finished up there. She joined him and they were soon stapling side-by-side.

"So what was the huddle about this morning?" she asked.

Mike stopped and looked at her. "You really couldn't hear us?"

She shook her head.

"Will always said he didn't think humans could tap into our telepathic communications. If you couldn't, even with our bond, I guess he was right," Mike replied.

"Why do you communicate that way?"

"It's faster…speed of thought, instead of speed of sound. Plus, it's private…apparently more so than we had realized."

"So, how do I get in on this 'conversation' of yours?"

Mike looked at her very seriously. "I don't know if you can, and that may be a problem."

"Well, could you at least warn me next time?" she requested. "Then at least I'll know you aren't ignoring me on purpose."

He nodded and squeezed her shoulders.

That evening Jan lay on her bed while the others made plans and preparations downstairs. She went through old family photo albums, now and then pulling out a photo and slipping it into a photo wallet. Occasionally a tear trickled down her cheek, and she would flip the page quickly.

Kimberlin knocked on her door, came in and sat on the edge of Jan's bed. "What are you doing?"

"Pulling out my favorite pictures," Jan replied. "I know I can't take them all so I'm creating two small collections – one that shows my family tree and one of just my mom, dad and me. I want to at least bring some of my memories with me."

Kimberlin flipped through the wallets. "Must be hard to decide which ones to bring."

Jan nodded.

"Michael explained what happened this morning…that you felt left out."

"No, it's more than that. Until he explained it, I thought I was being purposely ignored."

Kimberlin winced. "We won't let that happen again."

"It's ok now that I understand. All I need is for someone to explain things once in a while and I'll be fine."

Kimberlin nodded then left the room.

Jan snapped the wallets shut stuffing them into her hiking backpack. She had been warned to bring along only the essentials. As she looked around her, everything suddenly seemed essential. She yawned, stretched and left her room. Spotting Mike lying on his bed studying the schematics, she knocked and went in. He glanced up and smiled.

"Done packing?"

She shook her head as she sat on the edge of his bed. "Just taking a break."

He nodded and rolled up the schematics. "I've just got last minute stuff to pack. Will and I always kept a backpack ready…just in case."

"What a way to live," Jan remarked.

"You do what you've got to do."

She remained silent for a couple of minutes then took a deep breath. "Remember last night when we were kissing, and…."

Mike cleared his throat. "And…."

"You stopped. Why? Was it something I did?" she asked expectantly awaiting an answer.

He looked at the rolled schematics in his hands. "You women always assume that if something is wrong you're at fault. Why?"

"Because we're the easiest thing to fix," Jan replied, chuckling. "If we goof up, we know we'll make it right once we find out what we did wrong. Then we know the problem will get solved quickly."

"And if you're not at fault?"

"Then we know this is going to be a tough problem because a man is going to need to be fixed."

He made a face at her in protest.

"Hey, you asked."

He held up his hands in self-defense then grew serious. "You're not at fault, Jan. You didn't do anything wrong."

"So what is wrong?"

Mike laid down the schematics and took her hands in his. "Remember when Prince Charles got engaged to Lady Di, and they had to go through all that rigmarole to make certain she was a virgin, etc.?"

Jan nodded.

"As High King of Quentas, not only does my future lifemate have to be a virgin, but so do I. Can't take chances of some kid coming around saying, 'Hi, Dad. You never knew me, but I'm your son by so-and-so, and by the way, I'm older than the crown prince, so I get your throne instead'."

Jan raised her eyebrows. "Yeah, that would be nasty problem. But I don't recall any special checks to see if I was a virgin."

"The ring would have rejected you if you hadn't been," Mike replied. "Besides, I kind of sensed you might be. Between caring for your parents when they were ill then throwing yourself into your work the way you do…."

"You know me pretty well."

"Just a lucky guess."

"So what would happen if you slipped up and we made love?"

"That ring," he said pointing to the gem on her finger, "would reject you. It would fall off your finger and no one, neither you nor I, could ever put it back on."

"I thought you said it was stuck on for life,' Jan said giving it an experimental tug.

"No one else can break our bond, Jan, yet if we screw up, we will have done it to ourselves."

Jan stared thoughtfully at the ring for a moment. "I was always worried about guys rejecting me once they found out I wanted to stay a virgin, and some did. But I knew some girls who made love to their fiancées, and I always figured that would be ok. I mean, we were going to get married anyway, so I would never have been with anyone else. This," she said holding up the ring, "changes things a whole lot."

"It's more than just that," Mike said turning her to face him. "The more closely we bond, the more desperately I want to join with you. Our hearts are already one and our spirits are close. I want that oneness to be complete, but it's not time. I need your help, Jan."

"What can I do?"

"Stop me. We're living under conditions that I doubt any other High King has had to deal with. Usually the two people return to their families for a month or two after their engagement and don't see each other again until their wedding. But you're right here with me, right beside me, and God only knows when we'll be able to get married. I want you so badly."

He closed his eyes and in a moment a flood of passion erupted over her. She felt an urgent heat that sizzled through her veins and every nerve ending seemed extra sensitive to touch. There was an ache in her groin that powered the desperation in her heart. She closed her eyes and swallowed hard. As suddenly as it started, it stopped. She opened her eyes and saw that passion mirrored in Mike's.

"That's what you're feeling?" she asked in amazement.

"Most of the time," he confessed.

Jan took a couple of deep breaths to calm down. "Do me one favor," she said squeezing his hands, "and I'll do everything I can to keep you honest."

"What's the favor?"

"Don't project that onto me again. It's all I can do to keep myself in line. I don't think I could handle that intensity for very long."

Mike nodded in agreement.

At that moment Will poked his head in the door. "We're leaving in the morning," he announced. "Get some rest."

Jan's heart began beating wildly. "Leaving." Everything she had ever known and was familiar with would soon be gone."

Chapter 20

Jan quickly packed the remainder of the things she had planned to take then crawled into bed. She was far too excited to sleep and got up as soon as she heard Will stir in the room across the hall. He went downstairs to call Kimberlin and Terry, and Jan hit the showers. When she came out with a towel around her head, Mike was waiting in the hall.

"Well, hello beautiful," he quipped.

"Beauty is a process. It doesn't just happen," she replied disappearing into her room.

By the time he was leaving the bathroom, she was hauling her backpack downstairs. She loaded it and Will's into the RAV. Mike threw his in after theirs. In minutes Kimberlin and Terry had added theirs. They walked inside for a quick breakfast.

"Where exactly are we headed? Terry asked.

"The reservation," Will replied.

"They found it?" Kimberlin asked.

Jan saw the shimmer begin. "Wait, guys! I want to hear this part, too," she cried.

Slowly, as if waking from a dream, they all turned towards her. Her face burned bright red with embarrassment, but she stood her ground.

"This involves me, too, and I need to know what's happening. Please slow down so I'm not left out," she pleaded.

Mike winced realizing he had not even kept his promise to warn her. "She's right. It's really easy for us to slip into thought mode, but Jan really needs to be part of this conversation."

"Where on the reservation are we headed?" Jan asked turning their attention away from her.

"It's deep into mesa land," Will replied. "There's a spot in there where the Indians gather for ceremonial purposes. We'll be meeting them there."

"They don't usually let outsiders know where those places are," Jan countered.

"We're not entirely outsiders," Will replied. "When we first crashed on Earth, they hid us in mesa land from the military. We stayed with them for four or five years before I felt it was safe enough to take Michael into the community at large."

"The tribe adopted us," Mike explained. "They're our brothers. We visit for ceremonies several times a year."

Jan nodded. "So how long of a drive do we have?"

"Seven, eight, maybe nine hours," Will replied. "Depends in which canyon the craft is located."

"Are we ready to go?" Terry asked.

"It'll be cramped quarters, but we should be ready, "Will replied leading the way to the RAV.

While Terry sat up front with Will, Mike and the two girls squeezed in back. At first everyone but Will dozed as they headed east on the highway. Three hours into the trip Will pulled into a service area for a cup of coffee, and Jan and Kimberlin headed for the ladies room.

"Have you always been telepathic?" Jan asked.

Kimberlin scrunched up her nose as she thought. "Actually no, I don't think I was as a kid."

Having hit upon common ground, Jan pressed forward. "How did you learn?"

Kimberlin frowned. "I don't remember learning either. It's

like I hit nine or ten and I could."

Jan's heart sank, but when they came out of the restroom, Kimberlin was still deep in thought. "You know, there was a process to this."

"What?"

"I did have to learn some things, like clearing my mind and relaxing. If you're tense or have too much going through your head, you can't hear."

Jan tucked her hair behind her ear and stared off into space. "Some people claim to be telepathic," she said. "In fact, I had a girlfriend when I was about twelve and it seemed like we were psychically linked. We could finish each other's sentences, we knew what the other was thinking…it was kind of weird."

Kimberlin's eyes lit up. "But that's like what mine started with. Maybe you could learn to hear us. Once you get it down, it's like tuning a radio to your favorite station."

"I'd really like to try," Jan replied. "If I could only learn to hear you just a bit, it would help."

"We'll work on it," Kimberlin assured her.

They climbed back into the RAV, and Jan settled in to doze off again as Will pulled back onto the highway. Just as she was almost asleep, she heard, "Jan, can you hear me?" echo inside her mind. Her eyes popped wide open, and she snapped her head around to look at Kimberlin.

"Did you?"

Jan nodded, her eyes wide, then both girls broke out into big grins.

"Try it again," Jan prompted.

However, now that she was wide awake and excited, she could not hear her friend.

"Great," she grumbled. "I have to be nearly asleep to hear you."

"But at least we know you can hear us at all. We'll work on it till you can hear while you're awake."

Jan sighed. "So telepathy is a process. Oh, good."

They stopped one more time before getting off the highway

and turning onto a dirt road. It was late afternoon as they drove up into the mountains, down into the valleys and through the canyons of mesa land. They pulled into a small Indian village, rolled through its dusty streets and approached the outskirts, when Will slammed on his brakes. An Indian woman stood in the middle of the road blocking the way.

Mike rolled down his window. "Grandmother, it's us. Why won't you let us pass?"

She looked sternly at him. "Little Star, you have one with you who is uninitiated in our ways. She cannot go to the ceremonial grounds."

"But she has to, Grandmother," he protested. "She's my lifemate. She has to come with me."

"She cannot pass."

Jan groaned. "What do I have to do?" she asked.

Grandmother looked her over with piercing black eyes. "Come with me."

Will pulled the RAV over, and they all piled out. Jan went with the Indian woman alone. They entered a small hut near the edge of town. Jan was surprised at how clean and uncluttered it was on the inside.

A woven Indian blanket lay on the floor with a bowl, some corn meal, tobacco, several quartz crystals and an abalone shell filled with sage and cedar arranged around it.

"Lie here," Grandmother instructed, and Jan stretched out on the blanket.

Grandmother lit the sage and smudged the room and Jan's body while she hummed softly to herself. Then she sat by Jan's head and ran the quartz crystals over her body. Afterwards she placed one beside each ear and one at the top of Jan's head. In her mind's eye, Jan saw a swirl of colors and heard voices mumbling as if from a distance.

Grandmother began to rattle and sway. She shook her rattle down the length of Jan's body then brought it back to Jan's heart. She opened her eyes and gazed kindly at her.

"You have suffered much grief in your young life."

"I lost both my parents," Jan confirmed.

Grandmother nodded. "Yet, your heart is open. Good. You love Little Star. That is good, too."

She smiled seemingly satisfied.

Jan sat up and gazed at the older woman.

"You are unafraid."

"You're not here to hurt me," Jan replied.

"How do you know I don't have the power to hurt you?"

"I didn't say you don't have the power to hurt me. You just don't intend to," Jan corrected.

"And where do you feel this 'knowing'?"

Jan pointed to her stomach and to her heart.

Grandmother smiled. "Good intuition. Use it wisely. Listen and it will care for you."

She went to put away her things, but Jan stopped her. "Do you know how I can learn telepathy?"

"What do you want to hear people's thoughts for?"

Jan explained what had happened over the past couple of days and ended by saying, "I could hear Kimberlin when I was almost asleep, but not when I'm fully awake. How do I hear when I'm awake?"

Grandmother gazed at her, and her eyes drooped somewhat. "Breathe in and out very slowly. See your breath coming in and out, with each breath see it first go to your throat, then your lungs, then all the way down to your stomach. Just concentrate on your breath."

Jan did as she was told and suddenly heard, "Bride of Little Star is a good woman."

Jan stared at Grandmother and smiled broadly. "It worked!"

"Of course. You took yourself out of the way. Remember your breathing and follow your breath," Grandmother instructed. "Then you will always hear them."

Jan smiled, reached out and gave the older woman a hug. "Thank you for a very precious gift."

"You do it yourself."

"But you taught me how."

With that they left the hut and returned to the RAV. Mike looked at Grandmother hopefully.

"You know how to pick 'em, Little Star. Now you two be happy together."

Mike hugged the older woman.

"Don't hug me, find room for me in that vehicle of yours. I

don't plan to walk to the ceremony."

They looked at one another.

"I can squeeze in back," Terry offered.

"And I can sit on his lap," Kimberlin said.

"We'll manage," Will confirmed. "Go get your tools, Grandmother. Let's get this show on the road."

While they waited for Grandmother to get her roll, Jan whispered in Kimberlin's ear. "I can hear, Kimberlin. Even when I'm awake."

"Even now?" Jan heard faintly inside her head. She smiled and nodded. "But let's keep it our secret for now."

Kimberlin nodded in agreement. Grandmother returned and they all squeezed into the RAV and headed into mesa land.

The sun had set by the time they reached Larry's camp just outside the ceremonial grounds. Larry had supper ready for them, and they sat down for a quick bite.

"We found the craft in a little canyon about a mile or so away. Around midnight it drops its cloak and we could see it," he told them.

"How many appear to be on it?" Will asked.

"Six maybe seven. There is that tall woman and three more of her kind, plus two ugly men," Larry reported.

"Who are those ugly ones?" Mike wondered.

"I've given them considerable thought," Will replied. "I believe they are B'narians and that that spherical craft we encountered earlier this year was theirs."

"But I thought B'nar had a treaty with Quentas," Mike countered.

"Did," Kimberlin said. "I vaguely remember something about the Saracens invading B'nar as well."

"So we're up against the Saracens and the B'narians," Will mused. "I'd like to get a look at that ship. We have to figure out a way to get inside."

They lay back for a while and slept after the long drive. Around midnight Will shook them awake. They strapped on their backpacks and headed out following Larry and his brothers. Within an hour they spotted a glow coming from a small box canyon. They crept to the rim and peered down at the shiny metallic craft.

"I count three," Will whispered. "Two on guard and one seems to be repairing something."

"Do you think the others are inside?" Mike wondered.

"I don't know. We need to get a closer look."

At that point, the air began to shimmer and Jan recognized their familiar leap into thought mode. Rather than get frustrated, though, she began to breathe like Grandmother had taught her. Soon she could hear bits and pieces of the conversation.

"Go down," she heard Mike say.

"On one side," Terry said almost over top of Mike.

"Behind the rock there," Kimberlin was saying.

The communications were all jumbled as their mental communication moved much too quickly for Jan to process. She tried paying attention just to one voice but lost so much of the conversation that she finally gave up. When she stopped listening she looked around and discovered that she was all alone in the night. The others had made their plans and had moved on.

Tears of frustration and panic welled up inside her, but she fought them back. Glancing about she thought she saw one of her group members just down the slope from where she lay hidden. Cautiously she crawled over the lip of the canyon and began slipping down the steep slope. She was only a yard away from her target when she realized her mistake. A tall form rose out of the darkness, and she began scrambling to get away. Too late. A hand clamped down over her mouth. A powerful arm lifted her off her feet, and the Saracen carried her into the night.

The Saracen's long legs took the steep slope in stride and in no time he had reached the back side of the ship. He carried her on board the ship and straight to the captain. The tall Saracen woman glared at Jan and smiled wickedly.

"This is perfect," she purred. "We have the bride. The groom will always follow. This is even easier than I thought it would be. They will come straight to us now."

She glared at Jan. "How many are out there? How many came with you?"

"I-I don't know," Jan replied shaking her head.

"How did you find our ship? Who led you here?"

Jan clamped her mouth shut and cowered before the menacing woman.

"She's trained like the rest of them," her captor said.

"Then we'll extract the information from her like we do from the others. Take her to the interrogation chamber," the captain ordered.

Jan was dragged through the narrow corridors and pushed into a small room. A B'narian waited inside at a computer console. The Saracen guard shoved her into a large, padded chair that was linked via wires to the console. Her head was forced back between two padded clamps, while metal clamps were brought down over both her wrists and her ankles. When the B'narian brought the Augmenter discs into view, Jan's eyes grew wide with terror. He affixed them to her temples then arranged a series of electrodes in an arch over her head.

The Saracen captain leaned on the arm of the chair and glared at Jan. "You have no choice but to tell us what we want to know. We will not play with you as we did before. Refuse to tell us and you will die."

Jan's heart was beating wildly as she glanced about in fear. If only she had some way to contact Mike. In her mind's eye she saw Grandmother and heard her say, "Remember to follow your breath."

"That was so I could hear their telepathic conversation," Jan thought. "Will it work in reverse?"

She had no choice but to try. Closing her eyes, she forced herself to shut out the terror and the menacing faces. Grandmother's face appeared before her, and Jan followed her breath.

Outside, the group descended from the rim of the canyon and cautiously gathered near its mouth.

"I still only see the two guards and the B'narian performing the flight check," Will telepathed.

Suddenly his shoulder was shaken, and he slowly turned his head to see Larry who was frantically trying to get his attention.

"They have Jan," Larry reported. "Jim saw her get captured."

Mike who had just brought himself back to audio conversation looked distressed. "But she was right with us. I could even swear she was listening to us. Why didn't she follow?"

"She just learned how to hear us today, Michael," Kimberlin said. "Don't you remember what it was like? All those voices and not knowing which one to pay attention to?"

Mike's face became an anguished mask. "I've been expecting

way too much from her. What do we do now?"

"Do you know where they took her?" Will asked Larry.

He shook his head.

Suddenly Mike stared at the craft. "She's inside," he breathed. "They've got her inside."

"Where, Michael?" Will demanded.

He shook his head. "All she can manage is to call my name."

"But that's enough," Will said. "Try to keep her talking so we can home in on her. I've got a plan.'

Chapter 21

"Cooperate," the Saracen captain demanded.

"Why?" Jan retorted. "You'll kill me anyway. What do I have to lose?"

"A few hours of excruciating pain," the captain replied turning on her heel and leaving the room with the Saracen guard right behind her.

Jan studied the B'narian for a moment. "You're not like them," she remarked as he set up the equipment.

He shook his head.

"So why do you work for them?"

He looked up at her. "Work for them?" he spat in a deep gravely voice. "I do not work for them. I am a slave. I just do as I am told."

"But why?"

Tears rolled down his brightly flushed cheeks. "They hold our princess captive. Our people are connected to her psychically. Whenever one of us disobeys, they torture her. We feel her pain and hear her cries. We must not disobey. She must not suffer so."

"Have you ever tried to rescue her?" Jan asked.

"To disobey to that degree would cause her death."

"So my pain and death are ok?"

The B'narian shook his head violently, tears coursing down his cheeks. "No choice. I have no choice."

He finished his adjustments. "Please answer truthfully. You will feel little pain, and I will kill you quickly before they return to toy with you."

"I wish it were that simple," Jan replied, "but I have someone of my own to protect."

He looked at her with eyes full of sympathy then bowed his head over the console. "We will begin. What is your betrothed's name?"

"Mike."

"What else is he called?'

"Michael. Dr. Stellan. Little Stár," Jan said, in rapid-fire succession.

"What other name?"

"That's all I know," she replied and a mild shock went through her.

"He has other names, other titles…what are they?"

"Um, professor, researcher, uh…." Jan said scrambling to find alternatives to the title "High King."

"Interesting pattern here," the B'narian remarked. "There may or may not be something else in the background, I cannot tell. Let's go over these questions again."

Out in the canyon, the group stealthily snuck closer to the ship.

"Have you located her?" Will telepathed

"Can't. She stopped sending. They're interrogating her, I think," Mike replied.

"Ok. We've got to take out these guards as soundlessly as possible, then draw out the others. Once we have, we can board the ship and find Jan," Will said slowly turning and whispering to Larry.

Larry nodded and slipped away to join his brothers.

Mike crawled on his stomach until he was directly in font of the two guards. With an internal nod from Will, he suddenly sprang to his feet. The guards raised their weapons but instantly dropped what had become hot pieces of lead. Before they could look back up, Mike fired a bolt of energy at them both and they dropped to the ground. He waved the others forward as the B'narian ducked back inside.

In the interrogation chamber, Jan was bravely holding her own.

"Where is he from?"

Jan thought for a moment and received a stronger shock.

"Answer immediately," the B'narian ordered.

"But I don't know," she protested.

"Is Earth his home?"

"N...Yes," a stronger charge hit her, and she saw the letter "Q" light up in front of her eyes.

"You are definitely masking a second answer," the B'narian said. "I believe it is the one I really want. Let's try that again."

He set the power up a notch. "Now then. Where did he tell you he was from?"

Jan anxiously began counting under her breath. "He never said." She had reached five.

"Are you certain?"

"Yes."

"Where are his parents?"

"Dead."Ten.

"What did they die of?"

"I don't know." Fifteen.

"Who raised him?"

"His legal guardian." Twenty.

Another shock jolted her as she reached twenty-two. She frowned. "What did I say wrong?"

The B'narian studied the console. "You were definitely masking your responses. The patterns for numbers are appearing alongside your answers."

"Oh." Jan shifted tactics and began singing the first song that popped into her head humming the tune quietly to herself.

"Who has he told you he is?"

"Why do you want to know?" A stronger jolt coursed through her.

"Answer with an answer, not a question. Who has he told you he is?"

"A physics professor." Still another jolt. "Come on! He is!" she protested.

"Your thought-masking concealed a further answer. Cooperate, young lady, or you will feel more," the B'narian threatened again resetting the power.

Weary and in pain, Jan began to recite the alphabet. "Hurry, Mike," she pleaded inwardly.

"Where is he originally from?"

"I-don't-know."

The next jolt was intense and took her breath away. Jan closed her eyes as the room swam before her. A locomotive seemed to be charging through her head, and the B'narian's voice faded in and out.

"You-are-not-cooperating!" he shouted through clenched teeth. "Try again! What are his immediate plans?"

"I don't know." The next shock made her reel. "He usually acts and I find out later." she cried in defense.

The next jolt made her scream. Tears streamed down her cheeks, and her breath came in short gasps. "Please," she whispered. "I'm telling you…what…I know."

"Only I ask the questions," the B'narian roared.

"Yes sir."

"Where is he now?"

"I don't know," Jan replied weakly.

She hardly felt the next shock.

From outside the ship came the sound of gunfire.

The B'narian jerked his head up. "I do not need these interruptions," he fumed. He got up and turned to walk out of the room.

At that instant a blue glow spread from the ring and surrounded Jan. A bright bolt of blue light shot out of the ring and hit the B'narian. He fell back against the console, his head compressing the shock button. Jan's body began to convulse.

Outside the ship, Larry and his brothers had opened fire and a rain of bullets hit the ship.

The third Saracen guard came out as well as the B'narian who had been fixing the ship. Mike took out the Saracen with one bright bolt, while Larry brought down the B'narian.

"Quick! Inside!" Will shouted.

They ran forward and cautiously crept into the ship. Mike

motioned for Kimberlin and Terry to head toward the back and look for Jan. Meanwhile, he and Will edged toward the command deck. The door swished open, and a hail of laser fire poured out.

They flattened themselves against the wall and waited until the firing stopped. Mike ducked his head forward and shot a couple of power blasts while Will crawled inside on his stomach. When the laser storm started back up, he was inside crawling into position to aim a shot at the Saracen captain with Larry's rifle.

In the back of the ship, Kimberlin and Terry crept along. They opened each door along the corridor pointing a rifle in first before poking their heads in. Kimberlin, who was working the right side of the corridor, suddenly gasped.

"Terry! Hurry! It's Jan."

Terry rushed to her side then they tumbled into the room. Terry hauled the B'narian off the console and began powering it down. Meanwhile, Kimberlin tugged at the metal bands and head clamps until they swung back, peeled off the discs that had burned into Jan's temples and yanked off the electrodes that arched over her head. Terry joined her and tried to help.

"My, God, Terry. She's almost dead," Kimberlin breathed as she bit her lower lip to stifle her tears.

"We've got to get her to Will. He'll know what to do," Terry said gently lifting her still form.

They scrambled down the corridor and made their way to the front to join Mike and Will.

On the command deck, Will reached his position and took aim. The Saracen captain caught sight of him and turned in his direction.

"Do you think you can harm me with that measly weapon?" she cried.

She raised her laser gun and aimed it at Will, but suddenly dropped it and clawed at her throat. She was lifted off her feet and hung in mid-air.

"Where is my beloved?" Mike demanded.

"She will be…of no use…to you anyway…by now," the captain gasped.

"What have you done to her?"

"See…for yourself," she said pointing behind him.

He glanced over his shoulder as Terry entered the deck with Kimberlin following. In his arms Jan lay limp and nearly lifeless. He swung his gaze back to the captain.

"What-did-you-do-to-her?"

"Used an…amplified Augmenter," she replied with a satisfied and malevolent grin.

Fury surged through Mike as his power crushed the Saracen's body. In an instant, a power bolt completely disintegrated her and he stood gasping for air.

Terry laid Jan on the floor and Will hurried to her side.

"How bad is she, Will?" Mike asked kneeling beside him.

Will swallowed hard. "I'm not sure she's going to make it, Michael."

"You've got to do something," Mike insisted.

"Let's take her outside so I can get my pack. I may have something inside to stabilize her," Will suggested.

Not wasting a moment, Mike scooped her up in his arms and led the way outside. They were met by Larry, his brothers and Grandmother. She elbowed her way forward and looked down at Jan gravely.

"Put her on my blanket," she instructed. Mike obeyed instantly.

While Will rubbed the salve into Jan's temples, Grandmother prepared for her ritual. She tied bells around her ankles and passed a drum to Larry's brother, Jim. The other brothers had built a fire, and Grandmother used a burning twig to light the sage. With her prayer feather she smudged each person in the group then stood at the four corners of the circle and said a prayer in each direction. She looked up, then down, then closed her eyes as she went inward.

Grandmother began to chant, Jim began drumming and the brothers began a low hum. For a few minutes, Grandmother swayed back and forth then began a shuffle step dance around Jan's prone body. After one circuit she lay down beside her touching at the feet, shoulders, and hands. Jim continued the drumming until twenty minutes later Grandmother opened her eyes.

She crawled to her knees then blew into the top of Jan's head, into her forehead and into her heart. As she did, she muttered quietly.

"Eagle I give you for fortitude, and foresight. Buffalo I give you for the power and endurance to lean against the great winds that buffet you. Mountain Lion I give you that you may have the courage to walk alone and to survive no matter how harsh your environment."

With that Grandmother stood up looking worn and spent, and Jim ceased his drumming.

"Little Star," she said, "she will live, but you must find someone knowledgeable enough to reverse the damage that was done, or this," she said pointing to Jan, "is all she will ever be."

Mike gazed down at her still form then hugged Grandmother. "Thanks," he choked out scooping Jan up in his arms and carrying her back inside the craft.

Grandmother touched Will's arm. "This will break his heart," she said, her brow knit in worry.

"Don't worry. If we can make it to Quentas, we'll find someone who can restore her," he assured her.

The Indians watched sadly as Will, Kimberlin and Terry boarded the ship. Larry and his brother, Jim, handed the five backpacks up inside and stood back. In minutes the engines whined to life, and they watched as the craft slowly ascended skywards. It made some test maneuvers over the canyon before blinking its lights several times in farewell and jetting heavenward.

Chapter 22

"How will we find Quentas?" Terry asked maneuvering the Saracen ship out of Earth's atmosphere. The ship rose straight upwards without producing any uncomfortable g-forces.

"The Saracens conquered it years ago," Will replied. "It must be on their star map. They've made enough trips back and forth over the past three decades."

He bent over a console, tapped in a sequence of commands and a three dimensional holomap suddenly materialized over a section of the floor in front of them. The map floated upwards until it hung in the air at eye level before them. He had it turn in several directions but nothing looked at all familiar. However, when Will punched in Quentas, one light on the holomap glowed a bright yellow.

"I've got the coordinates!" Terry exclaimed as they appeared on his navigational screen. "We're going home!"

"Finally," Will breathed. "Now, if you're all set, I'm going back to check on Jan. After that, I'll see if I can help Kimberlin with the retrofit," he said heading off the command deck towards the back of the ship.

He found Mike in one of the crew's quarters on the left of the aft corridor. Mike had lain Jan on the bunk, but she had started convulsing and the seizures were threatening to throw her onto the floor. Will rushed to his pack, which lay against Mike's, pulled out a medical kit and got out a syringe.

"Hold her arm still, Michael," he instructed. "At least long enough for me to give her a shot."

Mike did the best he could and, after a brief struggle, Will was able to give her the injection. They waited beside Jan until the tremors slowly decreased then ended. Mike sighed with relief.

"Someone should stay with Jan at all times," Will said, "yet we need everyone we have to help with the retrofit."

"Let Michael stay with her," Terry said from the doorway. "I have the ship on autopilot, so I can lend a hand for a while."

Will nodded and left with Terry.

Mike remained by Jan's side. He held her hand and stroked her hair back from her face. When he noticed how shallow her breathing had become, he checked the ring. Inside, the fire glowed but dimly indicating how very low her life force had become. Tears of anguish trickled down his cheeks as he laid his head against the bunk and cried until he had no more tears.

Several hours later, Will found him sound asleep by Jan's side. He reached down and shook Mike's shoulder. Mike jolted, his eyes popped open and he glanced around.

When he saw Will, he suddenly became more alert. "How's the retrofit?"

"Going well. We still have several hours of work left on it."

Mike got to his feet. "I'll go help them."

"You need some rest," Will countered.

"No, I need work, something to take my mind off what's happened to Jan." Mike replied. "Will you stay with her for a while?"

Will nodded and sat down beside her. He waved to Mike as he walked out the door, then took out a medi-scanner and ran it over her body. He reset its calibrations carefully running it over her head along the pattern of wounds and marks from the electrodes. He studied the read out and shook his head.

"Jan," he said quietly. "I told Michael you were tougher than he thought. If there was ever a time to prove me right, now would be a good time."

Will rubbed her arms and hands, which had become cold, then laid back to get as much rest as he could.

Five hours later the retrofit was complete. Terry and Kimberlin chose crew quarters for themselves and were soon sound asleep on bunks of their own. When they awoke next, they would begin testing the retrofit before making it fully operational. Mike headed back to where Will dozed beside Jan. He shook Will's shoulder to rouse him.

"How is she?"

"Gave her another shot about an hour ago. She should be fine for another five hours."

"What's making her convulse?" Mike wondered.

"I did several scans," he said sitting up straighter. "There doesn't appear to be any damage to the spinal cord. The locus of the neurological damage follows a path along the arch where they had placed the electrodes when she was tortured. My guess is that a lot of neurological pathways have been disrupted so they're misfiring. Plus, there may already be some scar tissue building up, and the electrical impulses in her brain are probably ricocheting off of it"

Mike nodded. "Any chance that these pathways will heal eventually?"

"To a small degree," Will replied, "but not as much as she needs them to."

"Is there anyone who knows how to treat this?" Mike asked desperately.

"Your mother. We'll plot a course for Quentas, and she is the first person we'll seek out," Will assured him.

Mike sighed heavily and nodded.

"You need some rest," Will told him.

"I'm staying right here."

"Then let me find something more comfortable than this floor." Will left and returned a moment later with a mat from another bunk. "Here, lie down on this."

Grateful, Mike stretched out and fell asleep on the mat by Jan's bunk. Her next series of convulsions woke him, but they eased on their own. He fell back to sleep sitting up beside her.

Several hours later Terry and Kimberlin awoke. They headed down the corridor and stopped in the doorway to Jan's cabin.

"Should we wake him?" Terry wondered.

Kimberlin shook her head. "Let's run the tests without him. If all goes well, we'll be in hyperspeed by the time he wakes up."

Together they went to the command deck and began a series of tests on the retrofit.

"You know," Kimberlin said to Terry, "we make a good team."

"You certainly do," Will agreed entering the deck. "That run was smooth."

"Is that a go for a full run?" Terry asked.

Will nodded.

"Whoo-hoo! Hyperdrive! Kick it!"

Terry hit the control and the craft shot forward into space. Stars streaked past their narrow viewing ports becoming streamers of endless color.

"Remember to monitor those coordinates," Will warned. "We want to come out of hyperdrive into empty space, not an asteroid or a star."

With that word of warning, he headed back down the corridor to find the ship's galley. He discovered one in the midsections and began nosing around the stocks. B'narian, Saracen and human food was neatly stored in compartments.

"Well," he said to himself. "We've got to eat and our pack rations won't hold out forever. It may taste strange, but this food will have to do."

Will set about assembling a meal, then took a couple of trays forward to Terry and Kimberlin before returning to the galley for a tray for Mike. He came back with one for himself and joined him. Mike took a couple of stabs at his food then set the tray down and looked at Jan. Suddenly he saw her eyes flicker and open.

"Will," he said leaning forward, "she's coming around!"

Will dropped his own tray and leaned over her. "Jan…Jan, can you hear me?"

She looked up at him but showed no sign of recognition. However, when Mike hovered over her, she gazed at him and reached up to touch his face and smiled. Overjoyed, Mike took her hand and leaned over to kiss her.

"Jan, you're back with us," he breathed.

She just stared at him with a confused expression on her face and vacant eyes.

As the hours wore into days, the ship's performance against the retrofit went smoothly. Kimberlin began taking turns with Mike in watching Jan. As Jan got stronger, Kimberlin pulled out the photo wallets hoping that they would spark some kind of recognition or memory. Jan gazed at them but grew frustrated quickly when nothing in them was familiar to her. For the hundredth time she picked one up, leafed through it as if seeing the pictures for the very first time, then threw them down and lay staring up at the ceiling. Mike ducked into the cabin at that moment and stopped just in time to avoid being hit on the leg. He looked to Kimberlin for an explanation.

"She doesn't remember anything, Michael, and she can't seem to talk even though I'm sure she understands me," Kimberlin mourned picking up the photo wallet and putting it back in Jan's backpack.

Mike went over and sat beside Jan who immediately turned toward him and smiled in recognition. "I'm the only thing she seems to recall," he murmured.

"And that must be due to your bond and the ring," Will said from the doorway. "Without that, everything would be completely foreign to her."

Mike sighed heavily. "If only there were some other way to reach her."

"Have you tried contacting her through the ring?" Kimberlin wondered.

Mike stared at it then cupped his hand over Jan's. "Jan, can you hear me?" he telepathed sending his thoughts through the ring.

She stared at him. "Yes, I can hear you," came the internal reply, "but I can't seem to talk. I can't make words come out, just noise."

"Do you know who these people are?" he asked. "Do you know who I am?"

A tear trickled down her cheek. "At the moment, the only time I know who I am is when you say my name. My memories are all gone…all taken away. It's so empty in here."

Mike brushed the tear from her cheek then turned to the others. "She has complete amnesia." He shook his head sadly, got up and left.

Suddenly the ship was jolted sharply and the lights dimmed.

"What in the world!" Kimberlin exclaimed.

Mike ran back into the room. "We're under attack by some cloaked Saracen vessels. They've been hailing us, but we haven't been on their frequency."

Will leapt to his feet and dashed to the command deck after Mike. The ship took another hit, and they grabbed the nearest thing and held on.

Once on the command deck, Will frantically ran through the frequencies until he found the Saracen hailing frequencies. Simultaneously, he had the main computer search the data banks for previous transmissions. Finally locating the digibytes he needed, he ran the recording through the channel.

"Stop firing! Stop firing!" the late Saracen captain's voice commanded.

"Who is this?" came the broken reply. "Acknowledge."

"This is Captain Lolika of the Ferrel Bird."

Will's mind was trying to anticipate the conversation as he continued scanning through transmission recordings.

"We have been damaged," he found in the databanks. "Navigational controls are not responding."

"Then let us tow you to the mothership," the Saracen in the other vessel suggested.

Mike and Terry turned to Will, their eyes wide with alarm. "We can't," they whispered.

Meanwhile, Will was still frantically searching the databanks.

"Hold a course for Quentas," the former captain's voice commanded.

"Quentas is quite some light years away and…."

"Obey your orders!"

"Yes, Captain Lolika. As you wish."

Seconds later they felt the drag of a tow beam as it caught hold of their ship. The three of them breathed a sigh of relief and Will closed the comm port. An instant later, the computers began going wild.

"They're scanning the ship's computers," Terry cried in alarm.

"Michael, can you block them?" Will asked.

"If I try, they may detect me."

"Disengage from their ship," Will instructed. "With the retrofit, we can easily out run them. Michael, use your powers and disengage us."

Mike placed his hands on the console. Seconds later a bright blue beam met the tow beam and cancelled it. Their ship silently moved away. Instantly Terry punched in the hyperdrive having already set the new coordinates. They left the Saracen ship far behind, but when they returned to normal space, they came out right in front of a large Quentasian vessel that immediately attacked them.

"Hail that ship, Will! Hurry!" Mike cried as they were bombarded by high-powered fire.

"I'm trying to, but they must be on a subfrequency to escape detection."

"Open them all," Mike said. "Just contact that ship!"

The next hit took out one of the navigational rockets and the one after it damaged a power generator. The lights dimmed and nearly went out, while Terry began having difficulty steering their small vessel. Will opened all frequencies and began a frantic call for help.

"Stop firing! Stop firing! This is Lord Dehan and I'm bringing the Crown Prince home!"

Chapter 23

Static crackled over the ship's speakers as it took several more hits.

"Stop firing! This is Lord Dehan!" Will tried again.

"Lord Dehan?" came a broken voice.

"Yes, who is this?"

"Lady Elira," crackled the response.

Mike rushed to Will's side. "Mother! Tell them to stop firing and tow us in. Our ship is about ready to break up."

"Ihue? Can it be?"

"Mother, please. There-is-no-time!"

Suddenly the firing ceased and they once again felt the tug of the tow beam.

"Quick! Grab your packs," Will instructed. "Mike, I'll get yours; you get Jan."

Terry flew down the corridor with Will and Mike right behind him. He hurried back with his and Kimberlin's packs while Kimberlin dragged Jan's behind her. Mike scooped Jan up in his arms and cupped his hand over the ring.

"We're transferring to another ship. We'll be safe there," he explained.

"I trust you," she replied.

They hurried back to the command deck and sealed it off.

"Jettison the hull," Will instructed, "before it blows up."

Terry set off a series of charges that sent the hull tumbling away from the command deck. Seconds later a loud explosion rocked the deck and they saw a fireball outside the viewing ports.

"That was too close!" Kimberlin exclaimed.

"But just in time," Will breathed.

Soon they were gliding into a transfer port in the side of the Quentasian ship. The tow beam gently set them down on a landing pedestal. The comm crackled once more.

"As a precaution, exit your ship with your hands in plain view."

They opened the hatch and stepped onto the transport deck. Soldiers in Quentasian blue, white and gold uniforms circled them with weapons raised. Will glanced around them searching for one familiar face. Suddenly he spotted it near the entry port to the interior of the ship.

"Elira!" he called, overjoyed.

"Dehan? Dehan!" she cried in recognition. "Drop your weapons. This is Lord Dehan and Crown Prince Ihue!"

She threaded her way through the soldiers and over to the weary travelers. Will held her at arm's length for a moment then wrapped his arms around her in a long embrace. She turned and looked up at Mike.

"So much like your father," she breathed. "So very much like Ihan! Where did my baby go?"

"Mother, it has been a lifetime since then."

"And who is this?" she asked immediately beginning to examine Jan.

"My betrothed, mother. Can you help her?"

"What happened? What did this?" she asked carefully examining the wounds.

"An Augmenter," Will said quietly.

Elira's eyes opened wide and her hands flew to her own

temples.

"She was interrogated and tortured," Mike added. "We almost didn't get to her in time to save her life."

Even as he spoke, Jan began convulsing again.

"Quickly," Elira said. "Get a hover bed. Take her straight to the infirmary." She pushed Mike toward the bay door even as she spoke.

They hurried along the corridors as quickly as they could. Now and then Mike had to stop as the tremors nearly shook Jan from his arms. Finally they met up with the hover bed, transferred her onto it, strapped her in and whisked her to the infirmary.

The place became a hub-bub of activity as healers seemed to pour out of the wood work. Mike and Will flattened themselves against one wall to watch. In minutes the healers had given her a shot to calm the convulsions and had a hydropack attached to her left arm. Electrodes with transmitters were carefully placed at intervals around her skull and a scanner overhead monitored her vital functions.

Elira glanced up, spotted the two men and motioned for them to follow her into a side room.

"How is she?" Mike asked.

"Critical, she is not good, Ihue. How long has it been since this happened?"

Mike looked at Will who was busily trying to calculate the time that had passed since they left Earth.

"Anywhere from two days to a week," Will said. "We lost track of time in space."

Elira shook her head. "Most of her memory centers were destroyed. There is damage to the speech center and to the motor cortex. How long did she endure that device?"

Mike and Will looked at each other then down at their feet.

"We can't be certain," Will replied, "but somewhere close to forty-five minutes."

"I think the Ring attacked the interrogator," Mike added. "Gorlan and Marla found him dead on the controls. He was forcing down the shock button, so she got a sustained charge at the very end."

Worry creased Elira's brow as she glanced back at the young

woman who lay on the infirmary bed. "So few can withstand that instrument of torture," Elira said more to herself. "She is fortunate to have lived at all. I am amazed that she has lived this long."

"But isn't there something else that can be done?" Mike asked helplessly. "Anything?"

"I…am familiar with the suffering caused by that device," Elira choked out. "When the Saracens discovered that I was still alive, they used that device on me to try to discover where Dehan had taken you. Only an old Molluc remedy kept me alive and restored me to health, but I think your betrothed may even be beyond that."

"Try, mother," Mike pleaded.

"I have forgotten the formula, so I must think about this for a while." She turned and slowly left the room.

Mike watched his mother leave, then slowly walked back into the other room and approached Jan's bedside. He gazed at her still form, reaching out as if to touch her, then drawing his hand away. He hurried out of the infirmary and found Will waiting for him outside.

"They've found us quarters," Will said.

"Where?"

"Just across the hall in some unused healer's cabins. They figured you would want to be as close to Jan as possible."

Will led the way and showed Mike his cabin. "Try to rest, Michael. You won't do Jan any good if you make yourself sick."

Mike nodded and flopped onto his bunk as the door slid shut. He lay in the darkness with his eyes wide open and his hands clasped behind his head.

Suddenly a flickering light appeared at the foot of his bed. It steadily grew into the pale, shimmering form of Jan. In horror he sat bolt upright.

"Mike," she called weakly.

"Jan, I'm here!"

"Mike, help. I can't go on."

Trembling, he leaned forward. "What can I do, Jan?"

"I'm so tired…no more strength. Can't fight anymore. Help me, Mike. Please…hurry." As she spoke her voice faded while her form grew dimmer until it vanished.

In a split second, Mike leapt to his feet and dashed out the door and down the hall. He burst into Jan's infirmary room and rushed to her side.

Slowly he reached out and cupped his hand over the Ring. Sparks leapt out from around their hands. Ignoring them, Mike closed his eyes emptying his thoughts into her mind. Inside he instantly perceived the charred remains of nerves and the acrid, smoky residue left behind. He groped his way into the center of the destruction.

"Jan," he called softly treading deeper. "Jan!" His voice echoed in the emptiness.

Up ahead Mike saw a faint, flickering light and dashed toward it. He caught sight of her limp form lying just beyond a small wavering candle flame.

He gasped choking back the lump in his throat. "Jan…Jan, please don't leave me," he called across the gulf that separated them. "Please, Jan…fight for just a little longer. I need you with me. You don't understand…now that you've accepted the Ring, I can't live without you. You can't leave me now," he begged, his voice cracking under the strain of repressed tears. "Jan, I haven't even begun my life's work. There's so much to do, and there's no way I can do it without you. I need your help. I'm nothing without you. Please, Jan…don't leave me."

As Mike pleaded, the flame gradually grew brighter. While the flame steadied, the wax on the candle stopped melting and replenished itself. Jan's eyes flickered briefly, a warm glow creeping into her cheeks.

"That's it, Jan! That's the way to go!" he cheered. "You can make it. I know you can."

He reached out toward her awakening form, but a burst of blue light flooded the darkness and he found himself flying backwards through a long dark tunnel.

"I love you, Mike," she called. "I always will."

Mike shook his head as he came back to himself and, glancing down, smiled with relief at the healthy glow returning to Jan's face. He gently caressed her cheek and watched as her breathing took on new depth, becoming strong and steady. Once again her hand was warm in his.

Tenderly he kissed her hand, her cheeks and her lips. Exhausted, he stumbled out of the room and down the hall to his quarters. Already drifting into a deep sleep, he sank into bed.

The next morning Will pounded on his door. It took Mike a while to wake up and recognize his surroundings.

"Michael, let me in."

Fully awake, Mike hit the button that unlocked the door.

"Michael, it's Jan. She's awake and asking for you."

"She's talking?" Mike asked incredulously.

"Yes, now hurry!"

Mike leapt out of bed, hastily drew on the clothes Will threw to him, and dashed out the door and into the infirmary. He burst into her room, surprised to find her sitting up.

"Mike!" she cried holding out her arms to him.

He rushed over and embraced her.

"You came."

"Last night?" he asked.

She nodded then leaned her head against his shoulder.

"Mike…where…are we?" she asked haltingly.

"On a ship heading for Quentas, my home."

"Quentas," she repeated very slowly. "I… remember… something."

"It's ok. The fact that you're even alive is all that matters right now."

Elira turned from the doorway where she had watched the reunion and quickly found her office. "I never remembered that Molluc formula, yet she is still alive."

She opened her office door, entered and wearily leaned against the wall. "Their bond must be very strong, and she must love my son very much to face torture and death yet still live."

"She does," Will said from the shadows to her left.

Elira turned as he stepped closer.

"I believe you sent for me."

"Yes, I did," she replied. "I have been running tests on…?"

"Jan," Will filled in.

"And I have been doing some research. She has feeling in her feet and legs but no motor response," she explained. "How she is talking at all, I cannot explain."

"So what's the verdict?"

They heard a knock on the door, and Mike poked his head in. The light in the room increased, and Elira motioned for him to sit down.

"Ihue, she is alive. How, I do not know. My assistants tell me she was very near death last night."

He nodded.

"I have run extensive tests on her. She has major damage to the Broda Speech Center and the motor cortex. At present her speech and ability to move from the hips down have been affected."

"Go on."

"Scar tissue is building and spreading rapidly," she said. "Eventually she will return to being mute then slowly decline to a vegetative state and death."

Mike sat back in the chair as if a truck had struck him. "Isn't there anything that can halt the process?"

"Or reverse its effects?" Will added.

"A cortical transplant," Elira replied. "I will have to take tissue samples to determine the most appropriate method, but it is her only hope."

"What are the risks?" Mike asked.

Elira looked down at her lap. "Monumental. It could kill her, but without it she will certainly die a long drawn-out death."

"And if it works?"

"We can halt the process and possibly reverse it...by how much I cannot tell. All I know is that this procedure is her one and only hope."

Mike got up and walked back into Jan's room. He watched her agonizing struggle to sit up, understand speech or make herself understood. Elira laid her hand on his arm.

"How long does she have like this?" he asked quietly.

"Just a matter of montari."

"Months," Will translated.

"Is she able to make this decision for herself?" Mike asked.

Elira shook her head.

"Then do it. Whatever you need to do, you've got my permission. I want to give Jan every chance to fight that's available to her. If this is it, so be it."

"But if it kills her….?"

Mike squeezed his eyes tightly closed. "Quickly or slowly," he whispered. "Either way she dies will kill me, too."

Chapter 24

"We will start by taking a minute tissue sample from her brain," Elira said. "We will extract her DNA and insert it into the cytoplasm of cells whose own DNA have been removed. Once the embryonic stem cells have developed, we will then separate those cells into several clusters and cultivate the brain cells for the specialized centers in her brain," she explained. "Once we have enough medium, we will inject these newly cultured cells back into her brain. Certain neurological injuries do recapitulate certain developmental processes. With any luck, this may be one of them."

Mike nodded then walked over to Jan's bed and stood at her side. She smiled up at him. He cupped his hand over the Ring.

"Honey, mother is going to have to operate on you."

She frowned. "Operate?"

He struggled to find a way to explain. "Mother needs to take out some of your brain cells that have been damaged and replace them with some new cells."

Jan just stared at him.

"It will make you better."

A hopeful gleam lit her eyes. "Normal?" she asked. "Can

walk? Talk?"

Mike closed his eyes and nodded. "We're hoping."

"You think operate…be ok? Good thing?" she asked struggling with the words.

He nodded again.

She reached up and touched his face, and he opened his eyes to gaze at her. "Whatever…you say…I …trust you."

He winced hard. "I love you, Jan." His lips brushed her forehead then he turned and left.

Elira ordered full brain scans immediately. Using lasers and a magnetic probe, she was able to get several samples of tissue. She studied the scans as the other healers prepared the tissue samples in culture dishes. Will stood beside her eyeing the scans with a sinking heart.

"There's so much damage," he breathed.

"And the scar tissue is growing so rapidly," she added.

"How long before you can perform the other surgery?"

"Too long," she replied. "I am going to have to add a growth enzyme to the culture, but I have got to be very careful. Too much and the cells could go wild."

"With the growth enzyme, how long till you can operate?" he wanted to know.

"Twelve honti."

"Half-a-day," Will breathed.

"But here is my next problem. Jan must be awake during the second surgery. We must be able to communicate with her throughout the operation in case we get too close to important brain centers or complications arise," Elira explained.

"And I'm the only one who can connect with her," Mike said from behind them.

They turned and looked at his pale, haggard face and anguished eyes.

"So, I'll be there," he said simply.

"Michael, you're in no condition to do this," Will cautioned. "You're near the point of exhaustion yourself."

"And no one else can."

"You need sleep, Ihue."

"I've tried, but I can't."

"I will give you a mild sedative," Elira said. "Hopefully you can rest then."

Mike nodded and followed her to the pharmacy where she pulled out a small vial, pressed it against the skin on his arm and squeezed the vial. He felt a quick prick then a slow, drowsy sensation creeping in.

"Go to sleep, Ihue. We shall wake you when it is time."

Mike left for his cabin, and Elira spent several hours going over the brain scans and practicing the surgery on a three dimensional holographic model of Jan's brain that she had had the computer construct for her. Satisfied with her preparations, she left instructions with her assistant, a healer in her mid-thirties named Lornda, to wake both she and Mike at the time required for them to prep, then lay on a bunk in her office and slept.

Seven hours later, Lornda woke Mike, helped him go through the disinfectant process and gave him sterile scrubs to put on. Jan had been given a mild sedative and had already been moved into the operating room. He entered, pulled the mask off his face so she would recognize him and smiled at her. He cupped his hand over the Ring.

"How are you holding up?" he asked. "You doing ok?

Jan smiled sleepily.

"Good. Just hang in there."

Another healer around Jan's age, named Calla, came in with a tray of instruments and set it up beside her head. "I have to clean the wounds and prepare the surgical sites," she told Mike, who relayed the message to Jan.

Calla gave her a local anesthetic before clearing away the thick scabs that had formed around her temples. Jan tensed when the pulling and tugging became annoying.

"We will have to put her head and body in traction for the duration of the surgery," Calla informed Mike. "While she must be awake, she cannot move."

As Calla maneuvered the head clamps into position, Jan eyed them wildly and tried to push them away.

Mike took her hands and held them. "Honey, relax," he urged. "This is not going to hurt you. This won't be like last time, I promise.

This is just to keep your head still so mother doesn't hit something wrong."

Jan stared at Mike and whimpered while Calla positioned the clamps. Though she trusted whatever Mike told her through their mental bond, her terror was still plainly evident.

Scanners were maneuvered into position while other healers moved about the room. Viewing screens were placed at varying angles to the long narrow table that Jan lay on. An assistant brought Mike a stool to sit on. An older healer, named Soniora, passed straps over Jan's body to secure her.

Jan started crying and shaking, but Mike stroked her arm and hand.

"Honey, it's ok…it's ok," he soothed. "I wouldn't let them do anything to hurt you. You know that."

She looked up at him with tears welling in her eyes but calmed under his reassurance. She looked up at the big oval light that glared down at her and started in fright when Calla's hand, holding a hypodermic needle, came into view.

"Calla's giving you a shot to numb your whole scalp right down to the skull," Mike explained. "It's ok. Just hold still."

Elira entered and positioned herself at the head of the table. She took up her instruments and checked the scanning image of Jan's brain.

"Tell her I will begin drilling," she telepathed to Mike.

He looked at Jan and relayed. "Mother is going to drill some small holes in your skull with a laser," he explained. "You shouldn't feel any pain because your scalp and the tissues underneath it have all been numbed and the brain itself has no pain receptors. When she gets into the brain itself, you may experience some strange noises or have flashbacks because of the areas she's working near. So don't be alarmed. Ok?"

She faintly replied, "Ok."

Mike nodded to Elira who positioned the laser drill and began. Jan relaxed when she realized she could feel nothing at all. Mike told her when Elira was about to start or stop each hole. Elira changed instruments and telepathed new instructions to Mike.

He again connected with Jan. "Mother is going to insert a

microscopic laser and suction unit," he explained. "She has to remove the scar tissue that has built up before she can inject the cultured cells. If you're going to experience anything weird, it will probably be now."

Elira pushed the microscopic probe into the first hole she had made checking the scanner to make sure the tip was in place. The others watched on the overhead viewer as laser pulses sliced through the scar tissue.

While Jan felt no pain, weird noises like synthesized garble echoed in her head. For a moment it quieted as Elira turned on the suction, but the strange sounds started up again when she moved the probe to a different site. At the third site, words of all sorts randomly bounced around in her head like rubber super balls. Some were nonsense words, some were technical words, and occasionally they were even in reverse.

Once the speech center was clear of scar tissue, Elira inserted a different probe and relayed instructions to Mike.

"Mother's going to put in the cultured cells now. She said this shouldn't hurt, either."

Jan blinked her eyes in acknowledgement and patiently waited while a microfine tube was inserted and a pump was switched on. Again and again Elira repositioned the probe until the speech center had been completely filled. She took an appraising look at her work through the scanner.

"That looks quite good," she announced. "Moving to the motor cortex."

Lornda reached over, parted Jan's hair in an arched pattern from ear to ear and secured her hair with clips. She snipped off a few strands along the arch and took a razor to the stubble. Mike reached out for the strands Lornda was about to drop onto the floor. He pocketed them then turned his attention back to Jan.

The procedure followed the one for the speech center with Elira drilling the necessary holes with the laser and Mike relaying the information. However, this time when she inserted the second probe and began trimming away the scar tissue, more than just strange sensations assailed Jan. The sudden memory of the broken leg she had suffered as a child sent pain shooting through her right leg and she cried out.

"What's wrong, Jan?" Mike asked, concerned.

"Leg hurts."

Suddenly the cut she had received in an auto accident began to throb. Then the cramp she had had while swimming to the diving platform in the lake at summer camp gripped her side.

"Take it easy, honey. Hang in there," Mike soothed. He glanced up at his mother and telepathed. "She's having flashbacks of old injuries."

Elira nodded.

Jan experienced each injury as if it was happening at that moment, screaming at intervals with flashes of phantom pain. Mike struggled to keep her calm and still.

Suddenly as Elira repositioned the probe for the last time and began removing the last of the scar tissue, Jan began to spasm. Her body shuddered and convulsed threatening to break the straps holding her to the table.

"Administer an antispasmodic," Elira snapped. "Quickly!" She held onto the probe for dear life having shut off both the laser and the suction.

Calla ran to the medication table, grabbed the syringe and hastily administered the full dose. Within minutes Jan's spasms eased.

"Suction on," Elira said, and went to work finishing the scar tissue removal.

In the next instant, alarms on the monitors sounded off shrilly. Jan's heart rate and blood pressure were taking a nose dive.

"Her blood pressure is dropping rapidly," Lornda announced.

"I must finish suctioning, "Elira insisted.

"So cold," Mike heard Jan say.

A strange blackness began to creep up her legs toward her torso.

"Cold!" she cried again, her voice dying off.

"We are losing her!" Lornda cried.

"Shut off suction!" Elira ordered.

"Blood pressure…twenty over five," Calla announced, watching the monitors. "Heart rate, zero."

"Jan…Jan, hang in there!" Mike cried. "Please, hang in there."

Elira inserted the microprobe. "Pump on."

"But there is some scar tissue left," Calla protested.

"And we are losing her!" Lornda countered.

"Pump on! NOW!" Elira ordered.

The pump hummed to life, and the cultured cells began filling the last section of the motor cortex.

"Blood pressure…forty over ten…fifty over twenty…sixty-five over thirty…still rising," Calla reported. "Heart rate…thirty-three…forty…fifty-five…sixty. She is stabilizing."

The other healers sighed with relief and tears brimmed over Mike's lashes. Jan would live.

Chapter 25

As soon as the surgery was over, Elira gave Jan a heavy sedative, and the healers moved her into a special care room. Mike followed Elira into her office where Will waited for them. Anxious for news, he looked up as soon as the door opened. Mike slumped into a chair next to him and leaned back putting his head against the wall and closing his eyes.

"Well?" Will asked.

Elira took off her surgical gown. "We came very close to losing her."

Will tensed.

"But she pulled through and is stable now."

Will heaved a sigh of relief. "How long before we know how well the cultured cells are taking?" he asked.

"She will be heavily sedated for the next forty-eight honti, then we will slowly awaken her and run some tests," Elira explained.

"Two days," Will breathed.

"I could sleep for at least one whole day, myself," Mike said. "I'm exhausted."

Will and Elira both looked at him and asked at the same time,

"Have you even eaten?"

Mike looked from one to the other then furrowed his brow. "You know…I can't remember."

"Come on," Will said clapping him on the back. "Let's get some food into you before you keel over."

"I think I'm hungry."

"Hungry or not, it's time that you eat something," Will said, steering Mike out the door.

Elira shook her head and she watched them leave and Lornda enter with a report. "Ihan and I were so very fortunate to have Dehan as a friend."

Lornda watched the two men disappear out of the infirmary. "They seem quite close."

Elira nodded. "Too bad Ihan is not here to see Ihue. He would be so proud of him. Dehan has raised him well."

She sighed and quickly skimmed the reports. "Good, she is stable enough that I can get some rest."

Down in the ship's canteen, Will picked out some a la carte foods and brought them over to Mike, who could barely keep his head propped up. He ate then went straight to his cabin sleeping soundly for most of the next day.

Upon awakening he finally discovered the ship's showers, cleaned up and went to visit Jan. He found Kimberlin, now known by her Quentasian name Marla, peering in through the glass enclosure around Jan's room.

"How's she look?" Mike asked.

"Ok. I've been watching the monitors and her vital signs are all normal. The healers say that's a really good sign," she replied.

Mike visibly relaxed. "No one allowed in there?" he asked nodding toward her room.

Marla shook her head.

He sighed. "Well, as long as she's doing well, I might as well have a look around."

"Gorlan is down in engineering," Marla said using Terry's Quentasian name. "Come on. There are a few things down there that you should see."

Marla led Mike down to engineering where he found Gorlan

attempting to explain to the Quentasian engineers the design concepts they had developed on Earth. Mike joined the conversation, and his worries about Jan were temporarily forgotten.

Thirty-six hours later Jan slowly blinked her eyes open. The world around her spun in hazy swirls, and she closed her eyes. A moment later she tried again, and this time the world stood still. On her third attempt the room came into focus. Elira smiled down at her.

"You are back with us," she heard Elira say, but the words did not sync with the movement of her lips.

Jan stared at her trying to make sense of the off cadence.

"Can you hear me?" Elira asked.

After a momentary delay, Jan nodded.

"Do you know who you are?"

Jan thought for a moment then a name came to her. "Janielle Childen," she whispered.

Elira smiled. "Do you know where you are?"

Jan gazed around her at the completely unfamiliar setting then shook her head.

"You are in the infirmary on a ship headed for Quentas. Does that sound familiar?" Elira asked.

"Quentas," Jan repeated. Something about the word made her heart skip a beat. She brought her hand up to rub her eyes and caught sight of the Ring. She stared at it, an excitement growing inside her. She closed her eyes and the face of a handsome, dark-haired, blue-eyed man appeared in her mind. Suddenly she knew his name.

"Mike!" she exclaimed. "Where…Mike?"

Elira smiled. "I shall have him paged. He will be here soon. While we wait for him, I would like to perform some tests."

Jan nodded and patiently tried to perform the neurological tasks Elira presented her with. She struggled with some but managed to complete them all. As she finished, both Mike and Will breezed through the door.

"Mike!" she cried in delight as soon as she saw him. She immediately held her arms out to embrace him.

He wrapped her in a glorious bear hug and refused to let her go for a long moment. "You're back with us…finally!" he said gazing into her eyes, which sparkled with life and recognition.

"She is indeed much better," Elira said. "Jan knows who she is, who you are, and has vastly improved neurological functions. She is definitely out of crisis."

Mike and Will whooped loudly, and Jan laughed for the first time in weeks. When the men finished giving each other a high five, Elira explained the more serious side of Jan's recovery.

"Jan has a lot of therapy to undergo," she told them. She needs speech therapy and physical therapy to begin with."

"I walk?" Jan asked.

"Hopefully in time," Elira replied. "But we cannot say yet."

A shadow crossed Mike's face, and Jan frowned.

"I…will…walk," she said slowly with determination.

"We will work on that," Elira promised.

"How long will her therapy take?" Mike asked.

"Montari."

"And how long before we get to Quentas?"

"We were three montari out when we picked you up. To be honest that was a blessing. We only had enough fuel for a one way trip."

"What were you going to do once you had reached Earth?" Will asked, shocked.

"We hoped we could find what we needed in order to get back," Elira replied. "To be honest, we were…are quite desperate. If Ihue does not return soon, there will be no Quentas to return to," she said grimly.

A heavy silence filled the air.

"Well, Jan, you need to rest," Elira said at last. "When you next awaken, we will try you on some soft foods, and we will begin your therapy."

With that, Elira shooed Mike and Will out the door.

The two men walked toward the canteen in pensive silence. They picked up trays of food and sat down in a corner off to themselves.

"I don't like the sound of what mother said," Mike began.

"She just confirms what the captain has told me. Quentas is in desperate straights. They have maintained guerilla warfare out of underground bases, but their supplies are very low. The people who live on the surface are slaves of the Saracens, and they are stripping the planet of all of its natural resources."

Mike shook his head. "Just how are we going to be able to fight back?"

Will did not answer.

In the infirmary, Jan slept through the rest of that day and long into the next, only to wake to a silent, empty room. She propped herself on one elbow and looked around. Seeing no sign of movement outside her door, she lay back straining to catch any sound of footsteps.

"No one up," she surmised. "Must be…night. Not tired…don't want to sleep."

She struggled until she sat up fully and threw the covers off her legs. "It took Chet two…three months to walk…after brain tumor…was out," she muttered. Didn't have tumor…how long…for me?"

Jan stared at her motionless legs. "Part of brain like baby's. Must teach legs…move…now."

She took a deep breath, then slowly moved each leg by hand. She fell back, exhausted after only two tries.

"Whew! Gotta rest. Try later."

When the ship's morning rotation began, Soniora wondered at Jan's fatigue during the dressing change. Yet, an hour later when she brought Jan her breakfast, she seemed fine. But Jan was flushed and panting when Soniora came back for the tray.

"I must watch her more closely," Soniora muttered shuffling from the room. "Something strange is going on here."

An hour later, when she approached Jan's room, Soniora was astonished to find the young woman sitting up and manually moving her legs.

"What are you trying to do?" the old healer demanded bustling back into the room.

Jan started at her voice then sheepishly lay back in bed. "Trying to teach brain…move my legs."

"You are what?"

"Teach brain…to move my legs," Jan reiterated slowly. "Like baby. New brain now…must teach."

Soniora chuckled. "You are a smart one, that is what you are." She looked Jan over. "You will keep doing this, even if I tell you to stop?"

"Have got to," Jan replied. "I…must…walk…again."

Soniora nodded. "Stubborn, too. All right then, I will help you practice. You should not be performing these exercises alone. I will work with you three times a day, and we will teach your legs to move. But for now, you lie back and rest."

For the remainder of the week, Jan slept and woke to the sound of Soniora's warm voice. Each time they worked, Soniora bent Jan's legs further and increased the repetitions. Soon Jan could move her legs with the healer's help. By the end of the week, she was eager to give a demonstration.

"Please, I have to show Mi-i…."

"That is Prince Ihue, dear," Soniora reminded her.

"And Will…I mean Lord De-e…."

"Dehan."

"Dehan. Can I show them, please?"

Soniora studied her for a moment. "Why not? I will have them paged and Lady Elira as well."

The healer prepared to leave, but Jan called her back. "Soniora is there anything to read or to write on?"

"I will check the ship's library. What would interest you?"

"Literature…history…fine arts, maybe."

Soniora nodded and shuffled out. She returned a while later with a computer slate, a light pen, some data discs and an electronic reader. She showed Jan how to use them.

"Would you write…everyone's name… please?" Jan asked. "If I see them…maybe I'll remember."

Soniora carefully wrote out each name and handed the computer slate back to Jan.

"Thanks, Soniora," she said as the healer left.

The next morning after Jan ate breakfast, Soniora showed in Mike and Will, while Elira entered from another wing of the infirmary.

"So what's up?" Mike asked giving Jan a kiss.

"I have something to show," she announced.

Soniora pulled away her covers then, to the astonishment of her onlookers, her right leg rose off the bed, bent at the knee, and plopped back down. Everyone stared as she repeated the routine with her left leg. Her little audience applauded, and Mike hugged her enthusiastically. Elira hurried in upon seeing the demonstration.

Jan turned to Elira. "I will walk," she stated firmly. "I want to start therapy."

"I wanted to give you another week to regain your strength," Elira said, surprised by her performance.

Jan shook her head. "Now! Today! I want to learn to walk again."

Mike held her hand and her gaze. "Are you sure you're up to this, honey? Don't you think you're pushing just a little bit?"

"Mike, no! All those brain cells are new now," she said. "Now…I will learn fastest. I want to walk."

"But what's the rush?" he asked.

She looked at him, then at the others, then back at Mike. "I want to walk off this ship by your side," she said quietly.

"Oh, Jan! That's way too much to expect of yourself," Will exclaimed.

"I cannot let you push yourself to that extent," Elira said.

However, Mike gazed steadily into Jan's eyes. Visions of her floating off in a hover chair competed with visions of her walking by his side. "No, she's very serious. If we won't help her, she will try on her own."

"Ihue, can you not make her see reason?" Elira cried.

He shook his head and looked up at his mother. "No, I think she can do this. I've seen what she's like when she puts her mind to doing something. I think she's right. She knows herself, mother. I trust her judgment. Let her try."

Elira breathed heavily, then sighed. "All right. We shall begin today, but if you push too hard, you could do more harm than good."

"I will take that risk," Jan said firmly, "so I can walk by my fiancée's side. Nothing matters more right now."

Chapter 26

That afternoon Jan's therapy began with a session in the flotation tank. While floating inside the darkened tank, a video played that portrayed a pair of legs moving effortlessly in a full range of motion, plus walking across ground of varying terrain. The sensory deprivation of the tank, coupled with the video training would help to begin the development of new neural motor pathways.

Then Jan was taken to a small therapy room where the healers placed her on equipment that would help her exercise the various muscle groups in her legs and hips. To her surprise, Jan found the exercises were very hard. On the quadricep machine, she double-checked the weight setting.

"The sensation of weight has been turned off for now," Soniora told her.

"Really? Then why can't I do this?" Jan cried in frustration.

"Because you must retrain your body and mind all over again."

Jan fought back tears as she grimaced and finally managed one repetition, then two. She let the padded bar drop.

"I didn't think exercises would be so hard," she panted.

Soniora patted her shoulder soothingly. "It will get better. Just give it some time."

"Time is the one thing I don't have a lot of," Jan muttered under her breath.

Soniora moved her to stall bars located on the wall. "Place your hands on the rungs in front of you then walk them up until you are standing," Soniora instructed.

Jan did as she was told, but something happened when she went to stand. Before she knew it, her legs buckled and she hung from the last rung she had touched. Suddenly her fingers slipped, and she hit the floor with a thump.

"Ow! What went wrong?"

"Like a baby you must reprogram your brain to find your center of gravity and your balance point," Soniora explained. "Try again, only this time spread your legs further apart for a steadier base of support and lean forward a little as you walk up."

After Calla and Soniora helped her reach the first rung, Jan tried again. This time she stood upright for several seconds on wobbly legs before crashing to the ground.

"Very good. Much better," Soniora said. "Now you need to rest."

Jan sighed as they eased her back onto a hover chair.

"Does she need to go right back to bed?" Mike asked from just inside the door where he had stood watching. "Or could she stay up and have a look around the ship?"

Jan's eyes shone at the suggestion. "Oh, please, Soniora. I promise I'll come straight back when I'm tired."

Soniora pursed her lips before finally conceding to the request. "But not for too long," she admonished as Mike reached for the hover chair.

He guided Jan through the maze of corridors and pointed out sections of the ship he had already explored.

"It's an older ship," he remarked, "but they've kept it in good shape. Gorlan and Marla have already been able to help the engineers with some modifications that are improving its fuel efficiency."

Jan listened politely then asked. "Is there anyplace where we can see outside?"

Mike thought for a moment. "There is a viewing deck," he said changing direction and heading toward a darkened corridor near the outer edge of the ship.

Benches and portals lined the corridor, and he maneuvered the hover chair near one then hit a button that made a small screen slide back. Jan gazed out at the pinpoints of light in the vast universe around them.

"Wow! We really are in space," she breathed. "Sometimes I thought people were playing games with my head."

Mike gazed up at her face which was illuminated by the light from millions of stars that shone in through the portal. He leaned over and kissed her, thrilled to feel her hungry response. When they parted, a lone tear slid down her cheek.

"What's wrong?"

"You…still love me. Even like this?" she said gesturing to the chair and her legs.

Mike nodded. "Of course I still love you," he affirmed. "It tears me apart to see you like this but nothing could make me stop loving you."

Jan closed her eyes letting his words sink into her hungry soul. A new confidence radiated from her face. "I needed to hear that," she said at last. "I was so afraid my problems would make you change how you feel about me."

He shook his head. "Never!" He kissed her again then asked, "Is that why you're working so hard to learn to walk again."

"Partly," she replied. "But I also don't think this hover chair would make a good first impression on your people. I don't want them to think their future queen is a cripple."

"It doesn't matter what they think," Mike said.

"It matters to me," Jan replied. "How they see me will make a difference as to how they see you. I want you to be a hero for them."

He took her head between his hands and gazed into her eyes. "You ask way too much of yourself. If we force the Saracens off of Quentas, I'll be their hero."

"They won't believe you can or that your primary concern will be the war, if I'm not walking beside you," she countered.

"Jan, never mind what they think."

She yawned. "Man, I'm getting tired."

He kissed her then headed back towards the infirmary. Along the way, though, he became acutely aware of stares from the crew, most of which he was certain were aimed straight at the hover chair and Jan's legs. Before they got near the infirmary, her head bobbed on her chest. She was sound asleep by the time they reached her room. Mike tenderly lifted her off the hover chair and gently laid her on her bunk. He tucked her covers around her, kissed her cheek and left.

Mike continued to observe Jan's therapy sessions for the next few weeks. Her progress seemed to be agonizingly slow. In spite of how hard she struggled, it was several weeks before she stood between the parallel bars to take her first shaky hesitant steps. Jan bit her lower lip in desperate concentration as she shuffled forward - first one foot, then the other. At the end of the parallel bars, she sank to the ground shaking with fatigue.

"I-will-walk," Mike heard her mutter through clenched teeth as he scooped her off the mat and put her back on the hover chair.

While Soniora took her back to the infirmary, Mike and Will watched her go and conferred.

"She's really pushing," Mike said.

"Way too hard," Will concurred.

"I've tried to talk her into slowing down."

"No good?" Will asked.

Mike shook his head. "She's got it in her head that she's going to walk off this ship so she will make a good appearance for our people and nothing can shake her of that."

"Keep an eye on her," Will warned. "I know Elira's concerned."

Yet, unknown to any of them, Jan returned each night on her own to sneak a workout. Marla saw her leaving her room one night and followed her. When she saw Jan begin her therapy routine again, she ran over to stop her.

"Jan, what are you doing?" Marla exclaimed.

"I've got to keep pushing. We only have two more months till we reach Quentas. I've got to walk by then," Jan replied with determination.

"You'll kill yourself at this pace."

Jan eased off the stall bars and back onto the hover chair. She looked Marla squarely in the eye. "Mike's mother doesn't think I'll ever walk again."

"How do you know?" Marla asked.

"One night she came to check up on me. She thought I was asleep, but I was just tired and resting. She told Soniora that the worst damage had been to my motor cortex. She said I might get some use of my legs back, but she doesn't think I will ever walk again."

Marla stared at her in alarm. "Does Ihue know?"

Jan shook her head. "His mother doesn't want him to know yet."

"So you're trying to prove her wrong?" Marla surmised.

Jan shook her head. "I'm scared that she may be right, but I won't know unless I really try hard."

"But this hard?"

"Please, Marla. Don't tell anyone. Help me. I figured I was going to have a difficult time adjusting to life on Quentas as it was, but what am I going to do in the middle of a war stuck in this thing?" she said gesturing toward the hover chair.

Marla wrung her hands. "I'm so torn, Jan."

"Please, Marla. What if it were you?"

Marla took a deep breath then nodded. "Ok, but I'll come with you at night. Otherwise, you could get hurt and no one would find you for hours."

"Thanks, Marla," Jan replied as she continued to work on the machines.

Over the next few days, Mike heard bits and pieces of gossip about Jan and her hover chair. Gradually he began to distance himself from her therapy sessions until he barely came around at all. She would glance hopefully toward the door every time someone entered, only to sigh with disappointment when the person was not Mike. She called after Will one day before he could leave her therapy session. He waited until she had completed shuffling between the parallel bars then walked beside her chair as she headed back to her room.

"Where's Mike?" she asked directly.

"Um, he's taken on a project in engineering. They're working on a new propulsion system," he explained.

"And he's too busy to even come see me?" she asked, surprised.

Will looked away.

"What's going on, Will? What aren't you telling me?"

He turned to face her as she hovered beside her bed.

"He's…he's having trouble dealing with your disability," he said at last. "He decided to put some distance between it and himself till he was able to deal with it better."

Jan looked as if she had been slapped in the face. "I-I see…."

"Jan, don't blame him and don't take this personally. He has tried to come to grips with this, but it hurts him to see you in this condition," Will replied.

"And it's easy for me to handle being like this, I suppose?" she demanded tears stinging her eyes.

"No, Jan. Of course not…."

"Then why has he abandoned me?"

Will took a step back at those words and swallowed hard. "I don't think he realizes that you feel that way, and I don't think he knows what to do."

She nodded but said nothing.

"I'll talk to him," Will promised.

She just crawled over to her bed and watched him leave. She lay staring at the door with eyes that burned with angry unshed tears. A few minutes later Marla walked in to find Jan still staring straight ahead.

"Hey, what's wrong?" she asked, concerned.

"Mike seems to have a problem with my being disabled," Jan replied flatly.

"Who told you that?"

"Will. I asked why Mike hasn't come by in over a week."

"Oh."

"He's embarrassed, isn't he?"

"I don't know."

"Marla, help me get dressed," Jan said out of the blue. "Something other than these hospital fatigues."

"What are you going to do?"

"Pay him a visit he won't forget," Jan replied.

Marla left returning a few minutes later with a maroon crew suit similar to the one she was wearing. She helped Jan get changed and fixed her hair.

"Do they have makeup around here?" Jan wondered.

"I don't know," Marla replied. "I'm just glad I brought mine with me. Here's your makeup bag," she said handing Jan hers.

Fifteen minutes later Marla guided Jan out of the infirmary.

"Is he down in engineering?"

"I think so."

"Can you get me down there?"

Marla nodded.

"Good, let's go."

Twenty minutes later Marla and Jan entered the engineering quarters.

"I think he's over there," Marla said beginning to head toward a side portion of the complex.

"No! Take me around so I can see what people are doing. I don't want to be in anyone's way, but I'd like to meet some of the crew," Jan instructed.

Marla looked at her and a light dawned in her eyes. "I think I see what you're doing. Good thinking," she said heading towards where some of the crew kept tabs on the functioning of the systems.

They slowly walked up and observed the crew. Once they were noticed, Marla introduced Jan who then asked the crewperson about some portion of the job. Pleased to be recognized, most of the crew took the time to speak with her. Soon she had even met the head of engineering who was on his way over toward Mike.

"Just stay here for a second," Jan said. "Let's watch."

The head of engineering walked over to where Mike, Gorlan and Will were busy working on a design modification. He bowed his head to Mike as he approached then got closer to the table they were working on.

"Your betrothed is quite pretty," he said to Mike.

"My betrothed?" Mike asked, startled.

"Yes, I really appreciate your having had her come down and speak with my crew. Word spreads quickly on a ship of this size. She is a real inspiration. I can already see the way she has bolstered morale," the engineer continued.

"What?" Mike cried standing upright and glancing around. He spotted Jan and Marla. Jan waved.

Will watched the look on Mike's face and began to chuckle. "She fixed you real good, Michael," he telepathed. "You may not know how to handle her disability, but she knows how to relate to people, and she really knows how to handle you."

Mike gave him an annoyed look then froze when he saw Jan and Marla head his way.

"Hi, Mike," she said quietly as the chair gently whooshed up to him. "Will told me how busy you were on this project. I'm so used to being right in the lab with you that I decided to have Marla bring me down so I could find out what you're doing."

Mike looked at her unable to think of anything to say.

"I know I don't understand the technical stuff too well, but will you show me what you're doing anyway?" Jan smiled her sweetest.

"Um, we're…we're trying to develop a way to retrofit our propulsion design to the ship's engines," Mike replied, his eyes never leaving her.

The head of engineering stepped aside so Jan could get a closer look at the project. Gorlan began explaining some of the details, but whenever she did not understand something, Jan always redirected the question to Mike and waited for his answer. Eventually she began yawning.

"Mike, I think I'm getting tired," she finally admitted. "Can you break away and walk back up with me?"

He nodded and waved to Gorlan and Will. As they got into a lift that would take them back up to the infirmary level, he gazed at her and smiled.

"That was dirty pool," he said.

She shook her head, the smile gone from her face. "No. That was me proving myself to you…something I don't feel I should have to do. You abandoned me," she declared. "That hurt."

Mike was taken aback by her words and the intensity of the emotion behind them. "Jan, I never meant for you to think that. I just needed time to think all of this through."

"You do that, you know," she said, her eyes icy. "You run away when you get scared, or when you think you'll get hurt. You distance yourself just in case."

Mike ran his hand through his hair. "You're right. I do that. I'm sorry."

"It hurts, Michael. It especially hurts when it's about something I can't control, like this," she said gesturing to the hover chair. "I'm trying to get out of this contraption, but it's not easy. I live every day just to see your face and your smile." Tears had brimmed over her lashes and were coursing down her cheeks. "But when you don't come, and it's because of this…and especially considering why I ended up in it…." she said memories of the torture vividly flashing through her mind, "the pain is agonizing. How could you?"

Mike stood before her, helpless to defend himself against her accusations. "Jan, I'm so sorry."

"Sorry isn't enough, Michael. Sorry is for minor goofs. This hurts so bad, I can hardly breathe." Jan took a deep breath to calm herself. "You've been too scared and embarrassed to come around. Well, I don't want you around any more. Don't come back."

She maneuvered her chair out of the lift door as it whooshed open, headed down the hall, and entered her infirmary room. She struggled to rotate the chair then hit the button to close the door. When it clanged shut, she locked it.

Mike dashed down the hall, tried the door then stood on the outside looking in.

Chapter 27

Mike knocked on the infirmary room's door. "Jan, let me in. Let's talk. Please."

But the door did not budge and he finally had to admit defeat. He took a long walk through the corridors not particularly paying attention to anything – just walking. Will finally caught up to him and fell in step beside him.

"I heard that Jan locked you out," he said.

Mike nodded. "She's really angry. I mean really angry…and it's got me scared. How do I make this up to her?" he asked turning to Will. "What I did was unconscionable. What if she never gets over it?"

Will took a deep breath. "Give her what you've always taken for yourself…time and space."

"But how long…how much?" Mike wanted to know.

"Until she has clamed down, cooled off, and is ready to let you back into her life."

"But what if she doesn't? What if this is it?"

"Every couple has some fights, Michael. Some are worse than others. Do you believe that she loves you?"

"I thought she did. How can you shut out someone you love?" Mike wondered.

Will stopped dead in his tracks and eyed Mike coldly. "Yes, Michael. How could you shut out someone you love? Maybe when you're able to answer that question, you'll see your way clear of this mess."

Will turned on his heel and strode off down the corridor leaving his words ringing in Mike's ears. Mike watched him go with a sinking feeling in the pit of his stomach. Crew-members walked by him chatting to each other, but in the midst of so many people, he felt more alone than he had ever felt. Suddenly he was all too aware of how he had made Jan feel.

Determined to talk with her, he tried to find her and asked the healers when her therapy sessions were scheduled. However, Jan never showed up in the places she was supposed to at the scheduled times. Finally he waited in the therapy room for an entire day, but Jan did not come. Day after day he tried one tactic after another. He even tried to enlist Marla's help in sneaking him into Jan's room.

Marla looked at him and shook her head. "No way, Ihue. I do not want to be in the middle of this fight. You two will have to find some way to work things out."

"But how can I if I can't even talk to her?" Mike pleaded.

Marla shrugged. "I don't know, but I know I can't be part of the answer."

Finally he gave up and went back down to engineering to help Gorlan, only this time his heart was not in his work. Only a matter of weeks remained before they reached Quentas and he and Jan were already estranged.

Two weeks from their final approach to Quentas, Mike received a knock on his door late one evening. The opening door revealed a page with an announcement.

"Prince Ihue, your presence is requested in the healer's lounge at Suntar Eight on the morning rotation tomorrow."

Mike nodded and the page left. Curious, Mike sought out Will who had received a similar invitation.

"What do you think this is about?" he asked Will.

"I'm very curious," his friend replied, "but try as I might, I've been told I have to wait till tomorrow. Might as well get some rest, Michael. Something tells me that tomorrow promises to be very interesting."

Mike struggled to sleep and was up early the next morning. He was already in the healer's lounge when Will, Marla and Gorlan entered. Marla had a huge smile on her face, but no amount of prodding would make her divulge her secret. Finally the men gave up and settled in to wait.

Elira entered and took a seat then to everyone's surprise, the side door opened and Jan walked in without any support. Though her steps were slow, she crossed the room, walked up and down a flight of therapy steps and headed back toward the door where Soniora waited with a pair of crutches.

"She's done it!" Will whooped clapping Mike on the back. "She's walking!"

But Mike just stared at her disappearing figure. Before Soniora could close the door, he jumped up and dashed after her, catching her in the hall.

"Jan! Wait!" He rushed up beside her.

She stopped and turned.

"You did it! I'm really proud of you," he began.

"Am I more acceptable now that I can walk?" she asked quietly.

He shook his head. "No, Jan. It took your anger to wake me up and make me see how wonderful you are always."

A smile crept into her eyes.

"They still talk about your visit down in engineering," Mike continued. "They never even saw that hover chair."

"No, but you did," she said with a deep sigh.

"Jan," he said, his voice cracking. "I don't know of a good way to apologize for what I did. You've given me a lot of time to think about it."

"And?"

"You were right. I spend a lot of time running from what frightens me or has the potential to hurt me. But nothing could scare me more than the thought that you might not love me anymore. Please, Jan," he pleaded. "Give me another chance. I've been stupid, but please tell me I'm not unforgivable."

Jan dropped the crutches and melted into his arms. All of a sudden she started sobbing. "At first I hurt so bad thinking that you were rejecting me because I was disabled. I wanted to make you hurt as badly as I was hurting. Then I got angry and used that anger to fuel my therapy. But Mike," she said looking up at him, "revenge hurt even more. I've wanted to see you and hold you and love you, but I couldn't let myself because of what I'd said. I'm the one who needs to be forgiven."

Mike folded his arms around her, happy just to feel her near him once again. "I'm all for calling us even and putting this behind us starting now. I don't want to live one more second without you in my life. You can be in a hover chair or on crutches or whatever you need. The most important thing is you from the inside out."

"We're even," Jan confirmed. "This is over."

"I love you, Janielle."

She squeezed him with all her strength. "I love you, too, Mike."

Mike walked her back to the infirmary where Elira waited in Jan's room. Jan sat up on her bed, her legs dangling over the edge, while Mike stood beside her. Elira checked her over with a scanner then shook her head.

"I have no explanation for how you managed to accomplish this," Elira finally said. "By all rights, the neurological damage was so extensive in the motor cortex that you should not have been able to walk ever again."

"I had someone to inspire me," Jan said gazing at Mike. "Sometimes it was good and sometimes it was bad."

"That's behind us," Mike reminded her.

Jan looked down at the floor. "I've got to forgive myself now. That may be harder."

"Well, what is not hard is this," Elira said smiling. "I am discharging you from this infirmary. You are much too healthy."

Jan's eyes shone and Mike gave her a hug.

"You need to return for daily therapy, but you do not need to live here," Elira continued. "You also need to leave these behind," she said taking the crutches. "Walk slowly and rest when you need to. I have had a cabin opened for you next to Ihue's. You are free to go."

Jan gathered her things together and Mike picked up her backpack. Together they walked down the corridor to her new room. The door swooshed open and they went inside.

"Mm, you're right next door," Mike said holding her close.

"Again. Think it will be all right?" Jan wondered.

"This ship is a busy place," he replied. "News travels faster than gossip. Yeah, I'd say that will be deterrent enough."

Jan hugged him then sat down in a cabin chair. "Can we work something out between us?"

Mike sat across from her on the bed. "Like what?"

"I know that everyone needs time to think through things, so taking a time out is fine. But you pull so far away, I'm afraid you're not coming back," she explained. "Can't we devise some system between us where you take time out but still let me know you love me?"

Mike gave her words serious consideration. "How about I tell you flat out but at least eat meals with you or come back at night to say good-night? Nothing long…just short and sweet. Enough to remind you that I still love you, while I'm sorting things through."

"Oh that would make me feel so much better," Jan exclaimed. "I could handle the distance then because I would know it's not because of me."

"Ok, that's an agreement. Now how about something to eat?"

"Sounds good," she said walking out the door with him.

They strolled to the canteen and found Will already there. Jan sat down by him while Mike went to get their food.

"Everything's settled?" he asked

Jan nodded. "We worked out a deal about his needing time outs. Now if I can forgive myself for being such an ogre, I'll feel better."

"Just give it some time," Will said smiling.

"Elira released me from the infirmary…said I was too healthy."

"The news just gets better and better."

Mike set a tray before her and took a seat across from her. "Man, the crew is edgy!"

"We're getting really close to Quentas, and we could be attacked by Saracens at any moment," Will explained. "You two ought to do some PR work, visit some of the crew. It would really boost their morale."

"But what can we do given the circumstances?" Jan asked.

"As the new royalty, you two symbolize the last hope our people have. They're watching your every move," he said nodding to the crew seated around them. "They're looking to Michael, especially, for the fulfillment of nearly thirty years worth of hopes, dreams and desires for freedom."

"So just making an appearance helps?"

"Do what you did down in engineering," Will reminded her. "Take an interest. Show you care. That's all you have to do."

Suddenly a commotion broke out between two crewmen across the room. Mike got up and headed over. The argument had quickly escalated to a brawl as an auburn-haired man took a swing at a sandy-haired crewman. Mike pushed his way toward them, stepped in between them and caught the blows of their fists as they swung – one to his jaw and the other to his shoulder. The men stopped abruptly, staring at Mike in alarm as he staggered back against the wall. He shook his head to clear it, then grabbed the two by their arms and shoved them into seats at a nearby table.

"What seems to be the problem?" he demanded.

"Forgive us, Your H-Highness," they stammered. W-we did not know you were…."

Mike waved their concerns aside. "It was my own fault. I should have known better than to get into the middle of a fistfight. I'd rather discuss what started it."

"There was a problem with the maintenance log," the sandy-haired man replied sheepishly. "Some information was left out."

Mike frowned. "Was it vital?"

"No. It was routine," the auburn-haired man replied. "Things we do not always have time to write down."

"Was it?" Mike asked the first man.

"It is routine but when the next shift comes in, we cannot be certain the work has been done and start doing it again ourselves. It wastes time when the work has not been logged."

"So what could be done about it?" Mike asked. "Communication is important to any operation."

They nodded.

"How about a short-hand or a code of some kind?" Mike suggested. "A quick entry that tells what was done, when and by whom."

"What should we use?" the auburn-haired man asked.

"You figure it out. Get a discussion going between the two shifts and come up with something you can all agree on. But do it today," Mike said. He rose to leave.

"Then, you are not going to throw us in the brig?"

"Or put us on report?"

"Not this time. I appreciate your fighting spirit," Mike replied, "but let's save it for the ones who really deserve it – the Saracens."

The men sighed with relief as they watched him go.

Meanwhile, Jan and Will had taken back their trays, and she had spotted Marla sitting at a table surrounded by a group of crew-women. As she headed over to say hello, Jan realized that Marla was quite distraught. One of the women gave up her seat beside Marla so Jan could sit down.

"Marla, what's wrong?" she asked her sobbing friend. "What happened?"

Marla looked up at her with red swollen eyes. "It's ok, Jan. Don't worry about it."

"What do you mean, 'don't worry about it'?" Jan demanded. "You're my friend. Of course I'm going to worry."

Marla stared at her for a moment. "I'm your friend?"

"Yes," Jan replied, somewhat surprised. "What would have made you think otherwise?"

"I-I thought…just because of Ihue…I mean," Marla stuttered.

"I met you before I knew who any of you were, and we became friends long before Mike and I called a truce let alone fell in love. Now, girl, tell-me-what's-wrong."

Marla took a deep shuddering breath. "I didn't go to Earth till I was thirteen or fourteen. Father kept thinking that if the family moved around a lot, the Saracens wouldn't find us."

Jan nodded encouragement.

"I fell in love with a boy who was eighteen and we became secretly betrothed. My parents weren't angry when they found out. They had kind of figured it out already. But then the Saracens found us, and my father sent me to Earth with Gorlan so we could be safe."

"And your fiancée?"

"Stayed behind. He joined the Underground to fight the Saracens," Marla explained.

"So what's wrong now?"

"Daily lists come in of the casualties and…and…he was on the last list," Marla cried bursting into fresh tears.

Jan wrapped her arms around her, held her and rocked her back and forth. "Oh Marla. I'm so sorry…so very sorry." Jan squeezed back her own tears. "How awful."

The two young women clung to each other for a long while until Jan saw Mike waving to her.

"Marla, will you be all right for a while?" Jan asked.

Marla nodded.

"Mike wants me to go with him, but you promise me one thing," she said.

"What?"

"My room is now right next to Mike's. You come over no matter what the time is, you come over when you need me. I'll be there," Jan said.

Marla hugged her again. "Thanks, Jan…for being my friend."

Jan rose and went to join Mike who was standing in the doorway of the canteen and rubbing his shoulder.

"So how did you make out?" she asked as they strolled out into the corridor.

"I have a sore shoulder and jaw for my efforts. I don't know how much good I was able to do. Hopefully I was able to take the tension down a notch and get them to think of a more creative approach to problem-solving. What's up with Marla?" he asked.

"Did you know that she was engaged before she went to Earth?"

Mike's eyes widened in surprise.

"She left a fiancée behind and just heard today that he got killed doing his part in the war effort," Jan explained.

Mike grimaced. "Oh, my heart goes out to her. You don't know how important a lifemate is to a Quentasian. Some lose a mate and never consider anyone else."

Jan looked up at him, awed. "If I had died after they tortured me, would you have felt that way about me, too?"

They stopped in the corridor, and he reached out tenderly stroking her cheek. He nodded. "Definitely. If you had died at any point, it would have killed me."

At that moment a couple of young crewmembers passed by, and Mike and Jan overheard part of their conversation.

"Do you think that was a Saracen scout ship we picked up on scanners the other day?" the girl asked.

Mike's ears pricked up, and he guided Jan into step behind them.

"Must have been," her companion replied. "Why else would Captain Rian have put us on a full Suntarida rotation?"

"Yes, and he started those high powered scans yesterday, too."

The crewmembers turned a corner and their voices drifted away.

"That sounds serious," Jan remarked.

"Very. Cat and mouse is a deadly game to play in space," Mike replied, his brow knit. "C'mon, lady. Let's pay the captain a visit. I'd like to know just how much danger we're really in."

Chapter 28

Mike and Jan hurried through the corridors until they found the lift to the bridge. They got on and Jan experienced the unusual sideways ride up. Minutes later the door whooshed open to reveal the bridge. Their appearance surprised Captain Rian who quickly rose to his feet. He bowed to Mike and Jan then offered Mike his command chair. Mike awkwardly accepted it and slowly sank onto the great seat.

Meanwhile, Jan wandered about the bustling bridge observing the operations but staying out of crewmembers' way as much as possible. She gazed at the grid screen while the navigator ran a continuous check on their course. Then she watched as the communications officer worked to unscramble a very weak signal.

"Is that a Saracen communication?" Jan asked.

"No," the office replied politely. "It is from our main base on Quentas, but the Saracens are trying to intercept it." The officer knit her brows concern showing in her dark eyes. "One portion of the message is warning that there is a Saracen fleet lying in ambush, but the part with the coordinates is lost."

Jan wandered over to the helmsman while Captain Rian leaned over the communications officer studying the incoming message. Jan watched as the helmsman busily fielded flags from the ship's computers that gave him information about the engineering and propulsion systems. He became engrossed in the messages concerning the retrofit that Mike, Will and Gorlan had worked on.

Jan caught a flash on another screen and tapped the helmsman on the shoulder. "Excuse me, but what does all that on your screen about hyperspace mean?"

He whirled about instantly punching buttons on his console. "Captain, hyperspace countdown commencing."

A crewman immediately stepped up to Jan strapping her to a stand that rose from the floor. Behind her, Mike placed his hands on the command chair and closed his eyes. He could feel the ship hurtling through the vacuum of space. Slowly he brought his awareness inside the ship tracing the old and new wiring to the engines that were laboring to make the jump. He relaxed opening himself to the ship and sending rejuvenating energy along the wires.

Jan watched the blue glow that surrounded him and the command chair, awed at this exhibit of his powers.

All felt a lurch as the ship leapt into hyperspace. To everyone's surprise, rather than the usual lurching and jolting, it glided smoothly through the streaks of rainbow colors.

"Recomputing re-entry," the navigator announced. "Jump factor increased by 2.4956 times, Captain," he reported, amazement in his voice.

Captain Rian watched his Prince in awe as the ship returned from hyperspace, and Mike's eyes fluttered open. He bowed low as Mike rose and boarded the lift with Jan. The couple smiled as the lift doors closed then wearily leaned against its sides.

"Tired?" Mike asked.

"My legs will barely hold me. How about you?"

"It'll take me a while to recoup after that boost I gave the hyperdrive."

Back on the bridge, a security officer turned to Captain Rian in alarm. "Scanners detecting a shadow, Captain."

"Identify."

"Impossible. It is out of range."

"Switch to high power scanners."

"We are on high power, sirha."

The Captain sat brooding in his command chair. "Possible Saracen vessel."

"Very likely."

Captain Rian pressed the comm button on his chair. "All hands hear this. We are on Orange Alert. I repeat Orange Alert. Maintain watch posts."

He wearily turned to the security officer. "Keep scanning. I want to know the instant you make a positive identification of that vessel."

"Yes, Captain."

Even with no identification yet available for the ship that shadowed them, Captain Rian mobilized his forces to try to evade it.

"Cloaking device…on," he ordered.

The Science officer worked at his panel. Outside, the ship shimmered and wavered – now disappearing, now appearing.

"Cloaking device is unstable, Captain," the Science officer reported.

Captain Rian hit the arm of his chair with his fist, angrily muttering something under his breath. "Helmsman, alert engineering to gear up for another hyperspace jump."

"B-but, Captain. We just made one thirty minari ago. The ship cannot possibly be ready for a second jump."

"We will have to chance it," Captain Rian replied. "We must lose that ship."

The navigator ran the computations, and the helmsman locked in the coordinates.

"Counting down to hyperspace," the helmsman announced. "Five…four…three…two…one."

With a lurch, the ship entered the field of streaking rainbow colors once more. Though a little rough, the ship did not buck and heave as it once had. When they returned to normal space, the ship sailed smoothly into the field of bright twinkling stars.

"Scanners," Captain Rian barked.

"We lost it!" the Science officer exclaimed.

"Sirha," the helmsman said, "engineering reports that everything is normal, though they cannot understand how we were able to make that last jump."

"Just tell them, it was complements of our Prince," Captain Rian replied.

"Yes, sirha!" the helmsman answered beaming.

The Captain looked about the bridge. Gone were the drooping shoulders and worried expressions. An atmosphere of exuberance prevailed. Hope had returned with their Prince.

Near the infirmary, Jan watched Mike enter his cabin while she headed inside the familiar ward for a quick checkup. Elira ran a scanner over her as usual, but all was well. Jan hopped off the table and headed back into the hall. She stopped a moment when she saw Marla outside her room.

Hurrying over, she touched her friend's arm. Marla lifted her head, her eyes red from crying.

"You need a hug," Jan said definitively. "C'mon inside."

She opened her cabin door and led her friend inside. Marla sank into the cabin chair while Jan eased onto her bunk.

"It hurts so bad," Marla said hugging herself and rocking. "It's been so many years since I've seen him, but it hurts like it was yesterday."

Jan reached out, took Marla's hand and pulled her over to sit beside her on the bunk. "Mike explained to me how your people bond with one another," she said quietly. "I can't exactly share that feeling, but I know how bad losing someone feels."

Marla nodded tears trickling down her cheeks.

"I know when my parents died, it felt like nothing was ever going to make the pain go away," Jan continued. "Thanks for making sure my pictures made it with me."

Marla nodded.

"But I almost can't look at them yet. It hurts. I cry when I see them," Jan acknowledged, a tear brimming her lashes.

"How do I go on?" Marla asked. "How do I function?"

Jan gave her shoulders a squeeze. "For a while, you may not. You're in shock; you're in pain; you're numb…you're not supposed to function for a while. That's how your body and your psyche handles the grief."

"But this is war," Marla objected.

"And even during war time on Earth, men were shipped back home because they were too shell-shocked to keep fighting," Jan replied.

"Do you think I'll ever get over this?" Marla worried.

"Look at Elira," Jan said. "She lost Mike's father. Somewhere along the way, she had to have found the strength to go on."

Marla looked up, hope registering in her eyes for the first time. "That's true. I hadn't even thought about it."

"You will find a way," Jan assured her. "We all do. My suggestion…be kind to yourself. And when you can finally breathe without sobbing, find something meaningful to channel the pain into…something you feel your fiancée would have supported."

Marla nodded. "Thanks…this helps…a lot."

Jan gave her another long hug then saw her to the door. Once she left, she collapsed into bed and fell fast asleep.

The next day Mike took Jan to check out the ship's arsenal. The officer in charge took them on a tour of the hand-held weapons. Most were mere variations of one basic design – hand-held lasers. Mike noticed they had just enough power clips to use what was stored but no more. Once a laser ran low, that would be it.

"Have you ever used any of this stuff before?" Jan whispered.

"No, just some gadgets that augment my powers. How about you? Ever fire a gun before?"

"Does a BB qualify?"

"Not quite."

"Then I haven't."

"Would you like to try one of our short-barreled models?" the officer asked. "We have a target range through here," he said, gesturing toward a door on the far wall.

"No. That's ok," Mike replied. "I don't want to drain the power clips."

"Do not worry. We do keep extras for practice and use them on the lowest power setting. Six montari is a long time to go without shooting a weapon. The crew must keep in practice."

"Well, in that case," Mike said, reaching for the laser the officer offered him. "Want to try one?"

Jan shook her head.

Inside the target range, the gunman demonstrated the laser

pistol then handed it to Mike. "Keep your aim within the red line," he admonished. "Within that field the laser's energy is reabsorbed, rendering it harmless."

Mike nodded his understanding and took aim. When he touched the trigger, a bright bolt zipped through the air, hitting one of the targets on the back board. Following a muffled zap, his score was exhibited on a small screen above.

"What's a '95'?" Jan asked.

"Nearly perfect," the officer replied. "Five more points would have meant on center."

Within the next fifteen minutes, Mike scored several 90's, and even a couple of 100's. By the time he was ready to quit, he had taken out seventy percent of the moving targets, too.

"Why don't we go see the really 'big guns'," Jan suggested, bored with this exhibition.

"Good idea!" Mike replied handing the laser pistol back to the officer.

"Right this way, Your Highness," he said leading them to the nearest power-driven swivel-mount.

They entered an area only large enough for two or three people. A console with a stool and headset took up the space along one wall. The officer led them past it to a narrow ladder that he allowed Mike to climb. The ladder led up to the cramped quarters of the gunner's post.

"This gun and the other five like it," he explained, "all spin a full 360 degrees and swing through a complete 180 degree arc. The rangefinder uses computer-controlled laser optics that define and lock onto the target by means of visual cues. They represent the latest technology and have just one drawback; they draw 25,000 megawatts of power per shot. Because the ship is low on fuel, we can only power up three at a time. A lengthy recharge period makes direct hits crucial."

Mike slid out of the gunner's roost and led Jan back to the canteen. He ate his meal in pensive silence then took Jan to the bridge with him.

The Captain immediately rose to relinquish his chair as Mike stepped onto the bridge, but he motioned for him to remain seated. Mike toured the bridge, instead, before returning to speak with Captain Rian. He bent his head close to the Captain's and spoke in low tones.

"The officer in charge of the arsenal whom I talked to today says this ship can only power up three swivel lasers at a time, plus their recovery after each discharge is lengthy. Is there a reason for this?"

Captain Rian looked uncomfortable. "I assure you that only our best sharpshooters are manning them. They never miss."

"That isn't the point," Mike countered. "What do those sharpshooters do while waiting for a recharge?"

"They must simply wait," Captain Rian replied with a helpless shrug. "It was all we could do to salvage this ship and get it operational. It took almost two full decari to collect the amount of fuel we left Quentas with. I am sorry. It is the best we could do."

"But what if we end up under attack?" Mike pressed. "What then?"

"We will avoid attack at all costs, but if it comes down to a pitched battle…we will fight to the death."

Mike straightened, unnerved by the Captain's grim information.

"I must thank you for whatever you did to the hyperdrive yesterday," Captain Rain said quietly. "We had to power up for a second jump just thirty minari later. If we had not, we would not have lost the ship that was tracking us."

"Ship?" Mike asked, alarmed. "What ship?"

"We could not be certain," Captain Rian said cautiously, "but all indications lead us to believe it was Saracen."

At the moment, a cry of dismay erupted from the Science officer. "Saracen ship in Sectin six and closing!"

"Close enough for a hit?"

"Yes, Captain."

"If only hyperdrive would power up again," Captain Rian said wishfully, "but the cells are still low from our last jump."

"May I take the command chair, Captain?" Mike requested.

"My pleasure, Your Highness," he said smiling gratefully.

The Captain rose hurrying to check the scanners. Mike eased into place and tightened his grip on the arms of the chair. Carefully he retraced the lines to the main power units.

"Jan!" he called in a voice barely audible to others, but which boomed like thunder in her head.

She turned in surprise and slowly approached him.

"Let me hold your hand," he instructed, his lips not moving. "Before I gave you the Ring, I found it could augment my powers. I'm going to need it now."

Cautiously she stretched out her right hand. Sparks flew when his palm covered the Ring. She winced but held her hand in place.

"Hold on tight, honey," he whispered discharging his own power into the hyperdrive.

When she felt the numbing tingle from his power, Jan instinctively tried to pull back, but their grasp had already fused.

"We have visual on normal scanners," the Science officer announced.

"What make?"

"Adiva year prototype, sirha."

Captain Rian glanced at the couple who shimmered in the midst of a blue haze. "Helmsman, we need hyperdrive, now. Do we have enough power for a short jump?"

"One moment, Captain. Engine room reports an intense recharge, sirha. She is ready for a full jump!"

"Commence hyperspace countdown, now!"

"Counting down, sirha."

A blast flew from the nose of the Saracen ship. The crew held their breath as they watched the glowing streak speed toward them. Instead of exploding on impact, though, the phaser bolt hurtled through empty space. The Quentasian ship had vanished, its bridge bucking and reeling madly while the framework creaked.

Captain Rian had to shout to be heard over the squeal of the engines. What did you do?"

"I recharged the power units to full capacity," Mike yelled back.

"That is more power than this ship has seen in years. I do not even know if it can withstand the strain."

"Captain, engine room reports the hyperdrive is overheating. We could explode!" the helmsman reported.

"Take her down!" Captain Rian shouted.

"She will not respond! The circuits have fused and she is gaining speed!"

"Time to normal space, one minari, thirty-two secondari," the navigator announced. "If we do not slow down, we will be split in two!”

“Full reverse thrusters. Use booster and auxiliary power,” Captain Rian commanded.

“Booster on. Auxiliary powering up, sirha.”

Soon the scream of the thrusters could be heard above the roar of the ship.

“Captain, the ship is overheating!”

“Entry point overshot,” the navigator announced. “Recomputing entry to normal space.”

“I’m going to try something new,” Mike whispered to Jan. “I’m going to try to reverse my power so hold on tight.”

Mike closed his eyes concentrating with renewed intensity. With a mighty effort the ship finally began to slow.

“Countdown to normal space,” the helmsman called. “Five…four…three…two…one. Entry point achieved.”

The ship glided smoothly through the streaming colors of space and into the midst of a Saracen sweep pack.

Chapter 29

Captain Rian looked at the group of Saracen vessels all lining up against them. "Talk about all the luck," he muttered resuming his command chair. "At least we are nearly home. Those last three jumps cut the remainder of the trip by seventy-five percent. At least we have enough fuel to handle a dogfight."

"Sirha! Quentas is on visual!" the Science officer exclaimed.

"Saracen Adiva fighters at Sectin three," called the battle coordinator.

"Red Alert!" Captain Rian yelled hitting the main button on his armpad. "All hands to battle stations. This is not a drill. I repeat, Full Red Alert."

Throughout the ship, men and women scrambled to their battle stations. Suddenly, Saracen fighters swooped toward the ship with their guns blazing.

"Shields up," the Captain ordered.

A phaser bolt grazed the hull.

"Raoel is hit! Port Three is out!" the battle coordinator called.

"Seal Port Three."

"Who will replace him?" Mike asked.

"We could only spare three sharpshooters," Captain Rian replied.

Mike spun around, grabbed Jan, and headed for the lift.

"Where are you going?" Captain Rain cried in alarm.

"To the next available port," Mike called back over his shoulder.

"But, Your Highness. You might be killed!"

"We all might be if I don't do something."

The door closed and the lift whooshed along.

"How can I help?" Jan wondered. "I can't shoot anything."

"You won't need to. I had an idea earlier that I wanted to try on the swivels. Looks as if I've got my chance."

"Where do I fit in?"

"The swivels require teamwork and you and I, lady, are the team."

"And to think, I hate guns."

"Get used to them, honey. I have a feeling we'll be seeing a lot of them for a while," he said as the lift door opened.

They hopped out and Mike dragged Jan down the corridor, around a corner, and into Port Four lift. The lights dimmed as the ship took another hit. Eventually the doors slid back, and Mike hurried out with Jan stumbling after him.

He flipped the switches that powered up the console and yanked down the laser guidance helmet and drew her over.

"Here. Sit at the console and strap this on."

"What then?" she asked watching him climb into the cockpit of the swivel laser.

"I'm going to channel my powers through this laser. Thanks to the use of the Ring back there and the power reversal, I still have quite a bit of juice left." He fired up the weapon. "I need you to watch the grid and be my 'eyes' down there, while I'm concentrating up here."

"But that means I have to aim it," she protested. "You're the sure shot."

"Just get the fighter near the crosshairs. The final shot'll be mine."

"But how will I let you know?"

"Don't worry, honey. I'll know."

Mike strapped in quickly and placed his hands on the controls. "Let's see," he said glancing down. "Swivel is at my feet, tilt is my left hand, and fire is my right."

He closed his eyes speedily rebuilding the internal components of the weapon to accept his powers. Jan quickly sighted several fighters approaching from the side. As she turned the viewer to get one in line, Mike simultaneously swung around in the cockpit; they acted as if they were but one person.

"I've got one," she called.

But even as she spoke, the viewer was yanked out of her control and Mike fired. A burst of light accompanied the Saracen ship's explosion. It careened away slicing through the Saracen fighter behind it. The two crafts blew into a raging ball of fire. A robust cheer went up from the crew on the bridge, followed by another when Mike scored his second direct hit.

"Port Four again," the battle coordinator confirmed.

"If those two can keep that up, we just might make it," Captain Rian breathed.

Once again Jan zeroed in on an incoming fighter which Mike blew away. They took out ship after ship, but whenever they managed to open a hole in the pack, more fighters dove in on them.

"What we need to be is invisible," Jan moaned.

"Ship's cloaking device isn't working," Mike replied. Suddenly he leapt from the cockpit. "We do need to be invisible, and I know just how to do it. C'mon. Man this port."

"B-but…." she stammered as he took the helmet off her, pushed her toward the ladder and helped her climb up. "But how do I work this thing?" she cried watching him disappear inside the lift.

With a heavy sigh, she pulled down the guidance helmet and worked the pedals till the gun swung out to face the incoming fighters.

Meanwhile, the lift had deposited Mike on one of the lower floors. He squeezed out as the doors began to open and dashed through the corridors. He ran into the infirmary and burst into his mother's office.

"Quick! We have to meld our powers," he panted.

"But why?"

"We have to cloak the ship…make it invisible."

"Just the two of us?" she asked incredulously.

"We've got to try."

"It is impossible."

"Not if you have some help," came a voice from the open doorway.

Mike and Elira turned to see Soniora standing just inside the door.

"My powers may be old, but they are still useful."

Mike looked to his mother. She took a deep breath then nodded.

Soniora approached them and they joined hands. With closed eyes and bowed heads, they focused their concentration. A blue glow shimmered about them sinking quickly into the ship's floor. Blue arcs of energy zipped through the ship eventually leaping from point to point over the outside of the hull. Suddenly the Saracen fighters began flying in erratic circles. Their firing stopped.

"Cease fire!" Captain Rian yelled into his comm as soon as he realized what must be happening. "Cease fire! We must not give ourselves away!"

Immediately all firing ceased, and the helmsman deftly maneuvered the ship through the Saracen sweep pack. Soon there was nothing but open space between the transport and Quentas.

"Prepare to enter the atmosphere," the navigator called.

"Countdown commencing," the helmsman confirmed. "Four…three…two…one…entry achieved."

They glided smoothly into the atmosphere and gradually sank through the clouds. The ship passed over the blue and green globe below them until they finally dropped from the sky.

In the swivel cockpit, Jan gazed awestruck at the beauty of Quentas. Sparkling ribbons of blue water wound like snakes through lush, green valleys, while white-capped peaks rose high above the plains. Suddenly she gasped in alarm as the ship headed straight for the side of one of those snow-capped mountaintops.

Jan braced for the inevitable crash but, to her astonishment, part of the mountain slipped back and they glided inside. The great mountain door closed with a resounding clang. The ship drifted toward an extending platform then slowly lowered onto a large pedestal. In minutes, the ship was securely tethered in place by the hangar crew.

Mike and the two women shook their heads releasing their grip on each other. They had completed their task.

"Well?" Elira asked. "How did Jan take the battle?"

"Jan!" Mike cried. "Oh, no! I left her in charge of Port Four. Only I reconstructed it, and she can't power down!"

He raced out the door and zipped through the corridors. He leapt in and out of lifts at last stumbling into Port Four.

"It's about time, guy," Jan called from her perch. "With all this power you left me sitting on, I didn't dare move."

"Sorry, I almost forgot you were here."

"You what!"

"Mother, Soniora and I melded our powers. We were locked together until a few minutes ago," he replied climbing up beside her.

He grasped the joystick and quickly reabsorbed the energy. The gun powered down easily in response. He shut it off completely and eased Jan out of the cockpit.

"So, what do you think of Quentas?" Mike asked as they entered the lift.

"It looks a lot like Earth. It's beautiful…like the Swiss Alps."

"Too bad I missed it," he replied ruefully. "But maybe we'll get a chance to see it later. Right now, we'd better find the others and get ready to meet our public."

Jan groaned.

"Nervous?"

"A little. I'm wondering if they'll accept me."

"I do," he said kissing her. "That's all the acceptance you need."

They found Elira in her room. She had changed into a blue, A-line gown and was adding some final touches to her hair in preparation to disembark. She turned toward them when the door opened.

"Well, you two will blend in very well with our people," she remarked eyeing their uniforms. "At the moment, though, you need to stand out."

She pulled three amethyst-studded capes from her closet. "Wear these," she instructed handing them each one. She drew the third around her own shoulders.

Opening a small chest on her dresser, she lifted out a gold circlet. Motioning for Mike to bend down, she placed it on his head then stood back to admire its effect.

Elira shook her head. "If you and your father stood side-by-side, you could be twins."

She snapped the box shut.

"Now, Ihue, protocol dictates that, until I have introduced you as the Crown Prince, you must follow me. Lord Dehan and Jan will follow us."

Elira furrowed her brows as she looked at Jan. "No title?"

"America did away with titles when it became a democracy," Jan replied.

"No connection to aristocracy?"

"Two presidents were distant cousins, but I doubt that's what you're looking for."

She pursed her lips pensively. "Technically I am still the Queen until Ihue is introduced as the Crown Prince and I hand over the rule of Quentas to him." Elira glanced up at Mike. "Well, as my last act as Queen, I hereby declare," she said looking back at Jan, "that from this day forth, you shall be known as Lady Janielle."

Jan blinked wondering how to act or what to say.

Taking one last glance around the room, Elira turned toward the door. "I believe we are ready. Ihue, follow my lead, and Jan, look to Lord Dehan."

A sudden knock at the door startled them.

"Enter," Elira called.

"It whooshed back revealing a company of Honor Guards who entered to whisk them away. Elira walked with a graceful ease that made her appear to float, but Mike's gait was stiffer from tension and fatigue.

"You know, this is Michael's moment to shine," Will whispered as he fell into step beside Jan. "The impression he makes on his people now will be hard to shake off. He must appear every bit as royal as he is."

"He's doing a good job of it," Jan remarked watching the way Mike's cape breezed behind him. "He looks so different from the man I first met."

Will grinned. "He knows what to do. I've drilled him since he was a child."

"Will the people's impression of me be as unshakable?" Jan asked.

"A good first impression always helps," he replied, "but time is on your side. It's a long road from this landing to the coronation."

"At least I'm walking off this ship," she declared lifting her chin high.

"And right now, we couldn't ask for more."

They both faced forward quickly as they rounded the last corner leading to the landing ramp. Directly ahead, the first flank of Honor Guards marched solemnly down the ramp.

Elira paused in the doorway to survey the scene below. Then, with a spring in her step and a light in her eyes, she began her descent.

A voice boomed throughout the cavern. "Presenting her most Royal Highness, Queen Elira."

The hangar rocked with overwhelming cheers and applause from the people who crowded onto every gallery. In seconds Elira once more touched her feet on Quentasian soil.

"His Royal Highness, Prince Ihue," the voice roared.

The echoing cheers slowly faded as the crowd stared in awe at the man who descended the platform. Mike glanced about at the awestruck faces while feeling the pressure of every eye that was trained upon him.

"The honorable Lord Dehan and Lady Janielle," the voice announced with less pomp.

As Mike's feet touched Quentasian soil for the first time, Will and Jan began their descent amidst respectful applause. They were followed by the remaining Honor Guards. When the last guardsman's boot touched solid ground, the ramp slid back into the belly of the ship. The quartet was briskly escorted to a nearby platform where a graying, middle-aged man welcomed them personally.

"My dear Queen. It is with our greatest pleasure and joy that we, your people, rejoice at your safe homecoming."

He bowed low then turned to Mike. For a moment he could only stare in silence, then he shook his head as if awakening from a dream.

"My dear Prince. You have come to us at last, and in our hour of direst need. Your arrival is none too soon, and the aid of your powers will give us all renewed hope and courage. We have already heard how you used your powers to augment the ship's hyperdrive, took over a gunner's post to shoot down Saracen fighters, then joined with the Queen and a Royal elder to cloak the ship with invisibility till it was safely home.

"When we last saw you, you were a babe in arms who had to be whisked into exile to safeguard you from Saracen assassins. Forgive us, Your Highness, if we stare, but the man who returns to us is so completely the likeness of his father that, for a moment, we feel we are seeing one returned from the dead."

Mike nodded in a gesture of pardon and understanding. The spokesman bowed once again then turned to Will.

"Lord Dehan, we would also welcome you from your long exile. Surely your experience has been no less difficult. You have raised our Prince and have guarded him with your very life. How fortunate we have been to have had someone as devoted as you having sacrificed everything for our cause and our Prince."

While the crowd applauded, he turned to Jan and cleared his throat. Spotting the Star Ring on her hand, he took a deep breath. "And may we welcome the Lady Janielle of Earth to Quentas after so arduous a journey. It is my understanding that you have already faced our enemies and have courageously fought by our Prince's side in the recent space battle."

The spokesman quickly turned his attention back to Elira and, amidst great applause, once more presented her to the people.

She held up her hands for silence. "My dear people. There are no words to describe the joy that I feel at our reunion. At this time, though, I have a duty that gives me equally great pleasure. As my lifemate, High King Ihan, ruled you before, so now must his son. Crown Prince Ihue is Ihan's sole heir. I retire the authority of Quentas to his shoulders and present to you, Crown Prince Ihue."

Mike stepped forward, took his mother's outstretched hand and bowed low. The crowd went wild. When he straightened up, his mother, in turn, curtsied low and stepped back. He gazed out over the sea of eager faces as the entire throng leaned forward to catch what he might say. At last, he took a deep breath.

"My people. Lord Dehan has ceaselessly reminded me of your plight. From my earliest memories he has instructed me in our ways and has thoroughly prepared me for this day. I have finally returned to accomplish what my father once promised you…that your freedom would at last be won."

Hearty cheers roared in his ears at the mention of their hoped for freedom.

"Lord Dehan has not only been my friend and guide, but has also risked his life for me on all too many occasions. However, it gives me great pleasure to present someone very special to me; someone whom I hope will soon become special to you, also. Like Lord Dehan, she has also been my close friend and has risked her life for mine."

A murmur of surprise ran through the crowd.

"May I present to you…my beloved and future lifemate…Lady Janielle." He turned holding out his hand to her. Will gave her a subtle nudge.

Jan slowly walked forward, her cheeks flushed with excitement, and took Mike's outstretched hand. A slow smile spread across Will's and Elira's faces when Jan bowed her head to Mike and curtsied low. She raised her head and gazed steadily into his eyes reading the mixture of surprise, fear and appreciation that had welled up in them. With a warm smile he turned, Jan rising and following his lead. He proudly presented her to his people holding aloft her right hand.

The Star Ring suddenly burst into the greatest sparkling brilliance that had ever been seen. The murmur of uncertainty turned to cheering and applause as the dazzling brightness grew to blinding proportions. These having witnessed their return would now accept its firm approval.

Chapter 30

The Honor Guards marched up onto the platform and swept Elira, Mike, Will and Jan into a passageway despite the clamor of the people. The spokesman marched sprightly beside them as they headed down many damp, rock-carved passages toward the living section of the huge military fortress.

The spokesman turned to Mike as they walked. "Excuse me for not having introduced myself, Your Highness," he said. "I am General Adar, Commander of the Land Task. I thought you and the members of your party might like to retire to their quarters after your long journey and recent battle."

"Thank you, we would," Mike replied glancing about at this new subterranean world. "By the way, what is this place? Lord Dehan never described any underground complexes to me."

Adar smiled. "Lord Dehan is not at fault. These chambers were ancient and a very well-kept secret. We only re-opened them to escape the Saracen oppression.

"You see, at first we fled our cities and farms for the cover of the mountains. We banded together for safety and sent out rebel groups against the Saracens. They merely increased their patrols, ambushed our guerilla groups and destroyed many of our camps.

"Just when we were losing hope, a curious little people rescued us. They led us into their halls beneath the Mozern Range," he said, his hand sweeping the air above their heads. "We found the entrances to these ancient underground fortresses and continue to gather in as many of our people as we can persuade to join us.

"Now that you are here," Adar said proudly, "we can strike the blows that will crush these hated Saracens."

He punctuated his forceful statement by raising his fist dramatically and nearly bringing it down onto the head of a small, beady-eyed, glossy-furred creature that just managed to scuttle out of harm's way. It turned and harangued Adar with a loud burst of irritated chirps and squeaks.

"What is that?" Mike asked in astonishment.

"A Molluc," Will answered.

"H-How did you know?" Adar stammered. "We thought we had just discovered them."

Will laughed. "Just? How else do you suppose Prince Ihan escaped his brother's subterranean dungeon in time to marry the radiant Lady Elira? The Mollucan, their King, swore fidelity to the High Throne of Quentas in return for complete anonymity. Only those closest to Ihan ever knew."

"Well," Adar exclaimed. "Today has certainly been a day for surprises."

They entered a semi-circular suite of apartments. The main door opened and closed for them on command.

"This suite of apartments was readied especially for your arrival," Adar told them. "On the right is Que…I mean, Lady Elira's. Along the hall to the left in order are Lord Dehan's, Prince Ihue's, and Lady Janielle's. Each apartment has a balcony that overlooks our subterranean gardens. A series of walkways connects the balconies to each other and to the garden paths."

The four of them nodded as they took in their spacious common lounge paved with terra cotta tiles. In the center a marble bench encircled a refreshing fountain in which water plants floated on the bubbling water. Trees with twining ivy were arranged along the walls.

Since no one asked him any questions, Adar mustered the courage to ask a few of his own. "Your Highness," he said facing Mike. "May I inquire into the background of your future lifemate?"

"Jan is from Earth," Mike replied simply.

"Uh, yes. I had presumed as much. What I mean is…well… since the Saracen invasion, our people are quite suspicious of all outsiders. I realize that your Lady must have had very special qualities to have attracted your affection, but the people will want proof." He paused. "You mentioned that she has risked her life for you. Were there any witnesses? Do you have any proof?"

"Show him," Elira said.

Jan pointed to her hair, and Elira nodded. Slowly she pulled the hair back from her temples revealing the cruel, ugly, deep impressions that remained.

"Gorlan and Marla found Jan attached to the Augmenter and a mind-reading machine," Mike explained. "When they got to her, she was almost dead."

"The neurological damage was so extensive, I had to perform a cortical transplant," Elira said. "We nearly lost her in surgery and, even then, I did not think she would ever walk again." She placed her hands consolingly on Jan's shoulders.

"Her speech came back rapidly," Will added. "But it took montari for her to learn to walk."

Adar stared at Jan's scars, his hand traveling slowly to his own temples. "Many of us bear those marks for keeping secret the whereabouts of our Prince."

"She received higher voltages than anyone I have ever known," Elira said quietly. "It is a miracle that she is even alive."

Adar gazed at Jan with new respect. "I am sorry I had to ask such difficult questions, but our people will need more than just the Ring's acceptance."

Mike furrowed his brow but said nothing.

"Well, you have been tested in a manner our people can most easily identify with," Adar said, brightening. "Your pain has eased your way, my lady."

A sudden series of beeps disturbed the quiet and a light on Adar's belt blinked impatiently. "Excuse me, Your Highness," he said bowing. "I must go. I will send some attendants to your quarters shortly." He backed out the door swiftly disappearing down the hall.

"Well, let's see what they've prepared as quarters," Will said, first taking an appraising look at the lounge then strolling toward his apartment.

Elira had already opened the door to hers and was gazing inside.

"Guess we might as well get settled, too," Mike said to Jan. "In fact, I suddenly feel tired." He yawned. "Between using my powers to charge up the laser, then the meld to cloak the ship, I'm more tired than I had realized."

He crossed the lounge to a gold, filigreed door and pushed it open. After poking his nose around the corner, he disappeared inside.

Left alone in the middle of the lounge, Jan stared around her. She walked over and sat on the bench examining the water plants in the fountain's pool. She glanced up at the closed doors around her, sighed and got up. Wiping her wet hands on her crewman's uniform, she walked to the far end of the lounge, and tried to open her door. When it would not budge, she tried pressing a lighted, raised dome she found on the wall beside it. Frustrated when the door still would not open, she leaned back against the wall inadvertently covering the dome with her hand. The door whooshed open.

Cautiously she entered the small apartment and stared up at the vaulted ceiling over the lounge. Two arches in the far corner led into other rooms and she moved to explore them. The arch on the right led to a small, eat-in kitchen with a door to her balcony. The arch to the left led to a short hallway. The bathroom, complete with a treadmill for her continued therapy and a sunken tub, lay on the right while her bedroom lay on the left.

Jan entered the bedroom and lay down on the bed staring up at the ceiling. Finally she glanced about the room and noticed a wardrobe against one wall. She got up, opened it and began taking out the clothes she found inside. One-by-one she held them up to herself in front of a full-length mirror.

"That council gown looks especially nice," Elira said breaking the silence.

Jan started and dropped the white, Grecian, column gown.

"I am sorry," Elira apologized. "I did not mean to startle you. I knocked but I guess you did not hear me."

Jan shook her head. "No, I didn't. I guess I was lost in thought."

"Well, I came over to see how your quarters were, and if you were finding everything all right," Elira said helping her pick the gown off the floor.

She held it and several other outfits up to Jan. "Yes, I think they got the fit right."

"Will I really need this many clothes down here?" Jan asked.

"Each of these has a function," Elira replied. "Granted you may not need them all at once, but at some point in time, you will. Just ask me, though, if you have questions about what to wear. Believe it or not, a political council meeting is different from a Council of War, and you would dress differently for each."

Jan's eyebrows raised. "Guess I'll be checking my wardrobe with you quite often for a while."

"Mm, maybe. You will come to understand the protocol after a while and, once you do, many of the choices are common sense," Elira said. "Well, if you are settled here, I want to see how things are going at the infirmary."

Jan nodded and walked out into the lounge. Once Elira was gone, she quickly returned to the bedroom, shed the uniform and pulled on a pair of stretch pants and a tunic. Satisfied, she walked out into her kitchen then onto the balcony. She leaned against the railing staring at the vast expanse of garden below. The sound of footsteps on stone made her spin around.

"Hi! Didn't mean to scare you."

Jan broke out into a big smile. "Mike! How did you get over here?"

"Remember? The balconies are all joined by paths. The path that leads from my balcony leads to yours," he explained, his eyes twinkling mischievously.

Jan laughed and shook her finger at him. "Ah, ah, ah. You behave yourself.

"A man needs some way of getting to see the woman he loves." He wrapped his arms around her in a loving embrace.

After a while he let her go, and Jan turned to face the gardens while leaning back against Mike's chest.

"I can't get over how different this place is," she commented.

"Like how do all of these plants grow underground?"

"Unfortunately for that question, I took up physics not botany," Mike said. "I'm as stumped as you are."

Jan was silent for a moment before asking, "Your people aren't going to accept me as easily as we had thought, are they?"

Mike gave her a squeeze. "I guess not. Thirty years of domination by invaders can make the most open society close its hearts and minds."

"What will change their perception of me?" she asked. "What can I do?"

Mike leaned his chin on the top of her head. "I don't know, although I personally think you've suffered enough."

He turned her around to face him and looked deeply into her searching blue eyes. "I love you, Jan. I nearly lost you once, and I don't want anything else to happen that could jeopardize your life." He leaned forward kissing her deeply.

"But Mike," she protested when their lips parted. "What if they want you to send me back to Earth? What if they don't want me here at all?"

"Then they'll be sending me back with you," he said kissing her again. "They know they can't break my bond with you."

Mike tasted her lips again and longing seized him. "Mm, honey. You're right next door and now there aren't a whole lot of crew people around."

He began kissing her passionately wrapping his arms around her and pulling her closer. She could feel his taut muscles rippling under his shirt as her breasts pressed up against his chest. She closed her eyes as he held her head between his hands kissing her cheeks, earlobes and neck. As the heat surged through his veins, his kisses became more and more feverish.

Jan heard the sound of clippers, opened her eyes and caught a glimpse of a Molluc gardener. "Mm, honey. Don't you think we're just a little conspicuous out here?"

Mike glanced up and stopped momentarily. "So, let's move inside." He slid his arm down to her waist and gently led her into the kitchenette.

"I have waited months to have you all to myself without crewmen or healers around," he murmured running his fingers through her hair. "To think that someday you'll be all mine, and I yours."

Jan looked up at him wistfully as she placed her hands on his well-defined chest. "I wish that day were already here. I wish we even knew when that day was going to be."

"Mm, me too," Mike whispered kissing her neck.

Their lips met in a trembling kiss as he slowly ran his hands down her sides.

"Mike, we've got to be careful," Jan reminded him.

He pulled her closer to him.

"Honey, let's chill out a bit," she tried again. "Please."

He kissed her lips once more.

Suddenly a knock at the door made them jump and pull apart. Mike glanced down at her sheepishly looking like the little boy who had been caught with his hand in the cookie jar.

Jan laughed nervously and leaned her forehead against his chest.

"Who in the world?"

"Maybe your mother?"

Mike shook his head. "I saw her head down to the infirmary. She's in charge of it."

"Will? Adar?"

"Maybe."

She took his hand preparing to lead him into the lounge, but he did not budge. "Shouldn't we check it out?" she asked.

Mike pulled her back into his embrace. "Maybe if we ignore them, they'll just go away."

"That would be nice but highly unlikely around here," she remarked.

Mike kissed her one last time then heaved a sigh. "You're right. Lead the way."

They strolled into the lounge, and Jan opened her door. To their surprise, three little Mollucs entered and bowed low.

"Your Highnesses," they chorused rising. "We are your attendants."

Two of them approached Mike. "We are your chamberlain, secretary," they announced, each calling off the area of service in roll call fashion.

"I am your maid," the last Molluc said curtseying to Jan.

"I also bring a message to you both," Mike's secretary announced. "While you must take today to regain your strength after the battle, tomorrow at Suntar Eight, General Adar has called a Council of War. You, both, must be in attendance."

Mike and Jan looked at him startled.

"Until then, we shall take up our appointed posts."

Mike's attendants backed from Jan's apartment, but Jan's maid stared up at her whiskers twitching with curiosity. Jan glanced at her, and the Molluc quickly scurried into the kitchen.

The couple sank onto a lounger, the air knocked out of them by the announcement.

"A Council of War," Mike breathed. "So soon."

"Reality hits hard, doesn't it?"

Chapter 31

The next morning Mike, Jan, Will and Elira met in their common lounge. Jan had found a long blue sari-like tunic and matching slacks set which Elira had deemed most appropriate for attending the Council of War. As they all headed out from the suite, General Adar joined them. They walked the corridors in tense silence following where the general led.

In the office section of the complex, they entered a large room with an oblong table in its center and various holomap stations around its perimeter. Several commanders and generals from different bases sat around the table already. They all rose to their feet and bowed as Mike passed by. Five seats remained which the group then took with Mike sitting in the chair that was somewhat elevated above the others. The council members waited until he sat down before resuming their own seats.

General Adar rose to address the council. "Your Highness… ladies and gentlemen," he began bowing first to Mike, "this Council of War had been called to allow us to update our Crown Prince as to the status of the war effort and to begin developing the plans towards the final battle to rid the planet of the Saracens."

When the general sat down, the other council members each rose in turn describing the efforts their own forces were making in the war effort. As the presentations wore on, the listeners became keenly aware that each group was acting as a sole entity. One group was hoarding weapons, another food, while others had barely anything at all. The only common element was the incredible losses and casualties suffered by all.

Mike's brow furrowed deeper and deeper as he listened to each speaker. When the last person had finished, he looked to Adar who again rose.

"As you can see, Your Highness," Adar said addressing Mike, "our forces are depleted, and we have entered a very desperate time. Your presence is much needed and may be just barely in time. We have need of your wisdom and your powers, or else our people and this planet are doomed."

Mike nodded and Adar took his seat. "I would like to call a recess for one suntar and would ask that all leave except the advisors who entered with me."

The council members nodded politely, rose and quietly exited the room. When the door closed behind the last one, Mike stepped off the dais and took a seat next to Will.

"When you said our people were in dire straights, mother, you didn't even describe the half of it," Mike remarked.

"You have to hear it first-hand just to believe it," Elira replied.

"Why such chaos, Adar?" Will asked.

"Up until now, our people have had no single unifying force," Adar replied. "The Saracens disrupted the old alliances and the principalities broke away into their own sovereign units."

"What will bring them together?" Mike asked.

"Hopefully you," Adar replied. "I am hoping that the seal of the High King will bring their allegiance under one governance, and that we can finally assail the Saracens as a concerted force."

Jan, who had been listening carefully until now, spoke up. "I can think of two examples from Earth history that are very similar," she told them. "One was the invasion of the British Isles by the Romans, and the other was the wresting of North America from the Native Americans by the Europeans."

"Hm, history wasn't my strong point," Mike remarked.

"Well, in the case of the Roman conquest of Great Britain, there were many separate Celtic tribes who all fought independently. Frequently they were also fighting each other as well as the Romans. Had they rallied together, say under Queen Boudica, they could have prevented the Romans from conquering England."

"What about these Native Americans you spoke of?" Adar asked.

"Again, separate tribes with separate territories who fought singly rather than together. The greatest coalition of any of them were the Six Nations of the Iroquois who had banded together as a Federation. But once the Europeans were able to divide them, even the Iroquois Federation fell. General Adar is absolutely right in assuming the worst will overcome your people if they cannot be brought together under one leadership."

Will, Mike and Elira all nodded.

"So what should we do?" Mike asked.

"We need to send out the seal of the High King to all of the principalities and request their renewed allegiance to the High Throne," Adar replied.

"Will they swear allegiance to just the seal?" Will wanted to know.

"If not to that, then to what?" Adar responded.

"To me in person," Mike said quietly. "If I were to visit each principality in person, then they would swear allegiance."

"No," Adar said. "Not yet. The Saracens must not yet know you have returned. They must not know that our mission was successful. The ship returned montari sooner than expected. Let them think that we failed. Let them think that they drove us back and that we were unable to reach the help we sought. Let them be ignorant of your presence on this planet for a time longer."

"But what if the principalities refuse?" Mike countered.

"We cannot even find all of the bases. Those that we have found have representatives here this morning. Those we should be able to convince," Adar replied.

"Why can't we find all of the bases?" Will asked.

Adar sighed heavily. "There are pockets of heavy Saracen concentrations that we cannot pass through. Some of our people are totally cut off."

"What about the sacred paths?" Elira asked.

"Only the Royal Family may tread them and few remain. Those who do are either old, still in exile, or are only now beginning to return," Adar explained.

"What about the hidden paths?" Will questioned.

"Again only someone of the Royal Family may tread those paths and that person must first be approved by the Mollucan."

"Yes, and that approval is hard to come by," Will said pensively. "Ihan was the last to use those paths, and only as an emergency escape route. The Mollucan barred him from ever setting foot on them again."

"So we're back to square one," Mike said. "We can't contact all of our people, and those whom we can may be difficult to convince."

"But we must try," Adar said.

"Oh, I agree," Mike replied. "I just don't like the odds against our success."

Adar said nothing.

The Council of War was reconvened and a tentative plan outlined. They would contact the known principalities and request their allegiance to the High Throne of Quentas. Once allegiance was given, the principalities would be brought into a plan to divide supplies and responsibilities equally amongst them.

That afternoon, after a quick bite in a common canteen, Mike, Jan and Will toured the Mozern Complex. They were shown the quarters of the Underground guerillas, the vehicle hangars and the infirmary. They passed by several training gyms and a research lab. Here and there, Jan noticed areas marked "Restricted" and once even thought she saw a cloaked figure duck into one. Her curiosity was piqued.

When the tour ended, an Honor Guardsman escorted Mike on to sign the letters to the principalities and set the seal of the High King upon them. Jan and Will walked back through the complex together.

"Will, does the Mollucan know anything about the Star Ring?" she asked.

"To be truthful, he swears allegiance to that and to the Star of Quentas over even the High Throne," Will replied. "Why?"

"Do you think he would give me permission to use the hidden

paths?"

Will stopped dead in his tracks and looked at her hard. "What are you thinking of doing?"

"I don't know yet, but I do know that if your people are ever going to accept me, I can't just sit in a hole in the ground," Jan replied glancing up at the ceiling.

"Now, you watch what you do, Jan. If anything ever happened to you, Michael would crumble. His will would be crushed," Will warned her.

"But what if I could obtain the permission to use those hidden paths and could find the rest of those bases," Jan postulated. "Not only would I have a better chance of gaining your peoples' acceptance, those added bases could be exactly what we need to tip the scales in our favor. Is this really an opportunity I can pass up?"

"Jan, be careful," Will warned. "Whatever you do, be careful."

Jan watched as he headed toward the research facility while she went toward the infirmary for a check up. Elira ran a new set of neurological exams then had Jan meet her in her office.

"You have continued to gain function," Elira remarked. "It amazes me but maybe your system is more responsive to the implant than ours." She glanced at the Ring. "Or maybe the Star Ring is helping."

"How much function do you think I've regained?" Jan asked.

"I would say 85% at least."

Jan thought for a moment. "Do you think I could run again?"

Elira raised her eyebrows then cocked her head to one side. "Give it a try," she said at last. "I never thought you would walk, but here you are."

Jan nodded.

As Elira prepared to leave, Jan stopped her. "Lady Elira…."

The healer turned toward her. "Jan, only in formal settings do you have to call me by my title."

"What would you like me to call you?" Jan asked.

"Something more personal."

Jan's heart skipped a beat. "M-mother?"

Elira smiled as she ran the familial title over in her mind. "I never got to hear a child call me matra. Now that Ihue and you are here, yes, I would like you to call me mother."

Jan's eyes shone. "I lost my mother to cancer when I was eighteen. It's really nice to gain a new mom."

The two women hugged, then Elira held Jan at arm's length. "Now, what were you going to ask me?"

"It's about your people and their reaction to me," Jan replied. "How do you think they feel about me?"

Elira pursed her lips. "When they discover that the High King has taken a non-Quentasian bride, I do suspect there may be trouble. They cannot possibly know what Ihue has gone through on Earth, or what your people are like. All they know is their own suffering at the hands of the Saracens."

"Will they pressure Mike to send me back to Earth?"

Elira frowned. "There may be talk of it, though I doubt they will succeed."

"But will they be as ready to swear allegiance to him if I stay?"

Elira shook her head. "I suspect they will be wary of his decisions fearing that you will manipulate him against them."

Jan sighed. "These scars aren't going to be enough to convince them either, are they?"

"They will help, Jan, as well as Gorlan's and Marla's testimony," Elira said placing her hand on the young woman's shoulder, "but you will have to work hard in order to gain a measure of acceptance."

"Eli…mother, this place is going to be my home," Jan said. "I don't want to feel alienated and hated for the rest of my life. I don't know if I could stand it, and I'm sure it would affect Mike. I don't want to see him hurt, and a fight with his people over me is bound to leave him feeling bitter. It's going to set up a losing situation."

"Jan," Elira said hugging her. "All we can hope for is the best."

That evening Jan ate dinner with Mike in his apartment. She only half-listened to him recount his day to her. He noticed that she had not touched much of her food and finally stopped.

"Not used to Quentasian food?" he asked.

Jan did not respond but continued to stare at her plate.

"Hey, Jan! Jan?" He waved his hand in front of her face. She blinked and looked up.

"Are you all right?"

Jan sighed. "I'm sorry. I've got a lot on my mind."

"Like what?" he asked laying down his fork and leaning toward her.

"Your people accepting me, what the general said this morning in the council, how desperate things really are...." She looked him straight in the eye. "I don't know what I was expecting would happen when we came here but none of this was on my list."

Mike took her hand, got up and led her into his lounge. They sat side-by-side and he put his arms around her.

"We'll just have to make the best of the circumstances," he said at last.

Jan shook her head. "No, Mike. We have to find a way to be proactive...I have to find a way."

Mike took her hand and kissed her. "I told you, the Ring accepts you and I love you. That's all that is important."

She shook her head even harder and pushed away. "Stop being naïve! I've been talking to people, and it's going to be a whole lot more complicated than that."

"You will have to let those scars and the testimony of witnesses be sufficient."

Jan got up and paced. "Mike, I can't sit back and do nothing. I'm not like that."

"And I don't want you to get killed," he said earnestly.

"So you're going to protect the one over the many?"

"What exactly is that supposed to mean?" he asked narrowing his eyes.

She waved him away. "I don't know. I just know that I cannot hide in a hole in the ground and ignore the fact that people are dying."

Mike rose, stopped her and placed his hands on each of her shoulders to get her to face him. "And I know that I can't make good decisions if in the back of my mind I'm worried about what's happening to you. Nor will I ever be an effective ruler if you die."

Jan looked at him with an anguished face, her desperate dilemma shining in each tear that welled in her eyes.

Chapter 32

Over the next few weeks Mike's words haunted Jan. She saw him off to his official duties each morning then walked on her treadmill pushing the speed faster to keep up with her racing thoughts until she was running again. When she was not on her treadmill, she either paced in her apartment or wandered the gardens below. At night dreams assailed her sleep, and she tossed and turned restlessly. One night she dreamed Mike committed suicide because she found a way to aid the war effort but was killed. His death in it was so real, she slipped into his apartment from his balcony in the middle of the night just to reassure herself that he was still alive.

Finally she could take the inner conflict no more. She chose something from her wardrobe that appeared to look business-like and pulled it on.

"Where will you be today, mirsta," her little Molluc attendant asked.

"I plan to pay General Adar a visit," Jan replied.

"Shall I plan on your return for lunch?"

"I don't know, Teldank. We'll see."

Jan left the suite and found the general's office by asking

Honor Guards along the way. She peeked in his door and observed him hunched over some paperwork. Taking a deep breath and mustering her courage, she knocked on his door then entered. He looked up, surprised to see her.

"General Adar, I know I don't have an appointment, but I need to speak with you," she announced.

He folded his papers then motioned for her to take a seat.

"What can I do for you?" he asked leaning on his desk. "I have just a few minari to spare."

"I need to ask some questions," Jan managed at last. "I need to know the truth."

He nodded.

"What is my status on this planet in your peoples' eyes?"

Adar cleared his throat and looked uncomfortable.

She stared at him with a piercing gaze. "I want the truth."

He nodded. "There are many, even in this base, who consider you their enemy."

Jan took a sharp breath. "Why?"

"You almost look like a Saracen," he replied. "If you were eight to ten inches taller, I might suspect it myself."

"So this is really serious," she murmured.

He finally looked at her straight on. "It is more serious than Ihue knows or even Elira. The people may seek to destroy or even execute you."

She blanched then changed the subject. "How is the campaign going to rally the principalities?"

"Not as we had hoped."

"Will enough of them join together to gather against the Saracens for a final assault?"

Adar shook his head. "Not at this rate."

"And the seal of the High King is not enough?"

He shook his head again. "They believe it is a ruse."

"What would convince them?"

He stared at her hand. "The Star Ring."

Jan held it up. "You mean this?"

Adar nodded. "That has not been seen on Quentas for three decari. We may be able to fake many things, but we cannot fake the Star Ring."

She thought for a moment longer. "How do I find the Mollucan?"

Adar shrugged. "We have spoken to him only through messengers."

Jan stood and extended her hand to the general. "Thank you for your time and frankness, general."

He nodded then watched her leave.

Jan returned to her apartment and paced some more.

"Mirsta, you need to relax," Teldank said bringing her a cup of special Molluc tea.

"I know, but I can't." She accepted the tea gratefully. "The one person I need to talk to no one knows how to get to."

"The Mollucan?" Teldank asked whiskers twitching.

Jan nodded.

"Never approach him without a plan."

"So how do I develop a plan? Somewhere in the back of my mind, I feel that part of the answer lies in those 'Restricted' areas on this base. But I have no clue what lies beyond their doors or how to get to them."

'What if I could…get you past those locked doors?" Teldank ventured.

"How?"

"By routes the Quentasians know nothing about."

"The hidden paths," Jan breathed and Teldank nodded.

"Yes. I accept your offer."

"Then swear to keep all knowledge of the hidden routes secret, even from the High King," Teldank demanded.

Jan's eyes widened in surprise, but she nodded. "I swear to keep my knowledge of them secret, even from Mike. No one will ever learn of those routes from me."

Early the next morning, before anyone else was stirring, Teldank woke her. She bustled Jan out of the Royal Suite before Mike had even stumbled into his shower. Once in the main corridor the Molluc stopped, glanced about warily then pressed a small bump on the wall. To Jan's astonishment, a slab of the wall suddenly slid back. Teldank entered pulling Jan after her. The portion of wall silently moved back into place.

"Where are we?" Jan asked, peering hard into the inky

darkness.

"A Molluc tunnel. They go everywhere, especially to the 'Restricted' areas."

A moment later, a small light appeared to dance at their feet and illuminated just enough of the path for them to see their way. Teldank hurried off with Jan following quickly. Twenty minutes later the Molluc stopped, opened another wall panel, and cautiously poked her nose into the corridor. Satisfied, she withdrew it, pulled a leather thong from a pouch on her belt, and threaded it through a sprig of fresh herbs she had carried.

"Bend down," Teldank whispered.

Jan knelt so the Molluc could hang an herbal necklace about her neck. "What is this stuff?"

"'Num-wat' in my tongue. It will make others forget you have been there."

"You mean, they'll see me but not remember?"

Teldank nodded and handed Jan a white, one-piece suit with a pliable visor to cover her face. "Put this on, too. Num-wat works best when you are disguised."

"Where are we?" Jan asked stepping into the corridor.

"The Science Research wing. Follow me and speak no more."

Teldank led her down a long hall to a lab filled with busy technicians. One man scrapped an old machine to get parts to rebuild a second, more delicate piece of machinery. In another lab, a group of scientists struggled in vain to build a machine they could only draft on paper.

"Their task is nearly impossible," Teldank whispered as they watched through viewing windows. "These machines are nearly three decari old and are beyond repair. They need supplies, but we can only obtain them from the Saracens who took over all the manufacturing plants. Obviously the Saracens do not sell them to us, so our success at finding or stealing the parts we need is very low."

They ambled inconspicuously through the lab. Jan spotted Will in one and watched his futile attempts at experimentation without proper equipment or sufficient supplies. The bags and dark circles under his eyes told the entire story.

Teldank tugged at her sleeve and they passed on. After turning a corner and taking a quick glanced around, they ducked into a deep closet and found the entrance to another tunnel clear in the back.

"They need a factory and raw materials," Jan commented.

"With the raw materials alone, they could do more," Teldank replied, "but in the Med-Unit you will see why the supplies just do not reach them."

They scurried through the maze of tunnels stopping minutes later while the little Molluc poked her nose through a crack in the wall.

"Here," she said pulling back and handing Jan a robe. "Wear this and pull the hood up over your head. Crush a leaf of Num-wat and follow me."

Jan hurriedly shed the first disguise and slipped into the robe. She pulled the hood up over her head then followed Teldank into the hall. They quickly wormed their way into the Med-Unit. Young men and women Jan's age and younger lay moaning on the hospital cots.

"They received their wounds while raiding the Saracens" Teldank explained in a low whisper. "Many will die, and there are too few able to make the ranks to replace them. We lose young people like this everyday."

As Jan watched, a young man in one corner cried out in pain. Teldank held Jan back as healers rushed to his side. In spite of their efforts, he gasped twice then fell limp and grey against his bedding. A tear trickled down her cheek as she stifled a sob.

"Poor Marla," Jan thought. "I hope she's all right."

Teldank took her arm and led her to the treatment center where healers, among whom Jan spotted Elira, worked frantically over the body of a young woman. They ran out of medication and a young healer returned with news that there was no more."

"Medical supplies are dreadfully low. The problem is always the same," Teldank said sadly. "The runners just cannot bring back enough. Come, let us go."

She led Jan back to a Molluc tunnel that eventually brought them back to the corridor just outside the Royal Suite. Teldank hustled Jan into her apartment before anyone could spot them.

"Mike has no clue how bad things really are," Jan remarked.

"Maybe they are afraid to show him for fear he, too, would lose hope and would prefer permanent exile to a losing battle," Teldank replied.

Jan sank into a lounge chair. "Has he returned in time?" she thought aloud.

"Barely."

Jan looked at the Molluc. "But you believe there is still hope?"

Teldank nodded. "Only if one uses the hidden paths."

"Where all do they go?"

"Nearly everywhere on Quentas."

"The Saracens don't know about them?"

"Few Quentasians even know they exist," Teldank replied. "No one but the Mollucs are allowed to tread them."

"Could someone with special permission?" Jan pressed.

"It has never been done before."

"Yes, well, a Quentasian High King has never married an alien before," Jan pointed out. "Who is your king, Teldank?"

"No one except Prince Ihan and Lord Dehan have ever seen him before."

"Someone else may," Jan murmured. "Someone else may."

She wandered out onto the balcony, and Teldank brought lunch to her. She sat at a small round table staring out onto the gardens. Suddenly Mike bounded up her steps and plunked down in the seat opposite her. Jan's face lit up.

"What a wonderful surprise!" she exclaimed getting up and slipping her arms around his neck. "What do I owe this mid-day visit to?"

"I need a moment of peace and quiet," Mike said wrapping his arms about her waist. "The representatives from the principalities argue constantly and that furry secretary of mine is a nag."

Jan pulled him closer until his head rested against her breasts and he could hear her heart beating. "So you came over for some TLC?"

"Mm, you bet. I could stay here like this all day."

"Can you?" she asked hopefully as she pulled away, unfastened his shirt and massaged his neck and shoulders.

"Unfortunately no," he said taking her hands in his and stopping her. "In a few minari I'll be meeting with the Science Minister for a report on the state of research and development."

Jan winced thinking of what she had observed that morning.

Mike pulled her onto his lap and drew her close.

"If you only knew…." she began then stopped abruptly at the

sight of Teldank's whiskered face in the kitchenette window.

Mike had not heard, however, and was more intent on a long, deep kiss to help refill his low reservoirs. Jan pushed recent events aside and returned his kiss with a hunger of her own. Just when she felt she could hold her breath no longer, Mike's Molluc secretary, Tandk, waddled up the steps chirping and squeaking all the way. Mike pulled away from her and glared at the Molluc.

"Your meeting is in ten minari," Tandk dutifully reminded him.

"You know, I'm not an irresponsible child," Mike retorted. "I am watching the time."

"Just doing my job," Tandk muttered. "Just doing my job."

"Then wait for me on my balcony."

Tandk hastily scurried down the steps waiting impatiently at the bottom.

"Time to go?" Jan asked.

"Sorry," Mike said easing her off his lap. He kissed her cheek. "See you later," he added then descended the steps, once more bristling at his secretary's sharp outburst.

Jan followed unwilling to let him go so soon. She bounded down the steps after him, grabbed his arm, spun him around and kissed him hard on the lips. He slipped his arms around her waist once more.

Finally she pulled away and whispered in his ear, "You have to have something good to think about this afternoon."

A flush crept over him and he squeezed her tight. "Thanks. Wish I had this all the time."

She watched till he had disappeared through the door of his apartment then went back into her own. After a running session on her treadmill in which she managed to set a new stamina record, she lay down for a quick nap. She kept a watchful eye on her Molluc attendant that afternoon and, when Teldank left to return to her own village, Jan stealthily followed. Tonight she would meet the Mollucan.

Chapter 33

Jan hung back in the shadows as several Mollucs joined Teldank and slipped into one of their secret tunnels. Quickly, before the entrance could close back up, Jan squeezed inside and followed the dancing pinpoint of light up ahead. Several times she caught her foot on cracks in the floor and stumbled. Each time she remained perfectly still for a while hoping the Mollucs had not heard her.

Suddenly she hit a damp spot on the floor, slid and fell facedown with a loud thud and an "Ouch!" Ahead, the group of Mollucs stopped and turned.

"What was that?" Tandk squeaked.

"We have been followed," another said.

Teldank elbowed her way to the end and gasped. "Janielle. Why?"

Jan sat up and peered through the darkness at her. "I need to see your king, Teldank. I'm sorry. I wouldn't have done this if I weren't convinced that the need is urgent. Please, take me with you tonight."

"Quentasians are forbidden on our home paths," one stout little Molluc insisted.

“I’m not Quentasian, “Jan countered. “I’m from Earth.”

“A mere technicality.”

“But she does wear the Star Ring,” Teldank reminded them as it flashed a bright blue in the dark tunnel.

Her comrades were in a quandary.

“We must take this up with our Mollucan,” replied the stout one. “Come.”

They shoved Jan in between them and hurried on. After many twists, turns and dips, they came at last to a homey, beehive-like, underground city. The little group hustled Jan before their King at once.

“This woman followed us on our paths, Your Majesty,” the chorused bowing with their noses practically touching the ground.

“She is the chosen of the Crown Prince of Quentas, and she wears the Star Ring,” Teldank explained. “She is the one I have told you about.”

Jan looked at her attendant in shock.

“Yes, so I see,” replied the old, graying Molluc from his great, carved seat near the fire. Its flickering light caused shadows to dance across his wrinkled face, while his body remained wrapped in a blanket of shadow. “All but Teldank may go.”

The others hastily backed from the room, while Jan and Teldank remained before him.

He eyed the young woman from Earth with bright, beady eyes, his moustache twitching now and then.

"Ye-es, I can see what Teldank has meant about you," he said at last.

"Begging your pardon, Your Majesty, but just what would that be."

"That you are indeed an intelligent woman, not given to deceit. Your mind is like a waterfall; it never stops thinking. Your will is like rock; solid and determined. Your heart is like the ground; yielding and nurturing and big enough for all you were meant to do."

Jan stood in awe of this unusual assessment of her person. "Does this mean that you will help me?" she asked.

“Possibly…possibly. First you must tell me your plan.”

“Yes, Teldank told me you would want me to have devised a plan.”

The Mollucan nodded.

"To be honest, I've only begun to think about what I could do," she replied. "Until Teldank showed me what lay behind all of those locked doors in the complex, I didn't have a clue. Now, however, an idea is taking shape."

"Yes?" the Mollucan said in a voice filled with infinite patience.

"Our people need more resources, safer paths, and stronger lines of communication between principalities and bases," Jan began. "We need to locate the bases that have been cut off for so long, and we need to bring the peoples of Quentas under a single governing body. Those are the goals."

The Mollucan nodded. "But how can you accomplish these things. You are but one lone woman with no powers. Outside of the Royal Family you are feared and mistrusted."

Jan stared at the fire that burned on the hearth. "I realize my position, Your Majesty. Believe me, I am all too painfully aware of how I am perceived. I recognize that I can do nothing on my own, which is exactly why I need your help. The only way to contact the bases that have been cut off is to use the hidden paths. By using tunneled routes, instead of surface routes, safety would be increased for the raiding parties that go out, and we could increase our supplies that way."

Jan paused then continued quietly. "I can't tell Ihue my ideas because he's so afraid for my well-being that his own ability to think and act clearly would be impaired. He doesn't know that his own people consider me their enemy, and knowing it would only make him angry and bitter."

Her face took on a dark, brooding expression. "What I would like to do, with your permission," she said looking respectfully to the Mollucan, "is to become part of these raiding parties…a leader. Only I would want to have permission to lead my parties on the hidden paths that the Saracens are ignorant of."

The old Mollucan stared at her long and hard. Jan could see his silver-flecked bewhiskered face studying her intently; his eyes pierced right through hers. Finally he drew a deep breath.

"There is a secret group…a group loyal only to the throne of the High King. They are called the Elitists," he said. "I will give you welcome to use all the paths our people delve once the following contingencies have been fulfilled. You must become a leader of these Elitists. One of our guides will take you to their commanders' quarters, but from there you will enter alone, and you will pass all the tests without our assistance. Once you earn the leadership rank of the Elitists, seek me again. The ways of our paths will be opened to you at that time. Until then, you will not speak of our meeting, not even to the High King."

"I swear I will speak of our meeting to no one," Jan replied.

Satisfied, the Mollucan clapped his furry paws together and a small Molluc page came and showed Jan to a room for the night. Very early the next morning, Teldank woke her.

"Elitist runners are arriving. You must follow one to the Underground if you hope to enter."

Jan rose quickly having slept in her clothes and slipped outside her small room. A thin, wiry Molluc waited in the shadows. He leapt up as soon as he saw her and took off in a flash with Jan struggling to keep up. After a half-hour or more, they squeezed through a secret doorway into a restricted fortress corridor. The Molluc pressed himself flat against the wall motioning for her to do the same. A girl in dark clothing leapt from a side corridor and took off. The Molluc sprinted after her.

"Who is she?" Jan whispered having observed her strange clothing.

"An Elitist runner. I know no more."

The Molluc stopped before the door the girl had just passed through. "I go no further. May the Star guide you." He bowed before hastily disappearing.

Jan slipped quietly through the door, caught a glimpse of the girl they had seen, and followed her into a large learning center. She gazed about in amazement and confusion until, minutes later, she backed into the very girl she had been trailing. To her surprise, the runner instantly grappled with her.

"Who are you?" the girl demanded fiercely.

"I am Lady Janielle, Prince Ihue's betrothed. I suggest you release me."

"Prove it!" the girl challenged.

"Let go of my arms and I will," Jan countered.

"And let you get away? Huh!"

"Then check my right hand for the Ring."

The girl wrenched Jan's arm around painfully letting her go in displeasure when she spotted the Ring. "So you are."

"Am I free to go now, or do you plan to hold me for interrogation?" Jan asked stiffly.

"That is not up to me. Commander Behran will have to decide that."

The girl grabbed Jan's elbow and shoved her down the hall toward a cluster of offices. She knocked on a door then entered pushing Jan before her.

"Elitist Mara, what have you found here? A troublemaker?" the man behind the desk asked. Though in his mid thirties, his hair was already beginning to thin.

"She is a trespasser, sirha."

"Not one of ours?"

"No, sirha."

The dark-haired, mustached man looked Jan over carefully. A spark from the Ring caught his eye, and he stared at it in shock. He rose from his desk, took Jan's hand and held it up for Mara to see.

"Do-you-see-this-Ring?" he demanded.

"Yes, sirha," she replied nervously.

"I suggest that, should you ever meet out visitor again, you treat her with far greater respect." He released Jan's hand.

"But, sirha, she followed me and…."

"Then perhaps you should retrain, Mara. If this woman could follow you so easily, think of what a Saracen could do. You are dismissed."

The girl turned and hurried out the door. Meanwhile, Commander Behran offered Jan a seat. Quickly he pressed the comm-link button on his desk.

"So," he said eyeing her intently, "we meet at last. I never expected to have the privilege, if a privilege it is. You have a lot of explaining to do, while I try to determine what I have on my hands here – friend or enemy."

Jan stared at him suddenly realizing just how much trouble she was in. She rubbed her sweaty palms on her tunic and swallowed hard then lifted her chin and looked the Commander straight in the eye, ready for the worst.

"I'll answer whatever I can, Commander," she said beginning the face-off.

"Then start by telling me who sent you to spy on us?" he demanded. "Was it the Prince?"

"No, no one sent me. I came on my own."

"Then, just how did you learn about us?" he asked leaning forward on his desk.

"One of Ihue's cousins received word that her betrothed had been killed while we were on the ship that brought us here."

Behran's eyes darkened. "And what did she tell you?"

"Only that her betrothed was in the Underground and that it was top-secret."

"Then how did you find us?" he pressed.

"A couple of days ago I toured the complex. I couldn't help but notice all the doors marked 'Restricted.' Restrictions and locked doors make me very curious."

"So, you decided to find out what lay behind those locked doors?"

"Essentially," she replied not flinching under his steely gaze.

"Well, then. What can I do for you?" Behran asked with a conciliatory smile.

"You could satisfy my curiosity," she promptly suggested.

He eased back resting his elbows on the arms of his chair and steepling his fingers under his chin. "I can try," he said nodding for her to continue.

"Who are the Elitists?"

Behran studied her intently before replying. "They are a hand-picked group of young people, mostly around your age, who train for and carry out the most difficult guerrilla warfare against the Saracens."

"Then why all the secrecy? Why doesn't Prince Ihue know about them?"

"They are strictly a covert corps."

"Obviously," Jan replied. "But even on Earth, each country's leaders are at least aware of the covert corps in their nation and the objectives of their missions."

“Let’s just say it is for his own protection,” Behran said. “The Saracens think that there are just isolated pockets of resistance rather than an organized force. We would like to keep it that way.”

Jan bristled. “Commander, I truly hope you meant something other than what you said, because what I heard made me think you’re afraid the Prince would betray his own people.”

Behran blanched.

“How would the Saracens learn of the Elitists from him,” she pressed, “unless he marched out to them and announced it over a loudspeaker?”

“It is, uh, a little more complicated than that.”

“Oh, I realize,” Jan said narrowing her eyes, “because what you’re actually doing is protecting your own interests. You already know he’d be furious if he ever found out that instead of making progress during his exile on Earth, you’ve lost ground and have nearly lost the war. The resistance has nearly collapsed and he has returned to rescue a bunch of losers.”

“Wh-where did you get that information?” Behran sputtered.

“That I can’t tell you. But I’m right, aren’t I, Commander? Quentas has nearly lost this war?”

For a moment he held her gaze then looked away.

“I thought so.”

“So, what do you want? A surrender?”

“I want to join the Elitists,” Jan replied evenly.

Behran looked back at her and laughed. “Oh, yes. You want to join this band of losers. Now just why should I admit you, an alien, into our Elitist corps? Why would you risk your life and my neck for Quentas?”

“Because one day soon, your people are going to become my people,” Jan replied. “I want to know what’s really happening to them. If we’re doing so miserably in here, I can’t even imagine how desperate those people out there must be. They-need-help.”

He set his jaw.

“Plus, I need a way to prove to your people that I am not like the Saracens,” she continued. “Not only is it something I want, but Ihue needs your people to accept me. If they don’t, he’ll be crushed. You can forget about Quentas then, because he will no longer be thinking about your people.”

Behran placed his hands flat on his desk. "I appreciate these sentiments, but I cannot admit you.""

"And I'm determined to enter, somehow," Jan replied, her blue eyes flashing with determination. "This corps would be the best way for me to both prove myself and to help your people."

"Do us all a favor. Go-home. Return to Earth."

Jan shook her head. "If I do, Prince Ihue will follow. Then all your hopes and dreams will be gone. Besides I can't. Our ship nearly ran out of fuel, and I don't think you have another stockpile waiting."

Behran winced.

"Thought not. Quentas is stuck with me."

"Then return to the Royal Suite and forget you ever heard about the Elitists. If you become a model of complacency, you will at least win a few hearts."

Jan shook her head again. "That's just the problem. I can't forget. I can't forget the young people my own age who are wounded and dying and have run out of hope. I can't forget Ihue and all the dreams he has for his home. I can't forget that there are real people out there, just like me, who are lonely and scared. If I leave here, they'll haunt my dreams by night and my thoughts by day.

"If you send me out of here without giving me a chance to join the Elitists, then I'll march straight to Ihue and tell him all I know. I won't stop with the Elitists. I'll tell him just how severe the shortages are, how many people are dying and that we have all but lost this ill-fought war. Whatever his reaction is to the news, I know it's the consequences that concern you most."

Behran stared into her cold blue eyes that had turned almost steely grey. "You really would do that?"

"You'd better believe it."

"Then you leave me no alternative," Behran said reaching for his compu slate. He activated it and scanned the work calendar. "There is a physical stamina and agility test tomorrow that will be three suntari long."

"I'll be there!"

Behran let out a sigh of defeat. "Be here at Suntar Five. If you can pass the tests, you will be admitted as a trainee," he said, a smile barely evident on his face.

Jan swallowed hard as she rose and left.

Moments later, a screen rose form a slot in Behran's desk and General Adar's face came into view.

"Well, Behran, what do you think of her?"

"I do not know, General. I cannot get a clear sense of her purpose, and I would love to know how she found her way here."

"Could she possibly be a Saracen spy?"

"I almost do not see how. Their armed forces are comprised solely of men, and they have rarely sent out female androids because they are so defective. She is not event the right height or build for a Saracen. IF she is a spy, then she is either a masterpiece or has been hired from elsewhere."

"Maybe the masterpiece," Adar said. "Maybe she is the one tool that will finally break us."

Behran looked uncomfortable at the thought.

Adar scratched his chin. "Any possibility she can pass the tests tomorrow?"

"It's possible."

Adar drummed his fingers on his desk. "Do we dare trust her?"

Behran shrugged. "I would rather have her where I can watch her every move, than wonder where she is and what she is doing. In the ranks, one false move and we will have her."

Adar rubbed his chin thoughtfully. "And if she is not a spy?"

"Then we will have gained ourselves a very valuable ally."

Chapter 34

Early the next morning, after eating the special breakfast Teldank prepared for her, Jan retraced her steps to the Underground. She quietly slipped into the test center with the other Quentasian hopefuls – thirty in all. Nervously she moved to the end of the line and waited.

An Elitist walked down the line handing out brown, one-piece uniforms. Commander Behran entered through a side door and strolled to the center of the room.

"You have just been handed work suits. You have five minari to change and make your way to the gymnasium for the trials," he announced.

Jan followed the others to a locker room changing as quickly as she could. Her legs shook and her palms were extra sweaty. Finally, she slipped through a doorway into the bustling gymnasium just as another Elitist blew a whistle to signal the start of the trials.

Jan watched as those ahead of her began timed sit-ups. The plump young man ahead of her collapsed before his sixty seconds were up.

"Next!" the Elitist shouted.

Jan stretched out on the mat and began. The Elitist stared at his stopwatch then clicked the button. He entered her score on the compu slate and noted her position in the standings.

"Pass on!" he shouted waving her away. "Next!"

She hurried to line up with others who were facing a wall on which a net had been hung. Another Elitist stood nearby slate in hand.

"We take the first five to reach the top."

Jan glanced down the line and winced. "Fifteen! That's only one-third."

"Climb!" the Elitist yelled.

She dashed to the net with the others and began hauling herself up. Almost before she knew it, she had reached the top. A red flag popped out of the wall, which she instinctively grabbed. She held the flag in her teeth as she made her way back to the floor.

The Elitist took her flag, making a notation on his slate. "Pass on!"

Almost unable to believe her good fortune thus far, Jan followed the other four to the next test. On the floor, parallel lines had been drawn running a little over fifty feet.

"This is the agility trial," a female Elitist announced. "You must jump from one line to the other and so on down the line. If your foot goes over either line, one secondari will be added to your score. A laser will count the number of jumps you make."

Jan moved into place.

"Go!"

A push from behind caused her to fall. Her hand penetrated the beam.

"Move it!" the Elitist yelled.

Jan pushed herself to her feet and began jumping down the line. She crouched off to one side afterwards panting.

"Pass on!" the girl shouted waving her away.

Jan nodded and trotted off.

"This trial tests speed," announced a tall, wiry man. "You will run to the line and back till the yellow light flashes. I will take the top five scores."

Jan crouched near the starting line. The man dropped his arm and they took off. Jan ran until her temples pounded and her calves ached; back and forth between the lines. At last the yellow light flashed, and she collapsed onto the floor.

The man pointed to her. "Pass on!"

Gasping, she crawled to her feet and moved on to the last trial. Her heart sank when she saw the line of treadmills that had been set up in the middle of the gymnasium floor.

"My legs feel like Jell-O now," she groaned. "How will I ever make it through this one?"

She watched the group ahead of her as they concluded their endurance run, then leaned her head back against the wall and closed her eyes.

"Next!"

That now-too-familiar call jolted her, and she staggered numbly toward a treadmill.

"You will run for twenty-minari," the Elitist timer said. "During that time, the tension will be altered at random by computer to simulate various terrains. We will take all who finish." He looked at his stopwatch then lowered his arm to begin the grueling twenty minute test.

The girl to Jan's right collapsed on the first hill simulation. Jan grit her teeth and pressed on. A young man to the far left dropped during the quagmire simulation. Jan stumbled but kept on. Fast, slow, hard or mush; her legs burned and shook, but she did not give up.

Suddenly all the other treadmills stopped. While the others gratefully dropped to the floor, Jan continued. Anger welled up inside her, and she glanced toward the viewing booth. She spotted Commander Behran and General Adar glaring at her. A spark flared from the Ring matched only by the fiery light burning in her eyes. The spark leapt straight from the Ring toward the two men then zipped back and arced over the treadmill. The machine jolted to a stop in an instant, and she climbed off.

"Congratulations," Behran commended them over the loudspeaker. "You are now Elitist trainees. Your schedules are listed on the computer discs being distributed. I expect to see all of you in the training gym at Suntar Six tomorrow morning."

Jan turned to leave but an Elitist stopped her. "Commander Behran wants to see you in his office."

Nodding, she stumbled out the door, into the office complex and finally to Behran's office. She wearily sank into a chair, closed her eyes, and waited in the cool quiet until he returned and activated the lights.

"Now," he said sitting behind his desk, "your case presents us with some unusual problems."

"Such as?" Jan asked opening her eyes.

"Such as, what would happen if you were captured or killed on a run? How would we explain that?"

Jan remained silent.

"It seems we must protect you against that. Therefore, you will only be sent out with our most reliable run leaders," he announced.

She nodded. "However, I want no special treatment in training itself."

"And you will get none, I assure you."

Jan stared at him tacitly.

"The second problem is your residence. You will have to remain in the Royal Suite rather than live with the other trainees."

"Prince Ihue would certainly wonder where I was if I didn't."

"Exactly. Furthermore, the Prince may occasionally demand your attention taking you away from training and runs. Under these circumstances, send word to me through General Adar or Lord Dehan. As head of Science Research, he also works for the Underground. However, you are not to give your whereabouts to any other person."

Jan nodded.

"Training begins tomorrow. I will see you then."

Thus dismissed, Jan returned to the locker room, changed and trudged back to the Royal Suite. She slipped into her apartment where Teldank waited.

"Well?" the Molluc asked searching Jan's weary face.

"I made it," she breathed slumping onto a chair. "They weren't going to accept me, I'm sure, but this Ring seems to have a mind of its own." She kicked off her shoes. "My training starts at Suntar Six, so get me up early. I just hope I can even move."

"I have a hot herbal bath all ready," Teldank invited. "It is a Molluc remedy for sore muscles."

"Oh, that sounds so good. Help me up, Teldank. Otherwise I'll have to crawl to the bathroom."

With Teldank's aid, Jan got up and shuffled into the bathroom. She stripped and sank into the steaming, bubbly water where she lay breathing in the minty scent of the herbs.

She sat out on her balcony to eat supper and was surprised to see Will walking over. His face wore a dark expression as he climbed her steps and sat down across from her.

"You know," Jan said.

"Yes."

"You're angry."

"Worried," he corrected.

She nodded.

"Do you know what you're getting yourself into?"

She took a deep breath. "Yes and no. I can't tell you where all of this is going to lead me."

"You've spoken with the Mollucan," he said watching her face carefully.

"Will, please don't ask questions about things I can't talk about," she replied glancing away.

Will finally smiled. "If you're under his protection, then you'll be all right."

Jan raised her eyebrows and looked back at him.

"All right, this is the plan. If Michael comes looking for you, you work with me now in the Science Labs and sometimes for Elira. We'll both cover for you."

She nodded. "You know, Adar doesn't trust me."

Will sat back with a surprised look on his face.

"He and Commander Behran were watching me during the last test and weren't going to let me finish."

"Maybe he just wanted to be certain of your commitment," Will speculated.

"You should have seen the reaction from the Ring."

Will frowned.

"It's a very uncomfortable feeling to be considered the enemy."

Will patted her hand. "You will win them over, Jan. I know it won't be easy, but in the end you'll see."

She watched him leave, sighed and went inside to bed.

Starting the next morning, Jan learned that novice training was physically oriented, aimed at increasing strength, endurance, speed and agility and lasted for two hours each day. Afterwards, special training concentrated on rock-climbing and jungle warfare. Specially designed areas of the cavern and its underground river simulated all the temperature zones and terrains for survival training.

Eventually afternoons were filled with classes in cryptography and the tribal dialects as well as customs, mannerisms and clothing particular to each. Tribal dances were gradually added to the folk lessons.

Six weeks later Jan's class re-ran through the testing ground. Jan passed easily this time and was assigned to an Elitist officer for her first run. She was surprised when Marla approached her with two other trainees. They walked outside once the meeting ended.

"I am shocked to see you here!" Marla exclaimed. "What made you want to be an Elitist."

"It's a long story beginning with I'm an alien and ending with I'm under suspicion of being an enemy," Jan replied. "How have you been?"

"Busy. This is the toughest job on the planet. Is everything covered with Ihue?"

Jan nodded.

"Now to figure out how to cover that Ring," Marla said.

"Already taken care of," Jan replied showing Marla her hand. "Due to general sentiment against me, they had Dehan disguise it for training as well."

"What about your hair? We have no blond Quentasians."

"Dehan devised a special hair color that I wash in before going on a run and wash out with a special shampoo when I get back."

"Good, then you had better use it tonight. We will be going out tomorrow."

Jan said good-bye and headed back to her apartment.

Over the next few weeks, Marla took her small band out on message runs posed as a troop of entertainers. They jolted along heavily-guarded topside roads, stopping at each Quentasian village and town. Each night the troop went to work as huge bonfires burst into flames in the center of the town square. Then the four young people would leap high into the air whirling and dancing about the flames.

Villagers would eagerly gather under the watchful eye of Saracen soldiers whose weapons were ever at their sides. When all eyes were trained on the troop, the girls would move closer to the crowd mesmerizing the people with their more intricate, sensual dances. But, from the corners of their eyes, they would watch the men stealthily load the wagon.

On their final trip home through the foothills of the Mozern Mountains, they suddenly found themselves faced with a Saracen roadblock.

"Halt!" the Saracen leader shouted.

Gerhan, who sat driving the work beasts, reigned them in.

"Who goes there?"

Marla crawled onto the buckboard beside Gerhan. "We are Gensies, sirha. Our papers." She shoved a packet at the Saracen.

The other Saracens leapt into the cart dragging Jan and Hushan from the wagon. They threw their belongings to the ground while the "Gensies" waited in tense silence.

The Saracen leader eyed the foursome suspiciously. "Supplies have mysteriously vanished throughout the valley this past week."

Jan suddenly spotted a familiar-looking plant. She edged over for a closer look.

"You would not happen to know anything about it, would you?" the Saracen asked stepping over to her.

She plucked a sprig of leaves before meeting his gaze. "No, sirha. No supplies except our food. We dance to entertain…see?" She whirled about in classic Gensy fashion while crushing the leaves of the plant as she twirled. The Saracen blinked staring about him uncertainly. He turned ordering his men away.

"We will be watching you," he warned still blinking his eyes in semi-confusion.

That night, however, the cart slipped out of sight during a torrential downpour. Inside the Underground, they unloaded the largest shipment of supplies in months; all were hidden in a double false bottom.

Two weeks later, they made another run, taking to the Eastern plateau where the monstrous Stonbots lurked. Each was the size of a large tree. As they stepped out onto the plateau, three attacked the runners with a hail of laser fire. As the Elitists ran, they leapt and somersaulted out of harm's way until they suddenly found themselves on the brink of a high cataract. Its frothing waters plunged into a deep, clear pool below.

"Dive!" Marla yelled leaping forward into space.

Gerhan and Hushan followed immediately, but Jan remained on the edge, rooted to the spot and paralyzed with fear as she stared at the long drop and the frothing water. A laser bolt hit the rock at her feet startling her. She glanced back then leapt into mid-air as the Stonbot fired again. She screamed the entire way down until she hit the water like a boulder and sank far below the surface.

A hand grabbed her wrist. Jan opened her eyes to see Marla gesturing for her to follow. They swam to the bottom and into the mouth of a long, dark tunnel. Finally, the two girls burst above the surface of the water gasping for air. They tread water in the midst of the pool in the Well of Souls.

Gerhan and Hushan grabbed their hands and hauled them onto the rim of the well where they lay panting.

"H-how often d-do you d-do that?" Jan finally stammered.

"Only when we have to," Marla replied. "Next time you will be prepared."

"I'll never be prepared," Jan muttered shivering at the thought of that precipitous leap.

Strangely, that evening in his bed at Mozern, Mike tossed and turned, his pillow soaked with sweat. Bright lights flashed past him as his legs pumped to send him racing over slick ground or leaping from wet rock to wet rock. Suddenly he stood at the edge of a falls; next thing he knew he was plummeting through the air, only to land in boiling, churning waters. It seemed that his lungs would burst for want of air as he clawed at the water around him.

He awoke sitting straight up in bed and shook his head to clear it. "That dream was too vivid to be just a nightmare," he muttered to himself. "But whose life am I tapping into? I could have sworn I felt Jan's presence in that dream. But that's impossible! She's in bed only an apartment away."

He sank back into his pillow unable to shake the thought that she was in danger.

Chapter 35

Three days after Jan's initiation to the Well of Souls, Commander Behran solemnly handed out the solo assignments to the Rank One recruits. When he got to Jan, he handed her a sealed envelope saying, "Take this urgent message to Commander Terin of Metara Five. You have seven suntarini in which to complete your mission. Now go with all skill."

Obediently, Jan snuck out slipping unseen past Saracen outposts by day and huddling in dark gullies by night. By the third day, she had entered Metara Five.

"Take me to Commander Terin," she demanded wearily.

The guard who had confronted her, whisked her through a maze of corridors to the office complex. He led her into a room with a low desk behind which sat a short, plump, balding man. She handed him the message she had concealed on her person and sank into a chair.

"So, Commander Behran congratulates me on my fortieth year of life," Terin chuckled.

"What? Do you mean I sat in gullies for two nocturini and three suntarini to deliver that?"

"Yes, and you made it with time to spare. I do not celebrate for another suntarin."

Jan rose to leave shaking her head in disbelief. She retraced her path even quicker than before marching straight into Behran's office the moment she had returned.

"Ah, Lady Janielle," he greeted. "So nice to see you have returned safely."

"Thanks, and Commander Terin adds his 'thanks.' His 'birthday' greeting arrived a suntarin early," she spat in disgust.

"Yes," Commander Behran said, "and if you remember your training in cryptography, a 'birthday' is especially important."

Jan thought for a moment then her eyes widened.

"That was a message upon which the seal of the High Throne of Quentas was affixed. Commander Terin's 'thanks' was his pledge of allegiance."

She took in the importance of the message she had just delivered. "I'm sorry I forgot its importance. Guess I have nothing to complain about."

"And neither have we for the moment. Not only has the message been delivered, but the messenger returned which proved her loyalty and she returned in record time. There was the fear that the next time we saw her, she would be found trading secrets in enemy camps."

A chill went through her. "So this was a double test?"

Behran nodded. "You were shadowed all the way, and I have your Rank leader's report on your run. You are clean for now."

"You still doubt me?"

"Less than I did but yes."

She nodded then rose to leave.

"I have not dismissed you yet."

"I'm dismissing myself for the present," she replied walking out the door.

"Just be back here in two suntarini," he called after her.

With her heart heavy, Jan rushed back to her quiet, lonely apartment. Teldank met her inside with a flurry of excitement, not having expected her for two more days. After a refreshing shower and a change of clothes, Jan wandered out onto her balcony. Hopeful of catching Mike at home, she strolled along the trail that linked their balconies. Mike's angry voice reached her ears, and she spotted him arguing with Tandk.

"I told you to cancel that meeting and I meant it," Mike yelled and slammed his door.

He stalked out onto his balcony, and she bounded up the stairs toward him.

"Mike!" she called running up to him and throwing her arms about his neck.

He caught her up in his arms and swung her around. "If you aren't a surprise for sore eyes. I don't get to see you nearly enough," he murmured giving her a hungry kiss.

"I know. It seems we're always missing each other."

"Especially now that you're helping out Will and mother."

Jan's face went blank for a moment, but she quickly covered. "Oh, well, I told you I couldn't just sit around in a hole in the ground and do nothing."

"Well, I'm glad you're at least occupied in a safe place," Mike said giving her a tight squeeze.

She grimaced at his words. "If he ever knew, he'd kill me," she thought, "or at least be furiously angry."

"Hey, I don't have a lot of time right now. How would you like to watch me at weapons practice tomorrow morning?" he asked. "I can guarantee you've never seen some of the toys I get to play with."

"Sure," Jan replied brightening. "Just make certain someone comes to wake me. On my days off I have a tendency to sleep forever."

"It's a deal. I'll send Tandk over." Mike kissed her again, said good-bye, and headed inside.

The next morning she heard Tandk's shrill voice as Teldank tried to quiet him. Jan got up, threw a bathrobe on and poked her head into the lounge.

"It's ok, Teldank. I wanted him to come get me."

Teldank bustled into the kitchenette muttering under her breath.

"You have twenty minari, mirsta," Tandk informed her.

Jan hopped in and out of a quick shower, gulped down breakfast and met Mike in the common lounge. After a hasty kiss good morning, they headed toward the gymnasiums. Mike headed into the locker room area, while Tandk led her to the viewing booths on an upper level. They entered one, sat up close to the smoked glass and waited in anticipation.

Below them, Mike strode across the training gym. A coach followed carrying a large, smooth white cylinder.

"What is that thing?" Jan asked as Mike took the weapon from his trainer.

"It is an energy amplifier," Tandk replied. "Some members of the Royal Family use it to augment their innate powers. Watch."

The gymnasium lights dimmed and holographic images sprouted up all about Mike. A labyrinth of walls appeared. As soon as it was completely laid out, his trainer nodded and Mike edged inside.

Stealthily he snuck along glancing about him as he went. A holographic enemy darted out at him, and Mike hastily ducked back. Pointing his finger, he moved back out and changed the image of the enemy into a bush. After a powerful blast through his weapon, the change became permanent.

Mike cautiously crept around it continuing through the maze. He checked each twist and turn before moving forward. Suddenly another image crept up behind him. Mike spun around, blocking the attack with his weapon, before somersaulting backwards out of the way.

He sprinted down the next long stretch, only to be surprised by a third image that sprang at him from atop a wall. Mike leapt aside just in time, rolling to a better vantage point, then he fired a bolt of sizzling power through his weapon that momentarily blinded the two observers in the booth.

"Wow!" Jan exclaimed. "That was amazing! That thing must increase his powers by at least ten times!"

"It also holds much of his own energy in reserve," Tandk explained. "Since it only amplifies small bursts of power at a time, it keeps him energized for the next discharge. Once he has mastered it, it will augment his powers by at least forty times."

Impressed, Jan headed back down to catch Mike as he left the locker room. He gave her a quick hug when he came out, then guided her along beside him.

"So, what did you think?"

Her eyes shone mischievously. "That you look great in a uniform."

He caught her in the ribcage tickling her briefly. "About how I use that weapon, silly."

Jan stopped giggling and grew serious. "I am very impressed. Tandk was telling me how it works. I can think of dozens of instances where having you present with that weapon would be invaluable."

"Oh and how would you know?" he asked eyeing her curiously.

"Um, from the stories the guerillas bring back," she replied glancing away. "When I work with your mother, I get to hear quite a few."

They reached the council chambers where they would part.

"I just hope that I actually get to use it someday," Mike said. "Practice is all well and good, but it's a weapon that could do some damage to the Saracens."

He gave her a quick kiss then entered the council chamber. Jan heaved a sigh of relief.

Two days later she began her training in explosives and espionage. At the end of each week's training, they infiltrated the Quentasian countryside targeting key Saracen outposts. Jan returned from her fourth run totally depressed.

Teldank handed her a cup of tea as she sank into a chair. "This run did not go well?"

"We completed the mission."

"Then why are you distressed, mirsta?"

Jan stared at the opposite wall not having touched her tea. "I've watched four of my friends get killed in the last four weeks and seven more are in the Med-Unit. Two more girls were captured on this run, and Marla's doubtful we'll ever see them again. I feel sick all over, Teldank. At night I break out into a cold sweat, too afraid to sleep and even more afraid to lie awake."

Teldank blinked a couple of times as she studied Jan. "I am sorry about your friends. But you must remember...you have a chance to make a difference, to lessen the risk for all."

Jan merely sank deeper into her chair. "I just hope I actually make Rank so I can."

The next week, she joined her squad as they were briefed for their trial mission.

"The main Saracen communications network covers the Sasawn Valley west of Hellsman Peak," Behran informed them. "Your mission is to close down this network and reduce the Saracens to messenger runs and fly-overs. That will make them more vulnerable to our attacks. Do your job, but be careful," he added emphatically. "We may need that network down, but we need you to return safely and whole even more."

The group of fifteen headed out. They split up scouting out and skirting around roadblocks. They climbed Hellsman Peak and had rejoined in the foothills above the Sasawn Valley when, suddenly, Saracens leapt at them from every side.

"We will hold them off," the green leader telepathed. "Take a small group and go on."

Marla, the grey leaded, grabbed Jan, Gerhan and a girl named, Tanza, upon receiving this message. As soon as she saw an opening in the fighting, they dashed through and kept on running.

"Hurry!" Marla urged as they crept up on the expansive target sit. "Let's blow this thing and get back to help the others. Gerhan, take the sector towards Thira I's rise to alpha; Tanza, take the sector towards Endel's rise to gamma; Jan, take the sector toward Thira I's set to omega. I will take the sector toward Endel's set. Set your explosives and leave. We will rendezvous at the ambush. Now, move!"

The foursome snuck inside the complex creeping silently between the girders that held up the antennas and the buildings. At each stop, they set a new explosive. Soon fleeting figures dashed from the grounds. Suddenly there was a rumble and a ground-shaking boom. A fire-ball lit the sky.

Back at the ambush, they stealthily approached from all four corners. The runners met in the center staring about them in horror. Their friends lay scattered across the ground smoke curling up from the fatal laser wounds they sported.

"Too late!" Marla cried. "We were too late!"

The others glanced about anxiously. Jan and Tanza checked some of the bodies for signs of life.

"Marla," Jan said. "Let's go! The Saracens haven't been gone long; the bodies are still warm. They'll be back for us, too."

"She is right," Tanza added.

"But I should have known. I should have felt it," Marla moaned.

She stared at their dead friends, frozen with shock. Finally Gerhan took her arm and pulled her along. They hid in a mountain cave straggling back to Mozern three days later.

As they sat before Behran in the conference room, no one spoke. All heads were bowed, their hands lying limply in their laps.

Eventually the Commander rose and cleared his throat. "Our loss this run is almost more than we can bear. The Saracens have discovered seven more of our routes over the past montar making runs more dangerous than ever. There is so little to say. Marla, you have earned a medal of honor; Tanza, Gerhan and Lady Janielle, you have all earned Rank Three with commendations. There will be a suntarin of mourning tomorrow for your comrades. Suntarin after, please meet in the library for Phase Four training."

Jan stumbled blindly back to her quarters and sank deeply into a chair.

Teldank stared gravely into her ashen face. "What can I do to help, mirsta?"

"Nothing, unless you can revive the dead." Jan took a deep, shuddering breath. "Out of fifteen runners, only four of us came back, Teldank. Somehow I was one of the lucky ones, but how much longer can that last? What happens if I don't come back one day? What if I end up on the ground with a smoking hole in my back? What would they tell Mike? What would happen to him? Am I trying too hard to prove myself?"

Teldank gazed at her pensively. "No one would blame you for quitting, mirsta. The risks are very high and rising. But what of your special opportunity to prevent such slaughter? Can you turn it down?"

Tears streamed down Jan's cheeks. "I-I don't know, Teldank. I j-just don't know. I'm scared that I'll go out and never come back or worse. If the Saracens ever captured me, they'd flaunt that in Mike's face and bring him to his knees. Even if he didn't give in to their demands, his spirit would be crushed; the whole rebellion would be destroyed. Is this opportunity really worth these risks?"

"Only you can decide," Teldank said quietly. "Just remember, you, and you alone, have been extended the Mollucan's offer. This chance will never come again."

Teldank watched Jan leave to wander the gardens in solitude. Two days later, Jan woke early; gone before her little maid had arrived.

Chapter 36

While Jan worried, Mike had mounting frustrations of his own to deal with. A new squadron of troops was ready for his inspection. While Jan was working on learning the techniques to earn Rank Four, he marched down the tunnel corridors between two military aides and strolled onto a large, subterranean parade ground. Row after row of young people stood rigidly at attention. They held their heads high raising their left hands to their right shoulders in salute as their Crown Prince passed by.

"They're so young," Mike whispered to General Attica who was on his right. "I taught students older than some of these soldiers." His eyebrows raised imperceptibly as he passed a thin, red-haired, freckle-faced boy of fifteen or sixteen.

"Many are your own age, Your Highness, but some," the general said with a nod toward the boy, "are much younger."

"But why?"

"These are all that are left to us."

"But what about the experienced fighters? Where are their fath...vadreri and unclas?" Mike persisted.

"Most were killed during the early resistance. Now, these young people flee to our centers to avoid capture and imprisonment in the mining pits. Those people too old to pose any real threat hold out as best as they can in the towns and on their farms. We work with what we have," the general explained helplessly.

Mike shook his head in dismay.

Several days later, after a grueling weapons drill, Tandk led him to one of the vehicle hangars. Mike was met by a flank of saluting fliers.

A burly man hurried forward to greet him. "Prince Ihue, so good of you to come, Your Highness! Commander Doberi at your service."

Mike nodded. "I understand there are some fighters for me to inspect."

"Right this way, Your Highness," the commander said gesturing toward the vehicle pit. "We have implemented our latest modifications and have reconstructed the crafts we had before the invasion."

He led Mike past sleek speeders standing on solid pedestals. "These are our finest Delna X land and air craft. They have been completely rebuilt and are at your disposal."

A pilot stood stiffly beside each craft a gleaming helmet tucked under one arm. As Mike strolled by, each one gave him a snappy salute. The commander followed beaming proudly.

"Would you care to sit in one, Your Highness? A pilot could explain its operating functions to you."

Mike glanced hastily to Tandk, who nodded slightly. "Uh...yes. Of course," he replied to his enthusiastic guide.

Commander Doberi led him to one of the highly polished speeders. The pilot saluted before stepping aside, allowing Mike access to the rungs mounted on the sides of the vessel. Mike took the steep climb in stride and swung himself into the cockpit. The young pilot clambered up beside him and nervously explained the vehicle's operations. "This lowers the safety restraints," the pilot said pressing a button and watching a padded harness encase Mike's shoulders.

"Once in place, we check fuel level, oil pressure, stabilizers, thrusters, boosters, and pulsers on this panel here," the pilot said leaning awkwardly across Mike to push some buttons that caused a series of lights to blink on the panel and messages to print out on a grid to Mike's left.

Mike squeezed against the seat as the pilot nearly fell into his lap. Embarrassed, the pilot righted himself then continued his explanation.

"When we have determined that all are functioning properly, we use the forward panel to operate the jet thrusters. They give us our lift and speed, while the pulsers correct stability and horizontal hold. Our engines and boosters combined give us a total speed of five hundred honti-a-suntar per spec."

Mike glanced dubiously at the craft.

"Over here are the weapons panel. Our magnamat, side-mounted blasters are designed to counterphase the Saracen's terra-shields. The explosions are great when we can get a hit." The young pilot laughed nervously, but his face quickly resumed its blank shield.

He reached overhead and pulled down a suspended visor.

"Our laser scanners track at over five honti. However, I have heard that a new scanner is being tested that may up that to ten. With that one, we would be able to hit the Saracens before they ever knew we were anywhere around."

Mike kept nodding his head politely while looking at the confusing sequence of panels. He placed his hands on the sides of the vehicle and scanned the inner workings, one grid at a time. Finally he thanked the pilot, hauled himself out of the cockpit, and shinnied to the ground. He scowled at Tandk.

"That thing is a piece of junk. It would fall apart in a light breeze," he telepathed.

The Molluc stared at him as the message registered, shook his head, and scurried toward the commander.

"What your pilot tells me is impressive," Mike said diplomatically.

"Nothing like the 'days gone past', of course, but they are the best we have. That one there is tops on our Delna X Squad."

Mike nodded before hastily taking leave of the beaming man.

Outside the hangar doors, Tandk scuttled along forcing Mike to jog to catch up.

"What is going on here?" Mike demanded. "If that's the top of the line, our forces are in big trouble. And why wasn't I given blueprints and specs to review before this inspection?" he asked grabbing the Molluc's ear between his thumb and forefinger. "I've never been so ill-prepared for anything in my whole life. I used to prepare for my university classes better than this. You made me look like a complete idiot out there."

"There is only one set of blueprints and the manufacturing staff needs them," Tandk squeaked. "Besides, they did not notice. Your presence lifted their morale."

"Is that all I'm good for?" Mike growled under his breath. "From now on I want you to schedule time for complete briefing before something like this. I will never go out there again when I've been rushed."

Looking up and catching a few curious glances from several passers-by, Mike slowed their pace. He released Tandk's fuzzy ear and the Molluc rubbed his smarting appendage. At that moment, Mike darted away through a crowd of Quentasian officials. Tandk uttered a cry of dismay and rapidly pursued the disappearing Prince.

Council meetings were going no more smoothly than were the tours and inspections. While a majority of the reachable principalities had sworn allegiance to the High Throne of Quentas extracting cooperation from them was far more difficult. Only the most senior officers recalled the days when all the principalities had acted under the sovereign authority of the High King. Most had no such memories to guide them. As a consequence, requests to more evenly distribute supplies and food were met with hostility and resistance.

Daily Mike listened to their bickering and mediated their arguments. Daily his frustration grew until he was reliving each council meeting in his sleep. On one such morning, he yelled "GENTLEMEN!" and sat bolt upright in bed just as his chamberlain, Ndak, knocked and entered. Both Prince and Molluc started in surprise.

"Headache?" Ndak asked once he head regained his composure.

Mike nodded as he swung his legs out of bed and held his head in his hands.

Ndak left and Tandk entered.

"Your schedule is full this morning," Tandk puffed.

"Lighten it," Mike demanded.

"But, Your Highness…." Tandk protested.

"No 'buts,' Tandk. I don't leave here till I can think straight, and with this migraine that will be quite a while. Oh, and check on that tour I wanted Jan to join me for. I want her cleared for it, and you can tell that to Adar."

Tandk sputtered as he backed from the room while Ndak entered with the medication.

After a while Mike dressed and took a stab at his breakfast. When that did not appeal to him, he went over to Jan's apartment and knocked at her kitchenette door. Teldank greeted him.

'Is Jan here?" he asked staring past the Molluc to search the inner rooms. "I wanted her to join me on a tour today."

"I am sorry, Your Majesty," Teldank replied with an awkward curtsy. "She rose early this morning to continue her work with Lord Dehan."

Mike drummed his fingers on the door jamb. "You'd think Will would give her some time off now and then. I'll have to speak to him later," he said under his breath. "When will she be back?" he asked the Molluc.

"Most likely sometime after dinner. But if she returns early, I will tell her you called for her."

He sighed. "Ok. If she's back by Suntar Eleven, have her meet me in the High Office Complex, Level Three."

Teldank bowed her head in acknowledgment and closed the door.

Meanwhile, Jan sat in the library, her head buried behind a viewer as she soaked in the contents of yet another map cartridge from the stack that lay beside her. Every day for weeks she would be studying maps, charts and the history of Quentas. At the end of the six weeks of Rank Four training there would be an extensive and detailed test to pass. As she absorbed the information from the latest tape, she heard the slow shuffle of feet behind her.

"Hello," said a weathered voice.

She glanced up at the wizened old man who beamed down at her.

"Forgive me for this intrusion, but I am Garik…the Research Librarian and Royal Historian. I could not help but notice the ring you wear." He took her hand to get a better look at the violet stone. "Lovely façade, but…." he said making a slight gesture that sent the cover tumbling, "yes, as I suspected, it is the Star Ring. You are the promised of the Crown Prince."

Jan blinked in astonishment.

"Are you part of the Royal Family?" she asked recognizing his royal powers.

"A very old member," he replied, "which is why I have taken notice of you. Come. I have something to show you that no one else may see," he said hobbling off.

Jan remained rooted to her seat, so he turned back to her.

"Come along. This is more valuable than anything you will ever glean there."

He moved his hands in a circular manner and Jan's eyes took on a glazed look. Hypnotically she rose and followed him. He passed a withered hand over a small, dome-shaped light on the wall. Immediately a wall panel slid back revealing a dusty secret room.

"Come," he urged beckoning to her. "In here are all the secrets of the Palatial City, plus the Sacred Paths or 'Elra.' Come see. They are for your eyes only."

With her eyes focused in a blank stare, Jan shuffled into the strange room. Garik gave her a throaty chuckle and he, Jan and the room all disappeared.

Wherever that little room was actually concealed within the library, Jan could not tell, for when she blinked her eyes, she was completely inside it; no exit was visible in any direction.

"On Quentas, only those directly connected to the High Throne may view these artifacts," Garik explained laying a dusty old book on a table before her. He reverently opened it, slowly and carefully turning its brittle yellow pages. "The paths you will find in these books will be the only paths that can possibly bring you to the Crown on the Hill alive." With a throaty chuckle, he hobbled off leaving Jan to wonder where he had disappeared to and to absorb the volumes of rare materials surrounding her.

Brow furrowed, Jan scanned the ancient maps and manuscripts. "He's right!" she thought. "This stuff is more precious than gold. But how will I ever learn all this and the maps I have to know for the tests, too?" She chewed on her lower lip. "If I get to the library an hour early each morning, and stay an hour or two late, I should be able to pick up a lot of this stuff. It'll be tough going, but there's nothing else for me to do. The more I know about this planet, the better off we'll all be."

Having decided that, Jan rose extra early and slept little for the next six weeks. During that time she learned all of the old road systems that belonged to the pre-Saracen empire, the present road system, plus the foot paths and trails that crisscrossed the planet. In her extra time, she learned about special secret and sacred paths that traveled beneath the palatial city and out into the mountain ridge beyond.

By the exam date, she had completed the required Elitist map cartridges along with the archival documents. After the long, grueling test, Commander Behran joined them in the large lecture hall.

"I am pleased to say that you all made Rank Four. This is the suntarin you have all waited for. You are now run leaders. Not only have you completed your training runs more efficiently than any other group, you success rate has also been higher. I wish I could send you straight out to do some damage to the Saracens, but their garrisons are so heavily entrenched in this area, that we are forced to wait until they decide to move. Enjoy this brief respite but be prepared to move out at a moment's notice. Once the Saracens leave the valley, we shall be on their backs and pushing them hard."

Jan left the meeting deep in thought. With a decisive nod, she glanced about then seemed to melt into the walls.

Chapter 37

Jan ducked inside one of the Molluc tunnels Teldank had shown her months before. Carefully she sought out the paths she had tread only once before to the Molluc village. At last she saw the beehive-like cluster of homes carved into the cavern walls. She was met at its entrance by a small Molluc page who immediately took her to the king.

“You have returned,” the Mollucan said as his page backed from the room.

"I've returned just as I promised. I've just been made a run leader, which is the signal we agreed upon."

"But they have given you no assignments?"

"The Saracens have garrisoned the Mozern and the valley around it. We have no choice but wait till they move on. Either I train now or never."

"Yes, I agree," he mused. "Tomorrow you will begin to learn our paths. Although none but our people have ever used them, you will now. Till tomorrow," he said quietly.

An aged Molluc woke Jan in the early morning hours. He led her to the Holwicol - the Hall of Knowledge. There, young Molluc-messengers awaited him in the flickering firelight. Jan sat beside them listening as the old Molluc imparted his knowledge of their secret paths with patience and diligence. The tunnels would lead them far beneath the Saracen ambushes, and the herbs would play tricks with their enemies' minds. The days stretched into weeks. One morning the old teacher came no more for Jan. Instead, a page escorted her into the Mollucan's presence.

"The Saracens are moving away and Elitist runners will go out soon. Use what we have taught you to spare all our people and destroy the Saracens. That will be 'thanks' to us."

"I will do the best I can," Jan replied and hurried from his chamber.

Once in the tunnels leading back to the Underground, her face took on a determined look. "Now I can begin these raids in earnest," she said aloud. "Now I can make a difference."

Upon her return, she found that Commander Behran was already gathering his leaders together and handing out assignments. Jan accepted hers then looked at her young runners with mixed emotions.

On impulse, she hurried to catch Behran in his office.

"Commander?"

"Yes?" He glanced up from his desk.

"I have a favor to ask of you."

He studied her for a moment. "Go on."

"I would like the group you have assigned to me to be mine on a permanent basis...even as they move up through the ranks."

"May I ask why?"

"I can only tell you that it is because of the paths I may use and an oath I swore," she replied.

He stared at her hard. "Is this some sort of trick?"

"No, sirha. However, I am bound by oath to say no more."

Behran thought for a moment. "I will consider your request while you are on this next run."

"Thank-you, sirha."

Jan returned to her group and gave them instructions. In a matter of minutes they were moving along tunnels, invisible to the others as they began their first long run.

Several weeks later, Tandk hurried into Mike's room first thing in the morning. As usual, Mike had swung his legs out of bed and was holding his aching head.

"Good morning," Tandk chirped authoritatively. "Your schedule is full, so you must get started."

"Is there any way out of this God-forsaken hole in the ground?"

"Wh-what?" Tandk sputtered and whistled in surprise.

"Is there any way to get above ground?" Mike asked raising his head and staring intently at the Molluc.

"B-but why do you wish to leave the safety of the tunnels?"

"Because I'm tired of being so safe."

"But surely you must have a better reason for wishing to face the Saracen threat?" Tandk countered.

"Answer me with an answer," Mike demanded, "not another question. Is there a way to get above ground?"

"Y-yes, Your Highness. There are several...."

"Then-get-me-out-of-here!"

"Wh-what do you mean, Your Highness? Wh-what for?" The Molluc followed worriedly as Mike paced the floor.

“So I can see exactly what’s happening to our people living out there,” Mike replied gesturing toward the ceiling. “I’m tired of just receiving reports. They’re skewed to make each principality appear successful, and they conflict left and right. I’ve got to see what’s going on out there for myself.”

“There is no other way, Your Highness?”

"None!" Mike replied with unmistakable finality.

Tandk sighed in defeat. "When does Your Highness wish to go?"

Mike stood with his arms crossed. "How far in advance do you made up my schedules?"

"A suntarin or two at most."

"Then put it down for the next day that doesn't have your furry pawprint on it yet," Mike ordered.

"I-I'll have to get clearance from General Adar," Tandk said stalling.

"I am clearance. If Adar doesn't like it, send him to see me!" Mike shoved past the frazzled creature and into the shower.

Tandk whistled, chirped and buzzed, while Ndak set out the

Royal Uniform. He hovered about Mike as he dressed.

"I can speak to Adar this morning while you are at your weapons training session. Only he and a few others can help you."

"Then do it!"

"Y-yes, Your Highness," Tandk replied meekly bowing his way out the door.

Mike pulled on the tight-fitting trousers and stretched uncomfortably. He stalked out to the balcony for breakfast but merely stared darkly at his plate.

"Should we show him the note?" Ndak whispered cautiously. "It is two or three montari overdue."

"Definitely not!" Tandk snapped.

"Then what should we do with it?" Ndak asked anxiously.

"The same as we have with all the others...Destroy it!" Tandk exclaimed grabbing it from Ndak's paw. "If His Highness were ever to discover that we have failed to give them to him, he would have our heads."

Tandk opened a door in the side of the wall and shoved the note inside; then, slamming it shut, he pressed a button marked INCINERATOR. It blinked a dull red twice before going out.

Several minutes later, Mike stalked out the door of his quarters, Tandk hustling after him. The Molluc stood outside the gymnasium till he saw the session begin. Immediately, he scuttled away disappearing and reappearing at intervals till he suddenly popped up in General Adar's office.

"We have trouble," he squeaked.

"What has happened?" the General asked peering over his desk at the stubby nose and beady black eyes that stared up at him.

"It is the Prince. He is getting restless and beyond my control."

"Give him more to do."

"It has gone beyond that." The Molluc paced frantically quickly burbling out the story while Adar's frown grew. "We cannot send him out there," the Molluc concluded breathlessly.

"No question. It is far too dangerous," Adar agreed.

"But the Prince is insistent."

"I shall merely deny him clearance."

"He said to tell you he is 'clearance'," Tandk said in a small voice. "He said to speak to him personally if you have any problems with that." His voice grew even smaller.

Adar shook his head worriedly. "This is serious."

Tandk nodded. "I cannot safely return without an affirmation."

Adar brooded. "I guess we have no alternative than do as he requests."

"B-but the danger...."

"He will merely observe."

"It just is not safe," Tandk countered.

"Neither is his increasing frustration . He is not like his father happy just to be busy. He has in mind the job he was meant to do and is determined to get it done. With his father's powers and the mounting tension from his frustration, who knows what he could unleash?"

"Then how soon will you allow him to go?"

"Tell him...in about one week."

Adar watched the Molluc hustle away then hit a comm button on his desk. Moments later Will's voice replied, "Yes, Adar."

"Come to my office, immediately."

"Trouble?"

"Definitely."

When Will entered Adar's office, an Elitist Team greeted him as well. "A new run going out?" he queried.

The general groaned. "Yes, and I have no choice. For the moment what I need from you is a disguise for this one," he said, holding Jan's face by her chin. "A disguise that not even the Prince will recognize."

Will's mouth dropped open in shock and he sank onto a chair. Jan looked at him anxiously.

"Adar, you can't possibly mean...?"

"Just to observe," Adar added defensively.

"No way! He absolutely cannot go!" Will fumed. "He could get captured, or killed, or...."

"I know, I know. My sentiments exactly. But he insists and has legally overridden my decision."

"Let me talk to him, Adar," Will pleaded. "Maybe I can convince him."

Adar shook his head. "Tandk said his condition is becoming

dangerous. I do not think even you could reach him now."

"I told you I should have remained at his side as his advisor," Will stormed.

"I-I should have let you, but I-I needed you here so badly," Adar said helplessly. "I never thought things would get to this point."

"But this is madness!"

"I know, but he has tied my hands. Since I must send him out, he has to be guided by our very best. I can only trust him with Marla and Janielle especially."

"Adar, he'll detect her in an instant," Will protested. "Their bond will call to him and the whole plan will be uncovered."

"And that is my biggest problem. What do I do with her?" Adar asked gesturing to Jan in a sign of defeat.

Will rubbed his hand over his head. "Adar, this game has got to end...soon. You are playing with dynamite, and somehow I'm caught in the middle."

"It is more than just me, Dehan. The entire Council agreed to Lady Elira's plan. With a little more time, we can make up for what we did not have until you came. Then we will be ready to present the entire strategy to him. Please, Dehan, just a little more time."

With a haggard, worried countenance Will led Jan back to his lab and sat her down. "Maybe if we mimic some of the worst torture wounds, he'll think his interest in you is morbid curiosity," he said heavily. "We'll have to heavily disguise your features. I can give you something so you will temporarily lose your voice…if only we could block him from sensing your bond."

"This is territory I know little about," she moaned. "I just know that when we're together it's like instant attraction and a magnetic draw. Even our dreams get mixed together. I have his dreams; he has mine. The only reason he has ignored mine is because he thinks I'm constantly down here with you or Elira."

"I know," Will said, the muscles in his neck tightening. "Jan, you've done some amazing things since you've become an Elitist and I would never tell you to give it up, but there are times when I wish you had stayed in your apartment and right now is one of those times."

He turned to a computer and began working on a stored image of Jan. In minutes he had created something that looked more like a death hag. "What do you think? Think he would know that was you?"

She stared at it.

“Hopefully if we camouflage you enough, he’ll get mixed signals like he does with your dreams and won’t guess your true identity.”

"Oh, Will. I hope so. If he ever finds out, we're dead."

Will groaned and nodded.

Chapter 38

For the next week Will worked on developing a disguise as gruesome and distracting as he possibly could devise. He worked with Jan trying one idea after another. Finally, desperate to comply with Mike's request and to provide him with the most knowledgeable guardians possible, he resorted to giving Jan a nerve block and to creating some real appearing wounds.

"Will this ever be reversible?" she asked worriedly as she looked at the changed image in the mirror.

"As long as you are back here within one week, I will be able to reverse the effects entirely," Will assured her.

"But what if we get stuck out there and it's longer?" Jan fretted.

"Then some of the effects may become more permanent," Will conceded. "I'll work on something to remove long term effects while you're out." He gave her a pat on the shoulder.

"Thanks, Will. I'd never be able to explain this to Mike, and I'm not sure I could live with myself looking like this for the rest of my life," Jan said.

As Adar had promised, at the end of that week Mike was

following Tandk along the quiet tunnels that honeycombed Mozern Mountain. Cautiously the Molluc guided him to an air vent that led to the surface. They crawled along silently until they reached an oval airlock. Tandk opened it and helped Mike outside. Mike blinked in the bright light of the sun then turned around to thank his secretary, but both the airlock and the Molluc were gone.

A small, furry hand tugged at his jacket. Mike glanced down his eyes opening in surprise upon seeing the thin, wiry Molluc at his side. His new guide held up one paw for silence beckoning for him to follow with the other. Mike scanned the landscape before starting after the nimble creature.

They shinnied down the steep mountainside into the blanket of early morning fog. Pebbles loosened by his boots preceded Mike. Soon they came to a low ridge that ran alongside a rutted, dirt road. The Molluc motioned for Mike to crouch low while they crept along its crest. The two silent companions continued in this tiresome position as the sun rose above the treetops burning off the protective mists. Eventually the Molluc ducked behind a clump of bushes and squatted on his heels.

"We wait here."

Mike crouched beside his guide. Eventually he sat on a prickly tuft of grass and watched the sun climb toward its zenith. He glanced around from time-to-time at the empty countryside.

"How much longer?" he ventured in a low whisper.

"Shh! Listen!"

Mike strained his ears until he managed to make out the faint creak of wagon wheels. As the vehicle approached, the creak and rumble grew louder. From around the bend appeared the head and body of a large, shaggy draft animal. The beast was followed, bit-by-bit by the wagon of a tinkerer.

"Now!"

They crawled out from behind the bush and jumped the few feet to the road. The wagon- master reined in his beast.

"What've ya got fer us t'day, Gurbn?" the man asked casually dropping the reins to his knees.

"Only a passenger."

"No herbs?"

"Not today. Tomorrow, yes?"

The wagonmaster nodded then lent Mike his gnarled hand helping him up. "We'll be back t'morra, Gurbn, less'n ya see the feather."

The Molluc nodded, leapt up onto the bank and disappeared behind the low ridge. Mike watched him go then glanced curiously at his host and companions.

"So, you're a wanderer, eh? We dunna get many footpads round now." The man flicked the reins, and his beast resumed its plodding pace. "Smart o' ya ta join up with a tinkerer. No one suspects us."

"So I was told."

"And what sights be ya come ta see out here, eh?" the man asked with a sweeping gesture at the rolling hills and parched wasteland below.

"I don't know...or at least I won't know until I see it."

"Vague 'nough, but it suits me. That's less'n them'll get outa me if they ever kitch me." The wagonmaster looked about him as if fearing that Saracens were lurking in the shadow of every tree and bush. Seemingly satisfied that the coast was clear, he turned back to Mike. "Well, ya might as well larn yar comp'ny, eh?" The man smiled broadly, deep creases forming about his eyes and mouth.

"Them in back are ma 'prentices, Durke an' Galin."

Two pairs of eyes popped open from under broad-brimmed straw hats which slid down at the offer of two polite nods.

"The girl back there's ma naptar, Marta. Good cook, she is, and a man's gotta eat at home and on the road," the driver said chuckling.

Mike nodded politely then noticed a thin figure shrouded in black that sat on the other side of his host. Neither face nor hands could be seen, not even a tell-tale lock of hair.

"I'm Gabrel, at yar service. To ma side here's, Seera."

The form turned towards Mike giving him a glimpse of glaring red eyes and skin as dark as coal ash. He gave a start in spite of himself.

"Dunna be 'fraid o' Seera," Gabrel said quietly, "though ah must admit, that's most folks' first reaction. She's what's left o' ma fam'ly...an gentle as this here ewan," he added nodding towards the plodding beast before him.

"Such a pretty girl, she was. Had a friendly smile 'n a pleasin' voice. She don't talk no more, but her ears got keener. She kin hear sounds long afore the rest o' us."

Mike settled back to enjoy the scenery, but his eyes kept returning to the huddled black mass on the other side. Something compelled him to stare at the unfortunate girl.

"What happened?" he asked at last.

"Ta Seera?"

Mike nodded.

"Oh now, sirha, that was 'them'."

"Them? You mean the...."

Gabrel cut him short with a curt nod. "Worst than most, she is. Got caught helpin' pris'ners 'scape...but it's past 'n done." He clamped his jaw shut, fixed his eyes on the ewan's haunches and said no more.

About mid-afternoon they jounced lazily into the blackened, charred ruins of a town square. Gaunt, care-worn women shuffled past them some giving an almost imperceptible nod.

"All right ya, shazbas! Out with ya! Go hetch up some business!" Gabrel called to the hat brims in the back.

The pairs of eyes popped open again.

Mike jumped down and walked around to the back of the wagon where he was surprised to bump into a very alert Durke. He spun around clumsily and upset the load of pots Galin was juggling in his arms. With a red 'collar' creeping up his neck, Mike hurried toward the front of the cart. Seera was sitting there testing the wagon rungs with her feet. He reached up to steady her, but she pulled back immediately.

"I'm sorry," Mike said in a quiet, gentle voice. "I won't hurt you. I just want to help you down."

The girl sat for a moment staring at him.

"She's a wee bit independent, sirha," Gabrel said coming up behind Mike. "Might as well let 'er be."

Mike took a few steps back.

"You can follow me," Marta curtly informed him dumping a load of pots, pans and assorted utensils into his arms. "I have deliveries to make."

She started off across the square with Mike staggering after her. She went from one cottage to another, knocking at each door and picking out the mended items to be returned. She placed whatever the cottagers offered her as payment into a sack she had thrown over her shoulder.

At each door, Mike peered past the menagerie in his arms and into the hut. The worn floorboards were bare of rugs or carpets; the two or three small rooms were sparsely furnished. Most had just a bed, a table and two or three straight-backed chairs. Shy, barefoot children in patched, but clean clothing hid behind mothers or grandmothers. Occasionally they peeked out with big, round eyes that stared from pale, hollow faces. Cupboards and shelves were empty, and the fuel bins held no wood or fire rocks. Though men's boots stood in several corners, no men were to be seen.

But what really captured Mike's gaze were the one or two pieces of exquisite finery each hut held that stood out from the stark backdrop. One hut might hold a finely sculpted, hand painted vase; another would have an ornately-carved, high-backed chair in a corner; and on the walls of others would hang gilt frames that surrounded either faded portraits or cracked mirrors.

As they hiked back from the far end of the village, Mike ventured a question. "Where are all the men?"

"Workin' for `them' in the mines and quarries. They'll be home at sun down," Marta replied with a toss of her head.

Mike frowned hard as he hurried to keep up. "Well, what about food and clothes...and fuel?" he asked. "No one seems to have enough of anything."

Marta turned on him. "Since when are Saracens s'posed to feed an' clothe their slaves? The fam'lies are allowed to garden in designated plots after they get their work done...say, after dark. That's of course, if'n the Saracens haven't a'ready tramped ev'rything into the dust."

Mike's mouth dropped open in shock. "B-but what about the children?

"What about 'em?"

"They're half-starved and half-sick."

Marta stared at Mike. "Let me give ya a clue, sirha. Saracens don't want no more Quentasian youngers. They keep the men and women too exhausted ta fight, the elders too ill ta protest, and the youngers too sick ta ever grow up. It guarantees their possession of Quentas. Eventually we all'll die out, leavin' the planet to them. That's after we've mined, drilled and quarried all its resources for 'em. All the Saracens'll have ta do is sit back an' enjoy it."

She started to walk again and Mike hustled to catch up.

"What is this place then? A concentration camp?"

Marta shot him a whithering glance. "This used ta be a manor plantation. The Saracen barracks were once an estate house. They forced the owners out and built these here shallies for people they round up. They put one nice heirloom in each shally ta remind 'em of what they've lost. Ev'rything else they smashed and burned."

She pointed to a still-scorched circle in the village square. "Now ain't that a lovely way ta live?"

Mike halted in mid-stride and gazed about him. Gradually he picked out things he had previously overlooked. Here and there were remains of stately walls and old gardens. Vestiges of ornate trim and once-polished metal still graced the 'barracks.'

A cool hand touched his arm and he spun around. Beside him, Seera stood staring up with her large, red eyes. She motioned for him to follow. He glanced up catching sight of the red and pink clouds the evening sun had tinted.

Seera led him back to the glowing cook fire Gabrel had started near the wagon. While they ate, a line of weary men in tattered, grimy clothing trudged into the village. Behind them marched Saracens, their lasers raised.

Gabrel rose, reached into the wagon then nonchalantly tossed Mike a hooded cloak. "It gets chill at night. Better wear this."

He passed more out to the others. Edging past Mike, he stooped down and drew the hood over the young man's head and face. "You're new. There'll be questions later. Let me do the talkin'."

Mike nodded while keeping a wary eye on the Saracens and the line of shuffling men. Suddenly one stumbled and fell. A child dashed from a doorway toward him, but a Saracen stepped into her path, laser pointed directly at her. Mike started to rise, but Durke and Galin grabbed his arms holding him back. Forced to sit and watch, his stomach twisted into one hundred tiny knots of fear and frustration.

"Why don't they let someone help him up?" he muttered under his breath.

"They're not of the compassionate bent," Marta whispered. "He'll be cold by mornin'."

"Dead?" Mike asked in horror.

"Surely. He's useless now."

"But what about his family?"

"They'll starve without 'im. Happens all the time."

"And you don't do anything about it?" Mike asked, astonished.

"Nothin' ta do if'n ya want ta see t'morra. Live ta fight another time's my byword."

Mike watched in stupified horror as the other men were forced to march past their fallen comrade. He clenched his fists, his mind racing.

"'I've got to help," he thought. "I can't let him die.

Chapter 39

As Mike watched the beleaguered men returning from the mines and agonized over the fate of their fallen comrade, an idea crept into his mind. He closed his eyes retracing the steps he had taken through the village with Marta that afternoon. He recalled the refuse pile the Saracens had heaped on the far side of the village. For a brief moment he felt the heat of its decay. He added to it the heat of his own anger and frustration with startling, but satisfying, results. In seconds an explosion rocked the village sending a fireball rocketing skywards. All heads turned to look as if one.

"What was that?" Gabrel exclaimed.

"Fire!" Marta cried. "Look!"

In minutes the square had emptied of Saracen and Quentasian alike as all hands rushed to put out the inferno. At that moment Mike made his move. He rose from the cookfire and crept to the man who lay sprawled on the quickly cooling flagstones. He glanced about anxiously as he bent down to lift him up. He was surprised to find Seera at the man's other side ready to help. He paused, smiled, then together, they pulled the man to his feet.

"Where do you live?" Mike asked.

The man gasped and moved his lips, but could make no sound.

Seera tugged at Mike's arm and gestured toward the line of shallies.

"Right. Show me the way, Seera."

Together, they dragged the man across the square ducking now and then into the shadows as Saracens walked into view, and down the row of small shanties. A door in one cracked open slightly and a dim light shone out. Mike and Seera pushed toward it and stumbled inside.

"Hurry! Over here!" the nearly frantic woman urged.

They made their way to a small room off to one side and carefully laid the man on the cot inside. The woman knelt beside him cradling his head in her arms and sobbing hysterically. Mike studied the couple noticing the woman's pale, lined face, though she did not appear to be much older than himself. He reached out, took her by the shoulders, and gently pulled her away.

"Go watch the street," Mike instructed. "I'll do what I can for him."

She stared at his solemn handsome face, looked back at her husband lying prone on the bed, then nodded. Still staring and nodding, she backed from the room, turned and rushed to the door.

"Go on," Mike told Seera. "Go back to the square. I don't want you here if trouble starts."

She made a garbled noise in protest, but Mike gently sent her from the room and closed the door. He sighed and hurried back to the man's side.

"I've never tried a power transference before," he said, half to himself and half to the man, "but here goes."

Mike placed one hand over the man's heart and the other on his forehead. He focused his attention inward, and for a brief moment, a blue glow surrounded his hands. Suddenly the power coming from his hands exploded into a burst of white light and the man's chest heaved. He took several deep breaths and color returned to his cheeks. Mike sighed with relief. He hurried past the woman and out of the shally without giving her time to say a word.

Cautiously Mike made his way back through the deepening shadows. At the last corner he nearly stepped into the path of an oncoming Saracen. A hand caught Mike's elbow yanking him back into the deepest shadows, and another hand clamped down hard over his mouth. Once the guard had passed, Mike breathed a sigh of relief and looked to see who his rescuer was. Seera led him out from the shadows and back toward the cookfire. Together, they took up their seats and waited for the others. In a while their friends returned sitting around the fire with them. They took up their now cold meals and resumed eating. Soon the square had turned to normal with people moving about in the shadows, and the Saracens had returned to their posts.

"What happened?" Mike asked nonchalantly.

"Garbage dump exploded," Marta explained.

"Self-combustion," Gabrel added.

"Where'd you hie off to?" Galin asked.

"No where special. I...uh...have a certain fear of fire," Mike replied, then leaned back staring silently across the square.

The sun finally sank behind the surrounding hills. Stars blinked here and there in the darkening sky above. Mike huddled closer to the cookfire with the others, but Seera sat alone in the darkest shadows. She raised her hands and pulled back her hood. Mike, eyeing the long, brittle braid of her hair and the blackish-blue hue of her skin, shivered slightly when her glowing red eyes fell on him. Hastily he glanced away as the shiver trailed down his spine.

Three Saracens strolled toward them ambling in a wide arc around the wagon before stopping next to the tinker.

"No new apprentices, Tinker," one warned.

"Not mine. My brodar's," Gabrel cried defensively. "He's just been articled. I'm merely tranportin' him from Sy ta Cag-can."

The guards eyed Mike suspiciously. "He has papers?"

"Like all the others," Gabrel replied reaching slowly inside his tunic and producing a sheaf of documents.

"These articles are somewhat stale," a guard spat throwing them back at Gabrel.

"It takes time ta make rounds," the tinker sputtered.

"And where was he during the fire?" the third demanded.

"Near 'nough. Not ev'ryone can be in the melee. Som'one had ta stay behind ta keep the ewan calm. With all the noise 'n ruckus, it was a'buckin' an' threat'nin to do some damage."

The Saracen moved toward his weapon but flinched at a touch on his arm. Seera moved among them beckoning for them to follow her away from the wagon. Mike watched her bring out three packs of thin cylinders from inside her cloak. The guards took and inspected them, while she signaled for them to go away. They laughed at her odd gestures but shuffled off nonetheless. Soon, pinpricks of fire dotted the square as the Saracens settled back to smoke. After a while, the Saracens' weapons dropped to their sides, and they stared straight ahead not seeing anything around them.

"Does it ev'rytime," Gabrel chuckled. "Weed's a bit heady for us, but it affects their systems quite right. Let's us keep an eye on 'em."

He rose stiffly and crawled into the lean-to pitched against the wagon where Marta and the other men were already stretched out. Mike looked around noticing that Seera had returned to her spot back away from the fire. He got up and moved over to sit beside her. She immediately drew up her hood.

"Please don't," he said lifting it back off her head. "You aren't really ugly, and you don't scare me anymore. You can leave your hood down."

She shook her head slowly and tried to raise the hood again, but Mike gently held it off her head. Finally she let her hands drop to her sides.

"Do you mind if I sit here?"

She motioned toward the lean-to.

"I'll head over in a bit, but I need some time to think," he explained.

Seera shrugged and nodded.

Mike edged closer staring moodily into the fire. He kept seeing the girl's blackened face in the dancing yellow flames. All of a sudden Jan's face flashed in its place. The visages alternated again and again and an intense longing swept over him. His arms ached to hold her again. In an instant, the images vanished as if with the flick of a switch. He glanced over at Seera and the longing welled up even stronger. He closed his eyes taking a quick gulp of air. When he blinked, his arm was encircling her rigid shoulders.

For a moment he froze then slowly pulled his arm away. "I-I'm s-sorry," he stammered. "I-I was thinking of someone else...don't understand why I did that."

Scrambling to his feet, Mike backed hastily away from Seera and the fire. He crawled into the lean-to and lay listening to the thump of his heart against his ribs. Soon the darkness and cold engulfed him.

Suddenly a bright shaft of warm light spilled over his face. He blinked sleepily and sat up yawning.

"We're headin' out," Gabrel announced. "Better come, too."

Mike scrambled to his feet and hauled himself into the wagon beside the others. Gabrel gave a cluck and a snap of the reins at which the ewan lumbered onto the road again. Mike's eyes drooped shut as the wagon jiggled over the ruts. Suddenly the cart jolted to a stop. Mike sat straight up and peered over the wagon's sides. They had climbed to the top of a knoll and had parked at its crest.

"What's up?" he asked crawling up next to Gabrel on the bench.

"Shh! Down there! It's 'them'!"

Mike looked down the hill scanning the valley before spotting a band of Saracens standing outside a small farmhouse barking orders.

"What are they doing?" Mike whispered.

"They're gonna torch the silo."

"Why?" Mike gasped in alarm.

"Hungry people make good slaves," Marta said creeping up behind the two men.

Mike watched in horror as a large flame-thrower was wheeled into view. He clutched at the seat, his knuckles turning white. Without warning, he sprang from the wagon and raced down the hillside toward the farm. He raised his right arm taking aim as he ran. A hand grabbed his, and the bolt flew out of him prematurely. He turned in time to see Seera land with a thud in a nearby thicket. He crashed through the brush after her.

"Are you all right?"

She sat up slowly, took his outstretched hand and tried to get her wobbly legs to support her.

"Sit down," he ordered.

She wrenched away from the firm pressure forcing her back to the ground.

"All right," he sighed. "Have it your way. But why did you stop me?"

Seera gestured toward the farmhouse.

"Yes, I know there are Saracens there. I was going to stop them."

She shook her head emphatically. She moved two fingers through the air like a lone person walking, while her other hand snuck up stealthily behind and pounced.

Mike watched intently. "You think it was a trap...that I would have been ambushed?"

Seera nodded.

They heard the leaves nearby rustle. Instantly she grabbed his hand and pulled him back up the hill toward the wagon.

"Get him out of here! Home base!" Marta ordered hastily.

Seera nodded and dragged Mike after her.

"Where are we going?"

She ignored him, and her clamp-like grip gave him no choice but to follow. He turned his head and caught a glimpse of Durke, Galin, and Marta dashing off into the brush toward the farmhouse. Gabrel was busy whipping his ewan to a remarkable speed. He headed it toward the hillside where no path was visible. In seconds ewan, cart, and Gabrel were gone.

Mike swung his head back around catching sight of a Saracen uniform in the process. He dove behind a boulder dragging Seera down with him. They crouched there for a moment watching the Saracen trudge by. As soon as he had disappeared, Seera leapt up and ran toward a copse of trees. They crashed through thickets and thorny bracken with the pounding of booted feet close behind. Though she led them straight uphill, the Saracens' labored breathing persisted. Two more Saracens unexpectedly leapt out of hiding, their weapons trained on the fleeing couple. Cornered, they edged back until their spines were pressed against a tree. Seera quickly glanced overhead, spotted a familiar mark then dropped her eyes to the ground.

"Well, well. What do we have here?"

A Saracen moved in for a closer inspection. "Seems one of you is new to this territory, though I think I know your sister," he said lifting Seera's chin with the tip of his laser. "We do not welcome newcomers."

His comrades edged closer. Mike and Seera huddled together. She slipped her hand around his wrist.

"I think we will take these two back to base and see what Conlinc makes of them. Maybe they can be convinced to tell where their friends are."

A loud rumble resounded from the valley below closely followed by a black cloud of smoke that rose above the treetops. Seera placed her free hand against the tree trunk directly behind them, seeking out a branch stub. She quickly rolled something around in her mouth until a short, transparent tube projected through her lips. With a short puff, she blew a small pellet to the ground in front of them. Mike heard a muffled click and jumped at the resulting poof of smoke. Seera tugged at his arm pulling him through a concealed doorway, while the Saracens opened fire in the thickening haze. When the smoke had cleared, Mike and Seera were no where to be seen. All that remained were the Saracens lying on the ground with gaping wounds in their chests. They had been caught in their own crossfire.

Chapter 40

The scenario with Seera and the Saracens played itself over and over in Mike's mind. In his sleep he heard the tramp of weary feet as the men struggled home from the mines. He heard the dull thud as their comrade fell to the stone slabs of the square. He could see the horror on the faces of the lone farmers watching as a flame thrower was positioned before their silo.

In the midst of the scenes, Mike ran from Saracens who were quickly closing in. He panted and gasped for air as he frantically clawed his way uphill. His head pounded, his legs ached, yet he forced himself on. An ember of anger inside him burst into the flames of full-fledged rage, and he turned to stand his ground. With all his pent up fury, he unleashed the full force of his powers at his tormentors; they melted like wax dummies in a museum fire.

Mike opened his eyes blinking at the grey stillness of his room. Suddenly he knew what he had to do. The council would either be convinced today, or the war would be lost.

Tandk knocked and entered. The appointment slate tugged out of his pudgy paws and flew smoothly into Mike's hand. The Molluc stared at him in awe, while Mike scanned the list and crossed off items as he went.

"Tours are a mere formality I no longer have time for," Mike said decisively. "I want a one-on-one meeting scheduled with each principality representative and each Task leader. Either I will convince them of the need for their complete cooperation when their competitors aren't around, or they are never going to be persuaded."

Mike handed the slate back to Tandk who bowed fearfully as he backed from the room.

Before Ndak could lay out his clothes, Mike flung open the doors on his wardrobe and chose his own suit. Ndak stood in the doorway watching Mike curiously.

"Do you need something for a headache today?" the Molluc chamberlain finally offered.

Mike rolled his head slowly from side-to-side loosening his neck muscles. "Thanks, but I don't have one, Ndak."

"For once I know exactly what I need to do," Mike said to himself as he stepped into the shower. "For once I have a plan."

He dressed, ate breakfast and scanned some valuable reports he had been forced to neglect for weeks.

Tandk entered bowing nervously. "Your schedule, Y-Your H-Highness," he stammered.

Mike swallowed a smirk with a gulp of his beverage. He took the proffered slate and scanned the list of the day's events.

"This is an improvement," he said reading to the end. "When am I scheduled to meet with the commander of the Air Task?"

"Next week."

Mike nodded and returned the slate to Tandk who beamed as he backed out the door. Then with firm resolve written on his face and, with anger flashing from his eyes, he marched from his quarters to the council meeting.

A respectful hush fell over the room when the doors opened and Mike strode to his seat. He signaled for the meeting to begin and sat down to business as usual. And as usual, the arguments flew back and forth past him. The Generals rose from their seats waving their hands in the air and banging their fists on the council table. They ranted and raved like furious clouds in a storm.

Slowly Mike also rose from his seat. The Heads-of-Council

haggled on. Gradually, though, they quieted as each felt a great, oppressive weight descend upon their shoulders. Some glanced up as if expecting to see a giant hand pushing them down.

Once in their seats, however, the oppressive weight lifted, but a will far greater than their own held them firmly in place. One-by-one, each head turned to view the solitary figure who stood resolutely in place. The understanding that dawned on the councilmen's faces swiftly transformed from surprise to fear. They had ignored their Crown Prince, and now they were going to pay the price.

Mike waited until every eye was on him. “Councilmen, I now have your attention,” he began. “For montari I have waited for you to show signs of cooperation as stipulated in the oaths of allegiance you swore to the High Throne of Quentas. I have patiently listened to the strategies you have presented. I have read your reports and your proposals. Nothing you have shown me suggests that you are working towards a cooperative working agreement, and without one this war is already lost,” he said forcefully, his will continuing to bare down on them.

“As for your proposals, your strategies, and your arguments, I reject them all. The only way we can attack the Saracens and win is with the combined effort of all of our resources pooled together. Only when the people of Quentas are reunified under allegiance to the High Throne can we hope to be victorious. However, to date no one here seems to even care about Quentas.”

Mike leaned forward bracing his body on the table with his fingertips. You are obviously too safe here in these cavernous halls. You have forgotten the malnourished, sickly children, the invalid elders and the men and women who struggle daily just to subsist. The men are slaves, the women worn and ragged, the lone farmers vandalized and terrorized, and all are without a shred of hope. I came here to free our people from the Saracens who oppress them and that is exactly what I intend to do."

Mike held each person's gaze in turn as he slowly scanned the room. "You, High Councilmen, are a sorry lot to be calling yourselves leaders. You each have a purpose that is all your own. It includes yourself and your own interest group. I have only one purpose, and it should be yours."

Mike wiped away the sweat that beaded on his forehead. "Lord Dehan raised me with only one goal in mind...free our people...free our people. Whenever I wished to take up some other challenge, he always brought me back to my primary goal - free our people. I have no other reason for being, nor will I have till Quentas has been rid of the Saracens."

He took a deep breath, the exertion of maintaining his will over the councilmen beginning to drain him. He stared at the council members with renewed vigor.

"This is now your only goal, gentlemen - free our people. I want new proposals that detail new strategies that will unify the people of Quentas into one fighting force. You have had three decari to prepare the garbage you've been handing me...but we do not have years. We do not even have montari. Instead, you have but two weeks, gentlemen; two weeks in which to reorganize. When the council reconvenes in one-half montar, I will review each of your proposals individually. At that time I will hear orderly statements, not this rabble. Gentlemen, you are dismissed."

The air about them snapped like a taut rubber band as Mike released his hold. He turned and marched swiftly from the great hall. Behind him, the councilmen sat in speechless awe.

Elated over his success with the High Councilmen, Mike strolled into the Royal Suite whistling. He stopped short as a furtive movement across the lounge grabbed his attention. He caught a glimpse of a lithe figure in skin-tight camouflage as it dashed up the hall past Will's door. Going around the fountain, Mike crept to the corner, edged around it, and spotted the fleeing figure as it ducked into Jan's apartment.

Mike furrowed his brows at once puzzled and suspicious. "Now, who would be sneaking around here in camouflage?" he muttered. "A spy? An assassin?"

Immediately adrenaline began pumping through his veins as he inched his way up the hall. When he stopped outside Jan's apartment and pressed his ear to the door, he could hear quick, muffled movements inside. A tingle flew up his spine, the hairs at the nape of his neck standing on end. Without hesitation, he passed his hand over the lock and slowly pushed the door open. Noiselessly he closed it behind him and scanned the lounge. Nothing seemed out of place, yet his stomach knotted uneasily.

He stood in the middle of the room, his hands on his hips then lifted his head as the sound of running water reached his ears.

"Someone's in the shower!" he breathed aloud.

Mike moved into the short hall and warily approached Jan's private bath. A spot on the floor caught his eye and he bent to examine it. "Mud and grass here? Underground? Now how'd that get down here when no one's allowed topside?"

With his anxiety heightened, Mike gently nudged the door aside, entered, and crossed to the shower. Slowly he reached his hand toward the opaque screen. Suddenly it swished back startling him. There stood Jan with glistening beads of water rippling off her silky, white skin.

Mike stood for a moment with his mouth agape. "Oh, boy," he whispered.

"'Oh boy's' not the word, guy." Jan grabbed for her towel. "Turn around," she ordered hastily wrapping it about her.

Mike sheepishly spun to face the door.

"You've got a bit of explaining to do," she said stepping from the shower.

"Uh...yeah."

She dashed past him and into her room. "Do me a favor," she yelled back.

"Anything."

"Stay right there till I say it's all right to come out."

"No problem," he replied.

Mike closed his eyes and swallowed hard. In his mind's eye he could see her glistening white skin, the soft mounds of her breasts. The fire that had risen to his face now seeped into the rest of his body. He opened his eyes and took several deep breaths.

"Ok 'Peeping Tom'," Jan called. "You can come out now."

Mike shook his head as if awakening from a dream. "Where are you?" he asked hesitantly stepping into the hall.

"In the kitchen. Want something to drink?"

"Yeah," he replied entering the kitchenette and slowly sinking onto a chair at the small round table in the middle of the floor.

"So, let's hear it." She set a glass of juice in front of him. "Do make this a good story. It's been ages since I've heard one." She slid onto the chair adjacent to his and watched his uneasy squirming with an amused smile.

"Look, I didn't know you were in here."

"And who else resides here?"

"No one. I mean…it's just…."

"Ye-es?"

"When I walked into the Royal Suite, I thought I saw an assassin heading for your suite. He was dressed in skin-tight camouflage and was acting suspiciously. I'm sure I saw him go into your apartment."

Jan started to chuckle.

"Look, this isn't funny. We could still be in danger."

She shook her head, her chuckling continuing and getting louder.

Mike scowled, his anger rising. "Fine, don't believe me," he said rising to leave.

"Oh, I believe you," Jan replied, "because I know exactly who you saw."

He turned toward her. "Who?"

"Me, though I never quite thought that outfit made me look like an assassin."

"You?" He sank back into his seat.

She nodded.

"But what were you doing dressed like that. Why'd you run?"

"I jog in that suit. It's made of something like Lycra-spandex, comfortable really. I'd been out in the gardens but when I heard the door open I ran. I didn't expect Will, since he's in the lab, and I figured you'd still be in council. Since I didn't know who was coming in, I thought it would be best to duck into my apartment and change."

"Yeah, you wouldn't want someone like Adar catching you like that," Mike agreed sitting back down beside her.

"Speaking of catching," Jan said rising. "Hold on." She dashed to the lounge to lock her door.

Mike watched as she ran from the room. His eyes remained riveted on the slender legs that jutted out from beneath her short tunic. He rose and met her half-way catching her in his outstretched arms.

"Mm, Jan, I love you," he breathed embracing her and hungrily kissing her lips. He found their taste intoxicating and kissed them again.

Jan gently pulled away, took his hands, and led him to one of the deep, cushiony loungers. She pulled him down next to her while he eagerly wrapped his arms about her again. He smothered her with another long kiss.

"By the way, what was all that about?" Mike asked coming up for air.

Jan gazed into his deep-blue eyes and traced his lips with her finger. "I wanted to make certain no one could come and drag you away, like that fuzzy secretary of yours."

"No need to worry. I shook up council this morning. In fact, I'm off for two weeks while they scramble to reorganize. As for 'Furry,' he's in hiding, I think." He leaned closer giving her another ravenous kiss.

"Mm, it seems like forever since I last saw you," Jan murmured.

Mike kissed her once more then sat back. "It has been. Take my word for it." He quietly studied her flushed face, slender neck and low-cut tunic.

"Just how long is forever?" Jan wanted to know.

He leaned his elbows on his knees and began counting the weeks on his fingers. "Five months," he whispered then groaned. "It's been five whole months. I had no idea it had been so long."

"Hmm, you missed my birthday." Jan sank back against a cushion and curled her legs up under her. "It was a couple of months ago. I had really hoped you could break away for at least a few minutes for that. I even had Teldank bake the equivalent of a cake."

Mike grimaced. "Oh, Jan. I'm sorry. Really I am. I had no idea."

"I left you a note. In fact, I've left you a lot of notes that you haven't replied to."

Mike looked at her strangely. "But I've never gotten any notes."

"You had to have," she objected. "I put them right into that little furry's paws."

"Which furry?" Mike asked suspiciously.

"Your secretary."

Mike drummed his fingers on the lounger. "Why that conniving little Molluc! He had me running around like a chicken with my head cut off and never once mentioned any notes."

"Well, at least that explains that," Jan said with a gesture of helplessness.

"Yes, but I'd love to know what he did with them." Mike stared dejectedly at the floor and sighed deeply. "Look, Jan. I'm sorry about all of this. I never had any idea that my position and responsibilities were going to take me away from you this much." He ran his fingers through his hair. "I had no idea it had been so long since we last kissed or...." His voice trailed off.

Jan laid a hand on his shoulder and gently turned him back toward her. "You're forgiven, though I can't exactly say it's all right. I've been pretty angry sometimes that I could never see you. And sometimes I've been pretty depressed. It felt like I'd gotten dumped here while you went about your important business. But now I realize there wasn't a lot you could have done about it. However," she said, a mischievous smile playing across her lips, "since you've got all this time off, maybe we can make up little of what we've lost?" She turned his face till their lips met and kissed him as hungrily as he had her.

Mike wrapped his arms around her and felt flames leap up inside him as she edged closer. He could feel her gentle fingers as she ran them through the hair at the nape of his neck sending a torch searing through his brain. She caressingly ran her other hand up his arm and down his back, like a spark that set each nerve on edge. Jan pressed her body even closer to his, and a desire he had never known raged within him.

Slowly they tumbled over and sank into the billowy folds of the cushions. They lay side-by-side as he explored her mouth with his tongue. Her hot breath fed the flames that scorched through him. The scent of her hair and body sent him reeling on a giddy high.

Mike felt Jan's sensuous body next to his, felt her bare arms and legs as she wrapped them around him. As he let his hand slide through her hair, the desire to make Jan his welled up inside him. He let his hand glide across her shoulders to caress her chin, then down her slender neck to her chest and tunic, while the longing inside him became overwhelming.

"Jan," he whispered, "I want to love you. I want to make you mine."

He kissed her neck and ears, his heart throbbing and the blood ripping through his veins.

"I've never been this close to a woman before," he breathed kissing her earlobe, neck and shoulder. "I've got to join with you. I've got to make you mine forever."

He savored her lips as he reached up to pull the straps of her tunic off her shoulders. He found her hand blocking him. He merely shifted and tried the other strap with the same results. For a moment, he stopped kissing her and looked at her in confusion.

"What's wrong?" he asked sampling her lips again.

"Mike, we shouldn't be doing this."

"Doing what? It's just you and me, sweetheart. There's no one around for the first time since we met. Let's make the most of a beautiful moment like this."

"Mike, stop! We can't!" Jan cried more urgently this time.

He reached out a trembling hand and stroked her hair. "What's wrong, honey? Are you afraid?"

"Mike, we can't go through with this."

"But...I only want to make you mine," he said, bewildered at her resistance. "I love you." He kissed her lips and cheeks, tasting hot, salty tears.

"Oh, Mike. I want to be yours, too, but we can't. Your laws forbid it. We've got to stop before we've gone too far," she replied pleading with him.

Mike shook his head to clear it. "But who cares about the laws when it's just you and me...alone...together?"

"Mike, you know what would happen. The Ring would sense the change. It would know that we'd gone all the way and it would reject me...actually come off my finger. I'd lose you forever."

Chapter 41

Mike gazed down at her in confusion. "But you're already mine forever," he whispered, his lips brushing her wet cheek. "I don't want to lose you." Dull comprehension began filtering through the haze in his brain.

"Mike, I want you forever, too, and I want to be all yours as much as you want me to be," she said slowly. "But the Law of the Ring demands that we set an example of self-control. You set that ring on my finger; we're both subject to its law. I don't want to lose you because of one moment of pleasure together. I want us to last a whole lifetime."

Mike slowly pulled them both to a sitting position. He took a deep breath in an effort to resist what his whole body was still screaming for.

"I'm sorry, Mike," Jan apologized tearfully.

"Don't be," he replied. "You just saved us from the only thing that could ever separate us...ourselves."

He let her go and sat staring at the floor for a while. Gradually the fire inside him died down to glowing embers. He heard a rustle beside him as Jan left the room, but he did not look up. Minutes later she returned quietly sitting back down beside him. Eventually even this small distance was too great.

"Mike," she called quietly.

He glanced up noticing she had changed to a longer gown. He breathed a sigh of relief.

"Mike, would you hold me?"

He saw the tremble in her lower lip and the tears moistening her eyes. Gently, he reached out and put his arms around her drawing her close.

"Mike?" she asked timidly.

"What?"

There was a long pause.

"Do you still love me?"

He drew back in surprise. "Of course I still love you! If anything, I love you even more. Honey," he said gazing earnestly into her forlorn eyes, "you just kept me from making the biggest mistake of my life." He quickly hugged her to himself.

"I was really afraid that if I said 'no,' you wouldn't love me anymore. But I couldn't say 'yes,' or I'd lose you forever and end up exiled on Quentas. I was so scared, Mike. I didn't know what to do."

"You did the best thing you could have; you stopped us both. That decision took a lot of strength," he said quietly, tenderly caressing her face, "and right now I think I respect you more than anyone else I've ever known."

Jan leaned her head on his shoulder and snuggled close. Mike sank back into the lounger and, in a minute, she had drifted off to sleep. He sat for a while stroking her hair as he held her. Later, when she woke, they strolled out into the gardens along the stone pathways.

"I kind of feel guilty," Jan confessed, her arm in his.

"Why?" he asked, surprised.

"Oh, come on. Most guys would have said I was being a tease with that mini-dress I had on."

"Were you?"

"Of course not. With you in the bathroom, I just grabbed the first thing I could find and threw it on. But if I'd been thinking...I mean after you saw me in the shower...I should've known."

"Known what? That I'd had to repress all my feelings for you during the five months we haven't seen each other? That having you that close to me was going to make all my repressed desires to bond with you surface all at once?

"What?" A perplexed look crossed her face.

He held her head between his hands. "Honey, Quentasians develop a bond that lasts for life. Usually it builds up over a period of time; but we've had to spend so much time apart that it just burst through me all at once."

"Then...it wasn't anything I did?"

"Well, let's just say it wasn't the dress...but those kisses...now those were driving me wild."

Blushing, Jan ducked her head leaning her forehead against his shoulder.

"We've just got to spend more time together so it can't sneak up on us," Mike explained.

"Kind of hard to do in the middle of a war," she said looking up at him.

"War or no war, we have to be together...and from now on you've got a place in my life, duties or no duties."

She smiled up at him and kissed his cheek.

After a while, Mike dropped her off at her apartment. He was heading down the hall to his own, when Will strolled through the doors to the Royal Suite. The two men looked at each other, broad smiles lighting their faces.

"Well, this is a surprise!" Will exclaimed giving Mike a quick hug and a slap on the back.

"It sure is. Hey, I'm free for a while. How about you?"

"As a matter of fact, I'm off early tonight. C'mon in." Will ran his hand over the lock, and his door slid open.

Mike eagerly followed inside and collapsed onto a lounger. "So, what've you been up to?"

"Work for General Adar, and more work," Will replied easing into a chair. "But how did you finally get time to yourself?"

"I got tired of being ignored," Mike said. "I'm afraid I scared Tandk out of his fuzzy wits this morning. I haven't seen him since I forced him to reorganize my schedule before breakfast. Later, I took over the council meeting. It's about time I had a break from their constant bickering."

"What did you do?" Will asked raising his eyebrows in surprise.

"I exerted my will over the whole lot of them."

"You what?" Will asked, his mouth dropping open and his eyes popping wide. "W-Why...I don't even think your father's powers were strong enough to accomplish that. I mean, every last councilman is of Royal descent with powers of his own."

Mike looked a little surprised himself. "Probably if I'd known that, I wouldn't even have tried. As it was, I was desperate. I've been out there," he said gesturing to the walls. "I know what's happening to our people. We've already been here over half-a-year and we've done nothing for them. They can't hold out much longer. We need action not hours of futile debate."

"Yes, I've noticed they seem to be stalling," Will remarked wryly.

"Yes, well, I've some ideas of my own as to how things will happen. I want to see the Saracens ousted and our people reunited. One way or another, I'm determined it is going to happen...and soon."

Will frowned as he began discussing Mike's objectives. The two men discussed the particulars until, finally, Will shooed the young man out. He had no more than closed the door when he heard a soft knock.

"Look, Michael," he said beginning to open the door, "we can discuss this more in the morn...oh! Jan! I'm sorry." He swung the door wide open.

She quickly stepped inside and shut it behind her. "I had to wait till Mike left."

"You could've dropped in and...."

"And he would've wanted to walk me back."

"True."

"Did General Adar say anything to you?"

"Yes, as a matter of fact, he did. He and Commander Behran completed their review of the run leaders' records. He remarked that yours was the most outstanding, not only because of your high efficiency rating, but also because you've never lost anyone under your command. He sends his congratulations...you made Rank Six."

"B-But, that's the highest Rank!"

"You earned it," Will pointed out.

"But I skipped Rank Five. Is that fair to the others?"

"You also took out that Saracen ammo dump, a command post,

and the communications network they rebuilt without losing one man."

"But...."

"But nothing! No one else has ever done that. By the way, how did you do that?"

"Ah-ah-ah! My secret," she said smiling and winking.

"Ah-ha. Right." Will led her out to the kitchen for a cup of tea.

"Do you think General Adar would give me some time off?" she asked. "Like two weeks?"

"Can't say," he replied setting the steaming cup before her. "Oh! You mean because of Michael's little vacation?"

"Mm-hm. I'd sure have a hard time explaining why I had to be gone night and day for two whole weeks, Will."

"That's for sure."

"And he and I really need some time together. Please talk to Adar for me," Jan pleaded laying her hand on his arm. "Please, I don't want to go right back out yet. Not with Mike finally free to spend some time with me."

Will patted her shoulder. "I'll talk to Adar first thing in the morning and persuade him to see things my way."

"Thanks, Will," she said giving him a quick hug before heading for the door.

The next morning Will strode purposefully into the General's office.

"What can I do for you, Dehan?"

"Nothing for me, Adar. I need a favor for Jan. She needs a few days off."

"No can do. That girl is in high demand."

"Yes, by someone with much higher authority." Will glowered at Adar.

"Oh, that...uh...little problem with High Council, you mean?" Adar fidgeted uneasily.

"The very same. It seems that during his few days of freedom, a certain Prince expects to spend that time with his bride-to-be. You know her...the girl you send out on runs while the council sits and stews."

Adar stared at his desk. "You know it has been necessary, Dehan."

"Yes, well, it just 'necessaried'' itself into a dead-end unless you have a great explanation cooked up for the Prince when he asks where his beloved is for two whole weeks. Besides, this isn't a one-woman war. You do have other run leaders."

"True, but Janielle is the absolute best."

"She is also Ihue's best, and I can guarantee that he won't let her out of his sight for two full weeks."

"You are right," Adar admitted raising one hand defensively while pressing a button on his desk with the other. His computer monitor rose from its recess in his desk. "Let's have a look at her schedule."

"Now we're getting somewhere!" Will said leaning across the desk for a better view.

Adar scanned it while thoughtfully rubbing his chin. He tapped his fingers idly on the desktop a moment then reached for the keyboard. He began switching runs to other leaders canceling the least important.

"Well?" Will asked impatiently.

"I can clear her through till the middle of next week. There is one run she has to take. It is of top importance, and I cannot trust it to anyone but Janielle."

"You're certain?"

"Dehan, we have had trouble from the B'narians because ten years ago the Saracens captured their Princess. They have been holding her hostage ever since. We have finally managed to locate her, and if Jan can free her and get her to a B'narian ship, her government has sworn to pull out of Quentas. That would leave the Saracens to face us on their own. Our odds would improve immensely," Adar explained.

"So that's why B'nar broke the treaty," Will mused. "Well, in that case, I guess this schedule will have to do."

"Do not worry," Adar assured him. "It is a three suntarini run tops. You can work out a cover for three suntarini, can you not?"

Will groaned. "Yes, I suppose so."

With the welcomed break in both their schedules, Mike and Jan spent most of the next few days talking. Though he insisted on keeping his weapons' training schedule, with her watching each session from the observatory, the rest of the time he devoted to her. They strolled through the subterranean gardens getting reacquainted. On one particular day, Mike was more quiet than usual. He sat on a bench and pensively rested his chin on his fist.

"Something wrong?" Jan asked, sitting next to him and sliding her arm across his shoulders.

"Oh, I don't know." He sat up and stretched his legs out in front of him. "I guess I was kind of primed to be the conquering hero. You know, come in with guns blasting, have a great big battle and come home on the shoulders of a cheering throng."

"Like the quarterback of a football team who'd just scored the winning touchdown?"

"Yeah, something like that. I mean, Will always told me our people would look up to me."

"I do."

Mike smiled appreciatively. "I know you do, but you aren't a Quentasian, and they're the ones I'm supposed to be here for."

"Well, don't they?"

"Look up to me?"

She nodded.

Mike shook his head. "I'm nothing but a pawn to them; someone the High Council can use to make themselves look like heroes. Until I took control of that meeting, they yelled and shouted no matter what I did."

"Didn't expect you to take them all on, huh?"

"Worse than that. It was if they had totally forgotten that I even existed and had only then woken up to the fact."

"But that's just the councilmen, Mike," she said squeezing his shoulders affectionately. "They're just a bunch of bureaucrats. They expect everyone to make a fuss over them. They're used to being important. But I doubt the people outside of Mozern see things the same way they do."

"But how do you know? How does anyone really know?"

"Oh, I think some do," Jan said quietly gazing off across the orchard.

Mike stared at her, wondering at the far-off look in her eyes.

Chapter 42

The leisurely days the Royal couple had together were over all too soon. One morning well into the second week, Jan crawled out of bed before anyone else was awake. She silently slipped into Will's apartment, made her way through the darkness into his bedroom and shook his shoulder.

"Will," she whispered.

He mumbled incoherently and pulled the covers up higher.

"Will," she said louder, as she shook him again.

"Mm? Huh?" He rolled over and opened his blurry eyes.

"Will. I'm off."

"What did you tell Michael?"

"That I'm helping you work on that final project in the lab, and that the results are necessary for the Science Minister's report to the High Council."

"Which means…?"

"You'll have to sleep in the lab till I get back," she replied.

"Because you told him we'd be there night and day," he concluded.

"What else could I do?"

"Nothing I guess," he groaned. "Oh, all right. I'll sleep in the lab again. Just make it your first stop on the way in."

"Promise," she replied slipping away without a sound.

Immediately after breakfast, Will moved his things to the lab and faithfully slept on the short, narrow bunk that pulled out from the wall. The first night passed slowly in spite of his grumbling, the second night he tossed, the third night he paced. All the fourth day and the fifth he waited anxiously to hear Jan's footsteps or voice. He jumped at each sound as his mind wandered from his work.

Meanwhile, above ground Jan had taken her group, comprised of Marla, Tanza, and Gorlan, along Molluc trails deep into Saracen mining territory. The Mollucs themselves had located the B'narian princess for her and, using the Molluc tunnels, she had been able to free the woman.

Now the five of them scrambled through cramped tunnels as they fled from the mines. Suddenly the ground shook and they heard a loud rumble from nearby.

"One of the shafts is collapsing," Gorlan said.

"Will this tunnel hold out?" Marla wondered.

Jan listened for a moment then spotted widening cracks in the ceiling. "Back! Back!" she cried pushing the B'narian princess before her.

They scrambled back the way they had just come. Seconds later, the roof of the tunnel tumbled in, showering them with dust. They coughed and gagged choking on the dust-filled air.

"Now what?" Tanza asked.

As the dust began to clear, it became obvious that the tunnel was now sealed. Jan surveyed the damage and made a decision.

"There's another branch, but we'll have to go back to the mine."

The B'narian princess stared at her rescuer, eyes wide in fear. Unlike the men in her society, she was small boned with delicate facial features. Now, malnutrition and torture had hollowed her cheekbones making her appear more skeletal. She shook her head closing her eyes against the memories of recent pain.

"We have to," Jan replied gently but firmly. "We will die if we try to dig our way out or wait for help."

The princess breathed heavily fighting an inner battle. Finally she nodded her acceptance of the plan.

"Lead on, Jan," Marla said. "Let's get going before the Saracens dig through the cave-in and discover this tunnel."

They painstakingly retraced their steps until they could hear the drills, shovels and occasional cries of pain from the mines. The B'narian princess flinched and whimpered with fear. Carefully Jan felt her way along until she spotted a tell-tale mark. Running her hands along the wall, she found a secret switch and pushed. A secondary tunnel branched off and they immediately followed it.

"Where will this tunnel take us?" Marla asked.

"A lot further away from the B'narian ship than I wanted," Jan replied. "Let's just hope there have been no recent cave-ins in this tunnel and that the Saracens aren't suspicious enough to garrison the area."

Her group members wore grim countenances as they pressed on.

By the sixth day, Will was frantic. He marched into Adar's office.

"Where-is-she?" he demanded.

Adar looked up and his face sank. He ran his hand across his eyes and rubbed his throbbing forehead. "I do not know, Dehan," he replied, shaking his head.

"What do you mean 'you don't know'?" Will leaned on Adar's desk staring incredulously into the General's bleary eyes. "Where are those scouts you sent out?"

"They brought back reports that the B'narian Princess had been rescued and returned to her people safely. The B'narians have since fulfilled their oath. They left Quentas at sunset yesterday, but...."

"But what?"

"There was an ambush after she was delivered to her ship. Since then, Jan's team has not been seen."

"What do you mean?" Will asked numbly sinking feebly into a chair.

"She simply disappeared...vanished."

"Captured?"

Adar shrugged helplessly. "We do not know, Dehan. There has been no sight of her, no word from her, and so far, no Saracen demands."

Will stumbled out the door and through the halls in a haze. He sat idly in his lab not even pretending to work. That evening he sat on the edge of his cot searching, via the agent of his mind, over the vast regions of Quentas. By morning, dark circles lined his bloodshot eyes. He met Adar on the way to High Council.

Adar peered into Will's face. "You, too?"

Will nodded.

"Anything?"

"Not a trace. I don't know how she could've made herself so invisible on a planet I thought I knew so well."

Reluctantly, the two men sat through the long, grueling meeting. Mike grilled each presenter sharply criticizing their new proposals. By the end of the day, Adar had yet to present.

"We got a lucky break today," he whispered to Will.

"Yes, but will we be so 'lucky' tomorrow?" Will countered as they went their separate ways.

In a cave deep within the foothills of the Mozern Range, Marla, Tanza and Gorlan waited anxiously. Now and then Tanza got up and soaked a rag in water from a small stream that ran through the cave. She brought it back to Marla who pressed it against Gorlan's shoulders. He winced.

"Does it look any better?" he asked.

Marla removed the compress and looked at the angry wound. "You need some medication. As soon as Jan gets back and we get you to the Med-Unit, you will be just fine."

Suddenly they heard scrabbling on the rocks at the entrance to the cave. Instantly alert, they grabbed their weapons and took up defensive positions behind stalagmites. They heard a peculiar whistle and breathed a sigh of relief.

"You made it back!" Marla exclaimed visibly relaxing.

"Yes," Jan replied taking some herbs out of a small pouch that hung at her waist.

"Did the Hallen reach his people?" Gorlan wondered as Marla began preparing the herbs Jan had handed to her.

Jan nodded. “I think we have some new, very valuable allies,” she said rolling out her bedroll. She turned to Marla, “It works better with hot water, but if you double the amount, it should work all right with cold.”

Marla nodded, and Tanza headed back to the stream for more cold water.

Jan stretched out on her bedroll. “Give me two hours then we’ll move out.” With that she rolled over and fell sound asleep.

That evening at dusk, four cloaked figures hugged the mountainside as they hurried toward the Mozern Base.

As Will hurried out the door, he bumped into Mike who followed him anxiously down the corridor.

"Dehan, is Jan still stuck down in that hole of yours?"

"Huh?" Will blinked his bleary eyes as he glanced up. "Oh, yes...yes, she is...hard at work, too. She took my shift so I could come to the council meeting, plus she was up all night. When I get back, she'll probably crash while I take over for a while."`

"Will she needs a break." Mike said firmly.

"She's the one with the endurance. I need her for these tests. Remember, Adar presents tomorrow, and this test is crucial. It must be perfected or we'll be missing the vital link in his plan."

Mike's face fell, and he sauntered dejectedly back to the Royal Suite. Will, however, marched straight to Adar's office.

"I just sent out a new group of runners," Adar said the instant Will opened the door.

"Any luck?"

"One spark of hope."

"What?"

"One runner had spotted Jan taking some unknown trail just prior to the Saracen ambush. However, the enemy has been camped out so heavily near there, we can only assume that she is remaining hidden till they move away."

Will collapsed into a chair. "What do we do, Adar?"

"We wait. She has to come out soon."

"But this is Ihue's beloved we're talking about. If anything happens to her, we'll be in front of a firing squad."

"I know. I realize that." Adar looked up. "I sent a team out to try to draw some of the heat away from where she was last seen. The rest is up to her. Jan is the leader I would ordinarily send out in a situation like this. If she cannot find her way back, then no one can."

Will nodded in resignation.

Back in the lab, Will anxiously paced the floor as precious time slipped by. He and Adar kept another silent vigil that night. In the morning, they slid wearily into their clothes and stumbled to the High Council.

Mike had no more than turned the floor over to General Adar when a silent figure, cloaked and hooded in deep forest-green, entered the chambers and slipped into an empty seat beside Will. Mike stared at the figure for some time, the face and form of Seera flashing through his mind. After a while, he returned his attention to the General's address.

"Your Highness, we feel that this is the only strategem that has any chance of succeeding," Adar was explaining. "We have discovered that the Saracen's main communicative and operative power sources are housed within the Palatial City and Palace, themselves. Also, there is the primary weapons factory and a satellite transmissions base there. Our plan would incorporate two small strike forces that would penetrate the City and Palace via the most secretive ways. The left flank would destroy the defense system, while the right flank would infiltrate the Palace and destroy the power and satellite installations. The instant the power plant had been rendered inoperative, our land forces would strike the main Saracen outposts across Quentas. We would utilize land, sea, and air strikes for maximum effectiveness. As part of our plan, messengers would already have notified villagers and farmers of our strike intent and time. They would be on the alert for our signal and would fight alongside our troops."

"And who will make up these smaller strike forces?" Mike asked.

"The left flank will be comprised of our top explosives experts. The right flank must be members of the Royal Family and their closest aides, due to the paths they will have to travel."

"Do you have anyone specifically in mind for the right flank?" Mike pressed.

"Yes, Your Highness, we do." Adar paused choosing the order of the team members very carefully. "We would, of course, need yourself and Lady Elira for your Royal Powers. We would also need Lord Dehan, our Chief Scientist, and Lord Garik, our Royal Historian and Antiquarian. I and my top aide, Commander Behran, would accompany you, and we would all be led by our highest ranking Elitist guide."

Adar focused his gaze on the cloaked figure, which rose from its place. As Mike watched, the image of Seera again flashed through his mind and a tingle flew up his spine.

"And who might this be?" Mike asked.

The figure reached up and threw back the hood and cloak. A gasp rose up from the audience, but Mike could only stare in shock hardly able to comprehend what he saw. He clutched the podium for support, his knuckles growing white.

Chapter 43

Mike stared at Jan in her Elitist uniform, his face draining of all color.

"I'm sorry, Mike," quietly echoed in his mind. "There was no other way."

He looked to Adar. "Is there no one else?" he asked hoarsely.

"We only have three top Elitists. Lady Janielle's success rate is the highest, though," Adar replied. "Even more importantly, she is the only run leader to bring back every member of every team alive. We believe there can be no other choice since the lives of the Royal Family are at stake."

Mike stared hard at Adar for many long, tense minutes. The general's face visibly contorted under the intense strain of bearing the Crown Prince's powerful gaze. Finally Mike took a deep breath and glanced up at the rest of the council.

"High Council will adjourn briefly. All members excluding General Adar, Lord Dehan, Lady Elira, and Lady Janielle, please exit to the adjoining conference room."

The foursome watched in tense silence as the other councilmen marched from the chambers. Mike waited until the Honor Guard had closed the outer door, then motioned for the others to follow him into the nearest anteroom. They straggled behind him in single file nervously anticipating the upcoming outburst. Mike waited until they had all taken seats.

"I don't know what has been going on, but we are not leaving here until I've gotten to the bottom of the matter. What I see before me smacks of lies and betrayal." He held their gazes, each in turn.

"Mother, you told me Jan was learning healing from you," he began. "This," he said pointing to Jan's uniform, "does not look like healing to me. Explain yourself."

Elira looked at her lap for a moment then up at the son she had never known. "Ihue, what I told you was partly true," she said quietly. "Jan did, indeed, learn many healing techniques, and even assisted me during some emergency surgeries."

"But not all the time," Mike pressed.

She shook her head.

"Why lead me to believe she was always safe with you?"

"Once Jan had become an Elitist, I was given orders that her training in healing was to be used as a cover for her Elitist activities."

"By whom?"

Elira looked down. "General Adar."

"And you couldn't countermand those orders?" Mike asked.

She looked back up at him. "When I turned the governance of Quentas over to you upon our return, my status was reduced to its pre-marriage level. I am very much subject to the orders of my superiors."

Mike studied her, a shocked expression on his face. "I…never realized…." he began.

"It is the law," she replied simply.

Mike turned his attention to Will. "Did you know what was going on, Dehan?"

Will grimly returned his gaze. "Not at first, Ihue. I knew Jan was concerned that our people viewed her as their enemy, and I knew she was seeking a way to prove herself to them. However, I didn't know she had even become an Elitist until I, too, received orders from General Adar to use work in my lab as a cover for her Elitist activities."

"Didn't you even try to stop her?" Mike wondered.

Will nodded. "I tried to warn her not to take such dangerous a risk, but Jan was determined prove herself to our people and win them over. In the end, I could not dissuade her."

Mike studied him finally nodding and taking a deep breath. He then turned to Adar, and the two powerful men locked gazes.

"General Adar, I do not know you well. I do recall now that at one point Jan told me she didn't think you trusted her. Would you care to explain your part in all of this?"

Adar stared at Mike for a long moment before opening his mouth to speak. "She was right. I did not trust her. Few of our people did, and those who trusted her were confined mostly to the immediate Royal Family."

"Why?" Mike wanted to know.

"Look at her," Adar said gesturing toward Jan. "Every aspect of her looks suggests some relation to the Saracens. It is as if they had created a petite female Saracen android with some sort of mental powers that could control you. Few who have seen her have not thought of this."

Mike studied Jan's features comparing them to those of Saracens he had encountered on Earth. Suddenly the resemblance was uncanny and a chill flew up his spine.

"So what were your plans for her?" he demanded.

Adar swallowed hard and fought to maintain composure. His face grew red under the increased pressure from Mike's powers.

Finally he gasped. "We only admitted her to the Elitist corps to keep her under surveillance. If she had made one false move, she would not have returned from that run. The execution would have been quiet and simple."

Mike stared at the general in horror. "You had plans to assassinate my beloved?"

"It was a general consensus," Adar choked out. "If she had had any Saracen connections, we would have destroyed them and her."

Fury began to build within Mike. "So now you've changed your tune. Why?"

"Because Jan proved to us that she was exactly what she claimed to be…a genuine human and not a Saracen spy. It has taken her montari of enormous effort, but she has gained the respect of the entire corps and of most everyone she has come into contact with outside of these halls."

Mike eyed him coldly. "I'm not through with you yet, Adar, but I will let the matter rest for now."

He looked at the others. "You are dismissed for now. Please wait in the Main Council Chamber. I would like to speak with Lady Janielle alone."

Will, Elira and Adar quietly rose to their feet and walked out the door. It whooshed closed and a long moment of silence followed. Finally Mike leaned over Jan.

"So, you wanted to earn everybody's respect," he spat. "Seems that you've done a marvelous job of it. Only one thing wrong...." He paused then pushed away from her chair. "You have lost mine."

"Mike, I...."

"You betrayed me...betrayed my faith and trust in you."

"Mike, I never betrayed you."

"No?" He swung around to face her again. "Here you let me think you were either safely tucked away in your apartment or were in the lab helping Will or were helping mother. But here all the time you were actually risking your life on dangerous runs. Why?" He paced before her white, shaken form. "Why did you lead me on to believe you were safe?" he demanded.

"Because you wouldn't listen when I tried to tell you how much danger I was in right on this base," Jan replied.

"You never...."

"I tried to several times, but you always cut me off saying that your acceptance and the acceptance of the Ring were enough. Only they weren't and you wouldn't hear me."

He took a deep breath. "I believed what I said."

"You were naïve and badly misinformed," she retorted.

"That doesn't excuse your actions," Mike replied.

"But it excuses yours?"

"I've had a lot on my mind. I can only deal with so much at one time."

"Yes," she said. "And the majority of the time it hasn't included me."

He glared at her. "So you run away to prove yourself. Do you understand what you've been doing out there? What would have happened if you had got killed? Did you ever think of that?"

"Every time I watched a friend get killed."

"Did you ever think about how I would feel if you got killed?" he demanded.

"Daily."

"Doubtful." He ran his fingers through his hair. "Did you ever consider what the Saracens would have done to you, to us, to me if you had been captured? My God!" Mike exclaimed, the thought gripping him. "You could have destroyed the whole resistance. Did-you-ever-think-of-that?"

"Yes," she replied, her lower lip quivering.

"Then, why Jan? Why in the world did you do it?" he demanded leaning over her. "This is insane! You're insane! I'm insane! Do you enjoy seeing me as a raving lunatic?" He turned away from her.

"No, Mike…please."

"Please, what? Please may I go on this run?"

"No. Please listen to me for once."

He turned toward her and crossed his arms in front of him. "Fine. I'm listening…for once. Why don't you start by telling me why you didn't run your plans past me?"

"I tried to, but I could never get a hold of you. If you'll recall, you had a very inefficient secretary who was excellent at losing my notes."

He nodded. "Yes, I later discovered some fragments in the incinerator bin. Go on."

"Well, if I couldn't get a simple message like 'my birthday's this week' to you, how in the world was I going to get something more complex across?"

"So, why didn't you catch me in between meetings or training sessions?"

"Oh, you mean you would have given me the whole five minutes you had between appointments? How generous of you," Jan spat. "This would have taken hours to discuss over a period of days, maybe some combined fact finding to determine the depth of your peoples' hostility towards me and some brainstorming sessions to figure out the best way for me to gain their trust and respect. But you didn't have hours for me. You didn't even have those five minutes. I've had to deal with this very personal threat completely on my own. You say I betrayed you? Why did you abandon me? Why did you just dump me in the middle of this place and treat me as if I only exist during those few minutes you think of me?"

Mike blinked at her charge. "I told you before…that wasn't my intention. I had no idea what the situation was like before we got here."

"You have an answer for every mistake you make."

"Yes, and I need an answer from you. How did you manage to become an Elitist in the first place when everyone hated you so much?"

Jan remained silent for a moment. "Many of the details I have sworn oaths to never reveal. Oaths," she quickly said as he opened his mouth, "that I take very seriously. What I can say is that the Mollucs helped me find the headquarters of the Underground. When I toured there, I saw a need, one I thought I could fill. I argued my way into the opening trials. From there on out, I trained and tested just like anybody else."

"'Just like anybody else'," Mike mimicked sarcastically. "Only you aren't 'just anybody else'!" he exclaimed pointing a finger at her. "You're my fiancée, or had you forgot."

"I am your fiancée," Jan replied, "but I am not your chattel. I'm not some animal you can own. I'm a person with needs and feelings, both of which you have ignored for nearly a year."

"You don't understand. I need you."

"When? During a rare ten minute break when you can take me down off the shelf and dust me off?" she spat, her anger rising.

"Of course not! Things just haven't been normal."

"You're darn right, they haven't been normal! I'm the useless fiancée of the Crown Prince of Quentas. I'm to stay home, mind my own business and scream for help when attacked."

"That's not what I mean."

"It's what I've experienced. No, Mike, I can't forget that I'm your fiancée, that I wear the Star Ring, that I look like a Saracen, that I'm an alien from Earth, and that your people hate me. Did you hear me? They HATE me."

She leapt to her feet and took a step closer to him as months of hurt and injustice erupted inside her. "I came here, Michael Stellan, because I loved you. I accepted this Ring," she said holding up her right hand, "so I could be with you forever. Only I discovered that weighty responsibilities come with it…one of which is to convince a planetful of people that I should marry their Crown Prince and take part in ruling them. A little difficult to do when you look just like the very people who have enslaved them for thirty years.

"I can guarantee that I wouldn't be very persuasive sitting cozily in my apartment doing needlework while people out there are fighting for their very existence."

Mike blinked, startled by her outburst. "But is this the only way you could prove yourself?"

She shrugged. "I don't know. It's the best way I could find on my own."

He nodded glancing at the floor.

"I do know that being an Elitist has allowed me to prove my loyalty and honest desire to serve these people. They know that I understand their suffering because I have suffered alongside them and have risked my life to help free them. Maybe, just maybe, it will be enough to break through their fear and hatred."

Mike sighed deeply. "All right. I'll concede that much. But I don't want you to be any part of this last run." He folded his arms across his chest giving his words an air of finality.

"But, Mike, they'll be sending you into the very heart of the danger. That's why they want me to lead - to make certain you get there alive. You don't always use restraint when you meet up with Saracens."

He crossed the room to her, stretched out his arms, and lifted the hood up over her head. He cocked his head to the side a moment and squinted. "Seera?"

She nodded. "Somebody had to make certain you returned for the next High Council."

Mike turned away.

"Don't-you-see, Mike? I have learned things the others haven't. The Mollucs allow me in their tunnels. The one we used to escape from the Saracens that day was Molluc. No other runner could have gotten you out of there, because the others don't know where the tunnels are located, how to find them, or how to open them. If you had been with anyone else, Mike, you would be dead right now and there would be no resistance."

Mike took a deep breath and sighed heavily.

"Please, don't you see? Because I wear the Star Ring, the Mollucan gave me free access to their tunnels. He gave me a chance to make a difference and I have. When we landed on Quentas, the resistance was actually losing. They had nothing to work with and were losing more people every day than they could recruit. But since I've become an Elitist, I've brought back more supplies than they've ever had, supplies Will has used to build better equipment. I've taken out more Saracen outposts to hold them back and brought back healing herbs for the healers to use on the wounded. Plus, I've brought back every person I've ever taken out with me...alive.

"That's why you need me now. I can take you through tunnels so the Saracens will never know you're there. Those other two runners could only take you by the best trails they know of and, in that part of the country, they're Saracen infested. You'd never even see the City, let alone get in."

Mike shook his head slowly lowering himself into a chair. "But how can I let you go, Jan, even for my own safety?"

She knelt beside him taking his right hand and stroking his long, slender fingers. "Because you've got a planetful of people out there who are counting on you to be their next King. Because I love you, and I want to make sure you finish this assault alive. Because I want to be a part of your life...an active part, not just a cheerleader on the sidelines."

Mike groaned. "All right. No more arguments. It goes against my will and my better judgment, but I concede."

Jan dropped his hand, rocking off her knees and onto her toes. She stared at the floor for a long, silent moment. "Mike," she said softly. "Has this ruined our relationship? Have you really lost your respect for me?"

He ran his hand over his face and across his chin before looking at her. "I don't know, Jan. I'm angry…furious right now. If you mean, do I still love you...I think so, otherwise, I feel very confused."

She nodded rising to her feet. "I'm sorry, Mike...very sorry. Nothing's turned out the way I thought it would. I wanted you to be proud of me. Instead, you're furious. It's not at all what I wanted." She turned and slipped out the door.

A light flashed on the Honor Guard's wristband. He glanced at it, then hurried to the conference room and called the councilmen back into the main chamber. Jan stood outside, drew the cloak around her, and pulled the hood up over her head. She returned to her seat sitting quietly next to Will as she had before.

"Well?" Adar asked looking to her for some word.

She neither moved nor spoke in reply, and he was left to guess at the Prince's reaction.

Minutes later, Mike strode back in and took up his position at the podium. His face was hard and stern. He gazed ominously at the assembly.

"I have made my decision," he announced tersely. "Though certain members of this council deserve strong disciplinary measures, I cannot overlook the fact that this proposal achieves the unity of our people in the destruction of the Saracens. It also takes into account every conceivable element we must face. In agreement with General Adar's choices, we will operate using all parties named in his proposal. Hearings on disciplinary measures will be postponed and rescheduled at my discretion, but will be no earlier than the end of our present conflict with the Saracens."

Mike paused, eyeing Jan's cloaked and hooded figure darkly. He pulled his attention back to the others.

"General Adar," he continued, "you have two more weeks to cement your plans and present a detailed outline of your proposal to this council. High Council is dismissed."

Mike turned from the podium and stalked out the door. He walked the corridors toward the Royal Suite with measured steps. Behind him, a dark figure followed, hidden and silent. It anxiously watched as he passed through the door into his apartment.

Chapter 44

Jan backed away from the Royal Suite and rushed along the labyrinthine corridors to General Adar's office. She hurried inside and collapsed into a chair.

"I'm sorry I'm so late, but...."

"Do not mention it. Your run was an immense success, and you managed to convince the Prince," Adar commended. "That more than makes up for it."

"Yeah, well, we aren't out of the woods with Ihue, yet. I only managed to convince him to accept your plan. Otherwise, we're still going to feel his wrath."

Adar nodded glumly. "The only thing we can do now is make sure our strategy works. Maybe he will just demote me."

"I'm glad it's so simple for you," Jan remarked acidly.

"Yes, well, I…uh...I guess your position is a bit more precarious," Adar admitted uneasily. He hastily cleared his throat. "Let's take a look at the hologlobe. There is one sector of your route that has me quite concerned. I need your opinion on it."

He pushed a button on his desk, and a wall panel slid back revealing a three-dimensional, holographic image of Quentas. It floated out into the room till it was situated between them.

"To the best of my knowledge, there is no safe route around the fort here and across the gap to the plateau beyond," he said, pointing from the peak enclosing the Star Chamber to the plateau that lay directly across the steep, rocky gorge.

The hologlobe rotated presenting the side being studied, and projected an enlarged image of the sector out from itself.

"Do you know any routes the rest of us do not know?"

Jan frowned and shook her head. "I'm sorry, General. To my knowledge, there are no underground tunnels in that region. A swing bridge used to be operated out of the fort, but Saracens now hold both it and the gap."

"Then to cross that sector, Core I would have to march out onto the plain as far as Rivnafor in order to ford the river, then double back and scale the cliff walls."

"Yes, but that presents two more problems," Jan pointed out. "Not only is Rivnafor now held by the Saracens, but the entire trek would take several days to accomplish."

"Yet, it appears to be our only route," Adar pressed.

"As far as I can tell."

"Then the only way to get Core I through that sector safely is to send a squadron against Rivnafor to draw them out."

"Too costly in lives," Jan protested. "Besides, we can't afford the time it would take to cross at that point and scale the cliff."

"I foresee no other way," Adar replied in resignation.

"There must be some other way," Jan said. She propped her head on her hand yawning in spite of herself.

"I am sorry, Jan. I am forgetting how long you have been without rest. You go to bed and I will put the problem to the committee."

"All right, General. But don't make anything definite till I've had a chance to sleep on it. I know there has to be another way to cross that gap, but I'm just too tired to think of it now."

Jan staggered wearily out the door and back to the Royal Suite. Elira was pacing the common lounge, while Mike's angry voice could be heard through the closed door to his apartment. Jan sidled around Elira, hurried past Mike's door, stumbled into her own apartment.

Meanwhile, two doors down, Mike paced and vented his anger.

"This whole thing is crazy! I feel like my best friends have betrayed me! Why, Will? Why did you ever let Adar talk you into this? How could you have let Jan go on those runs? You never would have done anything like this on Earth. What gives?"

Will shook his head trying to clear his vision which had suddenly clouded over. A throbbing ache pounded along the left side of his head like a rapid, steady heartbeat. He pressed the heel of his hand against his head in an effort to counteract the pain. "It's different here, Michael. On Earth, I was the decision maker. Here, I have to take orders from others. My position has changed," he slurred.

Mike stopped pacing to look at him. "You still have those migraines, don't you?"

"Yes," Will said wincing. "They've gotten worse since we returned...more frequent, too."

"Do you always know what you're doing when you get them?" Mike asked.

"No. I don't think so," Will admitted. "On Earth I could usually think, even with one. Here...." He inhaled sharply as the pain intensified.

"No use yelling at you," Mike muttered. "Tandk!" he called.

The Molluc scurried from the kitchen.

"Get Lord Dehan something for his migraine."

The Molluc bowed and left.

"Maybe you ought to lie down, Will," Mike suggested studying the man's strained face.

Will nodded weakly and struggled toward the door. Mike caught him just as he was about to fall.

"The floor's a bit hard, Will," he quipped. "Try a lounger." Mike dragged his friend to the one against the far wall.

Will was mumbling incoherently when Tandk returned with a small vial. Mike took it and emptied its contents into Will's mouth. In minutes he was sound asleep. Tandk brought out a thermo-blanket and covered him.

In her own room Jan sobbed into the pillows on her bed. The only other times she could recall feeling equally miserable were when her parents had died. Otherwise, nothing seemed to compare. She cried until her stomach ached and her eyes were heavily swollen.

Teldank came to the door and watched her heaving shoulders for a moment before quietly entering. As she approached Jan's bed, she began humming a soothing Molluc lullaby. She reached out and began to gently rub Jan's back. Gradually the sobs eased and the tears dried. Finally Jan lay peacefully sleeping.

Teldank shook her head and muttered to herself as she shuffled into the kitchenette. Ndak stood near the table and twitched his whiskers upon seeing her distraught face.

"She worked so hard and did so much, only to have him discount and devalue all of her efforts," Teldank said, a sad tear slipping from her eye. "She did not deserve the reprimand he gave her. It is as if he cannot see her worth."

Ndak nodded.

"All that work for nothing."

"Not for nothing," Ndak responded. "She has accomplished much."

"To a woman…for nothing."

Jan slept soundly for several hours, but as time passed she began to twitch. In an hour she was tossing in earnest eventually kicking her covers to the floor. "Something…warned…Saracens," she moaned. "Too many…in clear lands…can't travel…Palisade Plain…got to…find another way."

She dove under her pillow, wrapping it about her ears. "Saracens…on plain…fording…takes too long…must be…other way."

She threw the pillow to the floor, her hair drenched with sweat. "If we…could fly."

Suddenly her eyes popped open. That's it! Mike knows about flying!"

She was half way out of bed before stopping herself. "He's not going to want to see me," she fretted. "But this is crucial. I've got to try."

Jan forced herself to dress, went to his door and timidly knocked.

"Who's there?" came Mike's gruff voice.

"Mike, it's me."

He did not reply.

"Mike, I need to talk to you," she tried again.

No response.

She knocked harder. "Mike, please. There's too much at stake. Open-the-door."

Just as she raised her fist to knock again, the door opened by itself. She hesitantly stepped inside and peered at Will who lay on the far lounger.

"He's got a bad migraine," Mike informed her matter-of-factly. "The medication knocked him out."

"Oh."

Mike motioned toward a chair near the door, and Jan slowly lowered herself onto it.

"So, what did you come to say?"

"I need some help."

"Finally? You finally come to me?"

Jan choked back tears. "Please, Mike. I'm so exhausted right now. I haven't slept in days."

"Seems to me you chose that occupation. I take it that sleepless nights go with the territory," he taunted.

Jan looked like she had been slapped then glared at him and rose to her feet. "Michael, you have changed…drastically since we landed on Quentas. At one point in time I considered you to be such a caring man. Now, I find a cold, cruel dictator. If I could get this ring off," she said tugging at the Star Ring, "I'd throw it at you and say good-bye."

Tears brimming anew in her eyes, she fled his apartment. He watched her go then shook his head.

"You really think you are the most special, most important thing around here," Ndak squeaked.

Mike stared at him in surprise.

"Oh, I know. Pay no mind to Ndak who just quietly minds his own business and does his job. But for your information, I too am a prince. I am the Mollucan's eldest son. On the day that he dies, I will inherit his throne and all of the responsibilities that go with it."

"Does that include lecturing other princes?" Mike asked, somewhat amused.

"Only when I see a bad situation getting worse, when it could have been prevented. Then, yes."

"Look, I don't think you understand how things are…" Mike

began.

"I understand all too well. Teldank is my betrothed. I see your side; I see her side."

"Go on."

"You came here expecting to be a big hero and, instead, got swallowed up in bureaucracy. Your beloved has become the hero."

"You think I'm jealous?" Mike asked, surprised.

"Search your own heart. Only you know for sure. I do know that to expect a woman to sit by and wait for months for you to request her presence is a death knell to love. Not listening to her concerns discounts her feelings. You cannot treat a woman like a hat," Ndak said.

"But when we're together, it's great!" Mike insisted.

"For you…not for her. You need big moments; she needs hundreds of small ones. For you, you say "I love you" and feel it suffices for eternity. After a few suntarini, she can no longer hear the 'I love you.' After a few weeks, she can no longer feel the 'I love you.' After a few montari, she wonders what she has done to make you hate her," Ndak continued.

Mike's eyes were wide as he took in his chamberlain's word. "You think I'm in the wrong?"

Ndak nodded vigorously. "I know you are in the wrong. Your people have made her feel like the enemy and an outcast; now you have, too."

Mike took a deep breath as Ndak cut to the heart of matters.

"But there is another area in which you are very much amiss and that is concerning her being an Elitist."

"I don't want to hear about it," Mike said beginning to rise.

Ndak put his hand on Mike's chest and pushed him back onto the lounger with amazing force. Mike blinked in surprise.

"You-will-listen," Ndak growled. "You make me ashamed to serve you when I see how you treat her efforts and accomplishments. How many other women would agree to leave every familiar thing they have ever known, suffer torture to protect you, travel light years to a strange planet and try to make a life here for themselves. Why? Because she loves you."

"What woman, though preferring the safety and protection of a comfortable home, instead fights and suffers and endures to win over the hearts of a strange, hostile people. Why? Because she loves you. And how have you repaid her?"

"I-I…." Mike stammered.

"With neglect, ridicule and reprimand. For once in my life, I believe that the Star Ring is wrong," Ndak declared. "It may have accepted her, but it should have rejected YOU!" Ndak turned and angrily left the room.

Mike repeated what Ndak had said over and over. So many times he had dreamed of the dangers outside of Mozern. Now he recalled them to mind realizing that he had vicariously shared Jan's struggles. One scene jumbled into another as he recalled when he first saw her right after the torture. His stomach knotted and he stumbled to the bathroom, sick to his stomach as he recognized his incredible failings.

He staggered back out to the lounge and sat with tears streaming down his face. When Will awoke, he found a much humbled Prince.

"How are you feeling, Will?" Mike asked as his mentor slowly sat up.

"A lot better than you look. What's wrong?"

"Let's just say, in the words of that old Southern Baptist preacher you used to know, "I'm just a humble pilgrim; just a repentant sinner," Mike replied.

Will marveled at the change.

"I've been heartless towards Jan. How do I make up for my arrogance?" Mike asked. "How do I make up for the neglect?"

"Start with 'I'm sorry'," Will replied.

That evening Mike paced the garden below Jan's balcony as he tried to gather enough courage to face her. Finally he squared his shoulders and marched up the stairs.

"She's not there," a voice said from behind.

He turned to see Jan standing at the foot of the steps.

"I've been watching you for a while. Whatever you have to say to me, say it out here."

Mike slowly walked back down and sat on one of the lower steps. "Jan, I-I've come to apologize."

"Save it."

He shook his head. “I can’t. I’ve got to. I can’t believe the monster I’ve become.” Tears welled in his eyes threatening to storm once again.

Jan looked at the ground.

“I was jealous, Jan. Jealous that here you had become the hero I had wanted to be. So I grabbed for power and control instead."

She nodded still looking down.

“I didn’t know how to treat a woman, either. I didn’t know you need ‘I love you’s’ everyday. Since I’d said it once and I hadn’t taken it back, I figured that it sufficed. I-I didn’t know, Jan.”

She finally looked up at him. “I wish I could say I feel something right now. I can tell you’re in earnest. At this point even anger would feel better than the numbness I feel.”

“Please, Jan. I really do love you, and I really do need you in my life…as an active partner,” he added.

She sighed heavily. “I’ve spent a year proving myself. It’s your turn to prove yourself, Michael. Win me back!” She darted up the stairs past him.

“What did you want this afternoon?” Mike called after her.

She stopped but did not turn around. “Help.”

“Let me start by offering it,” Mike said hurrying after her. He touched her shoulder but received no response.

Finally Jan nodded. “Let’s go inside and I’ll show you where the problem lies.”

They went into her lounge and she reached into her pocket drawing out a small, multi-faceted prism. She threw it into the air where it burst with light. A holographic image of the pass and river to Rivnafor took shape in the center of her lounge.

"This is our hot-spot," she said quickly explaining the obstacles they faced and Adar's proposal. "It occurred to me that if we only had wings, we could fly across the pass. But it would have to be silent flight."

"A glider," Mike said rubbing his chin thoughtfully.

"That's what I thought, but there'll be eight of us, and a glider only seats two."

"Plus, they're too large for the area you have there and something that big would be easily spotted," Mike commented.

"Well, I guess that's out," Jan said dejectedly.

"No. There may be a way. What sort of air currents run through there?"

"Some good updrafts along the ridge," Jan said. "But we'd have to send out a team to explore them more thoroughly. Why?"

"What about using hang gliders. We built them once in the Aviation Club. They're lightweight, fully collapsible, silent and, made of the right material, difficult to detect."

"Hmm. I like the idea. Do you really think it would work?"

"I think it's reasonable. Better than the route Adar's proposing."

"Then I'd better fill him in so he can start working out the details," Jan said.

"While you're gone, I'll start working on the design."

Jan left to contact Adar. Mike went back to his apartment and picked up his compu slate.

"What are you drawing?" Will asked looking over his shoulders.

Mike looked up from the compu-slate he had grabbed. He sketched a few lines then held it up for Will to see. "Look familiar?"

"Vaguely. I know I've seen that design before."

"It's the hang glider I made for the Aviation Club that one year. Want to help me modify it?"

"Hmm. Let's take a look at it," Will said moving over to Mike's lounger. He sat beside him watching as he drew. "How far will it have to glide?"

"Hold a sec," Mike said reaching for a small keyboard that lay on the end-table. He tapped into the main computer and watched as the distance across the gap to the plateau flashed onto the compu-slate in its upper left corner. "We don't seem to have all the information we need."

"Talk to Jan. She should know the distances."

"Want to help us with it?" Mike offered.

"Yes, actually I have some ideas for wing material that could make it almost invisible," Will replied. "However, we can't finish the design till we know the direction and velocity of the wind currents around the gap," Will said.

Jan entered at that moment with a stern look on her face.

Mike looked over at her watching her face intently. "You aren't thinking of going out, are you?"

She glanced up at him. “A team is going out soon to check on Saracen movements. It could always extend its range and send up some weather balloons.”

“You are not going to lead it this time,” Mike declared.

She glared at him, stood up and began walking away.

“Jan, wait. I didn’t mean that.”

“Just let me do my job, Prince. I know my business well enough. Otherwise, leave me alone!”

Chapter 45

Mike watched Jan stalk out of his apartment and immediately regretted his outburst. "Tell me it's possible for me to learn to keep my mouth shut, Will. Please tell me it's possible."

"You will, Michael. You will."

Mike sighed, got up and headed for the comm-linc. "Let's transfer this design to your science lab computer," he suggested.

"Good idea. After lunch I'll go down to the lab and try out some formulas for a new fuselage."

Mike nodded and entered the command on the slate, while Will strolled out the door. Mike got a quick glimpse of Jan as she darted by. He turned off his comm-linc then headed out onto his balcony and over to hers. He caught her at her table. She got up to go back inside, but he stood in front of her blocking her escape.

"I'm sorry," he said easing her back onto her seat and kneeling before her. "I still want to protect you, even though you're well trained. I know you know your job and do it well."

"You're apologizing a lot lately," she remarked.

Mike took her hand. "I'll apologize and bite my tongue until I've got this right. I want you back. I want to make you feel loved.

I've never been so miserable in my whole life."

Jan's face relaxed and she gently ran her fingers through his hair. She kissed his forehead then nodded toward the opposite chair.

"Have lunch with me," she invited.

Mike smiled and took the seat she offered. She split her food sharing it with him. They ate in silence for a while.

"You'll be happy to know I'm not going on that run,' she said at last.

"No, why not?"

"Adar felt that it was fairly routine and that I need to conserve my energy," she replied.

"Hm. I could learn to like that man after all."

"Problem is I've got this bad feeling about it. Behran always called it 'trail instincts.' After a while you learn to trust them."

Mike squeezed her hand. "Well, let's just hope everything turns out ok."

Adar sent the team out the next day, and all Jan could do was wait. While she helped Mike and Will in the lab over the next couple of days, her mind was frequently elsewhere. She walked back to the Royal Suite with Mike not hearing a word he was saying. As they stepped into the common lounge, he stopped her and turned her to face him.

"You're really worried, aren't you?"

She glanced up at him. "I've got this knot in the pit of my stomach. Something has gone wrong, and Adar won't let me go out to see what it is."

"You shou…." Mike started to say, then bit his tongue. He took a deep breath trying to reword his concern. "I know you want to go back out there, but maybe things aren't as bad as you think."

She squeezed his hand. "Thanks. I just wish I could be certain."

Jan slowly headed for her apartment and disappeared inside. Mike walked into his, paced the lounge then went out into the gardens. As he meandered along the paths, he spotted a Molluc gardener trimming several blooms off a shrub. He walked over and picked up the flowers.

"These flowers look fine to me," he said. "How come you're

cutting them off?"

"Because when I remove some of the flowers, the ones that remain will be bigger because they will get all the nutrients," the gardener replied.

"What will you do these?" Mike asked picking several off the ground.

"Oh, these are useable as they are."

"Could I have a couple?" Mike asked looking at the unfamiliar plants.

"And why would you want them?" the Molluc asked suspiciously eyeing Mike from under his hat.

"I wanted to cheer up Lady Janielle," Mike replied smelling the flower.

"Oh, well, in that case, take a few, but not all."

Mike picked up several of the apricot and pink colored blossoms. He got up and waved to the gardener. "Thanks."

The Molluc waved and went back to his task. When Mike was far enough away, he took off his hat. Ndak nodded to himself, his whiskers twitching.

Mike ascended the stairs to Jan's balcony and knocked at the kitchenette door. Jan opened it, and Mike held one of the blooms out to her.

"How pretty! Where did you get it?" Jan asked.

"In the garden," Mike replied. "The same place I got these," he said bringing the fresh cut bouquet out from behind his back.

Her eyes sparkled. "Oh, Mike, they're beautiful. But won't you get in trouble for picking them?" She backed into the room and turned to show Teldank who, though looking at the flowers appreciatively, also wore a curious expression.

"The gardener was pruning the plant and said I could have a few, just for you," he replied gazing into her eyes.

She glanced down still unsure of her feelings. "Let me find something to put them in," she said hastily turning toward the cupboards and pulling down a cruet.

Mike placed his hands on the back of her shoulders and gently squeezed them. She stood still swallowing hard then turned toward him. He leaned over to kiss her lips, but she turned her cheek to him instead.

"I'm sorry, Mike. I-I'm not ready to…to take up where we left off."

Though disappointed, he nodded. "It's ok. As long as I can see you and spend time with you. Just don't send me away."

She shook her head slightly. "No, I want you to stay. I-I just wish I felt toward you like I used to."

"Me, too."

The next day Jan left the lab several times to check on the run's status. On the third day she nearly lived in Adar's office. Mike finally came, put his arm around her shoulders and led her back to the Royal Suite.

"I'm just so worried," she complained.

"I know," Mike said taking her hand and leading her into his apartment.

He sat her on a lounger facing away from him, took her long hair and gently pushed it over her left shoulder then began rubbing her tense neck and shoulders.

"Mm. This feels so good," Jan murmured then started to cry.

Mike stopped and turned her to face him. "What's wrong?"

"I just can't help thinking of all the other times when I so desperately needed to feel your touch and you were no where around. Even feeling good right now hurts," she conceded.

He wrapped his arms around her and gently rubbed her back. "You have no idea how sorry I am, Jan. But I can't undo anything I've done in the past. All I can do is try to make things right now."

'I know. I'm working on it, too."

"Do you want me to stop?" he asked.

"The shoulder rub? No, please don't stop."

He gave her a squeeze then turned her back around and kept rubbing.

Suddenly the comm-linc in his office beeped loudly. Mike leaned over and pressed a button on the end table.

"Yes?"

"Prince Ihue?" Adar's strained voice called. "Is Lady Janielle with you?"

"Yes."

"Would you two come to my office? The news is urgent."

Jan, who had been listening carefully, jumped up. "It's the run.

Something has happened to them."

"We won't know till we get down there," Mike said rising.

"If anything has gone wrong, I'm going to be pretty upset," she replied darting out the door.

Mike hurried after her and minutes later arrived in Adar's office, winded. Adar rose to greet them with a bow, his face remaining grave.

"The run? What happened?" Jan asked immediately.

Adar shook his head.

"You mean, no one came back?" Mike asked incredulously.

"Only one. She is in the Med-Unit."

Jan looked from one to the other, her face livid. "I told you I should have gone."

"But it might have been you," Mike protested.

She shook her head. "You still don't understand, do you? I know other ways of getting around…tunnels the Mollucs taught me as well as their tactics. My whole team would have been back by now, not just me. I knew this would happen. I just knew it!"

He hung his head. "Well, at least we can go see how she is."

Jan bolted out the door with Mike and Adar following.

"How bad?" Jan asked anxiously as Adar hustled along at her side.

As they neared the Med-Unit, Jan glanced through the ward's windows. "Marla!" she cried spotting Marla's matted, dark hair and blood-stained cloak. She dashed through the doors, the men following quickly behind.

"Marla! Marla, can you hear me?" she called kneeling beside her friend's cot and holding her trembling hand. "Are you all right? Marla, what happened?"

The other girl's lips moved slightly and her eyes fluttered open. She attempted a weak smile. "I got back."

"You sure did, Marla, and am I ever glad. But what happened?"

"Saracens...from the old fort...attacked us. Got the balloons up...took the tunnel...you showed me. Thanks."

"Did you get any information off the balloons?" Adar asked.

Marla nodded weakly. "Compu-disc."

"The usual pocket?" Jan asked.

Marla nodded again.

Jan reached for the mud-caked tunic on the floor next to her. She poked her hand inside and pulled out a round, flat disc.

"You do what the healers tell you and get better," Jan instructed squeezing her hand. "I don't want to hear that you've been fighting orders."

"But the last run...." Marla protested weakly.

"We would all rather see you regain your health," Adar said with a warmth his manners rarely betrayed.

Marla looked up at him and nodded.

Adar took the disc from Jan and walked away cradling it in his hand. Jan squeezed Marla's hand, then rose and took Mike outside the Med-Unit.

"That's my best friend in there," she stormed. "I don't know how badly she's hurt, but if anything happens to her, I'll never forgive you and Adar."

"But Jan...."

"No buts. Being an Elitist is my job. I was trained to do a job and I do it well. I really resent interference, especially when all my senses are telling me that sending a regular leader into a particular territory was going to mean big trouble for us."

"I'm sorry, Jan."

"Mike, you're trying to protect me. I know. I know how you feel. But you've got to realize that you can’t protect me when I'm in the service."

He sighed heavily and nodded. “I’m working on it, Jan. But it’s hard not to want to protect the one you love.”

Jan nodded and squeezed his hand. “For now I’m going to stay with Marla.”

“I’ll be back to stay with you. I just want to talk to mother for a moment.”

She nodded and watched him wander away then went back into the Med-Unit to Marla’s side.

Meanwhile, Mike let his instincts guide him to his mother’s side. She looked up in surprise then hurried over to greet him.

“That last run didn’t go well, did it?” he remarked.

“No.” Elira said sadly. “Only your cousin returned.”

Jan says she could have brought them all back.”

Elira took a deep breath. "She would have, Ihue. I know it. But Marla is not to be blamed for failing. All of the runs before Jan became an Elitist went like this one. Everyone knows that she takes trails that no one else knows of."

"I guess I really should have insisted that Adar let her go out after all," Mike said remorsefully.

"You cannot be blamed, either," Elira said quietly. "You love Jan and want to protect her.

Mike nodded. "I know, but this is war."

"Love does not understand war."

He sighed heavily. "How bad is Marla?"

"Thankfully not too serious. She has several laser wounds, a broken wrist from a fall, and an open gash. She lost some blood trying to get back here. She is weak, but she will be fine."

"Does she need a transfusion?"

Elira nodded. "We have started culturing blood cells from her stem cells," she said.

"Does she have a special blood type?"

"Royal," Elira replied. "We carry a particular set of antigens and proteins that the rest of the people do not have."

"Is that on top of blood type?"

She nodded.

"So type my blood," Mike said rolling up his sleeve.

"Ihue, I cannot."

"I insist. Jan and Marla were friends on Earth, and if there's one thing Jan needs, it's friends. If my blood matches, let's do a transfusion now."

Elira studied his earnest face then nodded. She led him to a lab area, took a small sample of blood and ran it through a computerized scanner. Within minutes the scanner had typed his blood and had checked for the antigens. They waited while it cross-matched with Marla's. Finally the results showed on a screen.

"Well, we have a match," Elira said. "Are you certain you want to do this?"

Mike nodded. "Absolutely."

"I will get Lornda to prep you," she said hurrying away.

Within half-an-hour, Mike lay on a bed in the surgical-med unit, a needle in his arm from which his rich red blood flowed through a clear tube into a bag. Jan entered and moved to his side.

"Marla's all ready in another room," she told him taking his free hand. "Why are you doing this?"

Mike gazed at her for a moment. "For one thing, Marla is my cousin. But even more importantly, she's your friend. If ever there was a woman in need of good friends, that's you. I want her to recover fully."

"Thanks," Jan replied brushing his forehead with her lips.

He closed his eyes as her breath caressed them. How he longed to hold her again.

Several minutes later the procedure was complete, and his blood was now infusing Marla with vitality. He remained on the bed feeling light-headed and a little weak.

"How do you feel?" Jan asked coming back in from checking on Marla.

"A little fuzzy," he replied.

"I brought you some juice and crackers. They'll help raise your blood sugar level. You'll feel better."

"Thanks," he said reaching for the juice then the crackers.

Finally feeling strong enough, he went in to check on Marla, who now had more color in her cheeks then back to his apartment.

Throughout the following week, the plans for the glider took shape. Mike took a break from the research and cornered Jan in the Royal Suite.

"What?" she asked, when he would not let her by. "C'mon, Mike. I have to go."

"You can't. I need to talk to you."

"But Mike, I have a meeting," she protested.

He took her hand and led her over to a comm-linc on the wall. He punched it and got through to Adar.

"General, Lady Janielle will be delayed from attending that meeting. Will there be a problem?"

"We need her presence. She is the main speaker."

"Can you reschedule it?" Mike asked.

Adar paused. "We can move it to after lunch."

"Then do it."

Mike turned back to Jan. "Ok, no meeting. Come with me."

She studied his face curiously but allowed him to lead her

through his apartment, out into the gardens and into a secluded spot deep within. He sat her on a boulder beside a deep pool then knelt before her taking her hands in his.

"Jan, I don't have a ring to give you; just my love. I know I've hurt you very deeply but punishing me isn't going to make things right. I promise to continue working on showing you love. But please. Take me back. Say you'll marry me all over again," Mike pleaded.

She stared at him in surprise and confusion. Deep emotions warred within her.

"I've been afraid that if I just accept you back, you'll go back to your old ways," she said at last. "I don't think I could stand it a second time."

"No, Jan, never! I may slip from time to time, but I will never sink that low ever again. I have truly learned my lesson."

Tears brimmed in her eyes and she nodded. He smothered her in his embrace kissing her and hugging her.

She gazed up into his eyes. "I love you."

Chapter 46

Towards the end of that week, Will called Mike and Jan to the science lab to examine the new material he had created for the fuselage as well as the scale model he had built.

"This material absorbs all visible light, rather than reflecting it," he explained. "Plus, it's lighter than Earth-made sailcloth and sturdier than nylon."

"That's some trick!" Mike exclaimed. "Looks really good."

Jan smiled but glanced anxiously out into the corridor where a group of runners straggled by. A puzzled frown crossed her face. She squeezed Mike's arm then hurried out the door after them.

Mike watched her go, gave Will a pat on the back, and followed the small group down the hall to Adar's office. As he entered, everyone was talking at once. He listened a moment then raised his hands. One-by-one the group fell silent.

"Now, if I could only train the council this well," he quipped before growing serious. "All right now. What's the problem?"

They all opened their mouths to speak at once.

"Whoa! Let's start with the leader of this run."

A young man shifted his feet nervously. "We did not even begin, Your Highness. Saracens stopped us before we got past the Mozern range."

"Every topside route is crawling with them," a young woman confirmed.

"But I need them to go out again," Adar said. "We need to know how many of the trails Core I and II will be taking have been infiltrated. We must know whether we have to alter the routes and our timetables."

"It is impossible!" the run leader declared.

"No, it's not!" Jan spoke up. "I can get a group through."

The room fell silent. Adar looked at Mike.

"She is right," he agreed. "She is the only one who could get a group through."

Mike sighed. "Runners, you are dismissed."

They glanced at Adar then hastily ducked out the door.

Mike waited until the runners had gone and the door had completely closed. "I would like to go with her."

Adar shook her head. "Completely unadvisable, Your Highness."

"Why not? She'll need a lot more protection than what you can offer her, and I've had a lifetime of experience fighting Saracens."

"Mike," Jan said, "when we go out, we avoid fighting Saracens at all cost. In small groups, we're not ready to wage battle. We use stealth and camouflage. We train and condition ourselves for speed and endurance."

"I've been working out every single day since we got here," he protested.

"And you're still breathless when you try to follow me from the Royal Suite to this office," she pointed out.

He frowned. "You're saying I'm out of shape?"

"Not for battle, but for speed and endurance, yes."

"So you're trying to say I'd be a liability."

"Diplomatically, yes."

Mike sighed in frustration. "I see your point. But if I need endurance now, won't I need it on the Last Run?"

"Which is why you, Elira and Dehan have been scheduled to begin conditioning sessions," Adar chimed in. "In fact, they begin this afternoon."

"You really need to take part in them," Jan said.

"I guess you're right," Mike conceded. "I guess I thought…."

"That if you went with me, you could protect me?" Jan asked cocking her head to one side.

He nodded.

"Have faith in me, Mike."

He held her close. "Promise me you'll be careful out there."

"I'm always careful," she said pulling back and gazing into his eyes. "The only thought I have in mind is to get back to you."

Mike drew her close again and kissed her long and tenderly.

Adar shuffled his feet. "Ahem! This run needs to go out as soon as everyone can be assembled."

Mike and Jan looked at him then she reluctantly pulled away.

"Right. I'll go get Tanza and Gorlan and get things set," she replied.

Mike caught her arm as she turned to dash out the door and gave her one last kiss. With her lips still wet, she slipped out the door. He watched her leave, an anxious frown creasing his brow.

Less than an hour had passed before Jan's group was heading out from Mozern. They literally had to crawl out of the secret Mozern exit and crossed the plateau warily. But once they had repelled down the cliff into the valley, they only saw deserted Saracen camps, which they skirted. By late afternoon they were creeping up the Gorgo Silan, the Gorge of Silence. At one rest stop, Jan climbed a tall tree shinnying back down just minutes later.

"There's not a Saracen in sight," she told the others.

"This is eerie," Tanza fretted. "Why would they be entrenched around Mozern and no where else?"

"Because they've finally detected the base," Jan said with a shudder.

Tanza looked at Jan as if thinking the very thoughts she herself did not want to say aloud. "If they have, the Final Battle is over before it ever began."

With uneasy knots in their stomachs, they sought the shelter of a cave for the night before retracing their path of the previous day. On the way out of the Gorgo Silan, they passed the team of runners from the Cliff Face Underground that were carrying messages to Star's End.

Jan stopped long enough to exchange information; they reported the same news - no Saracens.

Ill at ease, Jan brought her team around the Mozern Range by the back route. A Saracen patrol crossed their path nearly spotting them. With her anxiety heightened, Jan searched for a Mot-pont, an entrance to a Molluc trail. The enemy patrol circled back picking up where the threesome had just been, but the scouts were now below ground and on the run.

Meanwhile, Mike and Will worked on the prototype glider. Adar had had a section of the small-vehicle hangar emptied for them and had supplied them with the necessary materials and tools. Together, the two men decided on the appropriate revisions and worked to bend the lightweight, yet sturdy, frame into the proper shape.

Three days beyond Jan's scheduled return went by. Mike glanced up every time a footstep sounded in the hangar, only to sigh as a Molluc or an engineer would hurry through. Early one evening, a full week after Jan's expected return, Mike packed up his tools and walked out with Will.

"Heading back?" Will asked.

"No. I'm going to Adar's office," Mike said. "If she isn't back tonight, I'm going out after her."

Will furrowed his brow watching Mike stalk down the hall. He shook his head and turned toward the Royal Suite.

Meanwhile, Mike had nearly reached the office complex. He rounded a corner only to be surprised by a runner with a forest-green cape floating out behind her. She leapt out of a niche in the wall and dashed off.

"Jan!" he called.

She spun around and stopped to wait for him. He reached her side, drew her to him, and held her close for a moment. Finally he held her at arm's length checking her over.

"Are you all right? You're so late getting back. Did you have any trouble out there?" He anxiously searched her weary face.

"No real trouble. We had to hide out from Saracen patrols but nothing worse than that. I'm fine, Mike," she reassured him squeezing his arms. "I'm just a little tired."

He breathed a sigh of relief. "Are you too tired for a surprise?"

"Can I see it after I give Adar my compu-disc?"

"Only if you make it quick."

He walked her down the hall to Adar's office and waited outside while she slipped in to give Adar her report. She was back out in less than five minutes. Mike put his arm around her shoulders leading her through the corridors to the hangar. He stopped just outside and put his hands over her eyes.

"Hey! I can't see a surprise this way," she complained.

"I just don't want you to peek before I'm ready," he said guiding her past the small vehicle pits.

Mike stopped abruptly and dropped his hands. Standing in its corner rested a large, two-man glider with nearly transparent wings.

Jan gasped in astonishment. "Mike! It's terrific!"

"It's like one I built for the Aviation Club except for some modifications."

She walked all around it taking a closer look.

"Will and I put it together while you were gone. It helped make the time go by faster, though I can't say it kept me from worrying about you." He reached out for her hand, pulled her close and hugged her. "You don't know what a relief it is to see you back here all in one piece."

"Believe me, it feels good to be back." She gave him a quick kiss then turned back to the glider. "How do we go about testing it now?"

"Testing? What?" Mike asked turning her toward him and kissing her again.

"The glider, silly," she chided gently.

"Oh, that. Adar's having his engineers set up a smaller wind tunnel for a test," he replied reluctantly drawing back from her. "Will's busy building a simulator to train us on."

"That's a load off my mind."

"Let's take a load off your feet." He scooped her up carrying her out into the corridor.

"Mm. This is the safest I've felt in days," she confessed putting her arms around his neck and resting her head on his shoulder.

Before they even neared the Royal Suite, Jan fell sound asleep. Mike nudged the door open using his powers, gently eased her onto one of his loungers then got a thermo-blanket to cover her with. He kissed her forehead then sat nearby watching her restless tossing as she slept.

The next day they hauled the glider into the wind tunnel and rigged it for a stress test. While a technician operated the computer, they visited Will to help him try out his simulator.

The day after that, High Council, which had been postponed due to Jan's late return, finally reconvened and Adar presented his detailed strategy. It was complete with holomaps, lighted diagrams, a time analysis, and myriads of computations. When the meeting ended, the Royal Couple helped Will give the glider a final check-up.

"I think she's ready," he announced.

"Then we should do one topside test flight," Jan said.

"I thought you said Saracens patrols were crawling all over the Mozern," Mike countered.

"I did, but where I intend to take us no Saracen would be caught dead or alive."

Before sunrise the next morning, Jan led Will, Elira, Adar, and Mike along Molluc trails that surfaced near a secluded canyon. They pushed their way out and stood on a sunny ledge. Suddenly two large, winged men dropped from the sky.

"Who trespasses in Hallen-nor?" one, who was wearing a gold neckband, demanded.

Jan stepped forward, hand outstretched and palm up. Resting on her fingertips was a silver Saracen wardisc. "Take this sign to your Chieftain, Torak. He will remember."

The man took the disc and rose from the ledge with a powerful beat of his wings. The other Hallens landed crowding menacingly around the group. In minutes, the first Hallen returned bearing a red feather.

"Torak remembers," he said handing her the feather. "Go in peace. Keep this as long as you travel in our valley. You shall be safe from all harm."

He leapt skywards with a mighty down rush of air from his powerful wings. Jan watched him and his comrades ascend then led her party on.

"What was that all about?" Mike asked.

"Just returning a favor. Remember when I got back late from my last run?"

He nodded.

"Their Chieftain, Torak, had been blown out of Hallen-nor's skies by a sudden storm and was shot down by a Saracen disc. Quite a mean weapon," she commented. "It inflicts a lot of pain. Anyway, I was bringing my group out of hiding when I saw him fall. We helped him to cover, and I removed the disc. Then we got him back to Hallen-nor. He promised me safe passage through his valley...a rare privilege from a Hallen."

They climbed the ridge to a high slope and set bundles down.

"Ok, Will. Time us," Mike said dumping out the various glider parts.

Will stared at his chronometer. "Ok...Go!"

Mike and Jan dropped to the ground and scrambled to put it together, working as calmly and steadily as possible. Finally he twisted the last nut into place.

"Done!" he announced looking up at Will.

"Thirty-three minutes," Will said.

"Too long," Jan muttered. "We're going to have to practice putting this thing together."

"Think it will soar the distance?" Will asked.

"It should. It isn't much different from the one I flew on Earth," Mike replied.

"Yes, but you only took that one through practice hops," Will reminded him. "You never did get a chance to see how it handled in full flight. Plus, this one has to go a lot further than that one ever did."

"Well, if there are problems with it, now's the time to find out."

"Are you certain you marked this distance accurately?" Adar asked Jan.

"Definitely. In fact, I extended the distance a little," she replied. "If it can make it today, given the wind currents, it'll certainly make it across the gap."

"But shouldn't Adar and I make this flight?" Will asked, concerned. "What if Saracens come around, or something happens to the glider?"

"The Hallens will take care of any Saracens," she said glancing up at the large, bird-like men soaring above them. "No one has ever come into their valley without their permission. Believe me, you don't know how privileged we are to be here."

"And, if anything happens to the glider, I can use my powers to land us safely," Mike said.

"I have Mollucs waiting for us at the landing site," Jan added. "Of all the runs I've made, this one is the safest."

She and Mike donned helmets and strapped themselves into the dual harness. Will and Adar raised an airsock on a telescoping pole which they planted firmly between two rocks. The couple headed the glider into the wind and signaled thumbs-up. They ran forward and an updraft caught the wings lifting the glider from the ground. With a wave to Will, Adar and Elira below, they rode the thermals far up and out across the valley. As they soared, Mike took in the beautiful landscape below, so different from the countryside he had seen on his previous run.

"Like what you see?" Jan yelled.

"It's great!"

"Wish the rest of Quentas still looked this good. The Saracens have destroyed so much."

Mike shook his head. "It's no wonder the Hallens don't want outsiders here."

"Really! From up here, they can look across their borders and see what's happened elsewhere."

They continued to soar over the lush vegetation until they could finally see a twisting ribbon of blue sparkling through the trees.

"Our target's on this side of the river," Jan yelled. "If we make it, we will have flown farther than the distance across that gap."

Soon the trees thinned and a clearing opened beneath them. The sun glinted off a shiny object.

"There's our target," she announced.

They began a gradual descent till their feet touched the ground. Mollucs raced out from the surrounding forest to help them dismantle the glider. They followed the noisy Mollucs through the forest to the river's edge and loaded the collapsible glider onto the waiting raft, then pushed off into the current.

"Bring back memories?" Jan asked.

"Yeah, but it was so different then," Mike replied.

"I know. Sometimes I almost wish we could go back."

Chapter 47

From that moment on, work around the base rose to a feverish pitch in Mozern as well in the other Underground bases. Ground speeders, air craft, and sea vessels were readied, armed and loaded with supplies. Runners were dispatched to every quadrant spreading the news of the upcoming battle to the beleaguered people. They returned with news of low-key Saracen activity.

A restless eagerness swept through the base. Adar, Jan and Mike walked into one of the training gyms and found Marla climbing a rope that hung from the ceiling. Suddenly she lost her grip and slid several feet. Seeing the bystanders below, she slid clear to the ground.

"How is the wrist?" Adar queried.

"Sore, but improving."

"Sure you're ready to go on this run?" Mike pressed.

Marla looked to Jan for support then back to Mike. "Yes, Your Highness. I am ready and I plan to go on this run."

Mike glanced at Jan who nodded slightly. "As long as you're certain and your healer has cleared you."

"Right here," Marla said pulling a slip of paper from her sleeve pocket.

Mike read it before tucking it into his pocket. "Welcome aboard!" he said with a smile and a handshake.

That evening, under the cover of night, the land crews moved out of the Underground to secret topside bases and positioned themselves to strike. Sleek airships flew low over the quiet land disappearing into deep mountain gorges and canyons. The countdown had begun; the time to strike was at hand.

Half-a-week later and very early in the morning, the two Corp groups convened in one of the Elitist conference rooms. While the General gave a rousing speech on the "glorious" final battle, Jan crossed the room to where Marla stood. They wrapped themselves in their cloaks and slipped outside to wait.

"Good-luck," Jan said as Marla's eyes filled with tears.

"Good-luck, yourself," her friend whispered. "I hope we will meet again."

"Have faith and trust your instincts. We'll make it. We have to," Jan replied hugging her.

They leaned against the wall, waiting. Soon the groups filed out and lined up next to their respective guides. Marla and Jan escorted them to where their packs waited. For an instant their eyes met in a silent, shared thought. Then, raising their hoods over their heads, they took their groups down separate tunnels.

"Did Adar get off all right?" Mike asked as Jan led them out of the Underground.

"He, Behran, and Garik will leave shortly to alert the base at Mozer-pan. I just hope Garik won't slow them down too much."

Using Molluc tunnels, she led them through the length of the mountain range till they surfaced on a broad plateau. A Molluc messenger waited in the shadow of a bush.

"All is clear," he whispered.

"Let's go," Jan said handing him her pack and turning to the others. "The tunnels stop here, so we've got to be wary. For now our way is clear, but that could change without notice."

They inched nervously across the barren, windswept land. It was early afternoon when they finally saw the mists of the Cold Fell rising above the plateau surface.

"We've nearly made it," Mike said, relieved.

"Yes, the Mot-pont should be close by," Jan replied.

Suddenly the ground shook beneath their feet. Jan spun around in alarm. Two huge boulders slowly unfolded and raised upwards.

"Stonbots!" she cried.

Mike glanced over his shoulder at the approaching behemoths. They opened fire on the group narrowly missing them. Mike turned to fire, but Jan grabbed his arm pulling him after her.

"What are you doing?" he demanded.

"Do you want to announce your 'Royal' presence?" she hissed.

"What do you suggest?"

"Follow Tarkn to the Mot-pont. I'll draw them off."

"I don't know," Mike said uncertainly.

"Don't worry. We deal with these beasts all the time. I know another way down. It's just too hard for all of us to take it."

"All right. But be careful," he admonished.

She nodded and sprinted to catch up to Tarkn. "Take them to the Mot-pont. I'll draw them off," she said gesturing toward the Stonbots. "Meet me at the Well of Souls."

He nodded and watched briefly as Jan raced out across the open plateau. The giant, stone robots spotted her immediately and followed.

"Quickly!" Tarkn urged. "Mot-pont is this way."

Mike, Will and Elira hurried away from Jan and the stone giants that pursued her. Mike turned from time-to-time watching her evasive leaps and somersaults in utter amazement. Tarkn grabbed his arm pulling him behind a low scrub bush with the others. They all watched anxiously as Jan tried to outrun the Stonbots.

She dashed along the river, nearly to the plateau's edge. Suddenly she sprang from the bank to a boulder in the middle of the swift current. Like a mountain goat, she hopped from one slick rock to another till she reached the precipice of the falls where the torrent raged mercilessly.

"She'll get herself killed out there!" Mike cried as the Stonbots bore down on her.

"Tarkn, we've got to do something," Will agreed.

The Molluc merely sat motionlessly watching Jan with intent, beady eyes.

The next blast nearly hit the rock that Jan stood on. Before anyone could stop him, Mike dashed from behind cover. As the Stonbots reached the river bank, Jan leapt high into the air and Mike fired. She dove over the cliff slicing through the air. Above, a Stonbot exploded, and the small group disappeared down the tunnel the bush had concealed.

"She's gone!" Mike gasped as he was yanked inside the tunnel. "No one could have survived that leap!"

"None but the skilled," Tarkn countered. "Come, and say no more. We must make our way to the Well of Souls."

The group slowly edged its way along the dark Molluc tunnel. The only light came from a phosphorescent vein in the tunnel wall. Damp from dripping mineral water which ran along cracks in the ceiling, the floor angled steadily downwards. At the tunnel's end they found a narrow, circular stairway that wound down to the base of the plateau to a more level path. Tarkn cautiously led them along the subterranean corridor till an unsuspected warm breeze blew in their faces. They turned down a side passage following the draft of warm, moist air until flickering light penetrated the darkness.

"This way," Tarkn instructed.

They turned a sharp corner that led through a low archway into a domed, oval-shaped room. Mike glanced around observing the skull-lined border surrounding a pool of deep, crystal-clear water. A small red flame flickered in the empty sockets of each skull, casting faint, eerie shadows about the water's edge.

Behind the pool a low doorway led into a smaller chamber. Mike crept toward it to investigate stopping suddenly as a quick movement startled him. He crouched low waiting to spring as a dark silhouette moved through the low door. Ready to pounce, he nearly toppled over as a cloak swished back and Jan stepped into the dim light. He stared at her in amazement then wrapped his arms around her.

"I never thought I'd see you again," he said holding her at arm's length to look her over. "I can't believe you're still all in one peace!"

She gave him a quick kiss and a pat on the shoulder. "Did you really think I'd jump like that into the unknown?"

"You mean, you've done that before?"

"More times than I care to remember. And to think, I used to be afraid of heights."

"You sure didn't act like it a while ago."

Jan shrugged. "That leap is sometimes the only way to escape the Stonbots. They're programmed to seek and destroy. When I don't come up for air in the cataract pool, they assume I'm dead and switch back to surveillance mode. They don't know about the tunnels or the Well of Souls," she explained. "But we'd better get moving. We have to alert Plateau Face before going on."

She grabbed her pack from where Tarkn had set it and picked up a small lantern from beside the low doorway. She touched first its rim then its base; a dim light bathed the floor at their feet. Urgently, she hurried them along the paths keeping them climbing until they met with a dead-end. Jan felt along the wall and touched a small lever; a panel slid back. The group shuffled into an austere council chamber filled with people. The chairwoman glanced up from her seat at the head of the table.

"Your Highness," she said bowing her head to Mike. "You have arrived safely. We had begun to worry."

"We greet you," Mike replied nodding toward them. "I believe our guide carries a vital message for you."

Jan fished out the waterproof pouch she had carried strapped to her side and pulled out a flat disc. "This is from General Adar," she said handing it to the chairwoman. "The final coordinates you need are on it."

The woman nodded.

Suddenly a thunderous blow rocked the chamber, followed by another. Dust filtered from the ceiling as cracks zigzagged down the walls.

"The Stonbots didn't switch modes!" Jan cried.

"That is impossible!" the chairwoman exclaimed.

A chunk of ceiling fell onto the table with the next tremendous blow.

"But we have been discovered. Are you certain no one returned fire?" the chairwoman asked glancing nervously at the ceiling.

Jan looked to those in the group. Mike nodded. She sighed, turned back to the council, and opened her mouth to speak. A hand was laid on her shoulder.

"My inexperience with Stonbots has led to this," Mike explained. "I fired at one to protect our guide."

The chairwoman looked startled then punched a button on the table before her. "Evacuate Plateau Face immediately. I repeat… evacuate all personnel immediately."

The entire assembly rose and dashed to the antechamber as another blow sent the roof crumbling about their heads. Several people froze in the middle of the room.

"Go on! Get out of here!" Mike ordered. "I'll keep the ceiling up till you get out."

He stood in the doorway concentrating on the falling slabs while his own group rushed past him.

In the hall the chairwoman opened a wall panel which the assembly surged through. Mike remained fixed in the council doorway as thunderous blows rained dust and rocks on them. The last person finally ducked out of the room.

"C'mon!" Jan yelled pulling him away and shoving him through the entrance to the passage.

As the debris from both chambers tumbled down, she dove through the panel opening and toppled down the winding, stone stairway. She picked herself up bringing up the rear as they raced down the steps. Once or twice she turned listening intently as the echo of footsteps reached her ears. Hastily she pivoted and sprinted after the others. Before they had found their way to the bottom, a tremendous blast of dust and air sent her sprawling down the stairs. Dazed, Jan got up and crawled back up the passage. A few yards away, rubble blocked off the staircase.

"They've sealed us in," she muttered surveying the heap. "How did they know we were down here? This looks so deliberate. Something about this isn't right."

Chapter 48

Having lost sight of her group, Jan hurried down the remaining steps. She heard a sharp click. Fearing the worst, she leapt to the landing and stood staring at two closed doors. Though she checked the floor in front of each, she could find no clues to tell which one the group had just passed through. She finally gave up and opened the one closest to her entering the bustling sub-port. Anxiously she glanced about for someone in Core I camouflage. In the next instant, she was jolted by a tall, robust man as he hurried past.

"Hey! You are a little lost, are you not?" he asked stopping immediately. He took her arm leading her out of the mainstream of traffic.

Jan looked up at his friendly smile, warm brown eyes, and wavy brown hair. "I'm not lost!" she declared firmly. "I'm looking for my group."

"Oh! I see. They are lost." A mischievous twinkle lit his eyes.

"You're never serious, Lotar...not even on runs. But I am. Have you seen anyone wearing this camouflage?" she asked pulling at the sleeve of her uniform. She peered past him gazing at the dusky figures that bustled along the docks.

"And you have always been too serious," he said placing his hand on her cheek and turning her head till their eyes met. "Lighten up some. Have some fun, like me."

She felt his will bearing down on hers, and the fire and passion she saw in his eyes seeped into her burning a path from her head to her feet. She shook her head to clear it as he backed her against the wall pressing closer to her.

"I have not seen them, but I thought maybe this time you had come looking for me."

Jan wedged her shoulder against his chest attempting to push him away.

He laughed and kissed her cheek.

Jan whirled around landing her hand on his face with a resounding slap. A spark leapt from the ring another lighting her eyes.

"How many times must I tell you, Lotar. I am promised to Prince Ihue. I order you to stop this. NOW! I refuse to play this game you men devised. I am loyal, no matter what you may think!"

"Do you really believe that only one man can love you?" he asked in honey tones while stoking her hair.

She angrily knocked his hand away. "I don't care if one hundred men love me, Lotar. I can only love one...the Prince."

She ducked past him to escape, but he grabbed her arm pulling her back.

"Jan, consider how burdensome that `Ring' will become," he whispered in her ear.

"Lotar, stop!"

She shoved him away wrenching her arm free. "I've got to find my group, and this time I'm looking for the Prince. You're lucky he's no where around to see how you treat his fiancée."

Lotar stared at her in shock then glanced hastily about the port. Jan wrapped her cloak about her to hide the angry trembling that shook her.

"They must be in the other tank," he said dryly leading her out the door and to the other side. He quickly brought her to Core I.

Mike caught sight of them and hurried toward Jan. "What happened? Where did you go?" He took her arm, but she did not look up.

"I went back to check on a cave-in then chose the wrong door. This is Lotar," she added gesturing to the man with her. "He pointed me in the right direction."

Lotar bowed to Elira and Mike avoiding their direct gaze. With the formalities over, he backed away. Mike stared at him coldly. Once his back was turned, Lotar stopped as Mike's searching gaze penetrated his being before hastily retreating out the door.

Mike drew Jan aside. "Who is he?" he demanded.

"I told you, his name is Lotar. He was a run leader for Plateau Face before he got injured. After that, they made him an engineer."

"Then why do I get a very strange feeling from him...and you?" he asked gripping her arm tighter.

"Mike, you're hurting me!" Jan protested.

He threw back her hood eyeing her crimson face. "Why does he make me feel so uneasy?"

"Because he likes forbidden fruit," she replied cryptically.

Mike grabbed her right hand to examine the Ring. Jan instantly yanked it free.

"Thanks for your trust," she spat. "I really needed that."

She hustled off threading her way through the milling crowd. Mike stood dumbfounded watching her go.

Off to one side, an evacuation coordinator barked out orders to a busy crew. Jan spotted him and hurried over.

"Excuse me, sirha. Is there space available to accommodate a group of four?"

He scanned his compu-slate. "The crew for Submergible Six did not make it. It is at Dock Four. Destination?"

"Fortress Mound...I mean, Mundfortu."

"Got it. Board up."

Jan hastily read the remarks about their submergible's lost crew then scrambled back to her group with the news. "I found us a way out of here," she announced.

Elira sighed with relief.

"Where to?" Will asked.

"There's a submergible available at Dock Four. If we hurry, we can leave on it now."

"Then let's go," Mike urged.

Jan led them through the maze of cargo and hurrying people to a dock that stretched out into a subterranean lake. The ceiling was low near the shore leaving just enough room for an upright stance.

"This is it!" Jan announced pointing to the small, grey, grenade-shaped vessel.

Will and Elira quickly climbed the steps up to the entry eager to get below. Jan followed silently and slipped into a seat near a porthole staring out at the bustle on the dock. Men rushed to load equipment that had been salvaged in order to move it to other bases, while personnel waited to board other submergibles destined for alternate bases where their skills could be used. Now and then the small sub rocked, allowing Jan a glimpse of the murky water below.

Mike ducked his head as he entered the low chamber and hesitantly slid into the seat next to her. Above, deck hands sealed them in.

"Look, Jan. I didn't mean to be suspicious of you, but I think I deserve some explanation. I don't understand the feelings I picked up from Lotar and you."

Jan remained silent while the submergible's engines whined to life. They settled into a quiet hum as the craft idled in preparation for launching.

"Are you jealous that other men find me attractive?" Jan asked without warning.

"You mean there are others besides Lotar?" he asked, shocked.

She nodded. "The men sought every way possible to discredit me right from the very beginning. They knew if I slipped up just once, they could get rid of me. First it was just straight forward harassment. But long after the others gave up, Lotar persisted. He projects his own lust onto me trying to weaken my resolve. There are times when he has come close…it has been so hard," she choked out.

Mike stared at her in astonishment. Embarrassed and humiliated, she pulled her cloak about her and turned to look out the porthole.

"This is outrageous! I can't believe they'd do this to my fiancée. Why didn't you say something before now?"

"Heh! It was the same problem I had with everything else. I was an Elitist without your knowledge, so I couldn't come to you for help."

"Well, I'm not going to take this lightly. I want the names and bases of these men. When this war is over, they'll go on trial. I'll make examples of them. To treat you with disrespect is to break their loyalty to the Throne and to violate our engagement. You're as good as being my wife as far as our laws go."

"That sounds great on paper," Jan replied stifling a sob.

Mike reached out to her and she turned to him for comfort, hot streams of tears flowing down her face. He wrapped his arms around her drawing her close and laying his chin against her head.

"I'm so sorry, Jan. I don't know what to say to make you feel better. I never thought you'd have to go through any of this when I brought you here. If I'd known, I don't think I would have brought you."

"There you go again," she complained. "Sometimes I wonder if you're ever glad I'm here at all."

He gave her a squeeze. "I'm very glad you're here. I just hate to see the things you've had to go through. I wish I could have spared you from all of this."

"Me, too," she admitted.

She turned and looked back out the porthole. After a while she turned back to him. "Sometimes it's made me feel so degraded. When the men would finally leave me alone, I'd feel like I needed to bathe for a week…I-I just felt so dirty."

"You didn't do anything to deserve that."

"I know," she replied with a helpless shrug, "but it's as if something from them always hung around. If it hadn't been for Teldank and her herbal baths, I don't know what I would have done."

Mike studied her for a moment. "It's the part of themselves they projected onto you," he said quietly. He placed his hands on either side of her temples. "Like now."

She choked back a sob. "Very much like now."

Mike slowly moved his hands away from her head then back towards it. As he did, a dark smoke seemed to rise up from her crown until he freed it from her. He 'balled' it up and sent it flying through the porthole and beyond. "Feel better?"

Jan sighed deeply and relaxed. "Yes, thank you."

"That was his garbage," Mike said speaking of Lotar. "You

don't need to carry that with you."

Mike let his hands smooth down over her shoulders, gave her a quick hug, then relaxed his embrace and left his arm draped across her shoulders while his fingers played with her hair. A bell clanged on the deck, and the vessel rolled along the bumpy track into the airlock. The doors slammed shut behind them as the riverbank opened up before them. With a soft whoosh, they were shot into the current to be carried downstream.

"Have you ever taken a submergible before?" Will called back.

"No. They're reserved for emergencies," Jan replied.

"Like now?"

"Yes."

"But why do they not stand and fight?" Elira asked.

"The base is demolished," Jan replied. "If four of their own men hadn't been crushed when a roof collapsed, we wouldn't be enjoying this privilege. Instead, we would be out there with those Stonbots."

"But what about Tarkn?" Mike queried.

"He was gone before the Stonbots ever got near. You didn't see when he slipped away from our group in the Mot-ton."

"Crafty, aren't they?" Will quipped.

"And well trained," Jan added.

For the remainder of the afternoon, they rested and ate while their vessel glided smoothly downstream. As the sun set above them, its rosy rays filtered through the water lighting it with long, pink, shimmering streamers of color. As the sunset gave way to dusk, their craft approached an opening in the riverbank ahead. As it entered the cave, it rose slowly and ran up a short track till it stopped beside an empty dock. The four people inside got up and warily crawled out into the inky darkness.

"What happened to everyone here?" Mike wondered.

"Have they evacuated, too?" Elira asked.

"Could be," Jan replied frowning. "A skeleton crew was supposed to stay behind after the order to move out primary war machines was issued. But it's deserted now, and that's not good."

"Saracens?" Will speculated.

"Good possibility."

"Where are we, anyway?" Mike wondered groping his way around the dock.

"That's another problem," Jan said. "We're under Mundfortu. That's no where near our Mot-pont or the rendezvous point with Adar. We were supposed to veer away from the river and travel the back of the Stardent Range. Now, we're almost onto the plain itself."

"How bad is that?" Mike asked.

"Very bad. We'll have to travel above ground...in the open. But the worst part is that Saracens were crawling all over this sector at last report."

"Then how will we get past them?" Will asked greatly concerned.

"There is no way past them. We're going to have to go right through them."

“What!” Elira gasped. “Jan, we cannot possibly do that. That would be suicide.”

"Jan, this does sound dangerous, even by my standards," Will conceded.

"Hold on," Mike cautioned. "Let's hear her out."

Jan eased onto a cement piling. "Simply put - we have no choice. Those Stonbots demolished Plateau Face and our original route with it."

"That was my fault," Mike admitted.

"But that's not all. How'd they know the exact chamber we were in? They attacked that one first, then demolished the exact tunnel we took. It was almost as if someone had signaled them. At any rate, that attack forced us miles off course and into heavily guarded territory."

"What would you normally do?" Will asked.

"Put on disguises and waltz right through them. But we don't have time for that. Besides, none of you are trained to assume clan dialects or customs. Plus, we don't know how many Saracen units there are or where they're posted. The fact that this base is empty tells me the Saracens have been on the move."

"In other words, we run the gauntlet," Mike surmised.

"Well, when do we get started then?" Elira asked in resignation.

"Not yet. I'm going to tuck you three in HASR till I know what we're up against."

"Shouldn't I go with you?" Mike offered.

"I wish you could but no way. I'm nothing to them, but you're the jackpot," Jan reminded him playfully poking a finger at his chest. "Besides, if anything goes wrong here, you'd be the first to sense it. I'd feel better if you'd stay and defend them." She nodded towards Will and Elira.

"Ok, but you be careful," he admonished.

"Don't worry. I can guarantee that."

They picked up their packs and groped along the dark, damp passages behind Jan. Their footsteps echoed ominously off the surrounding walls.

"How about some light?" Elira asked tripping on a crack.

"Better not till we stop and listen."

They all stood still wondering at the eerie clangs and boot steps that echoed faintly down the long corridors.

"Something isn't right," Mike whispered in Jan's ear. "If this base is deserted, who's making all that noise?"

"Guess."

"Saracens."

"Probably. Now I know for sure why the base was vacated. We'll need to go on blind and silent."

"Definitely," Mike agreed taking Elira's arm to help her along the dark tunnel.

Jan moved on quickly and certainly. Soon she stopped again and ran her hands over the wall. Her finger hit a concealed switch and a low panel slid back. She helped the others crawl through before squeezing through herself and replacing the panel behind her. They mounted a narrow staircase that led to a small chamber containing a lantern and sleeping mats. Jan lit the lantern with a touch of her hand and hung it on a hook on the wall.

"What is this place?" Mike asked scanning the room curiously.

"HASR. Will knows this room well. He perfected the concept."

"Heh! Not quite," Will muttered under his breath.

"But what does HASR mean?" Mike persisted.

"Hide-And-Seek-Rotational. The rest of the base could be swarming with Saracens, but they'd be hard pressed to find you here."

"How come?"

"Because the room changes locations periodically when its inhabited."

"`Changes its location'?" Mike repeated incredulously.

"Mm-hm. Stand still and watch," Jan instructed.

She pressed a button, and a small panel on the wall slid back revealing a vertical keyboard. She pressed the key in the top right corner, and the room slowly revolved.

"What is happening?" Elira wondering.

"The room's rotating to close off the old entrance. If any Saracens had followed us, they'll only find a dead-end now."

She pushed a sequence of keys then turned to the others. "Hold on. The position shift may make you feel a little sick. Just stay in one place...and don't panic."

Suddenly the edges of the room began to shimmer with a bright glow which crept up the walls then across the ceiling and floor. As the shimmering, particled light touched each person, they felt a sickening, tingling sensation. Their forms wavered like flickering candles as the room became totally engulfed. Elira gasped when the room winked out.

They slowly spun through blackness and solid rock while HASR searched for a safe retreat. After it had settled into its new place, the glimmer retracted from the walls. Once it was gone, Mike and Elira felt their once-again solid bodies. Will just shook his head.

"We never could get all the bugs worked out of that ride," he grumbled.

"You're telling me?" Mike groaned.

Jan touched the keyboard and HASR rotated once more. "Sorry about the discomfort, but with Saracens in the complex, I didn't want to take any chances."

She entered another sequence and the panel lit up. "Now, I've put the computer on auto. It will sense intruders. If they don't have this," she said pulling a small, black wand from the panel compartment, "the red light will flash a warning, and the room will relocate."

"How often will that happen?" Elira moaned.

"Whenever a Saracen enters HASR's field," Jan explained then turned to Mike. "I need to leave the fortress and scout out the stretch between here and the gorge, ok?"

"I guess so."

"If I should, somehow, be captured and the Saracens follow me here, press that red button."

"But what about you?" he asked worriedly.

"I'll get away, don't worry. Now, I'll be back as soon as I can. When I get back, we'll have to move out, so grab a bite to eat and try to get some rest."

She reached up and kissed him before slipping out the door. Mike watched anxiously as she vanished down the dark hall. He stayed at the door till he could no longer hear her soft footsteps.

Will laid a hand on Mike's shoulder. "She'll be back. She always comes back."

Chapter 49

Jan slunk stealthily through the dark passages to the lift that carried her outside. She gazed up the strip of plain to the dark foreboding mountains that loomed over it.

"I've got to travel clear to the gap and back tonight," she thought. "Wonder how I'll make it."

Jan wrapped her cloak about her pulling up the hood. She glanced up at the starry sky and listened carefully to the night noises about her. Endel and Thira I, Quentas' two moons, hovered just above the horizon. She scanned the darkness picking out the Saracen patrol ahead. With trained agility, she leapt for the cover of the brush before sprinting around the enemy soldiers and on through the enshrouding gloom.

She sped on until Endel and Thira I were at their quarter points in the night sky. Jan glanced anxiously at her double shadow. Upon spotting three dots of flickering light, she skirted the Saracen camps finally reaching the narrow gap leading to the Gorgo Silan. Checking about quickly, she ducked inside the gorge and sat under a ledge to rest. A short while later she peered back out at the night sky. Endel and Thira I were crossing each other's paths.

Recalling the whereabouts of the Saracen camps, Jan altered her return route. Still, she glanced nervously about her at the eerie night shadows. The closer she got to the base, the more skittish she became. She dashed furtively between instances of cover, watching the way behind her warily. Once within HASR's field, she checked the wand.

"Trouble," she groaned. "Three changes since I left."

As she held it, the wand showed a fourth change in progress.

"Wonderful! The others are safe, but I have to cut right through the Saracens to get to them."

She glanced up at the sky and the setting moons. "I can't wait for another change," she muttered. "If I do, I'll never be able to get back inside the base."

Cautiously Jan slunk across the plain to an entrance and crept inside the base. She inched silently along the dark corridors keeping a constant watch for Saracens. The deeper she traveled inside, the more frequently she stopped to listen.

"I know they're here," she thought. "Why aren't they moving?"

She covered her mouth to stifle the scream of panic that had welled up in her throat. When she reached HASR`s last sector, Jan dropped to her hands and knees to crawl past.

"They're using EFI's*," she muttered frantically. "I've got to stay calm. It's just electronic pulses. Keep calm," she told herself.

She took a deep breath, let it out slowly and pressed on. "I'm certain I'm headed for an ambush. Wish Tanza or Marla or even Mike were here. Their Royal Blood would pinpoint it for sure."

As she continued on, Jan heard a swift movement behind her. Immediately she grabbed her necklace, yanked off a bead, and threw it over her shoulder. It hit the floor with a flash of blinding light and a puff of thick smoke; she leapt forward.

From up ahead booted feet shuffled quickly. She rushed straight for them and leapt into the air. As hands grabbed for her, she tucked into a tight ball somersaulting out of reach.

"So far, so good," she thought landing on her feet and running on. Yet, her panic grew. "Got to be more EFI's" she muttered.

Suddenly a blinding light was shone in her face. Jan dropped to her knees shielding her eyes with her hands and cape. Two booted men

*EFI's – Electronic Fear Inducers

stepped up beside her grabbing her arms above the elbows.

"So, what have we here?" one snickered.

"Another one of those blasted messengers," the other replied.

"Yes, but not just any messenger. Look!" the one with the light said holding up Jan's hand.

"This one again?"

"Yes, 'this one.' Only this time she will lead us to that Prince of theirs." He yanked the wand from her. "We shall crush their rebellion for good."

The Saracens wrenched her arms behind her back and dragged her along between them. Confidently they followed the wand to HASR.

Meanwhile, Mike was pacing in the dim lantern light. Will sat up watching him intently as he stopped to study the control panel.

"The red light's not on. What's wrong?" Will asked.

"That light may be off, but Jan's in trouble. I feel it, Will! Something has gone wrong."

He returned to pacing but soon stopped by the door; he detected a movement out in the corridor. Straining to see through the dim light, Mike caught a glimpse of figures approaching.

"What's up?" Will asked tensely.

Mike's eyes widened in alarm. "Saracens! They've got Jan!"

Before their enemy saw him, Mike fired a power bolt at the Saracens on either side of Jan. They collapsed to the floor, their bodies spitting electric sparks and acrid fumes.

"Nice try, Prince Ihue," a voice said from behind Jan.

Mike stared hard till he made out the vague outline of a tall Saracen. "Zorak! You've followed us an awfully long ways."

"Yes. I have made you my life's project. Come on out. This game is finally up between you and me. I have got someone of interest to you. You come out and I will let her go. A fair trade."

"No deal, Zorak."

"You always insist on being difficult. Oh, well."

Zorak lowered his eyes to his belt as he shoved the wand into a loop then reached for his laser. Seizing the opportunity, Mike fired a bolt that zipped past Jan's ear slicing into the Saracen's head. With a cry of pain, Zorak fell to the ground releasing his hold on Jan. She sank to her knees, grabbing the wand, while Mike leapt toward the panel and punched the red button. The room began to revolve.

"Hurry, Jan!" he yelled. "Jump!"

She readied herself to spring, when Zorak moved toward his laser, picked it up, and fired. The wand spun out of her hand.

"Jump!" Mike cried frantically through the narrowing entrance.

"Gotta find the wand!"

Mike fired a final bolt at Zorak who was readying for his last shot at Jan. Meanwhile, she searched the floor for the wand. Her fingers found it securing the cylinder in a tight grasp. She glanced up just as the doorway clicked shut and watched in horror as the wall began to shimmer.

"I've got to go with them," she said watching the glow intensify. "I've only got one other chance."

Mike, too, watched in horror as the door clicked shut and the shimmer began engulfing the room. He dashed to the panel frantically pressing the keys, but the glow marched on.

"It's no good!" Will yelled. "It can't be overridden."

"But she's still out there!" Mike cried in alarm.

Behind Jan, two more Saracens pounded down the passage. Just as they lunged for her, she dove into the midst of the bright glow.

As his body flickered like a wisp of smoke, Mike saw a flash burst from the wall and heard Jan's agonized scream. A solid figure collapsed onto the floor, and HASR winked out. It spun slowly through the stone walls of the base, picking at random a safe place to rest. As it settled into its new location and the others returned to their solid forms, Jan writhed and moaned in pain. Her features were distorted with angry blotches of light.

Alarmed, Will rushed over. "What happened? How did she get in here?"

"She leapt through the wall as we were changing," Mike replied.

"She what?!?"

"She came through the wall just before HASR vanished."

Will dashed to the corner and grabbed Jan's pack. "I hope she keeps a molecular realigner in here."

He threw her things about as Jan's moans increased to garbled screams. Slowly the patches of light grew tearing her body apart.

"Ah-ha!" Will exclaimed grabbing a small unit and hurrying to Elira. "Here," he said thrusting it at her. "I can't use this, but you can."

"What do I do with it?" Elira asked still confused as to what had happened.

"Place it on the bridge of her nose and across her forehead."

Kneeling beside Jan, Elira mentally activated the instrument. She grimaced as she aligned the instrument according to Will's instructions and desperately tried to stabilize Jan's tortured form.

"Cannot-do-it," she gasped. "My-powers...too-weak. Ihue, help me."

Mike grabbed the unit from her quickly channeling his powers through it. He gritted his teeth forcing the particles of light to solidify. For a moment, her body wavered.

"Come on, Michael," Will urged. "You can do it. You've got to."

"I'm giving it...all I've got."

"Use your link with her. Give it a little more."

Mike closed his eyes and found himself in shifting space. Reality and light-energy criss-crossed on divergent continuums. He cried out as pain assailed him.

"Concentrate on your own stability," Will instructed.

Slowly, ever so slowly, Jan's form became clear and her screams piercing. Mike grimaced and gasped for breath sweat drenching his hair and pouring down his face and neck.

"That's it!" Will cried. "Just a little more."

With one final effort, Mike forced out the remaining light particles and Jan became solid once more. Her limbs fell limply against the floor; her screams ceased. Mike sank wearily beside her.

"Is she all right?" he asked panting.

"I think so," Will replied beginning to check her over.

Elira hovered over Jan checking her vital signs. "Her pulse is irregular...respiration shallow."

Will reached for his pack, fished around inside and pulled out his medi-kit. He opened it and took out a small vial.

"What is that stuff?" Mike asked dubiously.

"Something to re-establish her internal equilibrium." Will collapsed it against Jan's arm. "When you design a place like HASR, you have to prepare for all possibilities. I'd always hoped the stabilizer and EQ-25 wouldn't have to be used, but I'm glad to have them when we need them."

They sat back as minutes ticked by waiting anxiously for Jan to recover. Mike held her hand watching for the faintest sign of life. At last her eyes flickered then blinked open.

"That was too close, Jan," Will chided. "It took everything Michael had to realign you."

"Believe me," she whispered. "I didn't plan it that way."

She tried to sit up then stand but swayed unsteadily. Mike grabbed her helping her to a corner where she collapsed beside her pack. Jan leaned against the wall, closed her eyes and sat panting. At last she took a deep breath, leaned forward and reached for her scattered things.

Mike knelt beside her. "You should rest." He took the pack from her hands and stuffed things inside for her.

"Can't rest," she replied. Dizziness swept over her and she shut her eyes against it. "The plain to the gap is swarming with Saracens. After this incident, they'll be heading straight for the base. We have to get out of here before we're trapped."

She struggled to her feet but collapsed right back to the floor.

"You're in no shape to go anywhere," Mike said.

"Let me take over for a while," Will offered. "I know this area pretty well. Tell me where the Saracen camps are, and I'll get us past them."

Jan nodded weakly and handed him the wand. She jerked her thumb upwards then leaned back. "Mike, get me out a glucogen pack, would you?" she whispered.

He grabbed the collapsible bottle and handed it to her.

Meanwhile, Will replaced the wand in the console and pushed the black button. As Jan drank the energy-giving fluid, the room slowly spiraled upwards. On the plain, a green mound appeared and four figures cautiously stepped from it.

"Where to?" Mike asked.

"Through the gauntlet," Jan replied.

Though stronger after her drink, she still leaned heavily on Mike for support while Elira carried her pack. A thick blanket of fog had settled into the valley and swirled eerily around them.

"At least we have cover," Will remarked.

"Best thing that's happened so far," Jan panted then stumbled.

Mike caught her placing her back on her feet. "Sure you're all right?" he asked anxiously as she trembled all over.

"Still feel sick and dizzy."

"Why do you not rest?" Elira pressed.

"Can't," Jan gasped. "We're sitting ducks out here. Too open. We've got to go on."

"Want me to carry you?" Mike offered.

Jan shook her head. She took several deep breaths then leaned heavily on his arm. "Go on, Will. I'll make it."

They started off, but Jan heard a faint noise up ahead.

"Saracens! Take cover!" she hissed.

They dove off the path hiding in the tall, wet grass. Moments later an enemy patrol tramped by within inches of them. They held their breath and waited.

"What was the message you received, Thov?" asked one.

"No survivors found at their base in the plateau."

"We tramped 'em good!" exclaimed another.

Several Saracens clapped hands with each other in a sign of victorious brotherhood.

"Do not be too cheery," the first admonished. "Conlinc radioed suspicious movements afoot in this region. First, we find deserted bases where we had never seen any before; now this group with its firepower."

"Yeah. Zorak said their Prince was back."

"We shall swat him down with the rest of his rebels."

The voices died away, but Jan signaled for them to remain in hiding. She waited till the last booted foot was out of hearing. Will watched intently for her "thumbs-up" sign. Mike helped her up and they pushed on.

"Where were those camps?" Will whispered.

"One dead-ahead...about a mile and a quarter," Jan panted. "One...maybe two and a half miles from there...towards Endel's rise. The other...at the base of Peda Lang - Long Foot."

He nodded and tramped on ahead.

As her system slowly recovered, Jan increasingly became able to speed up her pace. Will, sensitive to this, led them accordingly. He skirted the camps she had mentioned, though they were quiet now with but a lone, dozing sentry in each.

As they approached the mountains, Jan glanced about worriedly. She let go of Mike's arm, stumbled towards Will and, upon grabbing his arm, nearly knocked him off balance.

"What's up?" he asked catching her and himself simultaneously.

"There's still one patrol missing."

Warily they continued toward the mountain gap. Will spotted Saracens out of the corner of his eye.

"Over there!" he hissed.

"Quick! Off the path!" Jan said.

Will led the group off to one side, but the Saracens had already spotted them. They charged up the hill shouting. In minutes their enemies would be upon them.

Chapter 50

Will scanned the immediate area and spotted a copse of trees. He tugged at Jan's shirtsleeve and pointed upwards. She nodded and they hurried to the base of one tree. Mike and Will scrambled into its lower branches then reached down and pulled Jan and Elira up beside them. The foursome worked their way higher until they were concealed within the tree's foliage. They sat holding their breath as the enemy soldiers passed below.

"Could you get them away from here?" Jan whispered to Mike.

"I'll try."

He quickly scanned the landscape, spotted a clump of bushes and pointed his finger. In seconds, they were watching themselves shout and run down the slope. The patrol sprinted after the fleeing figures as the real group shinnied down from the tree.

"Where's the gap?" Will asked.

"This way," Jan replied leading them away from the Saracens.

They made a dash up the hill and disappeared inside a cleft in the mountainside. They dropped to the ground gasping for breath.

Jan pulled herself to her feet. "C'mon," she urged. "We've got to make the Gorgo Silan before High Sun."

They struggled to their feet and scrambled on over the rocky terrain. They edged along the narrow trail above the steep ravine. Jan stumbled over a tree root and slid down into the ravine bumping against the jagged boulders all the way. Eventually she came to a stop and sat at the bottom biting her lip and fighting back tears. Mike hastily slid down after her.

"Are you all right?"

She nodded. "I twisted my ankle on a root and bruised my arm. Man! What a clutz! No one's ever going to believe I was a successful run leader at this rate."

"Heh! You're just pushing too hard," he said gently feeling her arm then her ankle. "Nothing's broken."

She stood up and tried her ankle. "Not sprained."

"You're wiped out. You need to rest," he reiterated.

"Wish I could, but we can't stop yet," she insisted.

"Then let me help you up to the trail," he offered.

"Thanks," she said taking his outstretched hand.

They scrambled up the side of the ravine to where Elira and Will waited.

"Are you hurt?" Will asked as they crested the lip of the ravine.

"No, I'm just tired."

"I think that experience with HASR took more out of her than she knew," Mike added.

"Why don't we stop here?" Will suggested.

Jan shook her head. "It would be better if we got to the rendezvous point first then rested. Once Adar, Behran and Garik meet us, we'll have to push on in earnest. This is nothing."

With Mike helping her, they clawed their way up the steep ascent only stopping to catch their breath at the top. Once they stopped panting, Jan moved them on crawling along the top of the ridge. Near the mid-point, she stopped abruptly.

"We should be almost there," she panted scanning the terrain. "Ah-ha! Up there!" She pointed to a clump of bushes not far ahead.

They eagerly pushed forward stopping beside the bushes while Jan shoved them aside. Dumping their packs and pulling them along after them, they squeezed through the long, narrow fissure the bushes had concealed.

"We're here!" Jan announced. "There's a hollow down in the gorge where we can crash. It should be mid-afternoon at least before the others join us."

They slid down the steep gorge sides and scrambled into the hollow. Gratefully, they dropped their packs and sank to the ground.

"Grab a bite," Jan said pulling rations out of her pack and eagerly digging in.

The others wasted no time in joining her and ate in silence for the next half-hour. Satiated, Elira, Will and Mike slumped back against their packs and dozed. Jan got up and paced to ward off the afternoon drowsiness that crept over her.

The afternoon passed quickly, the sun finally passing its zenith and dipping behind the peaks. Becoming restless, Jan scanned the ridge above them and the shadows between the overhanging trees. She heard a crunch on the gravel behind her, jumped and spun around.

"What's wrong?" Mike asked.

She let out a sigh of relief. "It's only you!"

"Thanks. Who did you expect?"

"Around here...who knows?"

He sat on a boulder pulling her down next to him. "So, what's got you so nervous?"

"Adar and the others aren't here yet. I'm getting worried. Who knows what could have happened to them."

"What'll we do?"

"I should go look for them."

"Alone?"

"Yes, it's faster. Besides, you need to stand guard for the others."

Mike nodded. "I just wish you'd take someone with you."

Jan glanced at Will and Elira, who were sound asleep. She shook her head. "They need their rest. Don't worry about me. I'll be back."

"That's what you said the last time," he reminded her, "and look what you came back with."

"I got back, though, didn't I?"

"Yeah, but your 'companions' were most unwelcome."

Jan leaned over and kissed his cheek. "I promise to be more careful."

He watched as she rose and scrambled up the side of the ravine disappearing beyond the trees. In resignation, he leaned back against a boulder to watch and wait. The others remained asleep, even as darkness settled into the gully and Endel and Thira I crept back into the starlit sky. Suddenly a pebble bounced down the bank behind him. He spun around peering into the darkness.

"It's me!" came a loud whisper.

"Find anything?" Mike asked hurrying to help Jan down the rest of the way.

"No, not a sign of them. Any trouble here?"

"Nothing."

"Want some sleep?" Jan asked.

"No, you rest first. I don't think you've closed your eyes yet."

She shook her head.

"Didn't think so. I'll stand watch a bit more." Mike gave her a kiss then watched her crawl into the hollow beside the others.

When the moons crossed each other's paths, he crawled into the niche and shook Jan's shoulder.

"Hm?" she murmured sleepily.

"Can't stay awake anymore."

"Have they gotten here yet?" she asked sitting up on her elbows.

"Sorry. No show."

"Wonderful!"

Mike sank into his spot, while Jan crept over her sleeping friends. She huddled in the moons' light, her cloak wrapped about her shoulders. Toward daybreak, Mike awoke to the sound of angry voices.

"I understand the time factor, Janielle," came Behran's voice, "but Garik could go no faster."

"Is he going to slow us up the whole way?" she asked in a low, tense voice. "We've already lost a full suntarin, and we had no room for lost suntarini to begin with."

"He will just have to work harder to keep up, that is all," Behran replied.

"If he doesn't, the outcome could be deadly...for us."

She stalked back to her pack waking the others as she did. "C'mon, folks. Time to move."

Elira, Will and Mike sleepily crawled out hoisting their packs to their shoulders. When all had eaten, Jan started out. Soon they spotted the glint of sun off water and the world around them became hushed and silent.

"What makes this place so quiet?" Mike asked.

"The stones here absorb almost all sound," Jan explained in what seemed to be a loud whisper. "It's the best place I know of to sneak through. You can't be heard and, with the overhanging trees and ledge, you almost can't be seen."

They reached the stream bank and hiked along the side of it. They walked on silently all that day and the next watching the stream narrow. While the others plodded along wearily, Mike turned frequently to glance behind them or overhead. He fidgeted nervously at meals, and near dusk began to pace about the camp. He said nothing to anyone maintaining his solo vigil.

During the third evening, a twig cracked waking him from his sleep. He sat bolt upright peering into the darkness. A movement caught his eye, and he concentrated on that spot. Suddenly Mike caught a glimpse of the moons' light glinting off the white hair of a shadowy form crawling back into its bedroll.

"Only Garik," he grumbled lying back down and drifting off into an uneasy sleep.

The next day Jan continued leading the way up along the stream that tumbled over the flint-grey rocks. She purposefully kept them well under cover of the trees or cliff overhang to shield them from unfriendly eyes. Yet, Mike kept glancing about with increasing frequency.

When they stopped for a quick lunch, Jan strolled up behind him gently brushing his shoulder with her fingertips. He jumped as if he were being ambushed.

"Whoa! Take it easy! We're friends in this camp...especially you and me."

Mike let out a sigh of relief and settled back again onto his flat rock.

"What's with you?" she asked dropping wearily onto the stone beside him. "I've never seen you this jumpy before."

"Nothing really." He casually took a bit of his rations.

"`Nothing'!" she exclaimed, her eyebrows raised to peaks.

Mike glanced at her then chuckled. "Guess I can't fool you,

huh?"

"You're a little too obvious at the moment. C'mon. Talk. What's eating you?"

"Actually, I don't know," he replied. "Ever since we entered this gorge, I've had the feeling we're being followed and watched. Yet, every time I turn around, there's no one there. It could be because I can hardly hear anything, including my own heartbeat. It's driving me insane."

Jan gazed at the water splashing playfully over the rocky streambed. "It's called 'trail instincts.' The runners with Royal Blood always have the best." She glanced up at him. "But I've been feeling the same thing, too, ever since we left Mundfortu. That can only mean one thing."

"Saracens?"

She nodded. "I hate the feeling they give me, especially at night. They have a device called an Electronic Fear Inducer. It emits radio waves on a certain frequency that produce fear in everyone within its range. Somehow, combined with the dark they seem a lot worse. It's weird."

"Speaking of which, I saw something weird last night," he said chewing his last morsel.

"Like what?"

"Garik startled me out of a sound sleep last night. I'd been asleep for a while, but he was just climbing into his bedroll."

"Late at night?" she pressed.

Mike nodded.

"So, you've seen him, too," she said pensively.

"You mean, you've seen him?"

"Every night."

"Haven't you followed him," he asked surprised.

"A couple of times. I never got too close, though. It seems it was just 'nature calling.' He never has gone very far and he mutters to himself the whole way there and back."

"Hm. I never thought it could be that. Still, we ought to keep an eye on him. Something about Garik doesn't feel right to me."

"Me, neither." Jan stared at a swirl of water in the creek. "Do you think he could be a plant like that phony foundation guy, Joe?"

"Joe?" Mike asked, brow knit in thought. "Oh, yeah. I'd completely forgotten about him. I never thought of suspecting that in anyone here."

"What do we do to find out?"

"Something Will had me do back on Earth when we suspected you."

"Me?" she cried in surprise. "What did you do to me?"

He stared across the creek. "I'd really rather not say, Jan. I wasn't happy about doing it."

"Why did you then?"

He looked back at her. "To make sure you weren't being used against your will to get at us, or that you weren't in trouble…like Will and I had felt Pat was. He said if I found anything, it could save your life. That's all I ever considered."

"Did you?"

Mike nodded. "Once a tracking device and another time a control device. That's what gave you those awful headaches there for a while."

Her eyes lit up. "Oh, yeah. But what did all that do to me?"

"Not anything I care to discuss, but you probably have a lapse of memory somewhere."

Jan thought for a moment. "Is that why I don't remember the time I spent with you at the cemetery after Pat's funeral?"

Mike nodded glancing away guiltily.

"I always wondered why you told me I had fallen asleep, yet I felt so drained. Well, what can I do to help you with Garik?"

"Not much. I'll have to have half-an-hour or more so I can psych up to do it and hold his attention."

"I'll see if I can arrange a long break sometime. Hopefully, Garik will cooperate and move a little faster."

"Ok. I'll do what I can on my part."

Jan patted his shoulder as she got up then headed for her pack. "Time to hit the trail," she called.

As they hiked, the stream banks rose more steeply and the water rushed over the boulders strewn in its path. By mid-afternoon, they could feel the cool mist drifting to them from the falls above. The water beside them grew frothy. They glanced up at the glistening, majestic waterfall.

"This is Vedufala," Jan announced, "the Veil Falls that was discovered during the Haslen-dag. It hides an impressive set of tunneled passageways. The way going up to them is very slick because the rocks don't absorb much water. Be certain of your hand and foot holds. If possible, use the same ones as the person before you used."

She stepped up the wet, slippery, moss-covered rocks beside the falls. Elira followed her, while Will and Mike brought up the rear behind Adar and Behran in order to keep Garik moving.

"This is what your father and I used to do a lot of," Will said feeling for a handhold.

"Where did you use to go?"

"Right up White Peak, at the summit of the Mozern. Best piece of climbing you could ever want to do."

Mike struggled to edge higher. "When this is all over, you'll have to take me climbing around here."

"We will definitely go," Will said. "There are lots of great places on Quentas to tackle."

They clambered higher until they finally stood on a narrow ledge high up the face of the cliff.

"From here on out, we'll travel underground, but be prepared to get wet first," Jan shouted. "We're going through the falls, so hold your breath."

She led the way through a narrow part in the veil of water. The rest followed quickly except for Garik who lagged behind.

"Go on," he insisted to Mike. "I have to catch my breath."

The old man glanced furtively downstream while fingering something that dangled from his belt.

"I'm covering the rear," Mike replied sternly. "Now, get in there."

He grabbed Garik's shoulders shoving him through the falls.

Mike glanced back downstream glimpsing a bright flash a ways off. Several flashes repeated themselves. He blinked, but now they were gone. Shaking his head, he stepped through the veil. Yet, something other than cold mountain water sent chills racing down his spine.

Chapter 51

Behind the Veil Falls, the ledge continued forcing its way into the mountainside like a wedge. Towards its back a large boulder butted up against the cliff face. Jan led them to its side, where they squeezed through a crevice into pitch darkness. Suddenly a flame leapt into the air with a loud sizzle. It cast flickering shadows on the walls and a ghostly glow on peoples' faces.

"Everyone take hold of the shoulder of the person in front of you," Jan instructed. "I'm going to lead us to a cache." Her voice echoed eerily through the cavern's labyrinthine tunnels.

The group shuffled slowly down the path till they could push their way into a small chamber to their right. Everyone huddled in the dark waiting for Jan to find a lantern.

"How do you keep a charge in these lanterns?" Elira asked.

"This is a prime rest stop for runners because it's so well hidden. Every time they come, they replace the stored lanterns with fresh ones. This one's only about two or three weeks old." She touched the rim of the one she had just unpacked and stood back to admire its warm glow.

Mike looked around the small chamber catching glimpses of stone shelves and sleeping ledges that had been chiseled into the walls.

"What is this place anyway?"

"Ah, a good question, Your Highness," Garik said. "This used to quarter a family of stone masons. This part of the cavern is riddled with these small chambers."

"What did they do? Live here?"

"While the Elra to the Dome were being delved, yes," the old man replied.

Mike whistled appreciatively. "How many would be here at a time?"

"Oh, thirty or so, according to the records. Each night they were hustled to these quarters and the great doors shut and locked behind them."

"Which is the reason Garik's along," Jan said hauling out four more lamps for the others. "The doors open by voice commands. The matra for each is chiseled into the door."

"The hieroglyphs are so ancient," Adar said taking up the explanation, "that Garik is the only one who still retains enough knowledge to read and translate them."

"Yes. My grannavan was one of the scribes who kept records of the workers' feats," Garik said warmly.

"But that would make you...." Mike began.

"Over two hundred years old, so they tell me," Garik said, "though I cannot recall that that is true. I thought I recalled dying once, but I guess it was merely a long sleep. Besides, I do possess the ability to read the matras, so I suppose that what I have been told is true."

"And the fact that you'll have to read them and perform whatever task they require to unlock the doors is reason enough to get going," Jan interjected. "Between the doors we can make good time, but who knows how long it'll take to read and translate each matra."

The others nodded in agreement.

"We should use the 'buddy system' for safety," she said. "Let's pair one army to one civilian, with one man odd. Each pair will carry a lantern."

The others again nodded their consent.

"Behran," she continued, "you'll be responsible for Garik. Adar will be with Elira, and...."

"I take you?" Mike hoped.

Jan shook her head. "We're both army, in effect, but Dehan is technically civilian. You want to take Dehan?"

"I'd rather take you," he said in a low voice, accompanied by a mischievous grin.

"Yes, well, uh...."

"I'll take Dehan," he said winking.

"Good." Jan went back to the cache and pulled out more rations handing them to each person. She also gave each person a coil of rope and began pulling out weapons.

"Weapons?" Elira questioned. "What need of weapons do we have on these paths? Most of them are secret, and some are so sacred they can only be tread by Royalty."

"Besides, I am peace-loving," Garik croaked. "I have no desire to carry a weapon."

"Saracens don't care about sacred paths, and side passages have since been dug into the main leader," Jan replied curtly. "We will need weapons…just in case."

Out of the corner of her eye, she saw Mike open his mouth. "No. Don't tell them yet."

He stared at her hard realizing that her lips had not moved though he had heard her speak. "When did you learn telepathy?"

"In training. I'm not good. It's hard. Let's wait till we have proof, ok?"

"Ok," he replied mentally.

"Look, I agree with Jan. We ought to be prepared," Will said picking up a laser.

"I trained my leaders to be ready for any contingency," Behran added patting a laser rifle that already hung from his belt.

Mike rose to his feet and faced Elira. "We're at war, mother. Enemies have no respect for the sacred. You need to choose a weapon, though I agree that, due to his age, Garik should not carry one." He picked up a lightweight firearm and handed it to his mother.

"What's in there for me?" he asked Jan.

"You practiced the most with this," she replied pulling out a long, white staff.

"It augments the energy of someone whose powers are in their prime. Your father used one on occasion," Elira remarked.

"Yes, and I've gotten rather good with it," Mike said. "It's pretty handy. I think I'll take it."

Jan handed it to him. As soon as Mike touched it, the staff glowed. Suddenly it shrunk to the size of a pen, and he tucked it into his pocket.

"Ok, folks. Let's get ready to move out," Jan called. "Will and Mike, I'd like you to follow me. Elira and Adar will come next then Garik and Behran in the rear."

They hastily assembled and started off snaking along the winding stone paths. Mike glanced at the floors and walls as they jogged.

"These paths don't look chiseled," he remarked.

"They weren't," Jan replied.

"What made them?" he queried.

"Ancient volcanoes," Garik puffed from the rear. "What we are in now is the core of an ancient lava flow. The outer surface cooled quickly forming long, hollow cylinders for the molten rock to flow through."

"You can see the other sleeping quarters off to either side," Jan said swinging her lantern from side to side.

Mike peeked in the doorways as he trotted by. "Then we aren't in the 'Elra'?"

"No. The sacred paths are further on," Jan replied. "This is an 'Omra'; one of the paths kept secret since the Haslen-dag."

"The Elra were only for the Rites of Joining, New Life and Death," Elira explained.

"Yes, but we'll be using portions of them," Jan said.

"No! You cannot! They may only be tread in ritual!" Elira protested.

"This is war, Elira," Will reminded her. "Our survival outweighs everything else. When faced with annihilation as a people, ritual must be set aside in order to assure life."

Elira swallowed hard, shivering as icy fingers clutched at her heart. "But without the rituals, what is left?"

"Life," Will replied simply.

The passage began to narrow affording room for only one at a time. Suddenly Jan skidded to a stop, the others sliding into her from behind. A man-sized door stood before them with an Ionic column flanking either side. Jan touched her lantern then pointed her finger toward the door. Her light illuminated its surface on which had been carved several figures of varying races, dress, and customs. Garik elbowed his way to her side and squinted at the figures and transcriptions carved on it.

"This is the 'People's Gate'," he announced proudly, straightening up as he spoke to make sure the others had heard him.

"How do we open it?" Mike asked.

"A-hem! Yes, well, that...." Garik muttered bending closer to study the hieroglyphs. "Hold that light steady, girl," he snapped at Jan.

She tapped the lantern twice and the glow brightened.

"Ah, yes...better, much better. Now, let's see. It says here..."We are many peoples, of many lords, who are bound by oath for all eternity. Never again shall brother slay brother nor friend slay friend. Instead, we shall live always in harmony.""

"That was written after the terrible Haslen-dag," Elira murmured.

"But how do we get in?" Mike asked impatiently.

"I am getting to that, young man," Garik snapped waving aside his question with a gesture of his hand.

"Let's see. Yes, yes! Oh, simple!" Garik exclaimed gleefully. He stood back from the door and raised his arms. "Undide unide hallrus," he said, slowly and distinctly.

Everyone held their breath till they heard a loud creak. Slowly the old door swung open. With a cheer, the group pressed forward.

"What did that mean?" Will asked as Garik returned to his position in line.

"Why, it is simple. "Unity of heart unites us all."

"Hm. I like that."

As they pressed further into the mountain, Jan quickened the pace from a jog to a trot to a near run. Finally, a yell from the middle broke her concentration.

"We must rest," Adar called. "Old Garik can go no farther, let alone the rest of us."

Jan drew a long breath. "There's a niche just up ahead. We'll rest there."

She slowed her pace as she led them on eventually allowing the group to halt. Gratefully they sank to the ground. Here and there around them, seats had been carved from the rocks, and a mural depicting common people at work adorned the walls.

"Must we hurry this fast?" Behran asked.

"We lost an entire day waiting for you at the rendezvous point," Jan reminded him. "Core II is comprised of young, conditioned runners. If they're in position before us, our way into the Palatial City could very well be blocked. Our movements have to be timed to theirs. You know that."

Jan walked a ways off sitting in one of the chiseled seats. After a while, she glanced over at Mike noticing his dark, brooding face. "So, he's been urging me on," she thought. "Wonder what he's feeling that's got him so worried?"

She pulled out her rations then edged over to Mike. "What's up?" she asked. "You seem really worried about something."

"Not really. I just thought I saw something before I went through the falls. It's been on my mind ever since. Guess it was just the stream."

"Mike, don't underestimate your senses," Jan urged laying a hand on his arm. "I learned months ago to trust the instincts of Royal Blood. A lot of times one of my runners would be nearly panic-stricken, while everyone else would be calm. The higher the percentage of Royal Blood, the more sensitive their 'internal radar' seemed to be. I'll tell you, if it hadn't been for them, I would've run into a lot of ambushes. And now, here I am on a run with the person with the highest percentage of Royal Blood. Believe me I'll listen very seriously to anything you have to say."

Mike gazed at her thoughtfully. "Will always told me that when my father was near danger, the hair at the nape of his neck would stand on end."

"What happens to you?"

"My stomach knots up."

"So, what have you been feeling?" she pressed.

"Like my stomach's being squeezed into a ball. I feel like someone's been following us the whole way and they're getting closer."

"You've been pushing me, too, haven't you?"

He nodded.

"Are they just behind us or are some ahead waiting in ambush, too?"

"No, they're definitely behind us. I think I've been trying to outrun them ever since the cache. But the further we go, the tighter my stomach gets."

"Have you any idea of how many may be following us?"

"More than two or three, I think"

"Twenty?"

He shrugged. "I don't know how to tell."

"But you think we ought to push on?"

"Yes as fast as we can. Now I'm positive I saw more than just the stream."

"What?" Jan insisted.

"Back at the falls, I thought I saw the sun reflecting off the stream. Now, I'm certain what I saw were signals," he replied.

"It couldn't have been fish jumping?"

He shook his head. "No. The flashes weren't random. They were signals."

Suddenly a knot gripped Jan's stomach, too. "We need speed, and Garik's slowing us down," she groaned. "I wish he could've taught someone else those hieroglyphs, but there just wasn't enough time. Speaking of which, what about that test you were going to put him through?"

"I need at least half-an-hour."

"Well, it'll just have to wait for now. Maybe I can make the next break longer. At any rate, let's not tell the others," she added in a whisper. "No telling what Garik would do if he were found out."

"No, I agree."

She returned to her spot and reloaded her pack. "Break's over!" she announced hoisting her pack to her shoulders. "We've got to get going."

"So soon?" Garik groaned.

"Now!" she and Mike chorused together.

The others rose wearily and packed up their things.

"I'm changing the line-up," Jan said. "Garik and Will will come directly after me. Elira, Adar, and Behran will come next. Mike, I need you to take up the rear."

He nodded.

"Everybody ready?" she asked as they realigned themselves.

"Let's get going." She took off trotting rather than jogging.

"What is the hurry, young lady?" Garik panted from behind her.

"There's a second door and a bridge just beyond it that I want to cross before we rest again," she replied.

Jan pushed on through the dark winding passages for several miles. Their breath sent puffs of mist swirling into the black above.

"Have you no respect for the aging?" Garik asked stumbling.

"Jan, we can't possibly make that bridge," Will called. "Even I can't keep up this pace."

She frowned in frustration and gave in resignedly. The others flopped down in the first available spot. Mike, however, took Jan's arm and led her a little ways off.

"What's this bridge?" he whispered.

"It crosses a chasm in one of the main vaults. If we are being followed, and they do catch up to us on this side, we'll be trapped. They'll gun us down for sure," she replied tensely. "I want us to get to the other side before that. I'd thought of having you take out that bridge once we'd crossed it. Now, it's imperative that you do. If only Garik weren't so slow," she moaned.

"It's not just him, Jan. Everyone else is winded, too."

"What about you?"

"I'm so nerved up, I could go on forever."

"Running on adrenaline. Better load up on carbs and watch that you don't crash from that high," she warned him.

They sat in silence for a moment.

"You know, with all the others in our group with Royal Blood, it's strange that you're the only one feeling this," Jan commented.

"There are a lot stranger things afoot, I'm sure," he replied.

"That's what worries me." She shook her head. "Too many things have been going wrong for them to be purely coincidental. It all gives me a very uneasy feeling."

"I know what you mean."

Jan glanced about at the worn faces of the rest of the group. "From the looks of them, this had better be a longer stop."

"That doesn't sit easy with me," Mike said.

She shrugged. "Me, neither, but what else can I do? You might as well take advantage of it, though, and confront Garik."

"As soon as everyone lies down."

She nodded then went back to her lamp. When she touched its rim, the others' lamps went out completely while hers retained a faint glow. "Ok, folks. Naptime."

"Good," Adar said dropping right off to sleep.

The others huddled against the rocks, their heads on their packs, and quickly dozed off. Jan, too, lay her head back but remained wary even in sleep.

Suddenly she felt a hand on her shoulder shaking her. "Hm?"

"Wake up!" Mike whispered in her ear.

"What's wrong?" she asked sitting straight up.

"Garik took off as soon as you turned down the lights. He's been gone ever since."

"Which way?" she asked clambering to her feet.

"Back this way," he said pointing toward the path they had just traveled.

"That does it! Let's check this out. He's been gone too long this time for it to be any natural reason."

Jan took Mike's hand leading him back down the dark path. They had nearly traveled halfway back to their previous rest point before they finally heard Garik's shuffling steps. Jan pushed Mike back against the stone wall and shrank back into a crack in the wall herself.

"Dunna appreciate an old man's efforts...." he muttered. "Just doin' the best he can. Canna do no better for no one."

The couple held their breath as he staggered past then breathed a sigh of relief when he was gone.

"That sure didn't sound like the Garik we know," Jan mused.

"Where do you think he went?" Mike wondered, while she knelt and felt the ground.

"I don't know, but wherever it was, he got hurt. He's trailing fresh blood."

"I've got a bad feeling about this," Mike said.

"Me, too."

"We've been betrayed!" they both exclaimed.

Chapter 52

Mike and Jan peered into the darkness at Garik's disappearing black form.

"He's been contacting them," Mike finally said.

"The Saracens?"

"I'm positive of it. Let's go back and wake the others. We've got to get to that bridge."

"Ok. We'll take a Molluc tunnel I know of. I want to beat Garik back there."

"Ditto."

They hurried off then slipped through a narrow crevice a little ways on and passed through a Mot-pont. Hand-in-hand they dashed along its smoother, straighter route. They arrived at the rest point, grabbed their packs, and huddled together watching and waiting.

Ten minutes later, Garik staggered to his pack and sank down beside it.

Jan immediately stood up turning up the lantern's light. "We're heading out!"

Mike was busily shaking each drowsy sleeper; Garik, however, refused to budge.

"Leave an old man be," he protested. "I need a sound sleep."

"Don't give me that," Mike snarled in his ear. "Jan and I followed you out of camp. I know you're tired, because you just crawled into that sack. Whatever you're up to, you just forfeited your 'sound sleep.' If we didn't need you to open those other two doors, I'd leave you here for your 'friends'."

Garik grumbled and rose like a slinking dog. Each person hoisted his pack and picked up a lantern. Jan touched the rim of each lantern then its base. Little balls of light energy zipped out of the bases and danced like pixies at their feet. Though they were bright enough to light the path, they were low enough so as not to be easily spotted from another section of the cavern.

"How far to the bridge?" Mike asked quietly.

"About a suntar...an hour," Jan replied.

"I don't think we've got that long."

"We'd better get moving. Here, jab Garik with this. It's an upper," she said slipping Mike a tiny syringe. "Maybe it'll get him moving." She turned to the others calling in a louder voice, "Same line-up as before."

Mike pushed back toward his position stopping briefly beside Garik and grabbing his arm.

"What are you doing there?" Garik cried.

"Giving you something to keep you moving," Mike replied giving him the shot. "Don't hold us up this time, old man. Don't even squeak. I'm behind you, and you will feel my wrath. Too much is at stake here for me to waste my time on you."

Garik glanced at him fearfully then shuffled into line.

"We're moving out fast this time," Jan announced. "No more breaks till after that bridge."

She took off at a fast trot with Mike continually urging them forward. Now and then he would stop to listen to the ominous echoes that resounded about them. Then, heart racing and blood pounding in his ears, he would run and catch up to the others, urging them on at an even faster pace.

Finally Will slowed letting the others pass by. When Mike neared him, he picked up his pace jogging beside the young man. "What are you trying to do, Michael? Kill us?"

"Shh," Mike hissed. "We're being followed."

"Followed!" Will gasped in alarm. "Saracens?"

"Yes."

"Have you seen them?"

"Once, by the falls. Now I keep hearing their footsteps. My stomach's in a dozen knots, Will. We've got to make that bridge."

With renewed vigor, Will elbowed his way back to the front and prodded Garik on. Yet, now the path swam before him. Will clutched his head as a wave of dizziness swept over him.

"Can't have a migraine," he muttered. "Not now."

He fumbled in his pocket for a small pill. He placed it under his tongue and kept going.

"The door!" Jan exclaimed. "Hurry! Get Garik up here!"

She manipulated her lantern so the light shone only on the carvings of a King and Queen. Garik pushed forward till he was close to the door. He squinted in his effort to read the ancient writing.

"The Royal Gate," he mumbled at last.

"Obviously," Mike retorted. "Get that thing open!"

Garik stared at the inscription muttering under his breath.

"Um...'Lojalate ade Regnete'."

The others waited' 'but nothing happened.

"What's wrong?" Mike demanded.

"I cannot see clearly," Garik complained. "Not enough light."

"Can't chance anymore light," Jan telepathed to Mike.

"That's all the light you get. Try again."

"Um...'Loiolate ade Regnede'."

Again nothing.

"Never mind," Mike said. "Let's try something else."

He grabbed Jan's right hand and his mother's. Before they knew what was happening, a surge of power went out of them and a bolt of light hit the door. The beam bounced off ricocheting off the stone walls.

"Royal powers have no affect on this door," Garik informed them.

"Great," Jan groaned.

Mike studied the door. In the picture on it, the King held the Queen's right hand, a starburst shining from her finger. "No," he said slowly. "I think you're wrong. Let's try again, but this time repeat that last phrase you said," he instructed.

Garik sputtered under his breath then positioned himself beside the couple. Suddenly they could all hear the distant pounding of booted feet.

"Saracens!" Will cried.

"Try again, Garik," Mike commanded. "On my signal."

Mike took Jan's hand again then nodded to Garik.

"Loiolate ade Regnade."

As Garik spoke, a bolt of power leapt from the Ring to the door. A glow surrounded its perimeter and it opened with a click.

Behran caught a glimpse of lantern light some distance behind them. "They are coming!" he warned.

"Hurry! Over the bridge!" Mike ordered.

They dashed pell-mell along the dimly lit path. As they ran, Mike pulled out his pen-sized staff. It glowed briefly before growing to useful proportions.

"The bridge is just ahead," Jan announced racing down the chiseled stone steps.

Mike glanced over his shoulder catching a spark of light glinting off metal.

Jan's foot touched the bottom of the stairway. Ahead, she could barely see the outline of the bridge. "Got to risk more light," she muttered. She touched her lantern rim and it glowed more brightly. She quickly surveyed the bridge before glancing behind them. "Saracens in the gallery!" she cried in alarm as they took up firing positions.

"Over the bridge!" Mike yelled. "Hurry!"

Elira stopped to test the bridge.

"Go on!" Jan ordered pushing the woman forward.

Garik, Adar, and Behran crossed next as laser fire whizzed overhead.

"Go ahead!" Will yelled to Jan. "We'll cover you."

Jan dashed onto the bridge clutching at the guide ropes as it swayed sickeningly under their combined weights. She let her eyes drift downwards into the dark, foreboding abyss but quickly looked back up determinedly focusing on the opposite side. A laser bolt seared the air above her head and she darted forward.

"Go on, Will!" Mike yelled. "I'll hold them back."

Will dashed to the bridge and began running across. A laser beam hit one support behind him, and the bridge sagged with a horrible lurch. He clawed frantically at the guide ropes but kept moving.

Jan readied herself leaping with a somersault through the air to the safety of solid rock. Will continued sprinting forward on his away across the bridge.

Mike returned the Saracen fire with power blasts aimed through the staff. He somersaulted through the air avoiding their laser bolts, then fired another of his own. Five Saracens fell dead but more stepped up to take their place.

Mike turned and dashed toward the bridge. Before he could reach its steps, another laser bolt hit the remaining support. Will's scream pierced the air as the bridge collapsed into the abyss' dark maw.

"Will!" Mike yelled. "WI-I-I-ILL!" He froze staring into the dark pit that opened at his feet.

"Mike! Behind you!" Jan shouted from the other side.

He glanced back in time to fire another power bolt then looked again into the abyss.

Suddenly laser fire hailed on his enemies from the other side dropping many on the stairs and forcing the rest higher into the gallery. While Behran, Adar, and Jan continued to spray them with laser fire, Mike pointed his finger at the frayed ends of remaining rope. A stone span sprang across the gulf and permified with a shot from the augmenter.

With Saracens at his heels, Mike leapt to the bridge and sped across it. He sprinted the remaining distance somersaulting to safety just in time to spin around, aim, and land a power bolt in its center. With the sound of a thunderous explosion and a tumult of wails, the Saracens tumbled into the chasm along with the crumbling stone. Those remaining on the opposite bank sent a rain of laser fire at the group, as well as the roof. Mammoth stalactites dropped from the ceiling and pelted the ground around them.

"Get them to cover!" Behran ordered Jan motioning towards the back of the ledge.

Behran returned the Saracen laser fire, and Mike blasted stalactites out of the air overhead. Jan sent the others ducking behind a pile of boulders and into another tunnel.

Suddenly Behran heard a scrabbling sound, and a hand groped

over the chasm's edge. "Jan!" he yelled. "Help us!"

She dashed back to his side.

"Cover us while we see who is climbing up from the abyss," he instructed.

She positioned herself behind a boulder and fired non-stop across the chasm, while Mike and Behran snaked toward the edge. They grabbed the hand and pulled till Will's head popped into view.

"Will!" Mike exclaimed. "All right!"

They hauled him onto the ledge and dragged him back to Jan's boulder. Behran took up the firing.

"Get him into the tunnel," he ordered. "I will hold them off."

Will draped himself over the couple's shoulders, and they staggered off with the injured man. Behran watched them disappear behind the boulders before zigzagging toward safety. As he turned to fire his parting shot, a laser bolt caught him in the chest. He slumped to the ground amidst a hail of stalactites. His empty fist clenched, trembled, then fell limp.

Mike and Jan half-carried, half-dragged Will down the tunnel towards the lantern light. As they came into view, Adar and Elira jumped up to help them.

"Dehan!" Elira cried.

"Dehan?" Adar said incredulously. "By the ancients, I never thought we would see you again."

They eased him down gently propping him against a stalagmite padded with bedrolls. While Elira carefully checked him over, Jan returned to the tunnel peering anxiously into the darkness.

"It has gotten quiet out there," Adar commented coming up behind her.

"Commander Behran?" The echo of her own voice sent chills up her spine.

"He was right behind us," Mike said following her to the entrance of the passage.

Suddenly fear clutched at Jan's heart. She grabbed the nearest lantern and dashed back toward the chasm. "Commander Behran!"

Mike dashed after her chasing the bobbing will-o'-the-wisp ahead. Jan pushed her way around the boulder then skidded to a stop. Mike edged up behind her. Together, they peered through the dim light to where the commander lay buried in rubble. His lifeless hand appeared to beckon to them, while his face remained frozen in a grimace of pain.

Jan rushed to the pile falling to her knees beside it and clawing frantically at the rocks. "Help me, Mike! We have to dig him out."

He bent down, took hold of her shoulders and gently eased her away. "It's no use, honey. He's dead."

"No!" she cried in disbelief. "If we can move the rocks off him, we can revive him."

"He's dead, Jan. We can't bring him back."

Chapter 53

Jan stood for a moment in the dark silence facing the stone walls. “He can’t be dead! No! Behran can’t be dead!” she moaned, her fists clenching and unclenching as she squinted her eyes tightly closed.

“This isn’t right,” she whispered hoarsely. “He can’t be dead. He’s not supposed to be; he’s part of my team, and I’ve never lost anyone before.”

"Honey, there was nothing you could do."

"But I should've been there to cover him." She spun to face Mike. "Why are things suddenly going all wrong? First, they knew our exact location in the fort. How? Then we're followed all the way here and they got close enough to attack. How did they know where to find us? Now I've lost a man. Why? This-isn't-right. None of this should be."

Mike stood helplessly beside her not knowing what to do or say.

"Don't you understand, Mike? I'm responsible for all of you. I have to account for each person in this group. Only, now one is dead, and I wasn't even around to see what happened. He was my training officer, Mike, and I let him get killed."

"Wait a second, Jan! Your training officer?"

She nodded staring out across the now empty chasm.

"Then don't you think that if he trained you, he knew what to do for himself?"

"He sent me on ahead with you and Will," she said mechanically.

"Then he probably believed he would follow. He wouldn't have been in a position to train you, if he didn't already know what to do for himself. Jan, he made a rational judgment. Saracens just aren't rational. You obeyed the orders of your superior. You can't hold yourself responsible for the outcome."

She remained silent.

"C'mon," he urged placing his arms around her shoulders and holding her. "Let's go back to the others and keep going. Isn't that what Commander Behran would have wanted you to do? Finish this run?"

She nodded, her eyes fixed numbly on the dead body. Finally she buried her head against his shoulder, allowing Mike to lead her back into the tunnel. Her throat ached and her eyes burned with tears that refused to surface.

General Adar glanced up as they approached. "Behran?"

Mike shook his head signaling for Adar to say no more, while Jan headed straight for her pack. She opened it, drew out a medi-kit and handed it to Elira.

"Dehan's hurt," she said mechanically.

"Just some cuts and bruises," Elira replied. "I already checked."

Jan nodded absentmindedly turning in a circle to assess the others. She stopped when her gaze fell on Garik. "What about him?" she asked icily.

The old man groaned.

"He has a head wound," Elira replied, "but I am not certain what caused it. It is too crusty to be a laser wound."

"It's not," Mike replied. "He got that sometime last night."

Elira looked at Garik. "What is going on here?" she demanded. "What has he been up to?"

"We believe he may have betrayed us," Mike said quietly.

Elira stared at him in horror.

"We've got to move on," Jan announced oblivious of their

conversation.

"His heartbeat is too irregular," Elira countered nodding toward Garik.

"Can you stabilize him?"

"Temporarily."

"Good enough," Jan replied coldly. "He's one person I'm not waiting for any more. He's already cost us enough trouble and one life. I don't intend to allow him to cost us any more."

She slung her pack over her shoulder, grabbed Garik's pack and moved a little ways into the far tunnel. Elira tucked away the medi-kit and let Will lean on her. Mike and Adar followed dragging Garik between them.

They marched steadily for over an hour till the tunnel narrowed and squeezed between two round stalagmites. Beyond them, a small chamber opened up with two passages leading from it.

Jan dropped her pack and waited as, one-by-one, the others all squeezed through. She unhooked the laser from her belt, raised it to shoulder level, and blasted the stalagmites melting them together to form a solid barrier.

"Now we cannot go back!" Elira cried.

"We don't want to. Besides, this way the Saracens will meet with a solid rock wall if they do follow us."

"But what about these other routes?" Elira asked.

"The one to the right leads to an entrance near the top of the ridge. I've used that one before. They'll have to retrace their steps to the falls then climb the mountain to reach it. Considering that Saracens rarely stop for breaks, it should take them at least eight suntari to come that way."

"And the other passage?"

"That leads directly to the Star Chamber," Adar said quickly, "which, to my knowledge, has not been disturbed in over twenty years. I doubt they even know it exists."

"So we are safe?" Elira asked.

"For now, at least," Jan replied. "Let's get some sleep while we can. When we do move out, our pace will have to be fast. We've had too many delays."

Elira lowered herself to the ground, while Mike and Adar propped Garik against his pack. Finished, they wearily sank to the ground and their bedrolls. Will adjusted himself the best he could and nodded off.

Jan sat watching the others for a while. Finally, she picked up her lantern and walked up the tunnel that led to the ridge. She trudged along, her arms wrapped about her. Satisfied that the tunnel was indeed clear and worn out by her efforts, she returned to the chamber. She sat near the ridge tunnel's entrance and dozed fitfully while listening for enemy footsteps. Now and then her fingers would twitch, and a frown would cross her face.

Some time later her eyes popped open and she glanced about. Frowning, she propped herself on one elbow and strained to catch the slightest sound. The ridge tunnel was quiet and no muffled boot steps came from beyond her improvised rock shield.

"It wasn't Saracens," she muttered.

A low moan startled her. She sat up fully and touched her lantern. It spread a warm glow about the chamber. Someone moaned again. Jan crept over to Elira and shook her shoulder. Elira's eyes blinked open; Jan pulled out the medi-kit and pointed toward Will. Together, the two women worked their way to his side.

"What's wrong?" Jan whispered setting the lantern nearby.

"My ribs," he gasped. "Think I...may have...broken them."

"Why didn't you say something?" she chided. "I never would have made you walk all the way here without a painkiller."

"They didn't...hurt this…bad then," he wheezed.

Jan carefully opened his jacket and shirt. She and Elira could see the purplish-black bruises that lined his chest and sides. Gently she pressed each rib to check for a break pulling back when Will cried out in pain. Elira pulled a scanner from the medi-kit and eased Jan aside. She moved it slowly up and down his chest and sides.

"Is he all right?" Mike asked propping himself up on an elbow.

"No breaks," Elira announced.

"You're lucky, Will," Jan said.

"You do have some extensive bruises, though," Elira remarked.

"At least they heal quicker." Will smiled wanly.

Mike crawled over beside them.

"I think we should tape your ribs," Elira said. "The support might feel good to you." She turned to Mike. "Would you help him sit up and get his jacket and shirt off?"

"Sure." Mike eased Will into a sitting position and carefully removed the two articles of clothing.

Meanwhile, Jan fished around in her pack and produced a bandage. "Well, Will. This is your own invention; a bandage that works like a patch to release pain medication through the skin."

Will smiled grimly then winced as Jan and Elira began passing it around his chest.

"Never thought I would use it," he gasped.

"I'll bet you didn't," Jan replied.

"Is Dehan all right?" Adar asked sitting up sleepily.

"Just a badly bruised ribcage," Jan said. "Once we get this bandage on, he'll feel better."

Elira tucked the end in, and Jan and Mike helped Will back on with his shirt and jacket. When Jan took the medi-kit back over to her pack, Mike followed.

"How are you doing?" he asked quietly sitting down beside her.

"I don't really know," she said dropping down next to him. "I even went for a walk up this path," she said nodding to the opening behind them.

"Alone? Jan, that was dangerous."

"Probably, but I wanted to make sure no Saracens had been pre-posted there to attack us while we slept. Plus, I wanted some time alone. It didn't help much, though. I'm numb all over."

Mike reached over hugging her tight.

"It's not just Behran's death, Mike. I'm really worried. We made these plans so carefully but nothing's gone right yet. No matter what we do, the Saracens already seem to know about it. It's just amazing that Will's all right."

"No one will be feeling well in a while," an eerie voice called from the corner.

They all turned to see Garik glaring at them with fever-glazed eyes. Puss and blood were oozing from the gash on his forehead. They trickled down his face in rivulets.

"Wonderful!" Jan groaned. "One man's dead, a second's injured, and that old goat's delirious. We'll have Saracens on our back porch in four or five suntari and we should be moving on."

She pulled her medi-kit back out of her pack and moved over to Garik. "Elira, come help me with him."

Elira crept to her side and fished out the medi-scanner. She ran it over the wound then shook her head, perplexed. "The injury is only a suntarin or two old; we know that. Yet, the medi-scanner insists there is no wound. It is as if he were two men. What is going on Garik?"

He stared at her through haze-rimmed eyes as he reached a tremulous hand toward her face. "You were so beautiful on your joining day, Elira."

She leapt back staring at him in alarm. "I do not recall your being there," she retorted icily.

A wan smile spread across his face.

Elira backed away nervously and joined the men on the other side of the chamber. Out of patience with the old man, Jan returned to her pack and tucked away the medi-kit.

"Don't listen to him, mother," Mike said. "He's been our traitor all along. Now, from the looks of things, he'll soon be dead, and we won't have to worry about anymore leaks to the Saracens."

"Ah, but you will," Garik said cryptically.

"I do wish he would stop that," Elira complained.

"Soon I will," Garik replied. "But until my demise, consider this...there is another traitor amongst you. One who knows not his fate."

"Just what are you talking about?" Mike challenged.

"Let's just say that I know enough to make King Ihan's best friend his traitor as well as yours," Garik said sneering at Mike.

"How can you make accusations like that!" Mike cried leaping to his feet.

"You make them yourself, Prince," Garik growled.

"Yes, but I had evidence and a witness."

"Sit down, Michael," Will said reaching up and pulling him back down beside him. "He's a delirious, sick old man. Don't allow someone that pathetic to rile you. He knows as well as I do that I never willingly, nor knowingly, betrayed anyone."

"Ah, but I said that you did not know. That would certainly gain you a pardon."

"I see no reason why I should need a pardon."

"Then maybe you should pay attention to what I know."

"Just what could that be?" Mike demanded.

"Memories. Memories of events I never witnessed," Garik

replied.

"Like what?"

"Like your joining ceremony, Elira. And the fact that Ihan was late."

"He had to escape from Garin's prison," Will remarked dryly.

"With your help, of course."

"Of course."

"Then Elira and Ihan boarded a Spherestar Whisker for their honeymoon to Earth. It took off from the Seat of Our Fathers on Elrador, just as Thira I rose over the horizon."

"Y-yes, we did. We took the Jewel of the Crown that night," she admitted.

"Mm-hm. But when the Jewel returned to the Crown, there was something to dampen the crowd's welcoming enthusiasm...was there not?"

"Yes," Elira said shaking her head sadly. "King Ihuk, Ihan's father, had just been shot in an assassination attempt. We were rushed straight to his bedside."

"Hm. I wonder, Dehan, if the King would have been shot had you stayed at the Palace? Could you have spared the King his fatal wound?"

Will covered his face with his hands. "I've never forgiven myself for that. I had two directives to obey; the decision between them was hard. I should have stayed with King Ihuk, but Prince Ihan had made me swear to take his message of thanks to the Mollucan. It was his Mollucs who dug Ihan out of Garin's prison and helped him get to his joining ceremony just in time. Yet, the very same day that I left for Molluc-ham was the same day that King Ihuk was attacked."

"Ye-es. You would keep your oath to the Prince instead of the oath you had to the King," Garik purred. "Little difference that made, though. You were remaining loyal to the throne for on his deathbed, King Ihuk did abdicate to his youngest son, Ihan. It is possible that you wanted to insure that Garin would never get the throne."

"A good thing, too," Elira cried. "Garin was a raving, egocentric, power-lustful maniac. He cared nothing for anyone but himself. King Ihuk had sworn long before never to let Garin have the throne."

"Yes, and he succeeded in cheating Garin out of the crown that was rightfully his by birth...by abdicating to Ihan with his very last breath," Garik growled.

"But how do you know the precise moment King Ihuk abdicated?" Elira asked warily. "The only ones present were the Sanctimons, Ihan, myself, and...."

"Dehan," Garik sneered.

Elira glanced in confusion from Garik to Will, but the latter wore an equally surprised and confused look on his face.

Mike touched Will's shoulder before telepathing. "What's going on here? Is he trying to frame you for murder and high treason?"

"I don't know, Michael," Will replied likewise. "I never told a soul what happened in King Ihuk's death chamber...not even you. I honestly don't know how Garik knows so much. Yet, there's something so familiar about him, it sends chills up my spine. Only I could swear that I've never seen him before our return."

"There are more pleasant memories to dwell on," Garik recounted oblivious to their conversation. "First Quentas celebrated the Grand Coronation of a young King and Queen. Two montari later, a Royal pregnancy was announced. Though you were simply radiant, Elira, the father-to-be was restless...anxious...preoccupied as I remember. I seem to recall that he divulged to someone he felt that all of Quentas was in grave danger. He was most certain that he would die in the conflict to defend his people. Did he ever tell you this, Elira?"

"No-o."

"No, come to think of it, he did not want the young Queen to know. After all, a woman approaching her time of delivery should not have to worry about the inevitability of becoming a widow."

"But surely he never mentioned this to you?" Elira cried indignantly.

"Of course not! But he told someone!"

"Dehan!" Elira turned to face him. "Did my lifemate tell you this?"

Will ran his hand over his eyes. "Yes."

Elira stared at him. "How does this man know so much of what you and Ihan discussed?"

"I don't know, Elira. I don't know."

"Ihan always did share everything with you. He protected me

from the truth, telling me only what he felt was best," she said, the bite of envy edging her voice. "Did you ever divulge to anyone what Ihan confided to you?"

"No, Elira. I swear. I never spoke a word of it...not even to Ihue, his own son. I would never...could never betray my friend," he declared turning anguished eyes to her.

"Then how does he know so much?" she challenged pointing straight at Garik.

"I-don't-know, Elira."

"Something doesn't add up here," Jan ventured. "Someone's missing from this scene."

The others ignored her concentrating on the argument surrounding Will, instead. Yet, she stared at Garik searching his old, lined face and fevered eyes as if he could somehow be the key. He briefly caught her gaze. Suddenly she felt his eyes burn holes straight through her head and a sharp pain assailed her temples.

"You went into labor the day the Saracens landed, did you not, Elira? Almost as if they had been signaled. I mean, with his lifemate in labor, Ihan was loathe to leave her side. True, Dehan?" Garik sneered.

Will nodded without looking up.

"Then followed the onslaught of Saracens in an all-out attack on every sector of Quentas. The planet and its people were so beleaguered, that no one even cheered when a son, a Prince, was born. Come to think of it, Ihan wanted the news kept secret to prevent a full-scale attack on the Palace."

"Yes," Elira said, startled. "I remember my healer saying that the townspeople were learning of Ihue's birth from the Saracens. I remember thinking that was very odd."

"Ihan wanted to wait until you and Ihue could flee to safety before announcing the birth," Will commented.

"But," Garik sneered, "someone leaked the news. Because of that misstep, the Saracens stormed the Palatial City before the Queen and Prince could escape."

"Yes," Elira recalled. "Ihan brought Ihue to the Jewel, while Soniora, my healer, brought me by another route. But the Saracens cut me off from my lifemate and son," she cried bitterly.

"Too true. Ihan was forced to give up his son to Dehan to carry to the Jewel. He then turned back to rescue his beautiful lifemate. A laser was fired from out of nowhere and struck her down. Oh, Ihan was brave in his defense of her, but he was overwhelmed by the numbers of soldiers who were attacking. Meanwhile, his best friend stood in the shadows and watched him get killed, correct, Dehan?" Garik asked contemptuously.

Will sobbed. "I had no other choice. Ihan had made me swear an oath of loyalty to Ihue...had made me swear that I would let anything happen to his son. He forced me to promise to escape with Ihue and to guard the child with my life. I was not to consider anyone else's welfare...not even his."

"Meanwhile, your Queen and your best friend lay dying," Garik taunted.

"I had no choice," Will gasped. His shoulders heaved with the impact of the memory and the resulting pain from his ribs cut his breath short.

Throughout the chamber, the tension had drawn as taut as a rubber band about to snap.

Chapter 54

Jan replayed what Garik had said in her mind. "But where was Garin all this time?" she asked innocently.

"Jan, don't intrude!" Mike snapped. "This is none of your business, so stay out of it!"

Adar and Elira said nothing, but Will's face contorted with his effort not to cross Jan.

"Wait," Will gasped struggling to be heard.

Garik's gaze bore down on him, yet Will dared to continue.

Throwing his hands up to shield himself from Garik's possessed stare, Will pressed on. "Jan does have a point. I don't recall Garin being anywhere around when all of this happened. He missed the coronation, and he was no where to be found when the Saracens landed."

"He was exiled for kidnapping Ihan!" Adar snapped. "Everyone knows that! Where he went during his exile is anyone's guess."

"No!" Elira countered with difficulty. "He was not. Ihan and I spread that rumor to explain his disappearance after our joining. But Garin disappeared before he could be brought to trial."

Garik began to cackle softly, but it soon grew in pitch; he continued with the fervor of a madman. "You fools!" he shouted. "Can you not see? Garin never left you. He has been with you all along, heard all you have said, and saw all that has happened. How else could the Saracens have known about you, boy?" he said sarcastically addressing Mike. "How else could they have known where you had escaped to?" He sat up, drunk with his own power.

"But Dehan is the only one who heard and saw it all," Mike pointed out.

"Yes. Odd coincidence? Hm?"

"And only that," Mike replied firmly.

"Just a coincidence? Oh, really, Prince. Think harder," Garik challenged cruelly. "Somehow the Saracens always knew where you were living on Earth...no matter what city or state you had moved to. And...." he emphasized with raised eyebrows, "whom did they home in on? Was that not always Dehan?" Garik concluded victoriously. "Only then did they go for you." Pleased with his deliverance, his cackling experienced rebirth and grew to the point of hysteria.

All eyes turned to Will who sat hunched over on the ground. "I-am-not-a-traitor," he declared firmly. "I never led them to you, Michael. You've got to believe me."

Mike laid a reassuring hand on his friend's shoulder. "I know you didn't. I believe you, Will."

"You are wrong, Prince," Garik persisted. "Dehan was indeed the one. What one thing did you so persistently search for within the minds of all you came in contact with...even the girl you loved? Over and over again you looked for danger in everyone...everyone but your most loyal guardian and mentor. Why did you never perform a subliminal profile on him, boy?" he challenged derisively. "Why not see where your true danger has lain all along?"

Mike glanced at Garik then locked gazes with Will. "I did minor subliminals on you and never found a thing. Could you have an implant that's buried deeper?"

Will thought in stunned silence for a moment. "I suppose it is possible, though I always figured I'd somehow know if I had one...have some sort of symptom to give it away."

"But what about those migraines, Will? When did they start?"

Will thought hard. "Just a little before your parents' joining, but I didn't give it much thought."

"Then you could have one?"

"It's possible, though I don't when or how it could have been planted."

"What should I do, Will?"

"Check. Go ahead," Garik goaded watching their eyes knowingly. "Search him like you did all the others."

"Go ahead, Michael," Will said aloud. "He's just crazy enough to be right."

Mike took a deep breath then stared into Will's eyes. The air between them shimmered as he stretched deep into his friend's mind. He found himself on a path lined with doors. There, blocking the way to Will's deepest memories, squatted a crustacean-like creature. Horrified, yet drawn by curiosity, Mike edged closer surveying its multi-segmented, armor-plated body which narrowed to a whip-like tail that it had coiled beneath itself like a mainspring. He stayed away from its lobster-like front claws and mammoth, curved mandibles that protruded from a mouth oozing with green slime. Suddenly it swung its eyestalks around, caught sight of Mike and lunged toward him menacingly swinging its head and mandibles from side-to-side. Instinctively Mike leapt back, just out of reach.

"Destroy it, boy," Garik urged. "You must rid your friend of its presence. Only...killing it would mean destroying your friend, too." His voice drifted to Mike as if it were traveling down a long tunnel.

Mike crept around to the side of the creature. He spotted a long, silver disc lying along the length of its back. The beast lunged at him again, but he rolled out of harm's way.

A uni-control, trans-receiving disc," Mike muttered. "So that's how he did it. Will, himself, would have overridden the impulses, but this creature is easily controlled. It was set up as a buffer. Now, what do I do with it?"

He scanned the endless mist that swirled above him. "Will!" he cried. "Help me! What do I do with this thing?"

From behind the creature, Will's form materialized. He stared past Mike with glazed eyes.

"C'mon, Will! Snap out of it! I need your help."

Overhead, Garik's sneering face appeared. "That is it, boy. Destroy the creature. That is the only way."

"Will! Help me!" Mike called ignoring Garik.

"The disc...." Will gasped fighting the control. "Destroy the disc."

"That's it!" Mike exclaimed.

He crouched low then leapt for the creature's head. Although it bucked and reared, Mike tenaciously hung on. Despite the rough ride, he managed to keep his eyes trained on the disc; soon smoke rose from the shiny plate.

"You will never succeed, boy," Garik declared.

A power bolt caught Mike directly between the shoulders throwing him forward and completely knocking the wind from him. He glanced up and saw Garik's face as his laughter rocked the inner sanctum of Will's mind.

"The disc, Michael," Will's form gasped. "Keep trying. It's weakening."

Mike redirected his attention to the disc. This time it slipped from side-to-side, smoke billowing from its center."

"That's it, Michael!" Will called in a stronger voice. "It's almost free! I feel it!"

With one last, desperate effort, Mike fired an intense, blue power bolt at the disc. The creature reared up once more then both it and Will dropped to the pathway.

Without warning, Mike found himself being sucked through dark, empty space. At a blink of his eyes, he was looking at the cave and the others around him; Will lay unconscious at his feet.

Mike spun toward Garik, his face contorted with rage. "What have you done to him, Garik?" he demanded.

A gurgle rose from the old man's throat. His eyes rolled back in his head while a grey pallor crept over his skin.

"Garik's dead!" Jan exclaimed in surprise."

Elira rose and knelt beside Garik. She felt for his pulse or any other sign of life. "He is dead."

"Will may be, too," Mike said crouching beside his friend.

Jan handed Elira the medi-scanner. She crossed to Will's side, activated the scanner and quickly passed it over Will's body.

"No. Dehan is alive, just unconscious."

Mike breathed a sigh of relief.

"What was in there?" Jan asked, half afraid to hear the answer.

"Some sort of bug with a control disc. Garik must have figured that Will would override its impulses on his own, so he planted that thing in there with a control disc riding piggy-back," Mike explained. "Somehow he controlled him with that."

"You mean, that's how he knew everything that had happened?" she asked in amazement.

"Yeah. Everything...like when my grandfather was most defenseless...when I was born...where we were on Earth...everything. He-used-Will all these years."

Jan laid her hand on his shoulder. "I'm sorry, Mike. That's got to be hard to take."

Will moaned and moved slightly.

Mike bent closer to him. "Will! Will, can you hear me?"

"Garin!" Elira gasped suddenly.

Everyone turned to look in the direction she was pointing. On the floor where Garik lay, a phosphorescent mist swirled about his body. Two images vied for precedence; the wrinkled face of Garik, the historian, lay transparently over the younger, cruelly-handsome face of another.

"He has been with us all along!" Adar exclaimed in horror and astonishment.

Will moaned and rolled over.

"Elira, help Dehan," Jan instructed. "See how badly he's injured. The rest of us had better get ready to move on."

"Why rush?" Adar asked. "It should be at least two more suntari before the Saracens get here."

"I don't think so," Jan countered. "If Garik...I mean Garin...I...if he knew what was happening all along then something tells me those Saracens are on their way now. I mean...Garik always lagged behind to give the Saracens information and a chance to close the gap. Something tells me this little drama was another stall. Those Saracens are close. I feel it!"

"Then what shall we do?" Elira asked glancing up from the scanner.

"Get ready to run."

"With Dehan in this condition?"

"How bad is he?" Jan pressed.

"Well, not too bad. He is temporarily blinded but rest ought to restore his sight. Other than that, his system seems to be recovering from the shock."

"Then we'll have to carry him till he can walk," Jan decided.

Mike took her aside. "Look, Jan. I think I know of a way I can hold the Saracens off for you...give you some extra time to get away," he said quietly.

"What do you mean? How?" she asked skeptically.

"It's not exactly something I've ever tried before," he admitted. "And I'll have to go astral."

"Now just what will we do with the rest of you?" she wanted to know.

"Take my body with you. I'll catch up later."

Jan frowned. "I don't like this, Mike. It's much too dangerous."

"And if you don't go ahead with it, we'll have more Saracens on our backs than we'll know what to do with."

"You've got a sense of how many?" she asked anxiously.

"Yes, and it's more than a dozen."

"Mike, I hate to let you do this."

"Do you have a choice?" he pressed.

"I'm trying to come up with one."

"Honey, you don't have one."

She sighed heavily. "I know, but that doesn't make it any easier."

"It wasn't easy for me to let you come on this little trip, either," he reminded her leaning forward to kiss her lips.

"Guess I'm on the flip side, huh?"

He shrugged. "Sorry. I didn't plan it this way."

"I know," Jan replied. "Ok. Do your thing. Elira and I'll drag you. Adar can carry Will."

Mike gave her a quick hug then went to his bag and stretched out beside it. In the next instant his body was glowing blue. A moment later, he once again stood in their midst.

"Ok, folks. We're moving out," Jan called. "Adar, you'll have to carry Dehan. Elira, you and I will have to drag Ihue."

"But what is he doing?" she asked, concerned.

"Buying us some time. He'll join us later."

Jan slung her pack over her shoulders then grabbed Mike's.

Adar slung Will over his shoulder in a fireman's hold and picked up his pack. Elira and Jan carefully grabbed Mike's arms and began dragging his body off.

Jan stopped a moment and looked at Mike. "You be careful, you understand? You, of all people, I want to see again...in one piece."

Mike flashed her his award-winning grin. "I'll be fine. Go on. Get out of here."

He watched them go then turned back toward Garik. "Now," Mike said rubbing his hands together, "let's see how much I can remember of neuroanatomy."

Chapter 55

Jan took one last look at Mike's glowing astral form then, together with Elira, reluctantly dragged his body with them. Adar stumbled after them carrying Will. They disappeared down the Elra toward the Star Chamber as the sound of booted feet echoed in the distance from the ridge path.

Mike glanced hastily at his retreating group before collapsing into a glowing blue ball. The footsteps grew louder and husky voices reverberated within the chamber. The blue ball slowly descended until it had disappeared inside Garin's forehead. Angry voices could now be heard clearly. Suddenly Garin's image shifted and once again became Garik just as the first Saracen appeared in the passage.

"Which way did they go?" the first Saracen asked hurrying over to Garik's still form. "I said, 'which way did they go', old man?"

Garik's eyes remained closed and his face expressionless.

"Wake up, old man," the Saracen yelled kicking Garik's leg. "Which-way-did-they-go?"

Instantly Garik's eyes fluttered open, and his head and right hand rose off the ground. He pointed toward the sealed passage. "They went that way," he croaked.

"There is no more bridge."

"The Prince reconstructed it with his powers."

"Again? Blast him! But where are they headed now?"

"Back toward a side path their guide knows of."

"After them!" the Saracen cried.

He and his men dashed into the dark hole. As the last boot disappeared inside, Garik's arm and head fell back. The blue globe rose from his forehead and sped down the Elra after the Core I members.

Garik's body was once again engulfed in a swirling mist. Suddenly his flesh shriveled and his bones dropped into a heap of dust.

The sound of echoing boot steps reoccurred from the ridge passage. Minutes later, two Saracens shot out from it and slid to a stop.

"Which way?" the first asked.

The second held up a lantern. "Not that way. It has been blasted into a solid wall."

"This way, then," the first one said nodding toward the Elra.

They dashed off down the passage in pursuit of their quarry.

Racing ahead of them, the blue ball zipped toward Core I. In seconds it had caught up to and had disappeared inside of Mike's body. Once again the blue sheen engulfed him. Mission completed, he struggled to his feet.

"You made it!" Jan exclaimed with relief. She handed him his pack.

"Yes, but I sensed a couple of them following us. Here, Adar. Let me carry Dehan. We've got to move faster."

The two men shifted Will from one set of shoulders to the other then Jan led them on. Mike slipped and stumbled along behind her with his precariously perched burden.

Suddenly Jan called. "Rock slide! Go slow!"

They inched their way across the treacherous patch of ground hastily pressing on once their feet hit smooth rock again. Without warning, Jan stopped.

"I've got to chance some more light. Adar guard the rear."

Adar turned, his weapon at the ready. Jan touched her lantern with her index finger, and a thin beam of light shot out across this second slide area.

"This one's quite wide," she remarked. "We'll have to use our ropes."

She took off her coil tying it from her waist to Elira's. She took Elira's coil and strung it between her and Mike. She continued on till each member was secured to the person in front of and behind him.

"I'll go across first. Don't follow till I give you the signal," she instructed Elira.

Slowly, Jan edged her way onto the soft dirt and loose stones. When she had gone a quarter of the way across, she tugged on the rope. "Come on, Elira," she called softly. "Take it slow, and be quiet."

As Elira gingerly felt her way onto the slide area, Jan continued on across. At the half-way point, she swung her lantern signaling for Mike to start. With Will draped over his back and shoulders, he began inching warily across. Jan had reached the far side, Elira was nearing it, and Mike had reached the half-way point when shots zipped overhead.

Mike glanced back at Adar, who had just started onto the slide. In a far portion of the gallery, the Saracens were shooting at the rocks and mud above them. Frantically Mike pressed on. Without warning, mud and rocks began to shower down on him and Will. A second round of laser fire took out his foothold. Mike slid down desperately struggling to find a hold with his free hand. He stopped with a sickening jolt and dangled below the ledge.

"These ropes won't hold us for long," Will said grabbing hold of Mike's jacket.

"Glad to hear you're back in action," Mike quipped.

"That ride we just took did the trick," Will responded. "Right now, I'm more concerned with these ropes." He rubbed a hand along one feeling its tautness.

"I think that before they give, mother and Adar will join us down here."

"You can't get a foothold?"

"There's nothing to grab onto, Will. Believe me, I've tried."

A laser bolt shot past them scorching the air.

"That was close! Even I could feel that!" Will cried.

"Which is why I'm going to get you out of here," Mike said.

"How?"

"Remember all those exercises you put me through back on Earth? Especially the one where you blindfolded me and...."

"And you sent your math book flying through the front

window?"

"Uh, yeah. I wasn't too good back then."

"Please tell me you've improved," Will pleaded.

"Let's just say 'I hope so,' because I'm going to fly you blind to the ledge."

"Michael!"

"Trust me, Will. Have I ever let you down before?"

"Heh-heh," Will chuckled sarcastically. "There's always a first time."

Mike looked up toward the speck of light that shone from Jan's lantern. Another laser bolt buzzed past his head. He grasped both the ropes firmly then closed his eyes to concentrate. Slowly, the weight on his back lessened as Will rose into the air. Mike opened his eyes watching till he eventually lost sight of his friend in the darkness.

"Can't-see-either-the-ledge-or-Will," he said through clenched teeth. "Sure-hope-he's-close. He's-even-heavy-this-way."

On the ledge above, Elira caught a glimpse of an object rising out of the darkness. She grabbed Jan's arm. "Look! What is it?"

"Will!" Jan exclaimed completing the last knot on Mike's rope as she tied it off on a stalagmite.

"Am I getting close?" he asked.

"About another foot," Jan replied. "Then I can grab your hand."

"I hope Michael can hold out. We were a long ways down."

"How's Adar doing with those Saracens, Elira?" Jan asked keeping her eye on Will.

"He seems to be holding out," Elira replied peering back at the general.

"Let's hope so. We've got our hands full right here." Jan stretched out on the narrow ledge and reached for Will's extended hand. "Just a couple more inches, Will. Maybe if you stretch a little."

The two reached a little farther. Finally their fingertips touched. Below them, the tie rope from Adar to Mike snapped sending him swinging through the darkness. Will dropped with a jolt, but Jan's hand closed around his wrist and held him firmly.

"Elira! Help me!" she called. "I can't hold you long, Will. Find a hand hold."

Elira knelt and held onto Jan's ankles while Will groped about.

His fingers found a rock and he grasped it holding on desperately while his feet searched for a solid niche. Soon he was dragging himself onto the ledge beside the women.

"How do we get Michael up?" he asked panting.

"I don't know. Elira and I can hardly hold him now that we have his full weight. If I hadn't tied the rope off at my end, we'd be down there with him."

"Maybe with the three of us we can pull him up," Will suggested.

"We can try," Jan agreed.

"Adar has made it nearly half-way," Elira reported.

"He'll have to manage the rest of the way on his own," Jan replied puffing as they tugged at Mike's rope.

Below them, Mike was spinning in dizzying spirals through the air. Suddenly his head hit the underside of the ledge. He clawed at the stone for a hold. His rope halted momentarily just as a laser bolt blasted the rock next to his hand.

"I've got to get out of here," he muttered.

Laser fire zinged around him as the Saracens aimed their infrared scopes.

"What I really need is a shield."

He let go of the rock with one hand and pulled out the augmenter.

"Air molecules exist, even if I can't see them," he thought aloud while glancing around. "Well, here goes."

Mike aimed the augmenter at a section of the darkness and drew a large square. He fired a bolt and watched as it glowed in the center of the square. The Saracen fire bounced off the invisible shield.

"Now for a ladder."

Mike pointed his finger at the rope stretching between him and the women on the ledge. In seconds it became a rope ladder, which he then permified with a touch of the augmenter.

"That's more like it!" he exclaimed.

He reached overhead and began pulling himself up the face of the slide. Minutes later, his head popped up above the ledge. Elira and Jan grabbed his shoulders hauling him up beside them. Adar leapt to the ledge just behind them.

"That was some trick!" Jan exclaimed appreciatively. "How long will that shield hold out?" she asked slipping the ropes off their waists and gathering the lengths together.

"Not long," Mike replied. "It's only made of air. A shift in the air current will blow it away."

"Then we'd better get moving."

"I'll carry Dehan for you," Adar offered.

"No need," Will said. "I think I can walk now."

"Good. We could use the extra speed," Jan replied. "C'mon."

Will grabbed Mike's elbow and the party hurried after Jan. Minutes later, they heard the pounding of booted feet following them. They skidded around a corner and trotted through a low tunnel.

"I know this area," Elira panted. "We're headed for the Dome of the Heavens."

"And the Star Chamber," Adar added.

"We'll have to take refuge there," Jan yelled back.

"But we can't!" Elira protested.

"It's either the Chamber or the Saracens," Jan replied.

Elira pressed forward with the others. Jan stopped abruptly just ahead of her, and Elira plowed into her from behind.

"What is wrong?"

"It's this fork. I can't see the map in my mind clearly enough to remember which one to take."

"It is this way," Elira said heading off down the right fork.

The others lost no time in following her. They soon noticed that the further they went, the brighter the passage became. The walls around them glowed a milky blue-white. Suddenly all five slammed into a broad set of double doors.

"They are closed!" Elira cried.

"They are always shut and locked after each ceremony," Adar reminded her.

"But we do not have Garik with us to decipher the writing and pronounce the matra to open them," Elira fretted.

"We really have a problem," Jan agreed.

Mike glanced at the doors then back along the path. "Are there any Molluc trails in this area?" he asked Jan.

She shook her head. "They swore to stay away from all places of ritual."

They could all hear the hammering of booted feet from behind them.

"What do we do?" Elira asked anxiously.

"Cover the path, Adar," Mike ordered while grabbing his mother's hand and Jan's ring-bearing hand.

Power surged through them then blasted at the door. The bolt hurled back at them sending them sprawling. Mike shook his head to clear it as he rose to his feet.

"That's no good," he groaned. "It repels our powers."

He stared at the door. Suddenly, he noticed an oval-shaped notch carved in the center of one door. He grabbed Jan's hand and looked at the Ring. "I'll bet that's it!" he exclaimed.

He dragged Jan over to the door, turned her hand around, and fitted the Ring into the slot.

"Hurry, Ihue! The Saracens are almost upon us!" Elira cried.

She took up a position beside Adar, and the two of them started firing.

Mike stared at the Ring. Nothing was happening. "Guess I was wrong," he said trying to pull Jan's hand away.

"It's stuck! The door won't let me go!" she cried in alarm.

Without warning, streamers of blue light burst out from the edges of the Ring. It engulfed Jan's hand then her whole body. At this, she started shaking violently.

"Jan! Are you all right?" Mike cried reaching out to grab her away from the door. A power bolt shot at him throwing him against the opposite wall.

"Do something," Elira pleaded. "We cannot hold them off much longer."

A brilliant light burst through the crack between the doors. In response, they slowly swung back. Jan collapsed into a heap on the ground.

"Come on!" Mike yelled scooping her up in his arms.

Elira dashed through the open doors, followed by Mike carrying Jan. Will grabbed Adar's arm, and they dashed off after the others. The tunnel glowed about them growing even brighter as they ran. Up ahead they could see a magnificently carved archway.

"This is it!" Elira cried. "Hurry!"

With one final effort, they burst into the chamber and raced along its terraces toward the other side.

"There is another tunnel on the other side," Elira said dashing toward it.

Suddenly she skidded to a halt. "It is blocked! The passage is blocked!"

A loud rumble resounded behind them. Turning, they gasped in dismay as the tunnel walls crumbled about the pursuing Saracens. One of them fired his blaster, and the entire archway collapsed onto them, a heap of rubble and dust piling up all around them.

"We are trapped!" Elira sobbed. "There is no other way out!"

Chapter 56

Elira studied the two collapsed exits and groaned. “How will we ever get out of here?”

Mike lay Jan down and checked her pulse.

“How is she?” Adar asked coming over to see.

At that moment her eyes blinked open and she looked about her. “Where are we?”

“The Star Chamber,” Adar replied.

“The Saracens?”

“Dead,” Mike replied. “They blasted the archway and buried themselves in the debris. How do you feel?”

“A bit light-headed and tingly all over. Otherwise, not too bad.”

“Good,” Elira said. “Can you remember another way out of here?”

Jan looked at her perplexed. “What about the second passage?”

“It is blocked.”

Jan pondered this a moment. "Actually, we're the safest we've been so far. We may not be able to get out at the moment, but the Saracens can't get in, either. Considering the fact that Will should be resting after his experience in that last chamber, I suggest we make camp here and get some sleep."

"Sleep?" Elira asked incredulously.

"For now. We all need it. For once I can catch forty winks with you, instead of having to keep my ears open for Saracens. Maybe when I wake up, I'll be able to think of an escape route. For now, even I'm too tired," Jan replied rolling out her bedroll on an isolated terrace, crawling in, and immediately falling asleep.

"Should we not be digging our way out?" Elira asked. "What if our oxygen runs out?"

"If we dug at those cave-ins, mother, the whole roof might collapse about our heads," Mike pointed out.

"Besides," Will added, "we really could use some rest. Who knows? The next time I open my eyes I might actually be able to see again."

"And I am certain our oxygen supply will not run out," Adar said gazing overhead. "Somewhere up there, there is a vent hole...at least there used to be."

"I cannot see one," Elira countered scanning the ceiling.

"Maybe it's actually dark outside," Mike proposed. "Whatever, let's get some sleep."

He helped Will into his own bedroll and made certain that Elira had settled into hers before stretching out with his pack for his pillow and covering himself with his jacket.

After Mike had slept for several hours, he gradually became aware of a deep, booming voice disturbing his dreams. He rolled over, closing his eyes tighter, but the voice persisted. Finally, he lay back and listened to its deep base resonance as it slowly drew him from the depths of sleep.

Suddenly his eyes popped open and he glanced around. Remaining perfectly still, he strained his ears for any sound, but the voice was gone. Yet, two unseen hands seemed to tug at his arms, insisting he get up and follow.

Slowly Mike sat up and scanned the vault. The glow permeating the chamber pulsated like a heartbeat directing his gaze downwards. In the center of the cavern's pit lay a blue, star-shaped, multi-faceted rock that throbbed with a rhythmical beat. Captivated, Mike got up and cautiously made his way towards it. The closer he got, the more hues the glow took on as it swirled around him. Veins within the rock oscillated with corresponding colors.

"Prince Ihue," the deep voice said.

"Who spoke?" he demanded, instantly tense and alert.

"It was me," replied the voice. "Down here."

Mike looked down at the rock. Suddenly he heard footsteps behind him. He turned and saw Jan making her way toward him.

"What's wrong?" she asked coming to his side.

"I woke up thinking that someone had called my name. When I got down here, I still thought I heard a voice. But I don't see anyone."

"Oh, yes, you do," the voice responded, and now they both heard it.

Jan looked down at her Ring then pulled at Mike's arm. "Look! Look at the Ring!"

He took her hand watching as the Ring pulsated with the same slow, steady beat as that of the rock. "It couldn't be that rock," he muttered. "Or could it?"

"That is me!" said the voice cheering noticeably.

"It is that rock!" Jan exclaimed. "I don't believe it!"

"I'm not quite sure I do, yet," Mike said. "It's rather startling to say the least."

"So sorry," it replied slowly. "I did not mean to startle you. It's just that I am so very glad to see you. I have been so lonely these past few years."

"Excuse me," Jan interrupted, "but who...or rather 'what' are you?"

"Oh!" it said laughingly. "I really am this glowing rock down here. Your Ring is a piece of me, which is why it is living. My name is Tovorald, and I originally came from a solar system several galaxies away."

"Then how did you get here?" Mike asked moving closer and sitting on a ledge.

"Well, instead of collapsing into myself like so many other stars do or burning myself out, I exploded outwards at one end and sped across the universe. I lost more of my outer shell and speed with each galaxy I passed. By the time I reached your galaxy, I was traveling far too slowly to pass by. I was caught in its gravitational field and eventually spiraled down into Quentas where I found this nice hollow spot to land in. What is left of me now is my core or heart."

"You chose this spot?" Jan asked.

"You move of your own free will?" Mike wondered.

"Yes and yes. Actually I levitate when I want to, but I have been far too comfortable to move before this. It does get lonely here, though," Tovorald said sighing.

"Are you the only living star, or are there others like you?" Mike asked.

"No, in this and most other galaxies, I am the only living star. There have been a few others, but they are all like I was...a heart lying at the center of great outer crusts. It takes much energy to communicate that way and after a while, we give up and live in isolation. I much prefer the way I live now...able to converse freely with other beings."

"But how long have you been here?" Jan wondered.

"Not too long to me, but a very long time as you know it. Five or six thousand years, maybe more."

"It's strange that I've never heard about you before," Mike said skeptically. "Why don't the Quentasians know about you?"

"Oh, they do. They just do not understand my true nature. They have preserved memories of me in some of their legends, but their meanings have grown very dim. Even the purpose for holding their rituals in my chamber has been forgotten.

"You see," Tovorald continued, "when I first crashed through the dome's roof, I was far too hot to come near. But, hundreds of years later, your people began to hide in these tunnels and eventually made their way to this chamber. I was still just a hot, molten mass...not shiny and glowing like I am now. Though a few came close enough to talk with me, they soon fell ill and died."

"Radiation poisoning," Jan murmured.

"The others stayed well away from me," Tovorald said softly. "Yet, while these remnants no longer sickened from my presence, they were forever altered. They developed powers like my own, which they then passed on to their offspring."

"Genetic mutations!" Mike breathed.

"Yes. And these 'new' Quentasians used their powers to settle the strife in the land, thereby bringing peace to this planet."

"So, the radiation you emanated genetically altered the ones who stayed here," Mike mused. "Therefore they were the only ones who could pass this along to their children."

"Yes. And ever since, their descendents have worshipped me and declared that my chamber is Sacred. No one has lived in my home since, and they rarely visit me. It used to be that marriages, christenings, and funerals were performed here. I even used to preside over them. Lately, no one has come...until now."

"And now I understand the difference between Will and myself."

"I should say so!" Tovorald exclaimed.

Suddenly a ray of light popped through the vent in the roof of the vault. Mike looked up to pinpoint the opening.

"Wish we could get up there somehow," he said wistfully.

"You want to climb out?" Tovorald asked.

"We have to," Jan insisted. "If we don't, we'll never complete our mission and the Saracens will dominate Quentas forever. Many people will die...maybe even everyone."

"Saracens?" Tovorald asked, perplexed.

"Invaders who over-ran our planet over thirty years ago," Mike explained. "They've had our people enslaved ever since, but we're on a mission to rid Quentas of them."

"Well now," Tovorald said pensively, his glow dimming a little. "Hm...." Suddenly the star burst with color. "Oh, say! I do believe I have it! I can get you out, but under one condition only."

"And what might that be?" Mike inquired.

"When you become King, Prince Ihue, I want a new resting place. I am a living creature. I am not a sacred object to be tucked away. Now that this is known, I want a place where I can commune with other beings and have fellowship, not this dreary existence in this hold."

Mike nodded. "Granted. On my oath, you'll have just such a place when I become King. Now, help us get out of here."

Jan raced up the terraces and woke the others. They packed their rolls and uncertainly tackled the descent. Finally the entire group had gathered at the center of the cavern.

"What is down here?" Adar asked.

"The Star of Quentas," Mike replied gesturing to the glowing rock. "This is Tovorald, a living star, and the object of Quentasian veneration for centuries. He has agreed to help us get out."

"Have you some rope?" Tovorald boomed for all to hear.

Adar, Elira and Will looked at the glowing rock in startled bemusement.

"At least four coils," Jan replied having become accustomed to speaking with it.

"Two will be fine. Just lay them on top of me," Tovorald instructed.

While the others watched in amazement, Mike took Jan's coil and laid it with Elira's on top of the translucent rock. Tovorald's glow intensified, and a rainbow of colors swirled about the cavern. The coils were transformed into a solid shaft of light.

"Climb aboard," Tovorald invited. "You shall show the others how it is done."

Mike and Jan stepped gingerly onto the platform of light locking their arms about each other's waists. Slowly the light-shaft rose and the pair waved to the onlookers till they neared the ceiling and the vent.

When they had climbed onto the mountainside, Tovorald called up to them. "Remember your oath, Prince Ihue. I shall be waiting for your return."

Within minutes, Elira's head popped through the opening. Will's and Adar's soon followed. They stood on the mountaintop in the dazzling, early morning sunlight gazing below them at the blanket of fluffy white fog that carpeted the valley.

"It is so dense you cannot even see the spires of the Crown on the Hill across the valley," Adar commented in awe.

Elira gazed a moment longer before turning to Jan. "Where are we off to now?"

"I've got to get my bearings. I'd originally planned to skirt the Star Chamber and exit on the far side of the mountain. The hang gliders were stored farther up the side from that portal."

She strolled a few paces to the right surveying their position in relation to the glistening white peak that rose majestically above the fog. Another, lesser peak lay just beyond the deep gap that cut through the mountain range.

"I think they're down this slope," she declared finally. "Will, how are your eyes?"

"I can see light but not much else."

"Adar, you and Mike get on either side of him. The going is steep and rocky."

Jan took Elira's arm and, like a mountain goat, picked out a path down the boulder-strewn mountainside. They worked steadily downwards scrambling for a foothold here or a handhold there. Before long, they found themselves at the edge of the fogbank. Mist curled eerily about them hiding the sun from view.

Mike stared back up toward the peak. "Wow! You mean we were clear up there?"

"Must have been," Adar puffed.

"Ureka!" Jan cried from somewhere in the mists.

She soon returned approaching like a phantom through the fog and dragging a long, dirt-covered pack behind her. Mike ran to help and, in minutes, they returned hauling a second and a third.

"We haven't got a lot of time," Jan warned setting the pack down. "I'd planned to glide over the fog using it for cover, but the sun's already burning it out of the valley."

"Then let's get these babies together," Mike said ripping open a pack and organizing the pieces.

Jan and Elira opened the second pack, while Adar tore into the third.

"Wish I could be of more help," Will groaned.

"You can. Hold this," Adar growled shoving a pole into Will's hands. "Just hold it where I tell you to, and this thing will be together in no time."

In twenty minutes the sails were stretched taut between the rogollo-wing frames, and the giant 'birds' were perched on the mountain-side ready to soar.

"I'll never be able to guide ours," Will said glumly.

"None of us will in this fog," Elira moaned. "We are all flying blind."

"I hadn't counted on the fog lifting this soon, but the possibility had crossed my mind," Jan admitted. "Each of you should be able to use your telepathy to remain in contact with the glider in front of you."

"What about us?" Mike asked anxiously. "What do we home in on?"

"I parted with my pendant for a little," Jan replied sheepishly. "I didn't want to, but I figured you couldn't miss that."

"You're darned right!"

"Then see if you can sense it."

Mike closed his eyes momentarily and searched intently for the prize. Suddenly his face lit up. "Got it!"

"Which direction?"

"That way," he replied, his body shifting to point out the direction.

Jan pulled out a small windsock, raised it on a thin telescoping pole, and let it float on the light morning breeze. "The updraft's coming from the valley. We'll have to head into the valley and tack back. Think you can get us there, Mike?"

"To get your pendant back? You'd better believe it!"

Jan chuckled.

"Let's run a quick pre-flight check," Mike said. "Double check the harness attachment." He began walking around their glider checking brace wires, posts and wing surfaces. "Everything ok with yours?" he asked turning to the others.

"Elira's checks out," Jan replied.

"Mine, too," added Adar.

"Ok, then. Harness up," Mike said.

"One good thing about this fog," Jan commented strapping on her harness.

"What's that?" Mike asked.

"If it's so thick we can't see where we're going, then the Saracens can't see us for sure."

"True." He yanked on his harness to make sure it was well fastened. "Ready?"

"Yeah."

"Find the neutral position."

They adjusted the glider.

"Ok. Let's go," Mike said.

The pair began running headlong down the slope and into the wind.

"Wind's got it!" he shouted. "Just a little faster."

They sprinted the last few feet until the wind gently lifted them off the ground. They followed the contour of the slope building up speed. Then they pulled back slightly on the control bar trimming for maximum glide angle. Behind them the other two gliders took off in sequence and became lost in the fog. Slowly they tacked across the wind catching the rising thermals that took them far out across the valley floor.

Mike closed his eyes concentrating on the small, heart-shaped pendant he had given Jan back on Earth. In his mind's eye, he could see it lying on a tuft of dry grass, the mists swirling around it. Jan looked over at his tense face then peered ahead into the dense grey nothingness.

They glided for an inestimable length of time; the damp, chill wind whistled past their ears. The mists shifted growing thicker as they flew into the heart of the fogbank. Finally Jan could make out the shape of a dark mass ahead of them.

"The cliff!" she cried. "Pull up!"

They struggled to bring the gliders up, just barely succeeding in skimming the cliff face. The gliders wobbled as they climbed before leveling off and drifting evenly across the short plateau.

"I see it!" Mike announced pointing toward a spec of luminescence.

"Good. Let's take them down," Jan said.

Silently the great 'birds' dropped from the sky settling nose-up on the plateau surface. Their pilots shed the bulky harnesses and quickly collapsed the wings.

"Hide these things under some brush," Jan instructed. "We're deep into Saracen territory now. We sure don't need to leave our calling cards lying around."

While she tucked their glider away, Mike retrieved her pendant. He hurried back to her side.

"Let's put this back on where it belongs," he insisted.

Obediently, Jan pulled up her hair as Mike fastened the pendant around her neck. An instant later, the clank of machinery and the whine of air vehicles drifted up to them from the valley floor. A large dark silhouette whooshed overhead and an ominous foreboding gripped each one.

Chapter 57

As the dark forms whooshed overhead barely visible through the fog, Elira glanced up at them.

"What are they?"

"Into the bushes!" Jan ordered. "Hurry!"

She directed Elira toward a clump of scrub brush, and Mike all but shoved the others into the dense foliage at the plateau's edge. With everyone safely hidden, Jan squeezed Mike's arm then crawled on her stomach to the cliff's edge. She lay beside the rocks listening intently and watching the dark shapes of the passing speeders. Finally she crawled back to the group through the thinning fog.

"Our forces, combined with the villagers and the outlying farmers, must have struck. The Saracens are emptying the Palatial City, just as we had hoped."

"Good news then," Adar exulted.

"Yes, but it also means that Core II is probably a suntari closer to the City walls than we are. It should be the other way around."

The small group crouched silently beneath the bushes in the grip of fear, listening to the grind of the war machines passing below.

"Come on, Jan," Adar said sternly. "Show us the Harna, the

Last Tunnel."

She started as if waking from a dream then picked up her pack. With the others following, she scrambled up the slope and searched for the long-hidden entrance. Suddenly she let out a muffled cry as she tumbled through an overgrowth of bushes into a dark, damp passage. The others dove in after her as yet another speeder whizzed overhead. She lit their sole lantern setting it on the stone floor to one side.

Jan crossed to Will. "How is your sight now?"

"Good enough to see your blurry face," he replied grinning.

"How about your ribs?"

"They're still tender," he said gently pressing on his chest and sides, "but I'm not in pain."

"Good. That's a big improvement. If we put you in the middle, we ought to be able to make decent time."

She picked up the lantern and hooked it to her belt. "We've got to run, folks. No more long breaks. We've got to make the City when Core II hits it, since we have no way of letting them know we've been delayed. We're already behind schedule. We have to make up some of that lost time. If we don't, we're as good as dead, and so are they. Everyone ready?"

The others nodded.

"Then let's go."

Jan took off at a marathoner's pace while the others fell in behind her. Though they puffed, no one complained. They pushed hard running for a suntari at a time before breaking. Everyone dropped to the ground during each rest period, too winded to speak. After the second one, Jan worked her way back to Will.

"How much can you see now?"

"More. I can probably see a good ten feet away."

"Good. We need your sight."

She gave them a chance to catch their breath and take a gulp of water before getting them up and urging them on again. They set a quick pace rounding a sharp bend near mid-day. The next moment, they found themselves shinnying into a river bed.

"It is dry!" Elira exclaimed, stunned. "This used to hold the overflow from the reservoir." She glanced around. "What happened to the river?"

"The Saracens sealed the sluice gates and flooded most of the City in order to create a moat," Will explained.

"Yes, but Core II is scheduled to blast open those gates," Adar reminded them.

"Right and we've got to be inside the Palace walls before that happens or we'll be swept away," Jan added.

With stern determination, they set out once again scrambling up the dry river bed. It was smooth from the many years water had flowed over the stones and steep as well in its descent from the mountain to the Palisade Plain. They clawed frantically for hand and foot holds as they climbed. Jan urged them on with increasing fervor as she hastily glanced at her chronometer set to Quentasian time.

"We're cutting this awfully close," she muttered anxiously. "We've got to make the entrance to the Palace walls in time."

"How far is it?" Mike asked.

"It's still quite a ways, and it's all uphill."

Outside the City walls on the side opposite the reservoir, four pairs of shadowy figures crept silently toward the smooth granite. With quick agile moves, they scaled the side, climbed over the spiked top, and landed inside on padded feet. With knowing nods, they slipped away and fanned out into the City melting into the shadows. Now and then, they would glance at the faint orb above them as it peered through the grey fog.

One pair, dressed in sleek night-black, crept noiselessly toward a tall steel tower that bore several transmitter dishes. Stealthily they climbed up its great, cold legs, planting small black packs at specific intervals along the way. When the last pack was in place, they leapt to the nearby rooftops. Several muted booms sent puffs of grey smoke skywards. The tower wavered then toppled to the ground breaking communication lines and bursting into flames. The nearby rooftop was already empty; the black pair was gone.

Several blocks away, two Saracen guards stood motionless outside a barren and seemingly impregnable building. Next to it sprawled a factory belching thick smoke. Silently a twilight-grey couple slipped through the barrier that surrounded the complex, completely untouched by its sophisticated laser defenses. They scooted undetected toward the buildings, unzipped long pockets on the sides of their uniform legs and began assembling several high-powered bombs. They quickly strung wire between them and set the bombs at intervals along the buildings.

They sprinted toward an old well, opened a hidden passage and soon dashed through an underground tunnel. On their heels explosion after explosion rocked the complex sending Saracens and machinery flying through the air. Suddenly one enormous explosion sent a thick black cloud of smoke mushrooming into the sky.

Alarm klaxons rang throughout the city creating an oppressive din. Those few Saracens who remained there poured toward the blazes. Along the way they grabbed fire hoses and cranked open the fire sluices. They turned on the valves on the hoses and water gushed out spraying back the leaping flames.

Down the street, the third pair in soil-brown crouched beside a small brick building. Hastily they placed sticky white balls against the building's outer walls and several on the works inside. They dashed away just as the building disintegrated with a gentle poof. Near the raging fires, the Saracens suddenly pointed limp, empty hoses at the raging flames. Several more explosions rumbled sending the Saracens fleeing. The brown figures watched for a moment then closed a concealed panel within the wall of an old municipal building and made their way down a dark internal passageway.

Near the reservoir, a pair in aqua-blue pulled a set of mini-flippers out of the pockets along the length of the legs of their uniforms and slipped them onto their feet. They slid into the water without leaving a ripple and dove into its depths. A shaft of sunlight streamed through the clear water illuminating the ruins of once proud buildings. The pair surfaced near the dam, gulped a lungful of air, then dove once more and placed hydrobombs on the now rusted sluice gates before jetting away. As a plume of spray leapt high into the air, two aqua-blue heads bobbed to the surface on the other side of the lake.

In the underground-river duct, Core I crawled onto the upper level of the dry river bed.

"The secret entrance is just ahead," Jan panted.

Suddenly several muted thumps echoed through the tunnel.

"What was that?" Elira cried in alarm.

"The hydrobombs!" Adar exclaimed stopping in mid-stride and glancing overhead.

"And the water," Mike added.

"We're too late!" Will gasped as the thunderous roar of the wild torrent reached their ears.

The thousands of gallons of reservoir water rumbled as they made their mad tumble through the antiquated locks to their ancient underground course.

"Don't stop!" Jan urged, with a hasty glance at the rushing torrent. "We might still make it! We've got to try!"

Mike grabbed Elira's hand and tugged; Will and Adar scrambled after them. They dashed toward Jan who was holding the lantern aloft, frantically scanning the tunnel walls as she ran. A few seconds later she stopped and brushed away the dust and lichen from a stone, revealing the ancient Symbol of the Star.

"I found it! Hurry!"

Jan reached above her head searching for the concealed lever. Once she had grasped it, she gave it a tug but nothing happened. She glanced anxiously at the oncoming tide then doubled her efforts.

"What is wrong?" Adar yelled.

"It's stuck! Rusted!"

Desperately, Jan worked the lever. A slight crack appeared in the wall. "Come on!" she coaxed. "COME ON!"

She glanced on last time at the approaching torrent then hung her full weight from the lever. With a groan and a creak, the door swung open. Mike reached her side and grabbed the door's edge. Together, they pulled till the opening had widened enough for them to squeeze through.

"Get the others inside," he ordered. "I'll hold back the water as long as I can."

He turned toward the oncoming flood staring at it in total concentration. Sweat beaded on his brow, rolled off his face and dripped from his nose and chin as the rushing, pounding tide leapt closer. Gradually it slowed its mad pace finally frothing in place just under a foot from the tunnel door.

Jan reached out to Elira helping her up the final incline and into the dark passage. She glanced over at Mike's tension-strained face noticing the tremble in his arms and hands. She turned back toward Will and Adar.

"Hurry!" she urged.

They made a final dash up the slope and struggled into the passage. They tumbled inside and lay on the damp stone floor. Beside her, Mike stood shaking, his teeth gritted against the fatigue as the agitated tide inched toward him.

"Come on, Mike!" Jan yelled.

"Can't-move," he replied through clenched teeth.

Jan placed one foot in the doorway and reached out as far as she could toward him. "Give me your hand. I'll help you."

Slowly, with great effort, Mike raised his arm up toward her. Jan leaned out farther until their fingers met. She grabbed his fingers then worked her way down until her hand clamped around his wrist. Together, they struggled for a moment as the water lapped at their feet.

At last Jan sat back with her full weight and yanked. In that instant, Mike's concentration on the flood of water snapped. With a sudden jerk, he fell towards the wall and tumbled through the doorway. The couple rolled over each other into the passageway and lay winded on their backs on the floor. Outside, the suddenly released water hurtled past with a tremendous roar. It pushed against the ancient door, slamming it shut with a resounding clang and sealing it – forever.

Chapter 58

The Royal team all stood inside the passage, doubled over and gasping for breath. Mike crawled to a kneeling position, one hand clutching his chest. Jan pulled a small tablet from her pouch, got to her feet and staggered over to him.

"Take this," she said placing the tablet in his hand.

"What...is...it?" he wheezed.

"It's a protein/carbohydrate concentrate. It will bring your strength back. Go on, take it," she urged.

Mike popped it into his mouth and swallowed with difficulty then leaned back against the wall, his chin on his chest. In a few minutes he shakily rose to his feet.

Jan stood up beside him laying her hand on his arm. "Feel better?"

He nodded.

"I think we'd all better take a pro/carb gel," she suggested. "Then we have got to get moving."

Without hesitation, the others dug into their packs, pulled out a tablet and swallowed it down with a gulp of water. Mike swallowed a second one.

Jan acknowledged the nods, then climbed the ancient stone stairs to the tunnel above, the others following slowly. Once on the level passage, though, they took off with renewed energy.

"We don't have much farther to go now," Jan announced, as they ran up a slight incline.

Suddenly she came to a halt at a fork in the tunnel and looked uncertainly in both directions.

"Which way?" Will asked.

"I've got to think. I can see the map in my mind, but it's vague. I can't remember which path leads where."

She stared for a moment at the split. On a hunch, she walked a ways to the left, then returned a couple of minutes later and repeated her actions in the right tunnel.

"The left one contains the same damp air as this tunnel does, so it must be the longer route that leads inside the Palace," she muttered pensively. "But this other one...."

She turned to face it. "There's drier air in this tunnel...therefore, I suspect this leads to the gardens behind the Palace."

Mike set his face toward the left passage. The hair at the nape of his neck stood on end as an unseen hand strangled his stomach. He strained his eyes to see through the dark and caught a glimpse of a vague apparition floating down the dark tunnel towards them. The apparition brought up a sword that burst into flames. It aimed the sword straight at Mike challenging him to fight.

"I have to face it," he thought. "This is what I'm actually here for."

He thought about all that had transpired so far and the long journey to get to this point. Exhaustion washed over him as did a new resolve. "I'm the target, the prize," he thought. "I will fight and either win or die."

Without warning, he pulled Jan to him and kissed her hard. "Go on like you had planned," he said grasping the back of her head with his hand. "I've got to go to the Palace. Whatever I'm here for is waiting there for me. It has challenged me and I must accept. Just always remember that I love you." He released her and dashed down the left fork disappearing into the darkness.

"Wait!" Jan yelled. "Where will you be?"

She made to dart after him, but Will grabbed her arm pulling her back.

"No!" he commanded sharply. "Whatever he saw down there, he has to face himself. This is his fight, Jan. No one can help him now...not me, not even you."

"But he will be killed! I know it! I feel it! Someone has got to go with him!" she insisted.

"Not this time, Jan. We have our own jobs to do...he has his. We can't protect him now."

She gazed anxiously into the black empty darkness that had so quickly swallowed up Mike. Her stomach knotted in fear and grief.

"Be careful," she whispered. "Stay alive…for me."

Reluctantly she turned and led them down the passage to the right. The tunnel inclined sharply, and they followed it to its end. Jan felt around till she touched a rung.

"Up the ladder," she directed climbing the rickety metal. Without warning, she bumped her head. "Ow! Will, Adar, help me move this!"

The two men climbed up beside her hanging onto the ladder with one hand while pushing with the other. The roof refused to budge.

"Elira, you and Adar try your powers," Jan directed. "There's a hatch here and we've got to get out!"

Elira stared at the dark slab above them and Adar's hands glowed a faint blue, while Jan and Will pushed and heaved. Slowly it lifted and moved aside. They climbed out into bright sunlight.

"No wonder it was so heavy!" Will chuckled.

He stood, hands on his hips, staring in amazement at the tall marble statue of one of their ancient Quentasian forefathers. Its base rested on and was the cover over the tunnel.

Jan crouched uneasily in the shadow of the statue glancing warily about the Palace gardens. "Let's find some cover," she suggested.

Her companions nodded instantly on the alert. They slunk off into the nearby bushes.

In the shadow of the main gate, eight figures met and whispered quietly.

"Do you think they made it?" Grey I asked.

"I hope so," Brown II replied.

"We all do, but we cannot sit here wondering. We have to open this gate," Black I reminded them.

"Right. That should draw away the Palace Guards," Blue I replied. "Black I, Grey I, take out the Saracens in the gatehouse."

"Brown I, Grey II, prepare those explosives. As soon as those guards are out, we will open the gates," Blue I commanded.

The second team slunk stealthily into the shadows. As the remaining four watched, the Saracen gatemen suddenly toppled from their posts. Two dark heads popped up signaling that all was clear. The explosives team waved back and cautiously eased toward the gate. Within minutes, a silent puff of smoke spit from the locks. The remaining team members rushed forward to help push open the gates.

With sudden shouts of anger and cries of war, Quentasian soldiers drove massive land machines into the heart of the City. Farmers from the valley and townsfolk from nearby villages followed attacking everything Saracen.

Underground, Mike heard the wail of sirens and the heavy tramp of booted feet.

"Well, our forces are in place just as planned," he breathed.

With growing apprehension, he pressed on. Suddenly he tumbled to the ground, assailed by an unseen force. Waves of nausea passed over him making him tremble and sending a cold chill down his spine. He gazed into the empty darkness of the tunnel, a roaring inferno suddenly leaping into view. He saw the palace itself on fire and himself trapped in its midst. The vision passed quickly and he wearily sank against the cold, damp walls.

"I'm going to die," he whispered helplessly. "There's nothing anyone can do for me. This is my last fight. Oh, Jan. This isn't what I had expected it to be," he mourned.

He thought about what lay ahead for him, and then he thought of the others especially Jan. A look of determination grew on his face.

"If I have to die," he declared, "then I'm going to go down fighting...not lying here in some dank tunnel."

Gripping his queasy stomach with one hand, he struggled to his feet and staggered on down the passage. After several hundred yards, he bumped into a solid wall.

"Dead end!" Then he thought, "But dead ends to Jan are always doors."

Quickly he placed his hands on the wall and pushed; a panel creaked open. He peered out into a long, empty hall.

Warily he crept from the passage and down the hall ducking from one massive granite pillar to another. Countless corridors branched off to either side. Mike surveyed each before dashing across the open space and dodging behind another column. Finally the row of columns ended. He took a deep breath and sprinted toward the massive stone arch at the end of the corridor.

"The Throne Room!" Mike whispered in awe as he peered inside.

Cautiously he stepped inside the great vault. He gazed up at the arched and buttressed ceiling that opened above him trying to take in the immenseness of the room. Concealed doors in the archway suddenly snapped shut behind him echoing with a loud, reverberating clang. He spun around and tried to pry them open.

"There is no way out," a voice cried booming ominously about the empty chamber.

Mike turned glancing nervously at every nook and cranny. Stealthily he crept across the mosaic-tiled floor eyeing the columned balcony overhead with suspicion.

Without warning, a blinding light flashed into the room sending a searing pain tearing through his head. Instantly, he flung his arms up to shield his eyes from the burning glare.

"Welcome!" the voice boomed again.

The light went out and Mike gradually focused on the man now sitting on the white marble throne. As he stared at the man, his mouth dropped open. A familiar, though, hated form finally took shape.

"You're dead!" Mike declared staring in astonishment.

"No, not really," Garin laughed. "Merely tricks and illusions to lead you here to me. I shall never die, but you," he snarled leaning toward Mike. "You shall!"

Instantly a power bolt shot from the man's eyes hurtling across the room. Instinctively Mike rolled out of its path, sprung to his feet, and returned the fire. He scored a direct hit, but his jaw fell open in shock. Nothing had happened.

"You cannot kill me," Garin said laughing hideously. "I am all that is left of me...my mind...and you cannot touch that." He filled the great hall with his evil laughter. "No one can destroy me now, but I can and shall destroy you," he declared letting loose a barrage of power bolts.

Mike dodged them zigzagging for cover as he dashed to a nearby column. In an instant it changed into a roaring beast that viciously lunged at him with bared fangs. Mike stared in terror at the gaping maw before diving out of the way. He fired another power bolt at Garin as he rolled to the side. The beast dissolved before his eyes.

"Must have a weak point somewhere," he muttered frantically scrambling for cover behind another column. "If his mind is all that's left of him, he has got to have a weak spot."

Another bombardment of bolts spit past him, and Mike tumbled from hiding just as the column crumbled into a heap of dust. He dashed to yet another hiding spot and bent over panting hard. Yet, Garin gave him no time to rest preferring to follow him about the cavernous Throne Room flushing Mike out of every hiding place with a new barrage of power bolts. Already fatigued from the hard push to get to the City itself, Mike began to slow.

" I'd better find that weak point and fast," he fretted. "This game of his is too dangerous, and I'm already tired."

Chapter 59

Outside the Palace in the once lush garden, Will quickly took over for Jan. “We have three major networks to destroy,” he said. “The power source that fuels all the Saracens’ works globally is located in the bedrock beneath the Palace. While that thing is still in operation, the best any of us can do is to harass the enemy forces. We must destroy the Power Plant.”

The others nodded silently.

"We also have to black-out their Interplanetary Communications Systems to stop any further contact with Sarace. Then there's the Satellite Network that links their forces on Quentas to the mainframe coordinating their operations. Once these systems are out, the Saracens should grind to a halt," Will continued.

"This is where we split up," Jan announced.

"Right."

"I have the Power Plant," she said.

"You have that explosives pack?" Adar asked.

"Yes."

"Remember...just one minar on that timer," he reminded her.

She nodded then lowered a branch enough to peek through. After a cautious glance about the grounds, she leapt from cover and sped toward the Palace.

"I have the Satellite Control Station," Adar said.

"Right," Will confirmed. "It's housed in the old station building back along the ridge."

Adar nodded and slunk off dashing from bush to bench to broken statue. As he disappeared, Will turned to Elira.

"You have the communications dish and the signal station. Cut through the antenna's wires first then attack the control house; it's located on top of the knoll behind the Courses. That'll leave me with the computer banks. Be on the alert for guards and, when you're finished, return here as we'd planned."

She nodded then headed across the grounds hugging the lines of shrubs and bushes that stopped abruptly at the foot of a slight rise. At the top stood a gleaming white dish-antenna.

"To think they chopped down that beautiful grove of trees," she muttered angrily.

Elira glanced furtively about her before dashing up the hill. Once she had reached the dish, she located the cables at its base. After a few moments of concentration, they snapped with a poof of smoke. Satisfied, she slunk to the small control hut. Holding her laser at the ready, she edged around to the front, eased the door open and leapt inside. She stopped in her tracks.

"No one here! Not a soul!" She spun around. "This is strange."

Keeping to the plan, Elira smashed the control panels and blew the transformer units. She stumbled from the hut gagging from the acrid smoke that poured out behind her. The panel keys inside sparked just before bursting into flames. She managed to stagger back down the hill then collapsed, coughing, in the shadow of her fore-father's statue.

While Elira had been fulfilling her assignment, Adar had been working his way over the familiar Palace grounds. He raced between what instances of cover he could find on the windswept ridge behind the massive complex. He crept up to the control station and burst inside. The Saracen technician at the panel rose half-way from his seat, but Adar fired first. The technician dropped over the back of his chair without uttering a word.

Raising his weapon, Adar leapt to the control board and smashed it with the butt of his laser rifle. He spun around the room blasting the sensitive equipment. Finished, he dove out the door rolling to safety as the building exploded. After several moments, he slowly picked himself up off the ground and made his way back to the garden. He hurried to the statue and knelt beside Elira.

Meanwhile, Will sped cautiously through the familiar halls of the Palace.

"The computers have got to be on the far side," he thought. "I've got to hurry. Just hope there aren't many guards posted."

He put on an extra burst of speed. "Got to find that computer complex and shut down the mainframe." He glanced at his wrist chronometer. "Jan should be getting near that Power Plant. Don't have much time."

In the opposite wing, Jan was tentatively creeping along the long quiet corridors. She nervously glanced about for Saracen guards.

"According to the map, the old Power Station was located in the Deeps. Logically the new one should be, too," she thought.

She ran down the many passages she had memorized and soon found the steep, spiraling staircase leading into the depths below the Palace. Silently she inched down a stair at a time. After a while, she caught the sound of the steady hum of immense generators.

"Good," she breathed. "I'm on the right track."

Back in the Throne Room, Mike was racing across the tiled floor when a searing pain shot through his right shoulder. He gasped, grabbing the wound with his free hand, and ducked behind the dais. He sucked air in through his teeth as he clutched his shoulder squinting his eyes shut against the pain. Garin stood in the center of the chamber, laughing fiendishly.

"You-are-finished," he howled. "You are exhausted. I feel it! Make this easy on yourself. Come out now and I will end your misery quickly."

Mike shook his head wiping the sweat from his brow with the back of his hand. "I'm not finished, yet, Garin," he yelled back. "But when I do go down, I'll be fighting."

"Suit yourself," his uncle cackled.

Mike popped his head out to take aim but ducked back as a bolt came whizzing at him. It glanced off the dais, hitting something near the ceiling; Garin jerked back in pain.

"His weak spot!" Mike breathed hopefully. Frantically he searched overhead.

By now Will had found the Computer Center. Only one soldier guarded the entrance. Will cautiously poked his head around the corner and, using ventriloquism, threw his voice down to the opposite end of the hallway.

"Hey, buddy! Over here!"

Fearing an attack, the guard crept warily toward the sound and slunk around the corner. Will sprang from hiding, snuck into the computer lab, and glanced about him in surprise.

"This is the old model I played with over thirty years ago!" he exclaimed in surprise. "This is incredible! Wonder if they altered the password?"

He sat down at a console and ran his fingers over the keyboard. "Well, let's see what we've got here."

He typed in several commands and the password "IHUE." The screen instantly cleared and returned with a prompt for his access code.

"I don't believe it!" he chuckled, hurriedly typing in the old codes and commands.

The screen again cleared, and the menu scrolled down.

"Well, this certainly makes things easier," Will breathed then knit his brow. "Actually too easy. I wonder what's up?"

The light at the bottom of the stairs intensified as Jan crept silently toward it. She peered around the corner glimpsing a lone guard standing motionlessly in front of the entrance to the Power Plant. Quickly she withdrew and plucked a pen-shaped object from her pocket. She unscrewed one end and dropped in a thin dart she had taken from a case in her other pocket.

Quietly, Jan edged back around the corner and, taking careful aim, blew into the tube. The needle whizzed through the air striking the guard in the neck. He reached up and tore it out. He stalked toward the staircase with his weapon at the ready muttering angrily the whole way.

Jan ducked back, pressing herself flat against the wall, and counted, "Four...five...six...seven...eight...."

The guard collapsed heavily into a heap on the floor nearly at her feet. She breathed a sigh of relief then, peering back around the corner, scanned the area beyond the fallen Saracen.

"No more guards?" she puzzled. "That doesn't seem right. There's usually at least two or three near important installations."

Finally, she gathered her things and, darting past the slumbering Saracen, entered the power plant. She lost no time in emptying her pockets of their contents and began to prime the explosives packs.

"Something doesn't feel right," she muttered anxiously as she worked. "This whole set-up is almost too easy."

Several more power bolts had ricocheted off the throne before Mike spotted the mirrored ball that hung from the center of the ceiling. Sparks flew off it shattering small sections each time. With each new crack, Garin reeled and grew more desperate.

Mike stuck his hand out around the dais, the augmenter ready. Garin fired instantly and knocked the weapon out of Mike's grasp. It spun through the air landing well out of his reach. He glanced at it, popped out of hiding and fired a volley of power bolts at Garin. Crouching low, Mike leapt from the safety of the dais and painfully rolled to the nearest column. He fired another bolt then dashed toward the augmenter. He snatched it up and tumbled behind another column.

Mike sprinted from pillar to pillar until he had a clear view of the mirrored ball. He shot a hasty barrage at Garin while raising the white cylinder to eye level. He aimed at the ball, centering his focus on its attachment to the ceiling. Seconds later, it exploded into thousands of flying glass shards. He looked back at the center of the room; Garin's image was gone. Mike heaved a sigh of relief.

"You cannot get rid of me that easily," boomed a disdainful voice from the archway.

Mike spun around and stared, both in shock and disbelief.

"Have you enjoyed my illusions?" Garin taunted exhibiting a wicked grin.

Mike desperately glanced about the Chamber for an avenue of escape.

In the computer room, Will had typed in the final command, flipped a switch and was watching the lights blink out on bank after bank. The cooling fans slowed to a stop as the old behemoth powered down. He gave the computer a final pat before hurrying to the door. He peeked out, snuck down the hall then retraced his steps through the Palace. In three minutes, he had slunk back to the statue and was crouching next to Elira and Adar.

As she knelt beside the generator bank, Jan hastily connected the last pack of explosives. She grabbed the wire and ran it, along with the string of fuses, to a detonator box outside the door. She carefully connected each wire to the box and set the timer.

"General Adar, forgive me," she whispered. "Sixty seconds is plenty of time for me to get to safety, but Mike will never make it."

Jan set the timer to 3:00:00 minari, set the box on the floor, and flew up the stairs. She sprinted through the Palace dashing outside to join the others.

"That was way too easy," she puffed plopping down next to them.

"I know," Adar replied. "None of us met with more than one guard."

"That worries me," Will said.

Jan frowned, her mind racing. "None of this mission has gone according to plan."

"Yes, I know," Adar groaned. "We have been stymied at every turn."

Suddenly a thought crossed her mind and fear seized her, twisting her stomach into knots. "That thing...that horrible thing inside Will's head! It was warning them of our plans and reporting our progress! We weren't stopped here because we-were-expected; we've been used as decoys. They don't care about us!"

Jan sprang to her feet in alarm, intently searching the grounds. "Where's Mike? He's the one they want. We've been tricked!"

"He's still inside," Will replied frowning.

"No!! He should be out by now! The Power Plant will explode in two minari, fifteen secondari!"

Adar scowled, but Jan ignored him.

"I've got to go back for him. He may need help."

She leapt over the base of the statue intent on the Palace doors, but Will raced after her tackling her in the tall grass.

"No, Jan! You can't go back in there!"

"I've got to," she insisted squirming.

"There's still time. As long as Mike believes we're all safe out here, all he'll have to worry about is his own fight. If one of us goes back in, he'll lose it. He'll worry about us instead of himself, just like his father did. He'll get killed, just like his father did when he tried to protect Elira. Please...wait just a minute longer," he pleaded anxiously watching the Palace.

Inside the doomed structure, Mike stared at his uncle in fury and disbelief. Without warning, he rushed forward to tackle the older man. Garin grabbed the younger man, flipping him into the corridor. Locked together, the two men rolled over and over.

"You cannot kill me."

"You're not just an illusion anymore."

"No. I am something far more," Garin replied slyly. "I learned from my Saracen queen."

He pinned Mike to the floor with an incredible burst of strength. "My Saracen bride taught me how to build androids...beings with tremendous strength and the ability to live forever. I have combined that strength with my own powers. I am invincible as well as immortal."

Mike gasped and threw the man off him. "So that's where you slunk off to after my father married Elira. Prince turned traitor."

"It does not matter. You cannot overcome me, Nevu."

"You may have made yourself into an android, Uncla, but even you have to recharge."

"You cannot even wear me down," Garin retorted leaping at Mike who ducked at the last second. Garin flew over the top of him and landed on the floor instantly leaping to his feet. "I will kill you long before I weaken. My energy source is in this very building. Till it ceases, I can go on fighting forever."

"The Power Plant!" Mike cried. "It's due to blow any second."

He turned to flee, but Garin grabbed him grappling hand-to-hand.

"I-am-going-to-kill-you," Garin assured him a blue aura surrounding him and traveling down his arms toward Mike.

"Like-you-killed-my-father?"

The aura reached Garin's fingertips. "Just like I killed your father."

The searing hot current shot through Mike in waves. He screamed writhing in pain as it arced over his body.

"There is no escaping me now!" Garin gloated as Mike tried to wrench himself free.

Mike closed his eyes and held his breath. In an instant, the energy was sucked form Garin even faster than it was being supplied. The older man sank to his knees, feebly trying to pull away. Mike opened his eyes staring directly at Garin who glanced aside with a shriek of terror; Mike's eyes were glowing balls of white-hot fire.

Suddenly a blaze of power shot like a bolt of lightning from Mike to Garin. The acrid stench of burning plastic rose to the ceiling as the older man fell limply to the floor. A deep gash across his chest revealed his android hardware.

Mike left him where he lay, reeling past him to the nearest column. He fell against it and slid to the floor.

Without warning a deafening explosion ripped through the Palace rocking the walls and foundation. Garin's body convulsed then lay rigid. Mike coughed and gagged as the smoke reached his nostrils.

"Got to get out," he gasped.

Fire sprang up around him as smoke began to clog the corridors. Mike pulled himself to his feet and groped for the next column, clinging to it for support. Through the thick haze, he made out the vague outlines of a wall of windows around a door. He collapsed to the floor crawling a ways before struggling to his feet again and staggering on.

In the City, Quentasian soldiers had fought their way from the gates to the Palace joining Core I in the garden. They stood with the little group watching the Palace burst into an inferno of flames.

As the roof collapsed, Jan screamed. Amidst the flames, she saw Mike staggering blindly through the rubble. Overhead, a beam split in two and crashed to the ground pinning him beneath its weight.

Jan wrenched herself free of Will's steel grip and dashed toward the Palace.

"Jan! Wait till I get a hose!" Will yelled frantically. "We'll get him then!"

Ignoring him, she tore a strip from her shirt as she ran stopping at the fountain only long enough to soak it with water. As she sprinted toward the inferno, she tied the soggy cloth around her nose and mouth.

Flames blasted out from the building scorching the grass and tiles around it. Jan threw up her arms to shield herself from the flames and pushed her way inside. The oppressive heat sucked away her strength. She tottered, her knees buckling, but resolutely stumbled on with her eyes glued to the spot where she had seen Mike fall. The flames licked at the marble columns whose eerie shapes danced all about her. But up ahead, a pale blue specter made her blood run cold.

Chapter 60

There, flickering above Mike's fallen body was an ashen, ghost-like resemblance of his own self. Tears streamed down Jan's cheeks as she pushed on toward him. She reached out her hand to the wavering phantom trying to call it back, to prevent it from leaving. However, it grew transparent as she watched and a strangled sob escaped her throat as the grim reality of Mike's imminent death sank in.

Suddenly she caught her foot on a chunk of charred debris and stumbled to the slate floor. She pushed her shoulders up gazing at the wavering phantom.

"No, Mike," she pleaded. "You can't die. Not yet."

She picked herself up off the floor and surged forward.

"Mike, I love you. I need you," she sobbed. "What would I do on Quentas without you?"

Jan glanced at the Ring whose light was quickly fading.

"Fight, Mike!" she cried looking back at him. "Please fight...for me. You can't die yet!"

Tears flooded her cheeks as the apparition wavered then slowly dissolved into the surrounding waves of heat. Desperately Jan rushed forward stumbling over his body in her hurry.

A fiery beam lay across his legs pinning him to the floor. Somehow, though she would never remember how, Jan found herself tugging his body across the floor, the beam lying off to one side. Hot embers fell around them as the flames leapt higher.

Her rag having dried by now fell from her mouth. She was coughing and gagging on the smoke and fumes entering her lungs. Turning her head in an attempt to regain her sense of direction, she peered through the thick haze and caught a glimpse of several dark silhouettes in the doorway who urgently beckoned to her. One pushed forward aiming a jet of water at the flames that cut off her path of escape.

With renewed hope, Jan struggled to pull Mike toward her rescuer. Suddenly, a sharp pain shot through her head as a falling tile glanced off her brow. She stood for a moment in a confused daze before crumpling to the floor.

"Over there!" Will shouted pulling the hose after him as he surged toward the fallen couple. "Hurry! We've got to get them out of here!"

Two soldiers in protective gear pushed past him, while a third grabbed onto the hose and helped Will cover the fire. Hastily, the first two plucked the injured couple from the floor and rushed them outside. They laid them on the grass, well back from the gutted building, while a team of medics swarmed around them. Elira elbowed them aside and knelt beside the couple. She attended them both with feverish haste.

"Jan's pupils are dilated and unequal," she muttered. "Her respiration is...ninety-five!"

"That's high but not too bad for her," Will said coming up behind Elira. "Jan's norm is closer to between sixty-five and seventy."

"Still." Elira turned to Mike checking his repeatedly. “Ihue's is...barely there," she whispered.

Will knelt beside her watching as she worked.

"Ihue has a shoulder wound from a power blast, various bruises especially on his legs, and is suffering from smoke inhalation, as is Jan. They both have second degree burns; Jan's on her hands only; Ihue`s over twenty-five percent of his body."

Hastily, she brushed tears from her eyes as she turned to the medics. "Set up a hydration tent with elevated headrests and oxygen for each. Administer an antibiotic and saline hydropack, stat. Coat the burns with silver sulfadiazine and put cold packs on their bruises."

As Elira rose, medics swarmed about the injured couple, frantically working to stabilize them. Will reached for Elira's arm stopping her.

"What's wrong with them? Are they going to make it? Is that all you can do?"

She nodded. "Ihue's lifeforce is nearly exhausted," she choked. "He is also suffering from burn shock and smoke inhalation. With that combination, all I can do is relieve his pain and discomfort."

"And Jan?"

"She has a concussion and more severe respiratory burns. The burns on her hands are actually minor."

"Then what's wrong?" Will pressed.

"They are both exhausted. Jan pushed herself beyond her limits to get us here," Elira explained, "but with Ihue, the mystery deepens. His lifeforce itself is depleted...almost as if he had purposely expelled it, or else like it had been sucked from him. Whomever he fought inside the Palace nearly drained him of his life long before that beam struck him down."

"But will they live?"

Elira shook her head. "I do not know, Dehan. There is so little that I or anyone else can do now. Only their own will to live can possibly revive them."

With a shuddering breath, she rose again and sank down beside Mike. Gently she laid her hands on his head and tearfully called his name in an attempt to reach deep within him. But her voice echoed back to her from dark emptiness. She let her hands fall to her sides.

"He is truly beyond me," she whispered sadly.

Slowly Elira turned to Jan who lay nearby laboring for each breath of air. As with Mike, Elira touched Jan's head reaching deep inside, but she could sense only the faintest flicker of life. Hopefully she called out to Jan but received no reply.

Exhausted, Elira watched the medics carefully carry the couple to the hydrotent that had been hastily set up. They lay them on air mats, their heads and shoulders elevated to facilitate easier breathing. Quickly the medics left closing the flaps behind them in order to keep the warm, moist air in.

Momentarily Jan's eyes fluttered open and she looked about. But the world spun in dizzying circles blurring her surroundings. She squinted, intent on finding something.

"No, someone," she mumbled, her voice rasping. "Got...to find...someone."

A cool hand gently caressed her face.

"Mike," she choked out. "Where's Mike?"

"Lie still and rest," a voice replied from far away. "Do not worry about Ihue. We are caring for him."

A terrifying blackness pressed down on her engulfing her with its hold. Jan tossed her head, fighting its hold, but the darkness won and closed over her; she knew no more.

She awoke later and scanned the tent. Still she could see no one through the blurry haze. Desperately she struggled to raise her head and shoulders.

"Mi-ike...." she tried to call out but fell back coughing. "Got to...find him," she whispered.

Another fit of coughing seized her. She lay exhausted for a long moment then rolled off her mattress and onto her knees. Her limbs trembled with the effort, and the world around her took on a darker grey hue.

A third attack of coughing jarred her forcing her to stop. It left her shaking with sweat running down her back. Jan set her jaw resolutely and pressed on feeling the ground in front of her, one hand at a time, as she searched.

All of a sudden, she felt a lump on the ground. She ran her hand along the cold, stiff form till she touched a face. The lips were firmly set and no warm air exhaled past them or through the dry nostrils above.

"Mike," she cried hoarsely. "Mike!" she called even louder.

Great heaving coughs racked her body. She collapsed on top of him convulsing spasmodically. A searing pain tore through her chest and head and all went black. Almost instantly, she found herself spinning through a long, dark tunnel; a cold whirlwind gusting about her.

"Jan!" a familiar voice called. "Jan, where are you?"

She turned from side-to-side trying to locate the source of the call.

"Jan!"

"Mike?" She searched frantically as she spun. "Mike?"

Up ahead a pinpoint of light pierced the darkness. She picked up speed as she neared it. An abrupt change in wind direction sent her tumbling head over heels. She screamed in terror as she approached the bottom and hit with a sickening jolt that knocked the wind out of her.

Finally she managed to sit up and look around. To her surprise, she was hanging in mid-air in the midst of nothingness. Everywhere she looked a blue-grey haze swirled and shifted. Suddenly the mists parted as a dark silhouette appeared. Jan squinted as she stared at the approaching figure.

"Jan!" a voice called.

"Mike?" She scrambled to her feet and made her way toward the silhouette. The familiar figure broke through the thick clouds, and Mike stood before her.

"So, you've come here, too," he said wearily.

"Yes, but...where is here?" she asked drawing closer to him.

He put his arm around her shoulders and stared off into the dense nothingness about them. "I don't really know where we are," he said at last.

"Do you think we're...dead?" Jan wondered fearfully.

Mike took her hand and studied the Ring. Though it was dark and lifeless, when he tugged at the jewel it remained activated clinging tenaciously to her finger. He stared at it, puzzled.

"I don't know, honey. The Ring won't come off, yet it doesn't have a spark in it. Maybe we're neither dead nor alive." He gave her shoulders a gentle squeeze. "At least we're together. We'll be all right," he added reassuringly.

"But how do we get out of here? There's so much nothing. I feel like we're in limbo," Jan complained. "I want to go back."

"We'll find a way," Mike assured her. "I'm sure we won't stay here forever." Yet, as he spoke, he glanced about them wearing an anxious frown.

Suddenly a bright flash lit up the haze.

"What was that?" Jan cried.

"I don't know, but let's go find out. Maybe it's a way out," Mike said hopefully leading Jan toward the heart of the glow.

Another flash followed, and they hurried forward. The mists swirled and parted before them then closed in rapidly behind. Suddenly they found themselves in a circular area, their feet firmly touching a polished transparent blue surface. Veins of violet pulsed beneath the floor. Out of the adjacent mists came a tall man with pale-blue skin. His skin was a deep metallic-blue. He was clad in a long metallic-blue robe. He folded his arms across his chest as he studied them.

"Who are you?" Mike demanded.

The man continued to observe them for a moment longer.

"Where are we?" Jan asked.

Finally the man beckoned them to come closer. Mike kept his arm protectively around Jan's shoulders as they hesitantly approached the man.

"I am Tovorald as I would appear if I could assume human form," the man said at last.

Mike and Jan visibly relaxed.

"You have reached the halls of your fathers."

Mike's eyes widened in fear and disbelief. "No. That would mean that we're dead!" he cried. "But the Ring hasn't come off. We can't be dead."

"The Ring has not yet left your beloved's hand because the deeds of your life must be judged by your ancestors. If you have completed your life's tasks, you will join them in these halls. If your work was left unfinished, you will be returned to complete that work."

Jan looked up at Mike and he squeezed her shoulders.

Lightning flashed again and again just outside the circle. Soon four men of varying ages walked into the circle. They stood in a horseshoe off to Mike's left. He turned to study them and the youngest almost appeared to be his twin.

"Father?" he whispered.

The man's eyes shone, though he said nothing in reply.

"These are your direct ancestors," Tovorald said by way of introduction. "You recognize your father, Ihan. The next is your grannavan – Ihuk, then your great-grannavan – Iherig and lastly – the first to inherit my powers, Terak. They alone can judge your works and determine if your life is complete."

Chapter 61

Mike faced the men who had preceded him in his family's line. Though they wore neutral facial expressions, their eyes were loving and compassionate.

"Ihue," Tovorald said. "You must stand before your ancestors alone. Your beloved is only here because of your bond. Should your ancestors determine that your life's work is over, you will remain with them and she will return to the living."

Jan looked up at Mike, fear and worry etched on her face. He patted her shoulder reassuringly but a frown creased his own brow as he returned his attention to Tovorald.

"Should your ancestors determine that your life on Quentas is not yet complete, you will return to the living and continue until your job is done. Please step towards your ancestors alone."

Mike looked into Jan's eyes. "I love you…always," he whispered and kissed her.

Then releasing her he stepped onto a low platform just in front of his ancestors. Jan's eyes brimmed with tears at the thought of possibly losing him, and she held her breath as Terak spoke.

"Several hundred years ago Quentas was a planet in the midst of a global civil war. Two main lineages of people had colonized this planet but had failed to live in harmony. Thus the Haslen-dag - the War of the Two Clans – erupted. The Pesrar Clan wished to dominate Quentas; the Endara Clan sought to shepherd the people. In the end, the Endara were losing and found themselves being aided by a native people – the Mollucs. The Mollucs led us to underground chambers in which we could hide and from which we could sally forth and fight.

"In one such chamber we discovered a glowing rock which spoke to us. The first adventurers who approached it became sick and died, so we devised shields with which to protect ourselves and gradually approached it. Over time the radiation from the rock changed our genetic structure and literally 'rewired' us from the inside out. We developed similar powers to those the rock possessed and the rock taught us how to use them. With these powers we were able to fight the Pesrar and win. That was in my vedrar's day. He left the charge to me to unite the peoples of Quentas under a High King. I completed that task and passed the charge on to my offspring."

"With my generation that charge was broken," Ihan said remorsefully. "Invaders overran the planet and enslaved the people. The clans are no more except as the Royal House and the Commoners, but the old tribal delineations reappeared as separate ruling factions, and Quentas was divided."

"Let us see what you have accomplished, son," said his grandfather, Ihuk.

Behind them, as if on a big screen, Mike's life began to unfold. Beginning with the moment of his birth, they all witnessed each minute of his life. Mike grimaced as he relived the painful memories of childhood during which he was taunted and teased for being different. Time-and-again Will would pack him into a vehicle and they would take off for an unknown destination. Saracens had once again located their whereabouts.

His tumultuous adolescent years surfaced as he struggled with his identity, with his emerging powers and with first love. Mike crumpled to his knees when he re-experienced the "accident" that had sent Pat into a coma and ultimately to her death.

Time moved forward through his early meetings with Jan all the way up to the present war which once again united the peoples of Quentas in a common goal. Finally Mike struggled to his feet and stood again before his ancestors. They turned inward and conferred amongst themselves, before again facing him.

"You have done well in completing your mission," Iherig commended.

"Yes, the people are once again united under the Throne of Quentas," Ihan said.

"You may join us," Ihuk invited.

"No!" Jan cried. "No! Please no!" She sank to her knees sobbing.

Mike, too, was distraught. "Wait! I don't feel as if I have completed my mission on Quentas."

"It is not up to you," Iherig replied.

"We have decided," Ihuk said firmly.

"Wait!" Terak said. "I withheld my judgment. Now I would like to hear what our son has to say."

The other three men looked to their elder then bowed their heads in deference to his judgment.

"Go on, Ihue," Terak encouraged. "In what way have you not fulfilled your destiny."

Mike licked his dry lips as his brain churned in an effort to sort out his feelings and to devise a response to his ancestors

"Yes," he said at last, "I did manage to unite the tribes of Quentas under my leadership toward a common goal – ridding the planet of the Saracens. However, that is not the tone which any of you have used in speaking of the unification of Quentas."

"Terak," he said turning to the eldest. "You said the Endara Clan wished to shepherd the people, not just gather them together into a collective unit. I have done nothing to shepherd the people, and once this war is over, they will go their disparate ways and reform their principalities. Without a shepherd to guide them, they will not remain united for their common cause will be gone. Eventually they will disintegrate into factions so dissimilar that another global civil war will erupt."

Mike's ancestors murmured and nodded at his words.

"Furthermore," he continued. "I have not been able to prepare for the future. This beautiful woman," he said gesturing toward Jan, "is merely my betrothed. I have yet to take her as my lifemate. We have obeyed the Law of the Ring and have refrained from becoming intimate. If I join you now, there will be no heir to continue my line and to maintain the unity of Quentas. All that she and I have fought so hard for will be lost."

His ancestors' expressions were grave as they considered his words.

"We must speak amongst ourselves," Iherig said.

"Normally our first judgment is final," Ihuk added. "However, since Terak did not cast his vote, we must reconsider our decision."

The four men stepped back and drew together in a huddle. The mists swirled about them hiding them from view.

Mike looked back at Jan and their eyes met.

"I love you more than life itself," he telepathed. "No matter what their decision; never forget that."

She nodded. "I love you, too," she replied mentally.

They waited what seemed an eternity before the mists parted and the four ancestors returned.

"To change our decision is unprecedented," Iherig began.

"Yet, many conflicting factors are involved," Ihuk added.

"In searching your life, we came to the realization that you have several directives for your life. As a young man you mission was to – free your people. In order to accomplish that, you had to - unite your people. Now that they are united, you have yet to consolidate your power, and you must provide an heir to – continue the House of the Star."

"So you see, Ihue," Terak said stepping toward him. "You have already fulfilled portions of your mission on Quentas. However, within each of the last two directives are imbedded several others."

"So what are you saying?" Mike asked, his mouth dry.

"We are saying, Ihue," Ihan said stepping forward, "that your life is not yet over. You have a lot of work to complete and a beautiful bride awaits you," he added nodding toward Jan.

"There will come a day when we will meet again," Ihuk said.

"And you will join us then," Iherig added.

"But for now, return to the land of the living and complete your life's quest," Terak said decisively.

Tears of joy welled in Jan's eyes as she watched each of Mike's ancestors embrace him. Ihan held him close for a longer moment than the others.

"Take care of your mother, Ihue. She has lived a hard life. And take care of your beloved."

As Ihan rejoined the other ancestors, they faded back into the mists. Mike stepped from the platform and approached Jan. He wrapped her in his arms holding her close for dear life.

"The ancestors have given their final judgment," Tovorald said. "Their decree is law. You must return."

Mike looked up at him and nodded.

"You will not be spared the pain of your wounds, and your recovery will be long. However, you have a long life and many directives to fulfill. Go in peace."

The mists behind them parted, and Mike glanced at Tovorald who nodded. With his arm around her waist, Mike led Jan through the mists toward the void from which they had entered. Suddenly a great whirlwind caught them up and spun them around. It tore them apart flinging them in opposite directions.

"Remember your oath," Tovorald called.

"Mike, I love you," Jan cried.

Then the world became dark, cold and silent. Mike blinked his eyes open and glanced around. He was lying on his back on a mat inside the hydrotent. The afternoon sun lit up the yellow walls. He pressed his hand to his wounded shoulder wincing when he tried to sit up. His arms shook uncontrollably and he sank wearily back onto the mat. Turning his head to one side, he saw Jan lying beside him on an air mattress. He took a deep breath, reached out and touched her hand. Her eyes popped open, she turned toward him, and smiled. He squeezed her hand then wearily closed his eyes.

Suddenly they heard footsteps outside. They both opened their eyes as someone stepped inside.

"You're awake! Both of you!" Will exclaimed. "What a relief! We thought for certain we'd lost you. In fact, we did for a while," he added, sitting on the ground between them.

"What do you mean 'lost us'?" Mike asked again trying to sit up.

Will gently eased him back to the ground. "Let's just say you two had a close shave and leave it at that, ok?"

"I guess." Mike reached a hand up to his face, feeling the short stubble. "Speaking of 'shave'," he said, "how long have we been lying here?"

"Oh-h-h, about a week," Will replied.

"That long?" Mike said whistling.

"Seems longer," Jan whispered.

"Yeah. A lot happened in a week," Mike mused. "By the way, how's the battle going? Are we winning?" he asked earnestly.

"Yes, we're winning."

Mike and Jan both sighed with relief.

"It seems that your 'presumed death' raised the ire of the people," Will explained. "At this very moment, our forces are drawing a net around the Saracens to hem them in. It won't be much longer before their supplies and ammunition run out. Then we'll have them all."

"Will?"

"No more questions now, Michael. Go back to sleep. You both need lots of rest," Will said getting to his feet and slipping quietly from the tent.

"We really did die, didn't we?" Jan whispered.

"Then...you dreamed it, too?" Mike asked incredulously.

"That was no dream, Mike. It couldn't have been. It was too real."

"Yeah, I know." He closed his eyes sleepily.

"Mike?" she called softly.

"Mm-hm?"

"I love you."

He squeezed her hand. "I love you, too," he murmured drifting back off to sleep.

Outside, Will sought out Elira. "Jan and Ihue just came to!" he whispered excitedly in her ear. "They've come out of it."

"What? Are you certain?" she asked spinning around to face him.

"Corpses don't talk," he replied grinning.

She rushed out of the pavilion with Will close behind and headed straight for the tent. Once inside she stopped; her eyes rested a while on the couple who lay side-by-side, their hands clasped.

Elira crept forward and knelt beside Mike touching first his hands then his face. She could feel the healthy warmth radiating from them. She glanced at Jan's still form, her breath still coming in quiet wheezes. Elira sighed with relief, rose to her feet, and backed slowly from the tent. An army medic met her outside.

"Does the Prince live?" he asked, as she fastened down the tent flap.

Elira turned to him, a smile beaming from her face. "They are alive and resting comfortably. I believe they are finally out of danger," she replied confidently.

The medic beamed and hurried to General Adar. "The Prince is alive!" he joyfully announced without waiting to be recognized.

Adar looked up from his field table relief spreading across his worn face. "Bring me the run leaders," he ordered.

Minutes later Marla, Tanza and Gorlan hurried into his tent. He looked at them straight-faced for a moment then broke out into a broad smile. "I want you to spread the news...everywhere," he said. "The Prince and his Beloved are alive!"

The three Elitists whooped for joy hugging each other and dancing about Adar's pavilion.

"A-hem! There are several hundred thousand Quentasians waiting to hear this news, too," he shouted above their ruckus.

They stopped and tried to bring themselves under control before saluting and slipping outside. Seconds later, another war hoop split the short-lived silence.

Chapter 62

The runners hurried from the City and, with the help of others, spread the news that the Prince lived. In every village, farm and town the war-worn people rallied with new strength and drove the Saracens from hiding. The beleaguered enemy, having exhausted their supplies and ammunition, fled their attackers and took refuge in the surrounding foothills and mountains.

They camped in the shadows of the great peaks, lying down at night while wary guards stood watch. But from out of the bellies of secret tunnels short, furry creatures crept into the dead of night. They silently stole up to their tormentors killing both the watchful and the sleeping before slipping off into the night.

Those Saracens who did escape, fled in terror - an emotion new to them. They frantically left the "haunted" hills for the fertile valleys and canyons beyond. These alien fugitives wandered throughout the lush regions until death pounced on them from the sky. Those who had dared to enter the peaceful, lonely valleys were never seen again; their helmets and uniforms turned up hanging from the Hallen aeries in testimony of their grim fate.

Finally the Quentasian troops managed to round up the few

Saracens who did remain. Weaponless, half-starved or power-drained, they were marched to the same dungeons that once held the Quentasians in torture. Yet, even these strongholds could not hold the defeated enemy for long. Runners soon entered the City and headed straight for Adar's pavilion. Upon receiving them, he sat staring at their solemn faces.

"Well?"

A young man stepped forward. "Sirha, the Saracens are all dead."

"What?" Adar sputtered in surprise. "I ordered no executions."

"No, sirha. Suicide."

"Suicide?" Adar breathed, letting the news sink in. "All of them?"

"Yes, sirha. In the night. They are...all dead," the young man replied.

"It hardly seems possible...but then, they were a proud race." Adar looked up at the runners. "Go get some rest. There will be new messages to carry in the morning."

He escorted them from his pavilion and set his course straight for Elira's. After breaking the news to her and Will, they sat together inside.

"What should be done now? This was...so unexpected," he said, flustered.

"I...."Elira began.

"Tell Ihue," Will interrupted.

"But, he is still so weak," she protested.

"He should still be told," Will insisted.

Reluctantly she and Adar agreed. This time when they arrived at the tent housing the young couple, Mike was awake. After the circumstances had been explained to him, he lay for a long while in silence. Finally he turned his head toward Adar.

"Send the people home. They've done their job."

"But what do we do with those whose homes have been destroyed?" Adar asked.

"Set up field tents to house them temporarily," Mike instructed.

"What about those who have been separated from their families?" Adar pressed.

Mike closed his eyes for a moment, his head beginning to throb. "We will have to deal with that when the computer links are reconnected. For now get as many names and locations from people as you can. We'll run them through Mozern's computer."

"As you wish, Your Highness," Adar replied leaving to carry out Mike's orders.

Surprised by the Saracens' sudden demise, yet relieved that their long ordeal was over, the victorious people disbanded and straggled home. In every part of Quentas renewal began as the toppled walls of homes and buildings once again stretched skywards. Roads long left in disrepair were rebuilt to open up the familiar trade routes.

But in the City on the Hill, that once-proud Crown of Quentas, it was not so. The master architects and guildsmen sadly shook their heads as they surveyed the ruins of the Palace and City.

"She was so beautiful," one mourned. "Now look at her."

"Just what is the extent of the damage," Will asked, concerned.

"See for yourself," a grayed father instructed. "At least seventy-five percent of the City has been underwater for nearly thirty years. Now that the waters have receded, it is a bog. The rest of the City is charred and crumbling."

"How long will it take to rebuild?" Will asked.

"Years, even if all the craftsmen in Quentas were to shoulder the work," the first man replied.

"We will have to return to Mozern as soon as Ihue and Jan are strong enough to be moved," Elira quietly informed Will before turning to the craftsmen. "How long will it take to rebuild just the Crown?"

"Five montari at least," an engineer replied. "The wing over the power plant is beyond reconstruction. The remainder will depend on the condition of the foundation."

"Then begin with the Crown," Elira instructed. "We can rebuild the City around it."

"As you wish, Lady Elira," the men chorused.

Will and Elira left them to their monumental task and returned to camp. They hovered over the injured couple nearly day and night anxiously waiting for them to regain their strength. But Mike and Jan progressed ever so slowly with one long, weary day blending into the next.

Finally the day came when they were both able to sit up, though well-propped with many cushions. Elira left them that evening after administering their medication and sought out Will. She found him standing amidst the ruins of the Palace looking out over the Palisade Plain.

"Dehan," she called.

He turned slowly watching as she picked her way through the rubble. She stopped when she had reached his side.

"They are ready, Dehan," she announced.

"Are you sure? They still seem pretty weak."

"They are strong enough to journey to Mozern without endangering their lives. Besides, I have a more thorough range of medical equipment at my disposal there. My options are severely limited here," Elira explained.

Will nodded slowly. "I suppose you are right." He turned to gaze out across the broad plain again.

Elira studied him for a moment, then edged close and laid her hand on his arm. "You are sad, Dehan?"

He held his silence for a few minutes before finally taking a deep breath. "So much has changed...so much is gone."

"Ihan?"

He nodded. "He was more than just a friend to me, Elira," Will said quietly. "He was more like a brother, and Ihuk like my father. Ihue is a lot like them, and yet...." His voice trailed off.

"No one can take Ihan's place, Dehan...at least, not for us. You gave up everything for him...including the woman you loved. But there was a purpose, there had to have been a purpose," she restated emphatically. "He would not have demanded such a sacrifice if he had not foreseen the need."

Will nodded. "I know, Elira. In my mind I understand that. It's just that Quentas is such a lonely, lonely place with them gone."

She squeezed his arm tightly in a moment of empathy. Then, together, they picked their way back through the ruins and were secure in their pavilions before nightfall.

Early the next morning, Elira slipped into the hydrotent and roused the couple. She bundled them in warm, thermal blankets.

"Where are we going?" Jan wondered.

"To Mozern," Elira replied. "It will be a long trip for you two, so save your strength."

Army medics entered with hover stretchers, lifted the couple onto them, and maneuvered the carriers to the waiting transport. As soon as they were aboard and strapped in, the pilot maneuvered the transport to the height of the tallest trees. The engines rotated blasting the vehicle along above the ground. It sped down the Palisade Plain, through the Star's End Gap, and along the valley beyond. Toward evening, it approached the Mozern Range. As it closed in on the mountainside an opening appeared. The transport zipped inside and lowered onto its pedestal base. Elira lost no time in hurrying the couple to the Med Unit. She quickly set up their new medical regime, re-ordered the healers that would care for them, and placed Soniora in charge. The tedious days of recovery had begun.

Elira, satisfied that Mike and Jan were being well cared for in Mozern, returned to the City. In a flurry of activity, she organized the rebuilding of the Palace. Having remained long enough to see the workers begin, she embarked on a whirlwind tour of the planet. Along the way she astutely assessed the damage caused by the long Saracen occupation and extended encouragement to the people.

Three months later, Elira completed her long circuit. Upon returning to Mozern, she quietly sought out Will finally locating him on his balcony. They sat at his little table watching as Mike and Jan meandered slowly through the subterranean gardens.

"They seem completely recovered," she commented.

"Just about," Will agreed. "A montar ago they seemed to hit the peak of their problems. Since then their recovery has been pretty rapid. They still tire easily, and Jan still has fits of coughing now and then, but otherwise they're doing good."

"How is the work on the computer network coming?"

"Nearly finished," Will replied. "We're almost ready to start entering the names and locations of those dislocated people. Hopefully we can make short work of reuniting families. How goes the work on the Crown?"

"I flew by on my way back here," she replied. "The living quarters are nearly complete but the office wing and the technical wing are still in progress."

"What about the Throne Room?"

"That had to be razed to the ground," Elira explained. "But

Simona, the Chief Architect, discovered the original blueprints in a vault where they had been sealed centuries ago. They start construction on the Throne Room this week."

"Wonderful!" Will exclaimed then grew solemn. "You know, Quentas really needs its King right now," he said watching Mike hold up a low tree branch for Jan to pass under.

"No, not yet," Elira countered. "He needs something else first."

"What's that?" Will asked with a quizzical tilt of his head.

"He needs his beloved to become his bride." Mischief sparkled in Elira's eyes. "Ihue will definitely want and need a Queen by his side. I am certain that Ihan would have approved of Jan. However, if she is to become his Queen, she must first become a Princess."

"Even Ihan couldn't have conferred that title on her," Will pointed out.

"No, but she would acquire it through their joining, just as I did." Elira turned and faced Will squarely. "What we need right now is a Royal Wedding."

Chapter 63

"So," Will said thinking out loud, "you want Mike and Jan to marry now and…."

"And have the coronation later, when the Throne Room has been completed."

"Where will we hold the joining? The Dome of the Heavens was sealed off."

Elira smiled slyly. "I have had a crew secretly working on those passages. They are open and the walls and ceiling are being shorn up now."

"We'll need a Sanctimons," Will reminded her.

"I sent out a search party two montari ago. Word returned that one has been found on Pelaris. He received the news of Quentas' liberation exuberantly and is on his way back at this very moment. He should arrive any suntarini now."

Will stared at her for a moment then broke out laughing. "You've certainly thought of everything, Elira."

"Ready to tell them?" she asked.

"The sooner the better."

Elira called her Molluc secretary out onto the balcony and directed him toward the couple. Minutes later they climbed the steps and took the extra seats that had been brought out for them.

"We have a bit of an announcement to make," Will said.

"Oh?" Mike asked eyeing them both suspiciously.

"First let me make certain my assumptions are true," Elira said. "You do want Jan to rule at your side as your Queen, right?"

"Well of course," he replied slipping his arm around Jan's shoulders.

"That is what I had figured. For that to happen the two of you need to be married first. Would it be a hardship for you to have the joining ceremony before the coronation?"

Mike and Jan looked at each other then exclaimed, "No!"

"Good. The plans are already in motion. The ceremony should be in a few short weeks," Elira assured them.

Before dawn on a morning three weeks later, Elira woke Jan. She went through the Ritual of Purification with her and helped her slip into a glistening white gown with star chip accents.

"This is the Gown of Poornim..."Purity" around which you will wear the Belt of Fasur..."Fidelity"," she said buckling a broad, golden sash about Jan's waist. "Now, wrap yourself in the Cloak of Mosur..."the Mystery"," she instructed.

Elira threw the black cloak about Jan's shoulders drawing it closed in order to conceal her. That being the final preparation, the two women hurried through the dim grey corridors to an awaiting hover-skid. Their pilot whisked them from Mozern to the Stardent Range in a mere matter of minutes. Once it had settled onto the slope, the women stepped out.

On the far horizons, the twin moons were just setting. Jan drew the dark hood up over her head and approached the entrance to the Elra-med. As soon as the first rays of the rising sun had pierced the sky, she and Elira entered. Their trek to the Dome of the Heavens had begun.

The two women entered the great vault from one side while Mike and Will, allowed to attend by special request, entered from the other. Below them, in the center of the terraced vault, Adar, Marla and the Sanctimons waited beside a crystal podium.

Mike and Jan each took two steps into the great chamber then awaited the next suntari to be observed in absolute silence. While they waited, they sought a glimpse of each other from across the hall but could see nothing due to the black cloaks and hoods.

Gradually the hall grew lighter and all eyes anticipated the total manifestation of its source. Finally the bright shaft of light came streaming through the opening in the vault's ceiling. On cue, Will and Elira both gave their charges a nudge, and the couple nervously proceeded around the upper circumference.

They met near the middle of the upper wall and could at least see each other's face. Mike flashed Jan an excited smile which she enthusiastically returned. Then, together, they raised their hands to their heads very slowly removing their hoods and drawing back their cloaks.

"You're beautiful!" Mike silently mouthed, taking in the stunning white, blue chip studded gown enhanced by the golden sash.

Jan merely stared in awe at his sharply tailored uniform of deep royal-blue equally enhanced by a matching gold belt. She looked into his eyes finding them more intense than she had ever seen before.

Below them, the shaft of light was slowly edging its way across the floor. Mike glanced at Jan giving a slight nod. Simultaneously they pivoted toward the center of the room and slowly began the Descent of the Terraces.

Jan's knees shook and once she nearly fell. Mike instinctively reached toward her stopping at the last instant as he recalled the taboos of the ritual. Eventually they both made it to the landing free of mishaps.

As the shaft of light moved closer, they nervously approached the podium. They waited expectantly before Adar, Marla and the Sanctimons knowing that the appointed hour had almost come.

Suddenly the beam of light fully engulfed the crystal podium. For a few brief moments, a rainbow of colors swirled about the cavern, and an enharmonic bass throb could be heard from the region near the Star. All those present looked on in awe. And then it was over; the shaft of light moved on. The Sanctimons cleared his throat drawing the bystanders back to the ceremony at hand.

"My dear ones," he began. "Years ago the liturgy to this sacred ceremony was lost. But this is a new Quentas and a new age, so the vows have been written anew. However, there is one thing that will never change. A man will always need a companion to guide, support, and love him; a woman will always need someone to love, cherish, and lend her support."

He turned to his right. "Lady Janielle, do you vow that from this day forth you shall remain this man's faithful lifemate, companion, and guide...and that you will love him as none other can?"

"I do," she replied quietly.

"And Prince Ihue," he said turning to his left, "do you vow that from this day forward you will remain this woman's faithful life-mate, companion and protector...and that you shall love her as none other can?"

"I do," Mike replied huskily.

"Now, Lady Janielle...you must take one further oath," the Sanctimons said returning his focus to her. "Do you swear, by the Stone you wear and by the Star of the People, to abide by all the laws of our land and to pledge undying loyalty, both to the Throne of Quentas and to the one who shall sit upon it? And, furthermore, would you sacrifice your life for his and for the people you will now serve?"

"I do so swear."

The old official smiled kindly. "Then I now declare you lifemates for eternity, the Crown Prince and Princess of Quentas."

The witnesses applauded enthusiastically as Mike planted a kiss on Jan's lips. Together, they took a hover speeder back to Mozern and entered his old suite, which they would now share. Will and Elira uncorked a bottle of champagne that he had brought from Earth and had hoarded for this occasion. They offered a heartfelt toast to the couple, hugged and kissed them then left.

A parade of Molluc attendants entered and bowed to them. "We need to take your gown back to its storage container," the spokesman announced.

Jan nodded and disappeared into the bedroom where her regular clothes had been moved. Teldank, who had come with the gown attendants, helped her out of the long, stiff material and into more comfortable attire. When Jan opened the door, the gown attendants entered and began wrapping the star-studded gown readying it for its return to storage.

"That gown is similar to this ring," Jan remarked to Mike as they watched the attendants traipse through the lounge with the gown carried between them.

"How so?"

"It conforms to the wearer. It never needs to be altered," she replied. "It fits perfectly and comfortably."

He raised his eyebrows appreciatively.

The procession wound its way to the door and into the outer lounge. Teldank curtsied to the couple and left as well. Mike stepped up to the door as it closed, cupped his hand over the lock and briefly focused his powers on it. Jan cocked her head to one side when he turned back around.

"Just changing the lock," he replied to her questioning look. "Now only you and I can open it. No more intrusions."

With that, he crossed the room to her side, engulfed her in a hug and held her close. "We're finally alone, finally married and it's finally our time…the right time."

Jan ducked her head a little, her forehead rubbing against his chest. "I can hardly believe it. I've so looked forward to this day, yet now…after all we've been through…it feels so foreign."

Mike put his finger under her chin lifting her head till her eyes met his ardent gaze. "Are you having second thoughts?"

"No…just butterflies," she replied blushing.

He bent forward and kissed her. "I have to confess…so am I."

"I guess we've just been through so much," Jan speculated.

Mike nodded and rested his chin on the top of her head. "Yes, if you think about all of it, it gets pretty overwhelming."

"I try hard not to think about it all," Jan confessed.

"There are some things I think about," Mike admitted.

"Like what?" she asked gazing up at him as he dropped his arms down to encircle her waist.

"Like what a brilliant, warm, beautiful woman I've married," he replied quietly.

Jan's eyes widened. "I am?"

Mike nodded. "I remember how hard you struggled to understand the physics I explained to you back on Earth so you could write up that article for the lab. You, an English major, were writing a scientific physics paper. I know you struggled, but you really grasped the concepts well.

"And I remember Seera…one of your incarnations."

Jan nodded and glanced down.

"Once I got over my anger, I thought about the way you managed those Saracens and kept an eye on everything that was happening to keep us all safe. And I thought about what a brilliant woman I'd been privileged to love."

Jan caught her breath and looked up.

Mike kissed her then continued. "And I remembered how you helped the villagers on that run. I think if you could have made that refuse heap explode so you could get to that man, you would have done the same thing."

Jan nodded. "There were a lot of times I wished I had your powers, or you with me. That day I so wished we were there together as a team."

"You have such a big heart, Jan," Mike said. "You care so much and so deeply…not just about me but about everyone. When I'm with you, I feel so loved and so welcome. It's one of your qualities I treasure."

Jan squeezed him tighter.

"And to think, all of this is wrapped up in such a beautiful package."

"Beautiful!" she exclaimed.

Mike tilted her head upwards and gazed into her eyes. "Beautiful. I think your beauty struck me the very first time I saw you. It was as if feelings I'd buried all jumped to the forefront at once."

"I was in a T-shirt and jeans carrying a bookbag," Jan reminded him. "How in the world was I beautiful?"

"You had these blue eyes that sparkled, a smile that just lit the room and hair that framed your face," Mike replied. "I had tried so hard for years not to get close to another woman, and I knew I'd fallen as soon as I saw you."

"You did!"

He nodded and kissed her. "But today when I saw you in that gown…wow! That took my breath away. I just wanted to stand there and stare at you and never take my eyes off you."

Jan blushed heavily.

"And all I could think was…she's mine…wow," Mike continued.

Jan reached up and kissed him passionately. “You know,” she whispered. “If you keep talking like this…I’m not going to be able to help myself.”

“That’s what I’m hoping,” he said with a chuckle. “I’ve loved your brilliance, your heart and your beauty. I long to love every part of you.”

Jan caught her breath then kissed him again. He scooped her up in his arms.

“Time’s right this time,” he murmured carrying her into the bedroom and closing the door.

Chapter 64

In the days that followed the Royal wedding, Elira kept in constant contact with the builders in the City. One month after the wedding, she cornered Will in his office.

"How goes the work?"

"The Crown is nearly complete," she informed him.

"Wonderful!"

"It is time for the coronation."

Will nodded.

"What do the polls say?" Elira asked.

"The majority of the people are in favor of having Jan as their queen. She seems to have touched many lives in deeply personal ways when she was an Elitist," he replied.

"And if any object, we can always move into an Open Forum," Elira said thoughtfully.

"We would have to say very little, I'm sure," Will replied. "She has supporters enough amongst the people."

"Then it is time," she declared. "We shall set a date and call the people."

The next morning runners set out across Quentas to announce

the upcoming coronation. In response, masses of farmers, villagers, and noblemen took to the roads, all headed toward the City. The majority brought such gifts as they could spare. A few came armed after a fashion. Adar quickly increased the number of Armed Task in the City as well as withdrawing the entire Elitist force to the palace.

Meanwhile, Will and Elira explained the concept of the Open Forum to the couple.

“There is a small pocket of resistance to Jan becoming queen,” Will began. “Probably people who were too far away for you to reach while an Elitist.”

She nodded.

“Should the people call for an Open Forum, you can only act as moderator,” Elira told Mike. “And Jan, you must remain silent and let witnesses testify for you.”

“Almost sounds as if I’ll be on trial.”

“Your record will be on trial,” Elira corrected.

“And with a record like yours, you have nothing to worry about,” Will assured her. “Enough people will volunteer to speak on your behalf that we may not even have to speak.”

“So this is just a formality?” Mike said.

“No, it is very real,” Elira replied.

“We just aren’t expecting problems,” Will added.

The eve of their coronation arrived. With their belongings packed, Mike, Jan, Will and Elira boarded a transport for the City.

Jan stared back at the Mozern Range as they pulled away from the base. "That place is the only home I've known here," she thought sadly, homesickness sweeping over her.

In resignation she turned around, put her head on Mike's shoulder and dozed till the transport arrived in the City several hours later. They were met by a squad of Honor Guards who escorted them from the plateau to the living wing of the Palace and their new suites. As they marched through the newly reconstructed halls, Jan gazed in awe at the cold grey stone walls, marble columns, polished mosaic floors and colorful tapestries adorning the walls. Hesitantly she entered their new suite. She stopped in the doorway just staring.

"Now that really makes you feel like Royalty, doesn't it, honey?" Mike asked admiring the crystal chandelier, polished mahogany paneling and gilt furniture with the eye of a connoisseur.

"It looks like a museum," she remarked, still awestruck. "I feel like there should be "Do not touch" and "Don't sit here" signs all over."

Mike chuckled. "That's silly. All of this is ours. They're meant to be used. And just think; you'll never have to worry about the cleaning. A maid will do all the work."

"That's definitely a plus, but it will all take some getting used to."

"I'll bet you suddenly get 'used to' it all the first time there are dishes to do," Mike quipped.

"Well, now that you mention that, it's sounding much more comfortable all ready." Jan replied laughing.

They strolled through the rooms of their Royal Apartment then out onto the patio and into the gardens beyond.

The morning of their coronation dawned fair and bright. Mike arose as soon as the sky started to brighten and began to dress. An hour later he stood before a full-length, gilt-framed mirror adjusting his attire. Jan strolled in from taking her shower, and he turned so she could see.

"Well, what do you think?"

"Very regal," she replied admiring him. "Is that what you'll wear everyday?"

"No, thankfully. This is dress formal. My everyday attire will be far less pretentious."

"Oh," she said coming up to him and running her hands over his shoulders and down his sides. "Too bad. This uniform really looks good on you." She pressed up against him and smiled up at him mischievously.

"I'm…uh…glad it has that effect on you," he replied extricating himself from his wife's loving embrace. "I'll have to remember that for some other time. Right now, though, we need to hurry."

With a mock pout, Jan pulled away and hurried into their room to get dressed.

Half-an-hour later she came back out in a ball-length gown of royal blue. "Can you get this last fastener for me?" she asked turning her back to Mike and holding her hair out of the way.

As he deftly closed the fastener, a knock at the door startled them.

"Enter," Mike called.

Honor Guards entered and flanked the doorway.

"I've got to go, honey," Mike said kissing her before rising. As he stepped out the door, he turned to wink and flashed her a broad smile.

Jan waved as he disappeared then began working on her hair. Suddenly Elira stepped over the threshold.

"Need any help?" she offered.

"Mm. Could you hand me a couple of hair pins?" Jan asked.

Together the women finished Jan's hair. Once again Elira wrapped her in the Cloak of Mosur. Dimly they heard the trumpets sound from the Palace spires.

"It is time," Elira said, holding the door for her.

As the gates of the City were opened to the throngs that waited outside, the two women made their way through the newly constructed corridors. The excited multitude rushed through the streets and swelled up the broad Palace steps.

When all had gathered, a lone trumpeter sounded his notes. The Sanctimons and witnesses entered the courtyard above the people from the wings. Next, a single, clear note was sounded. The people gasped in awe as the great doors of the Palace opened and Mike strode forth. Behind him followed a lone figure shrouded in black. He faced the crowd momentarily then knelt before the venerable official. The concealed figure stood off to one side all alone.

The Sanctimons turned to the agitated crowd and cried, "Hear ye! Hear ye! We are gathered here today to crown our returned and victorious Prince the "King of all Quentas"."

Cheers of elation rang out from the crowd, but died as the Sanctimons raised his hand for silence.

"At his side, the Princess Janielle. It is the wish of our Prince that she, as his lifemate, should serve beside him as Queen."

At this a murmur rippled through the crowd. Several loud cries of "Hear ye!" resounded, but another more dissenting mood could also be detected.

"Is there anyone opposed to Princess Janielle ruling beside our King as his Queen?" the Sanctimons asked.

Several people shuffled their feet. Finally a tall, burly man worked his way through the crowd and stood out in front.

"I would prefer to have no King at all if she must be Queen," he announced.

Mike stepped forward. "Are there others who feel the same way?"

Several cries of "Yes" echoed through the throng.

"Shall I move into an Open Forum?" he asked.

At first Mike only heard one or two yes's but soon heard many more.

"By the will of the people, I now declare an Open Forum," Mike said.

A trumpet blast resounded across the courtyard. A ripple of uniforms dispersed throughout the crowd as Armed Task personnel positioned themselves to quench any trouble flared tempers might ignite. A small group of young people in dark hooded cloaks pushed down through the center and spread out at the foot of the Palace steps.

"The people shall present first," Mike announced. "I shall hear your arguments one at a time, so choose those spokespeople who will present. When you have finished, I shall listen to all those wishing to present on behalf of Princess Janielle. In the end, the fair majority shall decide. Is everyone agreed?"

A loud chorus of "Agreed!" returned to him in response. A hush fell over the throng as two people worked their way forward. Meanwhile, the burly man himself stepped away from the crowd insuring his opportunity to speak.

The Honor Guards took Jan by the elbows and led her to a station nearer the edge of the courtyard. She remained on her feet despite her trembling knees. However, her eyes never once left the ground for fear of looking upon the many angry, bitter faces.

"Bring forward your witnesses," Mike commanded.

Three or four persons climbed to the first level of the Palace steps.

"Present," Mike said.

The burly man put his foot on the lowest step of the second rise. "Your Highness," he began, "you have spent too much time away from the people. Indeed, I doubt you have ever known us," he shouted angrily. "What do really know of Saracens and their tyranny? Moreover, what do you know of the treachery and betrayal of our sister planet, B'nar, who aided the Saracen regime? At one time we felt we could trust our neighbors living on the nearest planets in this galaxy. We have since learned how wrong we were. If our sister planet could betray us, even under a sworn treaty...how do we dare trust you?" he asked gesturing toward Jan. He slammed the prongs of his hay fork into the solid granite steps and stepped back.

A woman in her thirties stepped forward in his place. She faced Mike, tearful and alone. Looking up timidly she took a deep breath. "Your Highness," she began weakly. "We understand how well you mean, but we doubt you are aware of much of our suffering. How could you know our sorrows when you have never experienced them. For instance, my children were taken by the B'narians for slaves. My lifemate was slain by the Saracens. You have experienced no such griefs, therefore you are freely trusting. But we have learned in pain that we can trust no one but our own. You have been joined to an alien, just like your uncla before you. Now leave us in peace to be ruled by you alone," she pleaded, weeping bitterly as she melted back into the crowd.

One after another stepped forward, each pouring out a similar tale of sorrow and grief. Some wept, others shook clenched fists at Jan, but all their stories had the same theme: the Saracens had killed and destroyed, and the B'narians had broken the treaty. Finally, satisfied that he thoroughly understood their concerns, Mike raised his hand for silence.

"I have heard your arguments against having the Princess for your Queen. Your main concern is the treason of our allies. You feel that, since sworn allies have betrayed us, we should never trust outsiders again. Considering the duration and intensity of your suffering, this would seem to be a reasonable conclusion," he acknowledged. "However, the Princess is also allowed a defense before the issue can be judged. Are there any who would come forward and speak in her favor?" he asked.

Two figures moved forward in the courtyard as one entity. A dark man in a handsome, gold-trimmed scarlet suit separated himself a little in order to address the crowd.

"My friends," he began. "You all know and trust me. Did not I aid Prince Ihan in his escape from his brother's dungeon in time to save all of us from Prince Garin's treachery?"

A murmur ran through the crowd.

"Was I not given charge of the infant Prince? Did I not carry him to safety? Have I not guarded him with my life returning him to you unharmed this past year? Have I not fulfilled my oath?" Will demanded, gazing steadily at the crowd and holding each glance in turn.

"Yes, but you are one of us," someone shouted.

"So-was-Garin," Will responded immediately, "and look what evil he did. Treachery is in the heart. He who allows it to reign in his heart is he who betrays his own. This is how treason found its way into the Royal Family, itself."

Some heads nodded in agreement.

"But, think, my friends. Would I have permitted our Prince to bring with him a treacherous, traitorous woman? Do you really believe I would not, first and foremost, have observed and tested her?"

The people in the crowd shuffled their feet uneasily.

"You all know better than that," Will continued. "Of course I would not have. In fact, I have known the Princess longer than anyone else with the exception of our Prince. I found her to be above reproach.

"However, while we were on Earth, we were forced to be extremely cautious. The Saracens utilized many methods in their attempts to trap and assassinate the Prince. We were forced to subject the Princess to subliminals to assure ourselves the Saracens were not using her as a decoy. We found that they had been, but because she would not cooperate with the implanted devices, she was suffering.

"This could easily have been the final proof of her character, but there were instances during which Prince Ihue's life was in danger when she demonstrated the most convincing proof of her nature. With no knowledge of his true identity and having sworn no oaths, the Princess remained loyal to him. In fact, she was instrumental in saving his life on more than one occasion.

"You spoke of the B'narians treachery and so will I," Will said, his voice rising in fervor. "Twice the Princess was captured by them on Earth. Even when facing the pain of personal harm, she retained her staunch loyalty to our Prince...out of love. Today she can say nothing in her own defense, but it is not needed. Her actions speak volumes, instead."

Will bowed to Mike then stepped back into line.

"My people," Elira said walking up behind Jan. "I have been your loyal servant all my life. I understand your fears because I have shared your agonies. I watched the Saracens kill my lifemate, and I underwent B'narian torture when I refused to divulge the whereabouts of my infant son."

Those closest to her could see the faint scars remaining in her temples.

"When I first met this young woman, she was nothing but a shell due to B'narian torture."

Elira drew back Jan's hood turning her head so the crowd could glimpse the deep, ugly scars still imbedded in the young woman's temples.

"You tell horror stories while believing my son and his lifemate to have been sheltered from such terror. I must contradict your thinking. My son has spent his life running from and fighting Saracen assassins. This woman felt B'narian torture because she refused to betray our Prince. Meanwhile, he was forced to watch the proceedings till he could give her aid," Elira said, her voice rising to a fevered pitch.

"You speak of aliens who make vows they are forced to break when their own peoples' lives are in danger. I speak of an alien who never took a vow but had the courage to remain loyal to our Prince out of love."

Elira paused, emotionally shaken.

"I submit to you," she challenged, "that the problem does not lie with deciding whether or not to trust this alien," Elira said moving her hands to Jan's shoulders. "Rather, we must decide whether to trust our Prince's decisions and be governed by them. If we cannot accept his choice of a lifemate and Queen, we will continually doubt his choices throughout his reign. I beseech you to search your hearts this day and weed out the roots of your mistrust. Replace it with belief and confidence in the man destined to rule you."

Elira gave Jan's shoulders a squeeze then dropped her hands to her sides and returned to her place in the courtyard. The people stared at Jan. Not a word was spoken, not a single sound was heard.

A tall, lanky farmer strode forward and stood on the bottom step gazing up at Mike and Jan. Though his hair was graying and he leaned on a staff for support, his body was still strong and his eyes still clear.

"Your Highness," he said to Mike. "I would like to speak to the people."

Mike nodded and gestured for him to go ahead.

The farmer turned around and faced the throng. "It seems to me," he said after a moment of silence, "that there isn't a lot ta protest about. Come now, Gerdan," he said addressing the burly man who had spoken up first, "who rescued your only son from the Saracens that day they swept the villages for slaves?"

Gerdan stared at Jan wide-eyed, as he caressed the head of the curly-haired boy at his side.

"Of course it was her!" the farmer confirmed. "And Helarna, who helped rescue your lifemate when the Saracens nearly killed him in the mines?"

A woman glanced up at Jan then bowed her head.

"I myself have the Princess to thank for a silo full of grain and a barnful of hay," the farmer said. "She always made certain we did not go hungry."

He looked out over the throng again. "Seems ta me we're a-beatin' a dead ewan here. This woman has a record of helpin' us and takin' care of us a'ready. What need do we have of rejectin' her? She's no Saracen…B'narian either and if her planet has more of 'em just like her, I say bring 'em on. But for now, let your anger and hatred rest. We destroyed the Saracens. They're gone. Why are we still a-fightin'? What's left ta fight?"

He nodded at Mike then slipped back through the crowd.

The Sanctimons stared hard at the people. "The Princess has been accepted by our former Queen, by King Ihan's most devoted friend and by many among you. Our Prince has chosen her for his lifemate and desires her to be his Queen. But there is one last and final witness…the Star Ring."

With that, he stepped to Jan's side, took her right hand, and held it aloft. "The Star Ring has accepted her. Do you still reject this alien? Can you still doubt our Prince's judgment?"

As if to punctuate his words with testimony of its own, the Ring burst forth with magnificent brilliance, bathing the peoples' faces in a blue-white glow.

Chapter 65

The people in the crowd could only stare, their hands raised over their eyebrows to shield their eyes from the Ring's brilliance. Gradually the glow dimmed and went out leaving the throng in speechless awe.

At last, one woman who had spoken earlier pressed forward and dropped to her knees on the stairs. "Your Highness...Your Honor...how could we have possibly known these things? We felt that all aliens must be alike. We assumed that in having been away from the center of our troubles, the Prince had been sheltered from our woes. W-we had no idea...." she said, her voice trailing off. She rose to her feet and retreated into the crowd.

Other voices of chieftains and noblemen began to call out.

"We were wrong, Your Honor."

"We judged in haste."

"Let her reign beside our Prince. He has chosen well."

From the back of the crowd, a chant was taken up which quickly spread throughout. "Long live King Ihue! Long live his Queen!"

Jan glanced up and discovered that her Elitist friends were forming pyramids on each other's shoulders. Once in place, they waved and shouted. She smiled through a haze of tears as the roar of the crowd became deafening.

Mike held up his hand for silence. As the crowd responded, he stared at the burly man who had remained in the forefront.

"The majority has ruled. How do you stand?" he demanded.

"Your Highness, please forgive my harsh words," the man began faltering. "We have been tormented and dominated by Saracens for so long. It is hard to let go of the bitterness created by such deep wounds so recently inflicted. Yet, even I would find it difficult to risk my life for someone of another race without an oath to bind me. Your judgment really was good, and I am put to shame. I will be governed by the majority decision."

A joyous shout rose from the multitude as the man melted into its ranks. Elira stepped over to Jan removing the dark cloak and hood. The crowd gasped in awe as the bright sun bathed Jan's gown dancing off the many fine chips of Star stone. Mike stared at Jan, too, as awed and amazed as their audience. For a moment he forgot the pageantry that was to follow.

Seeing the hesitation, Elira placed her arm around Jan's shoulders and led her to Mike's side. With a proud smile, she joined their hands. Mike swallowed hard as, together, they knelt before the Sanctimons.

"Let the trumpets sound!" the Sanctimons commanded.

In unison, the trumpets sounded a joyous fanfare from the Palace spires. "O people!" he called. "We are gathered here today to celebrate the coronation of the next King and Queen of all Quentas. A new age is arising from the ruins of the old."

He lowered his gaze to Mike and Jan. "We, your people, this day do crown you "King Ihue" and "Queen Janielle." We ask that you rule us with fair judgments, guide our course throughout our lives, never make our burdens more than we can bear, and protect us from all who would seek to harm and destroy us. May your reign be long and fruitful!"

He touched their heads and shoulders with the tip of the gem-studded ceremonial sword then turned to the young pages at his side. Each bore a cushion on which a crown nestled. He carefully lifted the largest one from its scarlet pillow and reverently lowered it onto Mike's head. After repeating the process with Jan, he graced their shoulders with deep-violet robes. As the Royal Couple rose from their knees, the crowd hailed them exuberantly.

Mike's gaze swept the cheering crowd. He again raised his hand for silence. "Oh, people of Quentas. Join together for this day in celebration. About our once proud city are pavilions where you may rest. And, near the shores of the reservoir, are tables waiting for you to partake of their bounty while my Queen and I remove ourselves from your presence to rest and prepare ourselves for our responsibilities to come. Rejoice, for Quentas has arisen from the ashes and is once again free and whole!"

Amidst renewed cheers and trumpet fanfare, Mike took Jan's hand and led her down the Palace steps. As the couple approached the throng, the people parted to let them pass but quickly pressed in behind them. The couple made slow progress through the crowd as people reached out just to touch them. Finally, Honor Guards elbowed their way to the new King and Queen opening the path to ease their way.

At last the throng ended. An Honor Guardsman held a gilt rope high enough for the couple to pass under. They walked across the empty ground toward the transport. Waiting beside it stood three cloaked Elitists who bowed as Mike and Jan approached.

"Marla! Tanza! Gorlan!" she exclaimed smiling.

"We wanted to see you off and being the King's cousin sure helps," Marla said hugging each one in turn.

"We are so happy for you," Tanza said hugging Jan.

Gorlan looked at each of them. "You know, Ihue, there was a time back on Earth when I didn't think you were going to let another woman into your life. I'm very glad you chose Jan."

The Royal Couple smiled.

"Speaking of letting a woman into your life…." Marla began.

"Oh, ahem," Gorlan said nervously fidgeting. "When you return, may I have an audience with you?"

Mike smiled. "Of course. I'll put you at the top of my list of appointments."

Gorlan grinned from ear-to-ear, but Jan caught a glimpse of Tanza's bright blush.

"This wouldn't happen to involve you, would it?" she whispered.

Tanza nodded.

"Honey? Ready to go?" Mike asked climbing the first two steps to the transport.

Jan took a deep breath and nodded.

"Then we're off!" he said giving the throng one final smile and wave before ducking inside.

Marla caught hold of Jan as she started up the steps. "Jan, be happy. You have what I will never have…a lifemate."

Jan gazed at her friend sadly, gave her one last hug then quickly disappeared inside the transport.

Seconds later, the couples' faces appeared at a side window. They smiled and waved to the crowd which responded with enthusiastic cheers.

The three Elitists hurried back beyond the ropes as the transport's engines whined to life. It lifted off the landing pad and took off with a quiet whoosh. As it zipped through the gates, the exuberant crowd ran along behind and a short way down the road out of the City.

Inside the transport, the Royal Couple sat back in their cabin seats. Two doors in the panel before them opened, and two drawers slid out. Mike took off his crown and placed it on one drawer with Jan following suit. The drawers retracted with the crowns and the doors slid shut.

Mike settled back comfortably while Jan gazed around them.

"I can't believe it's finally all over," she breathed. "All of the fighting, the waiting, the pain…over."

Mike held her hand in his. "We've been through it all, and we're still in one piece."

"And together," Jan whispered as he leaned over to kiss her.

Tired Jan leaned her head on his shoulder. "There's a part of me that would like to go home," she remarked.

"You mean…to Earth?" Mike asked.

She nodded. "Somehow things seemed simpler then."

"Eh?"

"Well, we weren't fighting a war," she pointed out.

"And we would never have lived in a palace."

"Touché."

Eventually their transport approached a clearing on a thickly wooded hillside. Mike nudged Jan, and she glanced out the window in time to catch an aerial view of the Swiss-style chalet Elira had had built for them. The transport landed in front of it, and they gratefully disembarked. While Mike stretched and looked around, Jan hurried inside. She found their bedroom upstairs and quickly shed the gem-studded gown. She opened the wardrobe pulling out a long, white gossamer dress, instead. She slipped it on then splashed cold water on her face from a basin that stood on a nearby table. Eagerly she crossed over to the window and gazed out over the wood mountainside and valley below.

Mike climbed the stairs and stopped in the doorway, studying her. "So, what do you think?" he asked entering and coming up beside her.

"The view is gorgeous," she said with a catch in her voice.

"But not home."

"We-ell, it is and it isn't," Jan replied trying to play fair. "I mean, it does make me think of Earth. But it's more like those perfect calendar pictures you'd get. It's great, except, they were places I'd never been to."

"Earth was always kind of like that for me," Mike said shedding the stiff jacket and slacks he had worn. "It felt like home, yet it didn't."

"What do you mean?" Jan asked turning to watch him pull on the closest equivalent to sweat pants and a T-shirt that Quentas could invent.

"Well, it was comfortable for me in that I was generally well-liked," Mike admitted, "when people had a chance to get to know me. Actually, I probably know the US as well as you know Quentas. I spent enough time moving around to escape Saracen assassins." His voice had taken on a sarcastic bite.

Jan sank onto the window seat as Mike continued.

"Of course, all those moves made it tough to make lasting friendships. I'd just get to know some kids, and we'd have to take off again."

"I'm sorry. I never realized."

"There were some other things you didn't know," Mike said moodily. "Like the fact that all through school, I had to study doubly hard. While Will insisted I get good grades in school, as soon as my homework was done, he'd start drilling me in all the Quentasian subjects, too. I'm certain I was "in class" about ten hours a day or more."

Mike crossed the room, sank into a chair, and stared out the window. He sighed deeply then looked back at Jan. "It isn't as though I haven't thought about going back to Earth now and then. I miss it, too. Believe me," he said chuckling, "when Tandk had my days so tied up, I was actually wishing for my old college schedule back.

"There are some things about Quentas that makes this place quite desirable, though."

"Such as?"

"I belong here," he replied simply. "I'm just like everyone else here. For once, I don't have to hide my powers and pretend to be someone I'm not. For once, my powers make me someone special... someone who's respected."

She nodded in understanding.

"I don't have to live in fear anymore. Even though the Saracens were in power while we were in Mozern, I felt safe. 'Safe' That's a word I never knew back on Earth."

Jan crossed the room and slipped her arms around his neck.

"Then, too, men here talk about women in a way I can understand. They're one-women men like me. They understand what this bonding experience is all about. Men on Earth could hardly care. They'd rather look at Playboy centerfolds." He shook his head. "I used to do a lot of acting in the locker rooms. There's only one woman who will ever turn me on," he said pulling Jan around to sit on his lap. "And that's because I love you."

They shared a lingering kiss before he continued.

"But most of all, Jan...I'm in charge here. If there's something I see as being unjust or unfair, I can change it. I can make life better for these people. I can make a real difference. And Jan," he said quietly, "I LIKE THAT."

"That I do understand," she said. "It's the same feeling I had when the Mollucan gave me permission to use their tunnels. It was like...well finally I could do something really important to help out."

"And did you ever!" Mike said proudly.

Jan gave his neck a squeeze. "It's just that there's so much of Earth we can't recreate here," she sighed.

"Maybe not all of it, but some of it we can," Mike said with a wink.

She looked at him quizzically. "Just what do you mean?"

"I'll show you."

He set her on her feet, got up and led her outside. They found a cobbled path that meandered away from the chalet and through a break in a tall privet hedge. They stepped into a well-sculpted garden full of blooming flowers.

Jan sniffed the air then took a closer look at the plants. "Mike!" she exclaimed. "These aren't from Quentas! These are good old tea roses from Earth! And this is a flowering crab apple tree, and that's a lilac!"

She hurried from one plant to another breathing in the familiar fragrances and admiring the pretty blossoms. "Mike, how in the world did they all get here?"

He chuckled, pleased to see her happy. "You'll have to thank Will for them. He somehow brought all these back in capsule form. He was going to experiment with them, but I convinced him that you need them more. He designed this garden for you as a wedding present." He glanced thoughtfully about him. "I don't know how he managed it, but he somehow sped up the growth process so they'd all be blooming this week."

Jan looked around appreciatively. "Well, this certainly does make me feel less homesick. I can't believe it! A piece of Earth here on Quentas." She took another deep breath. "If I just sit here with my eyes closed and breathe real deep, for a while I can be back on Earth again."

"That's what I thought."

The setting sun stretched long, rosy fingers across the evening sky. Gradually the sun sank and the sky darkened, stars blinking on one-by-one in the expanse above. As Endel and Thira I rose above the horizon, Mike tilted Jan's chin towards him and gazed longingly into her eyes. Her breathing quickened, her eyelids drooped, and a soft glow crept over her face.

Mike took her hand and led her along a brick walkway to a secluded nook complete with a bubbling fountain. He drew her close and hungrily kissed her parted lips. As she stretched her arms up around his neck, he ran his hands down her sides feeling her smooth, graceful curves. Slowly Mike lowered them to the ground stretching out on the fragrant mix of grass and clover. Jan ran her fingers through the hair at the nape of his neck while he kissed her neck and shoulders. As she smoothed her other hand over his back, he gently nuzzled her earlobe.

"Sweetheart, this is a moment that I'm going to enjoy forever," he tenderly whispered in her ear.

EPILOGUE

"I'm not terribly anxious to leave," Jan remarked a month later.

She stood at the loft window taking in the beauty and serenity of the gardens below. Several Molluc porters bustled in and out of the room in the process of removing their luggage.

"Don't worry. We'll come back," Mike assured her. "Besides, you can always come up here whenever you get homesick."

"I think I feel an attack coming on," she said mischievously. She crossed the room to his side and ran her fingers across his chest. "Let's stay a little longer before going straight back to the Palace."

"Ah-h, but we aren't going straight back to the Palace. I have a bit of a detour in mind," he added with a wink.

"Oh?" she asked, eyebrows raised in curiosity.

He merely smiled mysteriously, took her hand, and led her outside.

After making certain all their necessities had been packed in the hovercar, Mike tapped on the hood. The vehicle lifted from its pad and jetted on without them.

Jan watched it go in confusion, but Mike smiled secretively and led her around to the rear of the chalet where a small speeder was waiting. He helped her in then climbed into the pilot's seat himself and sent it flying. Several hours later they were fast approaching the Stardent Range.

"Now I get it!" she exclaimed understanding dawning on her face.

Mike set the speeder down on a grassy slope. He and Jan climbed out and hurried to the entrance of an Elra eagerly jogging along its brightening passages till they finally burst into the Star Chamber. As they neared the glowing vault, a deep voice rang out to greet them.

"King Ihue? Queen Janielle?"

"It's us, Tovorald," Mike replied entering the gallery.

"Then, you did remember."

"Now, Tovorald. Do you think we could possibly forget you?" Mike asked.

"Oh, no-o. Of course not. How silly of me."

"Are you ready to go?" Jan asked.

"Ready? I have been working myself loose from this base ever since your joining ceremony," Tovorald replied.

While the couple watched in amazement, he slowly levitated off the ground. He began floating toward the passage then stopped and rotated slightly.

"Well? Are you coming, too, or do I go alone?" he asked impatiently.

The couple chuckled.

"We're coming," Mike assured him as they hurried to catch up to him.

They jogged through the passage emerging into the mid-day sun, and climbed back into their speeder. Mike again set it into motion hastily following the blue Star across the Palisade Plain.

Dusk had already settled on the City by the time their vehicle settled onto its pad on the landing plateau. The couple hurried out and secreted Tovorald through back ways till they entered a dome-ceilinged observatory. A large, marble base was awaiting the Star.

"I wanted a place of honor for you, yet with a touch of privacy," Mike explained to the Star.

"But where are all the people?" Tovorald asked forlornly dimly blinking his usually bright blue light.

"They're asleep right now," Jan soothed. "It's night."

"Just wait till tomorrow morning when we open these doors," Mike said. "Then you'll see a crowd."

"Well, seeing that I have waited this long, I am certain I can wait the night," Tovorald replied with a sigh. "But at least I can see the stars again. How long it has been since I have seen my brothers."

Mike and Jan looked up through the glass dome above and smiled then backed out of the room and closed the doors behind them.

Early the next morning, the Royal trumpets blared from the City walls, and Honor Guards opened wide the Palace doors. As the people threaded their way through the Palace to the Observatory, Mike and Jan entered the bright, spacious room from a side door. Mike seated himself in a large, richly-ornamented chair while Jan patiently stood at his side. Together, they watched as the crowd continued to swell through the double doors stopping at the rope-barrier that had been set up. Once they were all assembled, Mike held up his hand for silence.

"My people," he began, "today I wish to dedicate the Palace and the Observatory to a very special friend. Throughout our planet's history, he has protected and guided our people from the sanctuary of the Sacred Dome of the Heavens."

The Star began to glow brightly causing the people to gasp and take a step back.

"This, my people, is the Star of Quentas whom our fathers revered before us. May he always be with us to guide and protect."

The crowd gazed in wonder at the glowing rock then jumped back, startled. It blazed momentarily.

"People of Quentas," a deep bass voice boomed. "It is with deep gratitude that I thank your King for honoring his promise to me. You are entering a new period in your history, and I ask for a more prominent place in your lives. May the peace you have won extend for generations."

The people applauded warmly but toward the back of the room several men from outlying principalities huddled close together.

"So, it is real," one mused. "Garin always doubted its existence and considered the star a myth."

"Well, this myth glows and speaks to us," commented another.

"Yes, but this 'myth' only gives the new High King greater power. Eventually he will not only shift 'surplus' stores around to less fortunate principalities. Soon he will seek to depose our sovereign kings," a third remarked darkly.

"But what can be done now?" the first man asked. "He has brought the star here. Everyone has seen it."

"Actually, he may have placed the star within reach," the third man noted.

His two companions looked to him with perplexed frowns.

"We do not understand."

"As of yet, you do not have to," the third man began. "For now, I only have ideas, vague shapes of plans, but soon…."

He was cut off by a sudden commotion. Jan doubled over beside Mike's chair, one hand clutching her stomach.

A pair of Honor Guards sprang forward and carried her from the room.

Mike urgently beckoned Will to his side and hastily whispered in his ear. He sat and only half heard the remaining message that Tovorald conveyed. When the star stopped speaking and the people gathered closer to inspect this newly appointed historical relic, Mike rose to his feet. He ignored the bowing people as he rushed out the side doors of the Observatory. He ran down the corridors to the Royal Suite and burst through the door heading straight for their bedroom. He stopped just inside the door. An old friend was hovering over Jan's pale figure. Worried, he hastened to her side.

"How is she? Is she sick?"

Soniora glanced up, smiling. "Oh, no. She is quite fine...just a bit tired."

"But she nearly collapsed," he protested taking another step forward.

Elira quickly moved toward him from the side of the room and put a restraining hand on his shoulder. "Relax, Ihue. She will be fine," she assured him.

"But what happened? Why did she collapse?" he persisted pushing past her.

Elira again tried to restrain him. "She just is not feeling well."

"But why? I-want-to-know."

Mike pressed past his mother and hurried to Jan's side. He gently eased himself onto the bed beside her and reached up his hand to stroke back her hair. Her eyes opened and she smiled wanly.

"Are you all right?" he asked earnestly. "What's wrong?"

"Not much," she replied laughing nervously. "I just felt a little sick."

"Jan," he said sternly. "Tell me what's going on."

"Oh, all right," she said pulling him closer. "I'm pregnant."

His eyes widened and his mouth flew open. "Pregnant!" he exclaimed. "You're pregnant?"

She nodded.

"But what happened in the Observatory?"

"I lost breakfast," she replied wincing.

"A simple case of morning sickness," Elira explained. "Nothing more."

"How long have you known?" Mike asked Jan.

"Oh, for a little while, I guess. I mean, I didn't really know, but I've kind of suspected."

"But why didn't you say something?" he demanded.

"Because I was afraid you'd make us cut our trip short, and I didn't want to leave the chalet any sooner than I had to," she confessed sitting more upright against the pillows.

Mike sighed and shook his head. "You're right. I would have rushed you back for a check-up. Call me over-protective."

He gazed at her tenderly and caressed her cheek with his hand. He slowly moved it down her body till it rested on her stomach. For a brief moment, an image flashed through his mind as a warm blue glow enveloped his fingers. "I still can hardly believe it," he breathed.

"Well, things like this do happen," Jan said a mischievous gleam in her eyes.

"I know, but to me? To us? I can hardly believe it!"

She reached up putting her arms around his neck, and pulled him closer. He put his arms around her as she kissed him then pulled back a little.

"Look, I have to get back to the Dedication Ceremony, but as soon as it's over, I'll be back," he assured her all in one breath.

"Don't worry. I'll be up soon. They just wanted me to lie down as a precaution," she said with a meaningful glance toward Soniora and Elira.

Mike patted her hand, then stood up and dashed from the room. He hurried back through the corridors skidding to a halt just outside the

Observatory door to catch his breath and straighten out his suit. When he strode into the Observatory his face was beaming. He resumed his seat before the people then held up his hand to silence the buzz of curiosity. The crowd leaned forward, eager for news of the young Queen.

"My people...I have good news to tell you," he announced. "The Queen is neither ill, nor injured."

Many sighs of relief were sprinkled about the room.

"Instead," Mike continued, "in a few short montari there will be a new Son of the Star."

The people cheered, and the Star flashed brilliantly. Life had indeed begun anew.

www.ingramcontent.com/pod-product-compliance
Lightning Source LLC
Chambersburg PA
CBHW030744030726
47497CB00001B/123

* 9 7 8 0 6 1 5 1 4 3 4 1 5 *